The Bookshop
DETECTIVE

Jan Ellis

WAVERLEY
BOOKS

Dedication

For Dad, the original "Harold".

www.waverley-books.co.uk
info@waverley-books.co.uk

The Bookshop Detective
published 2017 by Waverley Books, an imprint of
The Gresham Publishing Company Ltd.,
Academy Park, Building 4000, Gower Street,
Glasgow, G51 1PR, Scotland, UK.

ISBN: 978-1-84934-445-6

A catalogue record for this book is available from the British Library.

Printed and bound in the EU

Contents

Chapter 1: The Reading Room

It all began when Maureen saw the ghost ship.

"I'm telling you now, I saw it with my own eyes, as clear as day."

"But I thought you saw it at night," said Connie, pedantically.

"Twilight, actually. The sun was setting right behind it, which is why I saw its spidery outline so clearly."

"What's all this?" Eleanor, who had been gathering books off the shelves to make up a customer's order, now returned to the front of the bookshop to find her mother Connie chatting with their neighbour, Maureen.

Eleanor had been talked into giving Connie a part-time job and now her mother was half-heartedly tidying up greetings cards in between gossiping with her friend from Ye Olde Tea Shoppe across the high street. "Maureen's been making rum babas again and I think the fumes have gone to her brain."

Maureen, who had popped over to Eleanor's shop for a break from her customers, folded her arms under her substantial bosom and huffed. "You can mock if you like, Connie, but I know what I saw and what I heard."

"And what was that?"

"As I was telling your mother," she said, turning towards Eleanor, "I was up on the moor taking

Peanut for a walk when I heard this strange groaning sound."

"You hadn't trodden on the dog, had you?" Connie was really a cat person and thought her friend's Chihuahua was especially ridiculous.

"Ignore her, Maureen," said Eleanor, pulling up a chair and sitting beside her. "I want to know all about it."

"I was walking towards the headland when I heard a sound like timbers creaking or branches rubbing together, except there aren't any large trees along there, as you know." Eleanor nodded in agreement. "The wind had come up and was blowing in off the sea, which isn't unusual, but it was carrying this odd noise with it. Peanut had had a good scamper so we were heading back to the car, but there was something about the sound that made me stop and turn around." Maureen was pleased to see both women leaning in, apparently gripped by her story. "So I looked across to the horizon and there she was – as plain as the nose on your mother's face."

"There's no need for personal attacks." Connie leant back now, looking cross.

"Sorry dear," said Maureen, tartly. "It was the first comparison that came into my head."

"Okay ladies. I don't want any cat fights in my bookshop, thank you," said Eleanor. "Go on with your story, Maureen."

"There she was in the distance – a big wooden ship, just like the ones pirates have. And Johnny Depp."

Connie waggled a bookmark at her friend. "And how precisely could you see what kind of ship she was, at night and with your cataracts?"

"I had them done after Christmas and now I can see perfectly well. Doubt me if you will, Connie, but I know what I saw, and whether you choose to believe me or not is entirely up to you."

"What did your little dog do?" asked Eleanor.

"In what way?"

"Did she howl or anything? Aren't animals supposed to react to ghostly presences? I'm sure Bella would run off and hide if there was anything scary around. You're not much cop as a guard dog, are you?" Eleanor's Welsh spaniel, Bella, had wandered over and rested her head on her owner's lap.

Maureen's brow furrowed in concentration as she thought back to the event. "Now, it's funny you should say that, but Peanut did squeak a bit."

"Conclusive proof," said Connie, laughing. "If Peanut squeaked, it must have been a ghost ship."

Maureen pursed her lips. "I don't expect you to understand the ocean's mysteries, being a Londoner. You don't have the sea in your blood like I do."

Connie tried not to smile. "No, mine's full of Thames water," she said, patting her friend on the shoulder.

"Thanks for coffee." Maureen picked up her bag. "I'd best go back across the road and see how Anton is getting on with the cottage pies."

As she stood by the shop window watching their neighbour cross the street to the teashop, Connie turned to Eleanor. "All that 'sea in the blood' stuff is nonsense, of course. She's from the Midlands, which is as far from the sea as you can be in this country."

"So she's not local, then?"

"No!" Connie laughed. "I think she kissed a sailor

once in Weston-super-Mare and her late husband was a Devon man. But now she has Anton in her life . . ."

"Mother, really! You make it sound like they're up to no good when in fact he's young enough to be her grandson."

"Ever heard of cougars?"

Eleanor guffawed. "Yes, but I'm pretty sure Maureen is not about to pounce on Anton."

"I wouldn't be too sure. We may be ancient ladies but there's life in us old girls yet, you know." Connie winked and went to tidy up their coffee things.

"Spare me the gory details."

Eleanor stood at the cash desk and looked around her empire. The bookshop was empty apart from a Belgian couple in matching beige anoraks examining the postcard rack and an older gent looking at historical biographies. In the past, Eleanor would have fretted when the shop was this quiet but, in the six years she'd owned The Reading Room, she'd become familiar with the rhythms of the week.

Monday mornings were always deathly quiet, but she knew the following day would be better and trade would pick up even more on Wednesday, when the farmers' market was held in the town square. At the weekend, visitors came to Combemouth to walk along the prom, paddle in the sea and enjoy the town's seaside charm. Plenty of them also made a point of visiting Eleanor's shop to rummage through her enticing selection of books and pick up some postcards or a storybook to keep the kids quiet on the journey home.

While it was quiet, Eleanor decided to refresh

the shop window. Easter had been and gone and the bunnies and plastic daffodils decorating the space were beginning to look tired. It was time for a change.

Smiling to herself, she dashed back and forth between the shelves, going from science fiction and self-help to crime and romance, seemingly picking up books at random. When she'd finished the arrangement, she asked Connie to join her on the pavement to admire her work.

"What do you reckon, Mum?"

Her mother pursed her lips. "It's interesting, dear, but what's the theme?"

"I'll write out a title, then you'll see." Eleanor went into the office and found a blackboard and a piece of chalk. "This should do it," she said, slotting the board into its stand and placing it in the window. On it she had written "I Can't Remember the Title, But the Cover's Blue".

Connie chuckled. "That's very clever and I think it'll be helpful for those of us whose memories aren't as sharp as they were."

"That's an excellent point," said Eleanor, laughing. "Perhaps I'll do a red display next time."

Across the road, she could see Maureen and Anton giving her the thumbs up from the teashop, which now appeared to be full of shoppers eager for tea and a bun.

"We seem to have the Latvian vote." Eleanor waved back, smiling with satisfaction at a job well done.

* * *

Anton had appeared in town some months before, having journeyed from Latvia via London and various music festivals where he'd had a great time until his money ran out.

Graham, who ran the hardware store a few doors down from the bookshop, had found Anton sleeping in his doorway one morning and was not best pleased. He asked the lad to move on, which he did during the day, but in the mornings when Graham came to open up the shop, there he'd be, curled up on the tiled floor in his thin sleeping bag, his boots and few belongings in a tatty carrier bag to one side.

They weren't used to homeless people pitching up in Combemouth, so no one knew quite what to do. Being a civilised and friendly bunch, the locals talked to Anton, gave him warm clothes and bought him hot drinks and Cornish pasties from the bakery. But everyone knew that "something had to be done", not least because a pale young man sitting on the pavement rather spoiled the jolly effect of Graham's brightly coloured plastic windmills. Eventually, Eleanor called the police who gave Anton a lift into the closest big town, where there was a shelter for the homeless.

After a week, Anton was back in Graham's doorway saying the shelter was full of "druggies and alkies" who shouted all night and he was too frightened to stay. Could he perhaps sleep in the doorway again in return for helping out in the shop? And so Graham reluctantly let him work there. He also lent Anton a tent and allowed him to camp out in the tiny garden at the back of the premises. At the end of a fortnight, the tent was abandoned and Anton was kipping in the back room and making himself useful in the hardware store. The only problem was that

Graham couldn't afford paid help and Anton needed to earn some sort of living.

A meeting was held at the community centre where the shopkeepers decided to share out Anton amongst themselves – everyone needed help for half a day or a day here or there. So, the young man ended up working in the high street shops and sleeping at Graham's place in return for a few hours spent cutting up roofing felt and selling bin bags. It was a solution that suited everyone, not least Maureen who was happy to have a smart young man's help in the teashop.

Chapter 2: A Surprising Supper

When Eleanor told her husband Daniel what Maureen had seen from the cliff top, she was surprised by his reaction. Rather than laughing at the ghostly tale, as she had expected him to, Dan seemed to take it quite seriously.

"Oh, that'll be the *Santa Ana*. She's occasionally seen at this time of year, though not normally so early in the evening."

"Hang on a minute," said Eleanor, pausing from dishing out the bangers and mash they were having for supper, "are you saying Maureen saw a real ship instead of an apparition?" Daniel was such a sensible individual that Eleanor found the idea of his believing in supernatural events quite surprising. Her husband was an architect, a man focused on measurements and straight lines; a man who thought deeply and could be undemonstrative. When they had first met some two years before, she was sure Dan didn't like her. In fact, he liked her a great deal, but was struggling to cope with the fallout from a recent divorce.

Since then, Eleanor had discovered that Dan was sensitive and creative, which she guessed was what allowed him to believe in the unbelievable. They'd only been married for six months and Eleanor loved the fact that her husband constantly surprised her.

"I guess you could say she's both ship and

apparition. There have been similar sightings on and off for years."

"Sorry – you're going to have to explain this to me."

Daniel took the plates from Eleanor and laid them on the kitchen table. "According to legend, the ship Maureen described was a Spanish ship that was blown off course by the weather. She was on her way home, became lost off Ireland and foundered on Bonnie Sands."

Eleanor frowned. "Foundered? You're talking to a landlubber here."

"She was stuck on the sandbanks that lie four miles off the bay. It may look calm and beautiful out there, but this part of the coast can be treacherous at low tide."

"Couldn't the captain wait until the tide came back in then sail away?"

Daniel topped up their wineglasses. "That's not how it works, unfortunately. As the tide goes out, a ship will keel over and be broken up by the incoming waves, which is what happened in this case, apparently."

"How awful," said Eleanor, in between mouthfuls of mashed potato. "How did the crew get off?"

"Ah, now that's the interesting part. There was a terrible storm followed by a dense fog that meant no one could go out to the *Santa Ana* until the morning. All night long the cries of the sailors – and some of the womenfolk they'd picked up in Ireland – could be heard. The water was coming in, you see. When the rescue boats did eventually make it over there at dawn, she was gone. Completely disappeared."

"Sailed away? Sunk?"

"No one knows. All that was left was the anchor

and chain, which had been ripped away from her side."

Eleanor looked thoughtful. "But if she'd been broken up, wouldn't there be debris?" She winced at the thought. "Bodies?"

"You'd expect there to be tons of debris given the circumstances, but everything was gone. Sails, cargo, people. Puff! She disappeared into the fog. And the story goes that those poor Spanish sailors can still be heard praying and calling out, *Madre mia, sálvame.* Save me." Daniel came around from the other side of the dining table, grasped Eleanor's shoulders from behind and whispered the words into her ear in a singsong voice.

"Stop it Dan." Eleanor shivered and pulled away. "That's creepy. To think all those Spanish sailors died at sea – and so close to where we're sitting now drinking Rioja."

Daniel shrugged, pushing away his plate. "Do you think so? For one thing, we don't know for sure they actually died and in a way I find it comforting to believe old sailors keep sailing on."

"Don't say that – I worry about you enough as it is." Eleanor's husband loved to sail and she did some-times fret when he went off alone for hours on end. "To wander the oceans forever, never able to go home or see family and friends. It sounds awful. When I'm gone, I want to be properly gone, not pacing up and down the aisles of my shop, endlessly rearranging the non-fiction shelves and chasing up orders."

Dan smiled. "You do that anyway, darling."

"Exactly, but I can always stop for a cup of tea, which I doubt will be available in the afterlife. Ugh.

Fancy spending all eternity without tea. This is getting morbid. Put the kettle on, will you darling?"

When the dishes had been cleared up and they were settled on the sofa, Eleanor turned to Daniel. He'd been so unfazed by their earlier topic of conversation that she had to ask. "Have you ever seen a ghostly vessel?"

Daniel frowned, rubbing his chin. "You know, I'd completely forgotten about it until now, but I did see something once."

"Ooh, what happened?" Eleanor pulled up her legs and rested them over Daniel's lap. "I enjoy a spooky bedtime story."

"Let me think, now," he said, frowning. "I must have been about nine or ten years old and I was out in the boat with Dad when we saw what appeared to be a large ship in the distance."

Eleanor's father-in-law Malcolm was a retired engineer and mathematician and absolutely the last person she could imagine believing in creatures from the afterlife. "I'm stunned you and Malcolm saw a ghost ship and neither of you thought to mention it to me!"

"It was nearly forty years ago, El. And neither of us really knew what it was we'd seen."

"Fair enough. Go on."

Daniel dredged his memory for the details. "We'd been fishing for mackerel outside the bay, so I guess it was late spring. After a couple of hours, we had three nice fat ones for supper, so Dad decided to head back to shore. It was getting dark and we knew my mother worried if we stayed out too late – exactly as you do," he said, playfully squeezing Eleanor's toes in their stripy socks.

"Too right!" she said, wriggling around to face him.

"Anyway, that's when we saw a craft very like the one Maureen described. I remember the ship seemed immensely tall from where we sat on our little boat."

Eleanor sipped her tea thoughtfully. "Call me an old cynic, but couldn't what you saw have been a large yacht? Or a container ship?"

"What Dad and I saw definitely wasn't a regular boat – she had three or four massive sails and she wasn't displaying any lights, which was most irregular."

"Creepy!" Although it was evening, the curtains weren't yet drawn. Outside, the spring sky was turning deep blue as Eleanor tried to imagine the scene.

"I agree it's hard to rationalise. I guess you could say the *Santa Ana* is the Combemouth version of the Loch Ness Monster – no one has been able to prove the truth of her existence one way or the other. Personally, I think the vision is most probably all down to a trick of the light caused by the way the sun hits the horizon at this time of year. Or perhaps a play in the waves."

"I'm surprised I've never heard about this before." Eleanor was quiet for a moment, thinking about the shop. "Are there any books about this ghostly phenomenon?"

"I suppose there must be lots of books about ghosts, but whether there are any on the *Santa Ana* in particular, I couldn't say."

"I'd better find out and order some copies – they could be the focus of a great window display."

Daniel laughed. "Ghosts and ghouls? Isn't April a bit early to be thinking about Halloween?"

"It doesn't have to be about ghosts – we could have

something about pirates. They always go down well with the kids."

"And don't forget smugglers – folk like to hear about people bending the rules."

"You're right. What a shame there's no smuggling going on around here any more."

"That's what you think! Don't you remember the ship that foundered a few years back?"

Eleanor shook her head. "I guess it was before I moved to the area. What happened?"

"The hold broke open and huge containers littered the entire beach. Of course, being a tidy community we had it all cleaned up in no time."

"What was in the containers?"

"You name it: motor bikes, washing machines, footballs, bread machines . . ."

"Bread machines?"

"Yes, really good ones, too. And some rather smart trainers. Oops." Dan made a show of crossing one battered shoe behind the other. "Nothing to see here!"

"You're joking, right? You wouldn't take something that wasn't yours?"

"Salvaging an item or two from a beach isn't the same as helping yourself to something that's fallen off the back of a lorry in the high street. Things are different at the coast: it's a question of tradition." Daniel winked. "The first rule of the sea is: finders keepers. Second rule: ask me no questions and I'll tell thee no lies." He kissed his wife's cheek. "You didn't know you were married to a smuggler, did you?"

"Every day I learn something new about you."

"You don't know the half of it," said Daniel, with a smile.

Chapter 3: No Place Like Home

As Eleanor walked down the narrow staircase from the bedroom the next morning, she stopped and patted the rough white walls of her terraced cottage, the way you might the neck of a horse. It was a bit eccentric, perhaps, but no more eccentric than believing in ghost ships and she was convinced that houses absorbed traces of the people who had lived in them over the centuries.

Daniel raised an eyebrow when he saw his wife stroke the wall as she entered the kitchen. "Is there something wrong, darling?"

"Wrong? No, why should there be anything wrong?" Eleanor looked up smiling, her hand dropping down to her side as she stepped into the sunny room and poured herself a cup of tea from the pot Dan had prepared.

"I could have sworn I heard you say good morning to the wall."

"Not to the wall, silly." Eleanor grinned as she tipped muesli into a bowl. "I was saying good morning to the house. Don't you ever do that?"

Daniel shook his head slowly. "No, I honestly can't say that I have ever had a conversation with the masonry."

"It's not any old masonry – it's rock and rubble and

bits of horse hair and lime plaster. You should know that, Mr Architect."

"I'm fully aware of the vernacular building methods and materials, cheeky, but I have never felt moved to address a house, that's all."

"Ah, but you should. It's terribly rude not to."

"Sorry House."

Eleanor put her ear to the wall, listening. "House says you're forgiven. What about plants? Surely you speak to them?"

"Depends. I may speak to flowers but not veg."

"No wonder your carrots don't thrive."

"I wondered where I'd been going wrong. I certainly won't have anything worth entering in the summer festival yet again."

The social highlight of the year was the grandly named Combemouth Summer Festival and Country Fair, an event organised by the vicar and a committee of fierce ladies in stout skirts. Although Combemouth was technically a town, it was the size and had the atmosphere of an overgrown village. Part of this was down to its position squeezed around a quiet bay on the North Devon coast.

The town never felt more rural than during the festival, which ran for a week in June. Most of the activity took place at the sea front, but the event kicked off with a country fair in the grounds of St Cuthbert's Church where delights included ferret racing, falconry displays and fruit- and vegetable-growing contests. The "Best in Show" categories for these were earnestly fought over by dedicated gardeners. Anyone was free to enter their produce, but the prizes tended to be won by the same few highflyers every year.

"Having lived here all your life, I'd have thought you'd be used to the disappointment of constant rejection by now," said Eleanor. "The allotment crowd are impossible to beat."

"A man can dream." Daniel smiled. "Seriously though, we do need to make a decision soon."

"We do?" Eleanor wandered over to the window to look out at the pretty courtyard garden that ran along the back of the house. It was too early in the year for anything much to be growing, though she had managed to fill pots with multicoloured tulips. Down by the end wall was a patch of lawn dotted with crocus and grape hyacinth, and pale pink hellebores were starting to bloom in a shady corner. "The strawberry plants are in and maybe I'll try courgettes in the raised bed again this year."

"I'm not talking about fruit and veg." Dan came up behind his wife, resting his chin on her shoulder as they watched blue tits and sparrows dart between the bird feeders. They had married in the autumn. Christmas had come and gone, it was now spring and they continued to live in their own, separate houses. "I mean coming to a decision about where we're going to live, Mrs Pearce."

Do we have to decide, thought Eleanor? Couldn't they stay the way they were? But she couldn't say what she thought. She knew she had to get her head around moving sooner rather than later. "Yes, of course. Absolutely. I couldn't agree more."

Daniel allowed himself to feel a flicker of hope. This was what he wanted to hear. "Seriously? Good, because I've lined up a couple more places for us to see."

"Great," said Eleanor, turning to kiss him on the cheek. "Can't wait."

Daniel watched as his wife opened the kitchen door and stepped out into the cool spring day, causing the birds to scatter in alarm. Dan couldn't help noticing that Eleanor hadn't bothered to ask him anything about the houses he'd found for them and his heart sank at the thought of another fruitless afternoon of house-hunting ahead.

Chapter 4: Mind the Gap

The summer festival was one of the most popular events of the year and brought in people from all the surrounding villages as well as tourists in search of some seaside fun. All the shops along the high street did their best to make a splash and seduce potential customers. For her part, Eleanor liked to lay on special events, including readings and book signings.

"You're looking serious, boss."

"I'm not serious, Erika, I'm furious." It was late morning and Eleanor was in the bookshop with her assistant manager. After six years, Erika was still Eleanor's only full-time employee and they managed pretty well together with occasional help from her mother Connie and son Joe. "I thought we'd finalised all our events for the festival week."

"So did I – what's happened?"

Eleanor spun the shop diary around for her colleague to see. "I opened my emails to discover that the author I had lined up as our star turn has pulled out leaving me well and truly in the custard." She closed the diary with a bang.

"Oh dear, that is bad timing." Erika grimaced. "I suppose there's always Lavinia Threlfall if we get desperate."

"True – her Gothic romances might not be to

everyone's taste, but she certainly has plenty of devoted fans."

"Who – as we know – are guaranteed to turn up and buy books, which is brilliant, although the shop does smell of patchouli for days afterwards."

"Her readers are a loyal and interesting bunch, but I feel we've 'done' Lavinia. Do you remember the book launch a couple of years ago when we turned off the lights and draped the place in velvet?" Eleanor laughed. "The shop looked like something between a souk and a bordello."

"That's not an evening I'll forget in a hurry. It was one of our most lucrative events ever." Erika had been Eleanor's good friend and right-hand woman for five years and shared the responsibility for entering the shop's figures into their accounting system.

"It was also the night young Georgie came into our lives or Joe's, to be more precise."

"They make a sweet couple."

"They do. My son is a very lucky chap to have such a sparky young woman take him on. I'm sure a lot of girls would find his chilled-out, 'surfer dude' approach to life annoying, but Georgie loves him. I guess being an Aussie she understands Joe's obsession with throwing himself into the sea at every opportunity. It's a shame Georgie is hard at work in London and Joe's still dossing in my spare room." Eleanor frowned. Although Joe was now in his late twenties, he showed no sign of wanting to fly the nest. In that, he was quite different from his twin Phoebe, who was working near her father's new home in Canada. "Anyway, back to the matter in hand – this gap in the schedule. I need to find an author with a high profile locally, but whose books we can sell to both men and women – which definitely rules out Lavinia."

"Yes, there aren't many men who'll confess to enjoying her passionate tales about lords of the manor and buxom wenches with an unhealthy interest in fresh blood."

"No, sexy vampires are not easy to sell to our male customers. They are more likely to go for biography or history."

Erika chewed her pen, thoughtfully. "What about inviting the local history chap to talk about the lighthouse? Or the old farmer who was in the Secret Service? They always guarantee a healthy audience."

"They're both great, but neither of them has a new book out and everybody in Combemouth has already bought their stuff or heard their talks." Eleanor drummed her fingers on the diary and sighed.

"Never mind," said Erika, trying to sound encouraging. "The festival isn't for two months yet – there's plenty of time to come up with a plan."

"Two months is no time at all." Eleanor scanned the wall calendar anxiously. "I need a whole lot of luck if I'm going to find someone thrilling at such short notice. It would be good to come up with whizzy ideas for more window displays, as well."

"You mean after you've done the red and black ones?"

"I think you'll agree the blue window is one of my best ever." Eleanor smiled. "I'll have a chat with Dan later. He often has good suggestions."

"Aren't you house-hunting again this lunchtime?"

"Drat. Yes, I'd forgotten. Thanks for reminding me."

"You're really not enjoying it, are you?"

"Oh, I wouldn't say that. I like a bit of property porn as much as the next woman and it's fascinating poking around other people's homes and gardens. We've seen some lovely places – I can't imagine living in any of them, that's the problem." Eleanor looked at the clock. "Lordy, I'd better go or I'll be late. I'm sorry to duck out early, Erika – could you shut up the shop tonight?"

"Sure, no problem. Let's hope you find somewhere that's right for you both soon."

Eleanor chewed her lip. "I'm sure my long-suffering husband hopes so too."

Chapter 5: Making Plans

Daniel knew that to persuade his wife to move, he would have to find somewhere pretty special, but there was a problem: he was keen on modern buildings whereas Eleanor's tastes tended towards the old and crumbly.

"So, where are we off to today?" asked Eleanor brightly, as she climbed into the passenger seat of Daniel's car. "Ancient or modern?"

"I thought we could compromise and go for something late twentieth century. There's a 1960s estate on the edge of Waterborough I fancy taking a look at. It's quite a landmark. What do you reckon?"

"If you'd like to," said Eleanor, doing her best to sound upbeat. The town was twenty miles away, which was a problem in itself as far as she was concerned. One of the many joys of living next to the shop was that she had zero commuting to do. After a lifetime in London, this was something she really appreciated. Now the longest drives she had were trips up to the cliff top or around to the next beach to walk the dogs with Daniel. These were journeys she loved even on winter's days when the wind howled and waves crashed onto the sand.

Daniel gritted his teeth, determined not to be defeated. "I think you'll be pleasantly surprised by how light and airy new properties are in comparison to our ancient houses."

"Sure," said Eleanor, trying to sound positive when the voice inside her head was screaming "No!"

It turned out to be another unsuccessful session. Eleanor hated the houses and, although she did her best to be noncommittal, Daniel figured it out. Nothing was said, but a dark mood came over him that didn't lift until they were walking along the beach with the dogs. It's not easy to stay gloomy when you're in the centre of a whirl of canine noses, paws and tails, but still the couple walked back to Daniel's sea-front house in silence.

As Eleanor fed the dogs, Bella and Crumpet, her husband crashed around the kitchen, grumpily gathering ingredients for their evening meal. Daniel's place was fairly unexceptional, but he didn't care – he'd bought it after his divorce as somewhere to lay his head. Eleanor had done her best to make it homely and it was certainly less like a storage space thanks to her influence. The one thing Dan did love about it was the office right at the top of the building where he had dawn-to-dusk views of the sea. Other than that, he had no particular affection for it and had been looking forward to starting afresh with the woman he loved.

So far it hadn't happened and Daniel still spent far too much time trudging up and down the high street with bags of clothes, feeling annoyed when the shirt he needed for a meeting was at the bottom of the laundry basket at Eleanor's house and not in the wardrobe in *his* house where he had expected it to be.

He seemed to be in perpetual limbo, which was

not a nice place to be. Sometimes he wondered if he was being unreasonable. Why should Eleanor give up her home for him? Did full-time cohabitation have to be the only way? Perhaps not, but it was what he wanted most in the world.

Eleanor was keen to lift her husband's spirits so decided to distract him from the subject of houses as soon as they were ensconced in the garden with a drink. The garden was on a rise behind the house and from the top there were clear views of the bay. It was a perfect spring evening, the sea was calm and inviting and there was a hint of warmth in the air that seemed to hold the promise of summer.

"Dan, I've been thinking about the events we're running to tie in with the summer festival. I've suddenly got a gap and I wondered whether you had any brilliant suggestions for who I might convince to come along. I'm also in need of inspiration for a special Combemouth-themed window display while you're thinking about it."

Daniel shrugged. "Bookselling isn't my area, is it? You'd be better off talking to Erika."

"We talked about it this morning, but I wanted your thoughts." Noticing her husband's sombre expression, Eleanor frowned. "Is there something wrong?"

"No. Why should there be anything wrong?"

"You look ever so glum, that's all. I know you were disappointed about today's houses – we both were – but has something else upset you? Are the clients being difficult again?"

"My *clients* are no trouble." Daniel turned to his wife and sighed. "If you must know, I'm growing really tired of our way of living. I've tried my best to be patient and give you time, but I want to get on – to find a house and start married life properly. Is that so hard to understand?"

"No, of course not." Eleanor twirled her glass, chastened by Dan's tone. "I know you're keen to move and I'm sure we will find somewhere eventually."

Daniel laughed harshly. "What precisely does 'eventually' mean? How much longer is this going to take? Months? Years? It's sometimes difficult to drag you out of the shop even to look at the places that I've spent a lot of time and effort finding for us."

"That's not fair – we've seen loads of houses." Startled, Eleanor tried to take Daniel's hand, but he pulled away. "And I've been really busy – we've both been busy – since the wedding."

"The wedding was last year, El! At this rate, we'll still be living in separate houses when our anniversary comes around in the autumn."

"You're right, I know." Eleanor nodded vigorously. "We have to keep looking until we find the right place."

"I wish I knew what the 'right place' was in your opinion: I've searched online and showed you every available house here in town and in all the surrounding villages. We've looked at old houses and modern houses, terraced houses and semis, but nothing's ever right. I'm beginning to think perhaps you don't want to live with me. Is that it?"

"Of course I want to live with you, darling." Eleanor moved closer to Daniel on the bench, managing this time to catch his hand in hers. "I love cuddling up together at the end of the day and seeing you when I open my eyes in the morning, you know I do."

"But not *every* morning, is that it?"

Eleanor opened her mouth to speak but nothing came out as she tried to put into words her complex emotions. How could she explain, without hurting her husband's feelings, that she did enjoy the luxury of having the whole house to herself once in a while?

"Well, I think your silence says it all." Before Eleanor could answer, Daniel picked up his empty beer bottle and got to his feet. "I'm going inside. It's getting cold out here. Coming?"

"Don't let's argue, Dan, please."

"I'm not arguing." He walked down the steps towards the kitchen then turned towards his wife, his face tense and drawn. "I'll check on supper."

Damn it. Eleanor loved her new husband with all her heart and when they'd met and fallen in love she'd wanted nothing more than to be married to him. But her little house represented freedom and true independence: it was the first time a place had completely belonged to her. In her twenties she'd gone from her parents' home to sharing with girl-friends in France. Back in London she'd met and married Alan, had the twins – Joe and Phoebe – and now here she was with a whole new life.

She and Alan had lived in an Edwardian pile in what was now a highly desirable part of southwest London. Eleanor had loved it, but it had never been entirely hers, unlike the cottage in Combemouth she'd fled to when they divorced.

When the Wimbledon house was finally sold, Eleanor had felt a combination of things: extreme sadness that the place where she and Alan had spent so many happy years was no longer hers, and alarm that this stage in her life was over. She'd also been amazed at the astonishing amount of money they made on the sale, insisting to Alan that they make a one-off donation to a housing charity to assuage her vague feelings of guilt.

With the huge pile of cash coming her way, she could afford a characterless flat in the same part of London or half a terraced house miles from the centre of town. She made the effort to visit a few properties, but her heart wasn't in it. Nowhere was right under the circumstances: she had expected to be married to Alan forever, not to find herself having to start her life again in her forties.

The Eureka! moment came during a walking holiday to the west coast of Scotland. She'd plucked up the courage to go on her own, keen to escape from the well-meaning but oppressive advice coming from friends and family. Striding along a beach on Arran with a group of strangers had got her thinking: away from the city she could breathe. The air was clear and clean and, at night, she could look up and see stars shooting by instead of jumbo jets. In particular, it felt good to be away from the constant bombardment of traffic noise.

She spent one rainy afternoon of the holiday stretched out on her bed writing a list of the advantages and disadvantages of living in London and was surprised by how few positive things she could come up with. Yes, she loved the city of her birth, but there were plenty of reasons not to live there any more.

Why continue to live in the capital when she'd always loved the sea? The answer was blindingly obvious: there was no reason to stay if she didn't want to.

Eleanor returned from that walking holiday all fired up. In the evenings after work, she scoured estate agents' websites looking for a house and garden in a small country town. Buying a seaside cottage with a bookshop attached hadn't been part of the initial plan: it was pure serendipity.

Being a legal secretary had been a way to earn a living, but it was not something Eleanor could ever feel passionate about. On the other hand, she loved books, read voraciously and had a good financial brain. Why shouldn't she run a bookshop? Having persuaded herself it was worth a punt, she bought the house and the business, joined the Booksellers' Association, did a sales course, read lots of books about marketing, crossed her fingers and plunged in.

And here she was six years later with a successful shop, a home she adored – and a brand-new, loving husband who wanted her to move again.

Am I being selfish? she asked herself. The inevitable answer was yes, she was. She frowned, pulling one of Daniel's sweaters around her shoulders.

Light was fading as she picked up her glass and padded down the steps. Dan was the most important person in her life so she was going to have to bite the bullet and sell the cottage. She stopped in her tracks as an alarming thought hit her: would anyone want the house without the shop? She'd bought them together as a package and for centuries the two properties had been indivisible. The thought they might have to be split up was unthinkable – and she'd hop naked down the high street before she'd ever give up The Reading Room.

Chapter 6: A Long Walk

The next morning, the atmosphere over breakfast was pretty frosty but Eleanor chattered away as normal, deciding that the best thing to do was to ignore Dan's low mood and wait for it to go away.

After clearing up the dishes, Eleanor grabbed her hat and boots. "Ready for walkies? I thought we could take the dogs up on the moor today." She turned to her husband, hoping to bring a smile to his handsome face. "If we're lucky, we might spot Maureen's ghost ship."

"Actually, I think I'll go for a run along the beach instead, if you don't mind. Can you take Crumpet with you?"

"Of course, darling. Whatever you prefer."

Daniel nodded and went upstairs to change, returning a few minutes later in his jogging gear. Eleanor smiled, admiring her husband's slim figure encased in a sports top and shorts despite the chilly spring air. When they first got together, she had made a brave attempt at jogging but soon came to the conclusion that her running days were over. In her twenties she had loved to pound the London streets, especially running along the South Bank, which was entirely free of trendy cafés and tourists in those far-off days. Since then her body seemed to have shifted around and certainly wasn't built for speed any more. Bits of her jiggled alarmingly, so she decided to give up running and take up something like crochet or felt-making, activities less likely to remind her of her saggy bits. Of course, she hadn't done this either and instead stuck to walking and reading for exercise.

"Enjoy your run." When Eleanor put her face up for her usual morning kiss, she was sad when Daniel seemed to give it grudgingly.

After Dan had left, Eleanor grabbed her keys and headed out. It wasn't yet 8am, but she liked to go out nice and early before it became busy with other dog-walkers. She herded the two dogs into the vintage campervan that was her guilty pleasure and drove out of town and up to the moor. She never tired of the road, which curved up behind the town through narrow, shady lanes before reaching an area of high, open land known locally as the Top.

She parked in her usual spot then walked along the path, enjoying the crunch of gravel under her feet. The weather was blustery and the wind whipped in off the sea, tossing strands of hair across her face until she extracted a woolly hat from her pocket and pulled it firmly down over her head.

Walking along, hands tucked in her pockets against the cold, she thought about her life. She knew her stance over the house business was making Daniel unhappy, but she didn't know how to resolve it. What was wrong with her?

Before she and Dan married she'd generally been happy, but there were times when she had felt lonely, despite the presence of friends and family. She'd missed not having a husband around and the lazy comfort of being married to someone you knew as well as you knew yourself.

After a few months in Devon, Eleanor had succumbed to pressure from her mother and made a feeble attempt to meet someone. Connie was a huge advocate of online dating, having found her beau Harold that way. Eleanor's efforts at finding love were less successful: she'd had a date with someone called Ted who spent the whole evening telling her why printed books were dead. Eleanor wasn't averse to a lively discussion about the future of the book trade, but when Ted insisted that bookshops were a waste of time she made her apologies and slipped out while he was arguing with the waiter about the bill.

The second man she met had clearly used a photograph that was at least ten years old and which made him look considerably taller and thinner than he was. Again, she could have put up with it if he'd been pleasant and hadn't spent an hour talking about his ex-wife and telling Eleanor how much better she herself would look if only she lost a couple of stone and dyed her hair blonde.

The only hints of romance in her life pre-Daniel were two recent encounters with her long-lost French boyfriend, Christophe Vauban. She and Christophe had spent an intense few months together in their early twenties, but seeing him again after two decades had made her realise that love is twenty per cent attraction, thirty per cent luck and fifty per cent timing: Christophe had been perfect for her in her youth, Alan was the right person to marry and have children with, but Dan was the only man she wanted now and she felt incredibly lucky to have met him.

With Dan, it was as though everything finally fell into place. She had someone to share things with again: a person she could talk to for hours, who enjoyed reading, long walks and good food. They didn't always agree and Daniel had different tastes from her in many ways, but those differences meant their life was never dull. And for the first time in many years she experienced a true passion that stirred her mind as much as her body.

Eleanor stopped at the cliff edge, watching as waves rushed to and fro onto the rocks below. The power and motion of the sea excited and soothed her at the same time: there was something comforting about the regular rhythms of the tides yet the strength of the water as it chipped away at the stone was frightening, too. She thought about the tales of ships lost along the coastline and shivered.

She turned away, watching the dogs as they scurried along. Bella was head down and tail up following the scent of some small creature under the heather while Crumpet the terrier poked her head down every hole in search of rabbits.

Eleanor breathed in the honeyed scent of gorse, which always reminded her of Ambre Solaire: spring was definitely here and summer would not be long in following.

Up ahead, she caught a glimpse of a brand-new building. This was a house and meditation centre designed by Freya, Daniel's ex-wife. The building was set far enough back from the cliff top not to cut off the public footpath and to avoid collapsing into the sea the next time rough weather claimed a bit more land for the ocean, as it did with alarming frequency.

The complex was too far away for Eleanor to see it well, but from a distance she could make out what would become a "green" roof sloping back towards the town. She had to concede that Cruella – as she was known to Eleanor and her sister – was a damn good architect: planting banks of pink and purple heather on the roof meant that the building would be almost invisible from the sides once the plants had grown up. At the front, the opaque glass and polished copper of the sweeping semicircular wall reflected the sea and sky, so the entire building would soon merge into the landscape.

The damned woman was talented but, best of all, she was now based in London out of harm's way. It was Freya who had divorced Dan, so Eleanor had no reason to dislike her or feel jealous, but she was wary. It had taken many months for Daniel to reconcile himself to the break-up and his first wife still mattered to him a great deal.

Freya was a woman who liked to be in control, and Eleanor always worried a little when she knew her predecessor was in town. She knew from Daniel that Freya popped back occasionally to check on progress at the building site but was generally happy to leave the day-to-day work in the hands of her project manager.

The house and meditation centre had been commissioned the year before by an ageing rock star who went by the name of Bill "Fingers" Widget. Bill had enjoyed a long and successful career as the front man of Tryll Spigot, a band better known for ear-shattering volume than catchy melodies. Bill's arrival had caused quite a stir, but Combemouth residents had gradually taken him to their bosom and were now rather proud of their celebrity resident.

The building was evidently going to be a beauty and no doubt lots of Bill's show biz friends would flock there to meditate and "find themselves", but Eleanor couldn't help chuckling at the thought of how much the smelly cliff-top goats and inquisitive ponies who lived on the moor would enjoy nibbling Freya's carefully arranged vegetation.

She put her head down as the route took her close to the end of the drive, concentrating instead on the pale stones under her feet. The last thing she wanted was to bump into Freya who – as well as being annoyingly talented – also had the unnerving capacity to look chic even at 8am.

Eleanor turned away, following the well-trodden path that looped up and around the headland. It was quite a climb and she was distinctly out of puff by the time she reached the top and could collapse onto a handy rock, the dogs panting at her feet.

It was a stunning spot from where she could look up and down the coast for miles in both directions. To the east, the land fell away towards Combemouth; to the west, a chain of scallop-shaped bays edged the land, disappearing into the distance. Eleanor closed her eyes, raising her face skyward. If she could choose to live anywhere, here on the Top would be a pretty good spot. She loved the fact that it was different every time she came: the sea, the sky and the plants beneath her feet were constantly changing.

Her heart sank slightly as she remembered the issue that was spoiling things between her and Daniel. He was the most important person in her life and she knew it was important to sort things out between them.

"Come on girls – it's time we did some work." She clambered to her feet and set off down the rough path at a clumsy jog, the wind at her back making the return journey much easier than the ascent. Looking towards Bill's house, she caught a flash of red through the trees and recognised the car: Freya was in town.

Chapter 7: Sisterly Advice

Once Eleanor had settled the dogs into the campervan, she had an urge to talk to Jenna. Checking her watch she could see that if she rang now, there was a chance she would catch her sister before she became too busy with school stuff. Jenna was Head of Maths at a smart London school and could usually be guaranteed to come up with a sensible solution to most things.

How odd it was to be sitting in her van, gazing out over the moor at an expanse of blue-grey water while Jenna was stuck in an office surrounded by paperwork. Eleanor smiled, very pleased to be where she was. The phone only rang two or three times before her sister answered. "Good morning, Jenna. How are things? Are your pupils being good?"

"Oh, you know what the little beggars are like. Just because mummy and daddy are stumping up squillions for Clytemnestra and Figaro's education doesn't mean they behave themselves any better than kids in ordinary schools."

Eleanor laughed at the silly names her sister came up with "to protect the innocent". "You love them really."

"You're right – I do. But how are things with you? As idyllic as ever, I'm guessing."

"A bit less than idyllic, actually."

"What's up? Run out of Combemouth tea towels?"

"Ha, ha! My life does get a teeny bit more stressful than that, you know?" It amused Eleanor that city girl Jenna believed everyone who lived outside the capital enjoyed a totally carefree existence.

"Okay, tell me what's up."

"The usual – we're not making any progress with the house-buying business and Dan is getting pretty grumpy about it."

"I'm sorry Sis, I know you've explained it to me before but I still don't see the problem. I mean, why would you not want to live in the cottage with your lovely, adoring husband? It's not like me and Kiff – I mean, we've been married and living together for so long that neither of us would survive alone in the wild." Jenna was quiet for a moment, obviously thinking. "We'd be like a couple of wildebeest separated from the herd. I'm sure I'd be picked off by hyenas in no time."

"You paint an interesting picture, but I can't say I'm following your rather dramatic analogy."

Jenna sighed. "In plain English, what I'm saying is that I know you're fine living – almost – independently, but I need Kiff around. If it's any consolation, living with the other half does get easier after the first couple of years."

"I remember: the first two years with Alan were great. It was the last two that were dire. But I have no intention of living on my own – everyone seems to forget that Daniel and I are together more than not. The problem isn't about us living together. The issue for me is giving up the cottage."

"Yup, it does sound pretty daft when it's your marriage at stake."

"Woah! I wouldn't go that far Jenna!"

"Okay, teensy exaggeration. But do you have to sell up? Couldn't you keep the cottage but rent it out to carefully vetted tenants?"

"I suppose I could, but I'd hate to have strangers living next to the shop. It wouldn't be right."

"In that case, what about Erika moving in?"

"I asked her if she'd like to, but as she works in the shop she says she'd rather not live in it as well. And her flat in the 1930s block is pretty fabulous."

Jenna sighed. "You have an unnatural affection for that house."

"I know it seems bonkers to love it so much, but it's part of me." Eleanor was frowning now as she struggled to explain what she meant. "I've chosen everything in it – the rag rugs, the 'vintage' crockery from the charity shops, the Welsh dresser, the hand-tinted prints on the wall." She frowned. "And I know it sounds daft, but I can't bear the thought of the house being separated from the bookshop when they've been a unit for two hundred years."

There was silence from Jenna, which was not an encouraging sign. After a moment or two she spoke again. "If you refuse to rent out or sell your place and Daniel won't – or can't – move in with you, then I don't see a solution."

"Oh dear." Eleanor sighed, disappointed that her clever sister hadn't been able to come up with a simple answer. "That's worrying because, at the moment, neither can I."

"Don't worry – everything will sort itself out eventually."

"Well, if you or Kiff come up with any brilliant ideas, let me know."

"I will. Meanwhile, how are Mum and Harold? Still giving it their all down at the salsa class?"

"Yup, in fact Alfonso has given the group a new routine to learn for the summer festival so they've been busy practising their moves. You should see Harold in his Cuban heels – he cuts quite a dash, I can tell you. And you thought Mum's internet date was a scammer and Harold didn't really exist." Eleanor smiled to herself, knowing that Jenna didn't like to be reminded that sometimes she got things wrong.

"Yes, it goes to show that not even I – your wiser, taller, older sister – can be right every time."

Chapter 8: A Blast from the Past

As Eleanor sat in the campervan chatting to Jenna, Daniel was on his regular run around town. After a few circuits of the little park with its Edwardian bandstand and flower clock, he decided to call in at his father's bungalow for tea and a chat.

Malcolm opened the door to find his son in a sweaty heap on the front step. "Come in and tell me how you got on yesterday," he said, leading the way into the kitchen. "Were those houses any good?"

"One was dreadful, three were okay and I thought two of them had potential. Actually, the 1960s property was stunning – all clean lines and big views."

"It sounds quite promising."

"You might think so, but I can't persuade El to make up her mind about any of them. I'm starting to think she won't ever choose a new house." It wasn't the kind of thing Daniel ever talked about – if friends asked when he and Eleanor were going to move, he made a joke about being impossible to live with. His father was not the sort of man to get into conversations that strayed into "delicate" territory, but today he decided it was time to say what he thought.

Malcolm was immensely fond of his new daughter-in-law, but could see the strain living in two places was having on his son. "I know it's possibly an outmoded view, but it does seem only right that you should set up home together, now you're man and wife." He paused to give Daniel a mug of strong tea and a thick slice of Maureen's simnel cake, bought yesterday at Ye Olde Tea Shoppe. "I suppose I am an old fuddy-duddy. On the other hand, I do understand Eleanor's reluctance to leave that lovely cottage of hers. It is jolly convenient for the shop and she has done it up beautifully." He stirred his tea, thoughtfully. "Can you really not share it with her?"

"I've half-moved in, as you know. The problem is it's too small for two adults with as much stuff as we have – even after Freya cleared me out. Joe's with us at the moment and there's nowhere for my daughter to stay when she visits. And there's also the tiny problem that I need a decent-sized office to work in." Daniel was a traditional architect who still enjoyed building scale models out of balsa wood and working in pen on large sheets of paper, not just designing things on a computer. "We need more space, Dad."

"And Eleanor can't be persuaded to move in with you?"

"I've tried, Dad, believe me. And she probably would if I insisted, but I don't want to force her into it." He ran his hand through his hair and sighed. "Ideally, I'd like us to find somewhere we can create together."

"It hardly seems unreasonable in the circumstances." Malcolm smiled at his son. "I'm sure she'll come round in time."

"Time!" Daniel made a sound somewhere between a laugh and a cry. "We've been together over two years and married for six months. How much more time does she need?"

Malcolm frowned. "In that case, maybe you need to try a different tack: be firmer with her – tell her how concerned you are and set a deadline, perhaps."

Daniel laughed. "Eleanor's not great with deadlines. No, I'll have to be patient for a little while longer, that's all." As he said the words, he believed them, but deep down he wanted the situation to be resolved and he left his father's house with a heavy heart.

Jogging back down the hill, the thought nagged at him that his first marriage had failed and his second was not going as smoothly as he would have wished. How committed was Eleanor if she didn't want to set up home with him?

He had reached the end of the path where it joined the main street when he bumped into Freya looking cool and elegant in a pale blue dress, a pair of outsize sunglasses perched on her head.

"Well, hello Dan. And where are you going in such a hurry?"

"It's called jogging and I'm going home if you must know."

Freya arched a slender eyebrow in a subtle gesture that managed to convey amusement, curiosity and a tiny bit of disdain. "And where is home these days?"

Daniel stood with his hands on his hips panting slightly. He nodded towards the sea front and the bright red door of his house. It was known as The Widows' House because of the two women who had lived there before him. "You know perfectly well where I live," he said, immediately angry with himself for falling into Freya's trap.

"With Edwina?"

The infuriating woman always knew how to push his buttons for maximum effect. "My wife's name is Eleanor."

"Of course it is. Silly me." Freya smiled. "It's odd, but I could have sworn I saw you coming out of the bookshop cottage with bags of clothes the other morning. Don't tell me you still haven't persuaded *Eleanor* to move in with you." She laughed outright. "Or has your snoring grown so bad she makes you sleep half a mile away?"

Daniel could feel the pressure building at the base of his skull, partly as a result of pounding down the road from Malcolm's house and partly from being put on the spot. It felt as though he'd been caught out, even though he and Eleanor made no secret of their unconventional living arrangements.

"Why the hell do you care who I live with and where?"

"Oh, idle curiosity."

"Well, it's none of your damn business. Now, if you don't mind, I've got work to do." And with that he turned and ran towards his house, furious with himself for losing his temper when they both knew that Freya only had to ask their daughter Emily what Daniel's living arrangements were. Freya had played him for a fool, yet again.

Once at the house, he stomped angrily around the kitchen ruing the day he had let her take their very expensive coffee machine. He had bought the damn thing for her birthday only a few months before their marriage broke up and, yes, he could quite easily afford to buy a new one but it rankled nonetheless.

He made himself a cup of nasty instant coffee and headed for the shower where he hoped a blast of cold water would help push Freya's face from his mind. But it was not to be. Even though they ran into each other fairly regularly, Dan's heart always missed a beat when he saw Freya's familiar figure in the distance, a leather folder of architect's plans under one arm.

It had not been his idea to divorce and the pain of dividing up "stuff" had been hard, but nowhere near as hard as wrenching Freya from his heart. She was his first love and her abandonment had left him hurt and angry.

When they separated, Daniel told her to take whatever she wanted from the cliff-top house they had designed together, a decision he regretted when she emptied the kitchen of all their best knives and gadgets.

Freya really was the most infuriating woman Daniel knew, yet he couldn't help feeling proud of what she'd achieved professionally. Since their separation, she had gone from strength to strength and he had almost grown used to seeing her name in the tabloids as the "wacky" architect responsible for the latest startling development.

Although they had trained and worked together, Freya was always the ambitious one: whereas Daniel was happy to build modest extensions for a nursery school or the doctor's surgery, Freya was keen to work with clients who wanted one-of-a-kind homes built from scratch, which is how she had ended up working for Bill Widget.

Daniel picked up the mug of cold coffee and swished it angrily down the sink. Pushing the wet hair from his brow, he examined his face in the bathroom mirror. "When will you ever get the hang of women?" he asked his reflection. The face in the mirror had no answer.

Chapter 9: A Visit to the Library

Eleanor and Daniel both agreed to a break from house-hunting the following weekend, so Eleanor took the opportunity to walk over to the library in search of inspiration for new window displays. She tried to change them every couple of weeks and worked hard to come up with exciting themes, some of which were more successful than others.

Last summer she'd created a holiday window with buckets and spades and plastic windmills. Shifting what seemed like a ton of sand had nearly done her back in, but the deckchairs and picnic hampers did look very jolly and caught people's eyes.

Eleanor didn't always stick with traditional themes. A few months after she had taken over the shop, there'd been a craze for a series of dreadful erotic novels. She and Erika had had great fun dressing up the window with pretend bondage gear from Graham's hardware store topped up with some chains and spiky dog collars purchased from Purrfect Pets. Visitors had loved it and Eleanor had enjoyed watching the reactions of passers-by more used to her predecessor Mr Williams' sensible displays of books on military history. Eleanor thought it was a triumph, but there had been a number of "Outraged of Combemouth" letters in the *Chronicle* so she'd had to tone it down a little.

Mulling over ideas for the festival week, she'd come to the conclusion that focusing on history might be just the job. She could dress the window with bits and pieces begged and borrowed from friends and neighbours, then display children's classic storybooks, romantic sagas, books on collecting antiques and local history. She wanted to narrow down the local history part and to do that she needed to research what Combemouth was famous for in Victorian times.

Eleanor had browsed her own shelves and realised that, although she had plenty of walking guides, she didn't have many books on history or folklore, which was why she'd decided to check out the library. She had loved libraries until she became a bookseller, since when she worried that they might lure away potential customers. And librarians were a funny lot – fancy giving someone a book to read then expecting them to bring it back. Preposterous!

Stuffing a notepad into her bag, Eleanor headed over to the library, cutting down side streets to avoid the main road which was busy with shoppers and tourists dripping ice cream down their tops.

Peering through the glass door of the building, her heart sank when she saw Dismal Deirdre sitting at the information desk. She had expected one of the cheerful volunteers to be on duty, but she was out of luck. Eleanor hoped to duck behind the display boards and skirt past the librarian unnoticed, but it was not to be.

Form a vision of an old-fashioned librarian and she is likely to look like Deirdre: a thin, wiry individual in a tweed skirt. Her skin, hair, eyes and cardigan were all in shades of blue-grey, as though she'd been placed in a shop window and left in strong sunlight for so long that the colour had leeched out of her. She was the only qualified librarian in town, the others having been sacked by the council and replaced with eager volunteers in the latest round of "efficiency savings".

Deirdre felt herself to be far superior to them and certainly superior to booksellers who, to her mind, were nothing more than amateurs. Recognising Eleanor as she approached across the dusty carpet tiles, her thin lips formed themselves into a polite smile. "We don't often see you in here, Mrs Mace."

"Pearce – I'm Mrs Pearce now."

"Ah, yes. So you are. Congratulations, if I've not said it before."

You haven't, thought Eleanor, gritting her teeth. "Thank you."

Unlikely as it seemed, Deirdre had been a supporter of Daniel's ex-wife. Freya had been a member of the library's rather earnest book club, a fact of which Deirdre was immensely proud. She thought it lent the club gravitas to have a woman of Freya's creative talents among them. It wasn't every club, she liked to boast, that had an award-winning architect in its midst. Ironically, Eleanor had it on good authority that Freya couldn't abide Deirdre – something the librarian was blissfully unaware of.

Since she was now based in London, Freya's attendance at the book club was sporadic at best, and it seemed to Eleanor that Deirdre held her unfairly responsible for the departure of the group's most interesting member.

"How can we help you today? Looking for a book?" Deirdre chuckled dryly. "Of course, a little shop like yours is quite limited in what it can stock whereas through the library system we have access to every book in the country."

Eleanor smiled, suppressing an urge to grab the pencil that Deirdre was using to gesture at the shelves and jam it up the woman's nose. "I was hoping you could direct me to any books you might have about the local area."

"Local agriculture? Archaeology? Our geology and geography? Wildlife? Flora and fauna? Folklore? Folk music? If you can tell me exactly what you're looking for, I shall be able to direct you further."

The woman was so smug and insufferable that Eleanor couldn't bring herself to give her any more information. Instead she said, "Oh, nothing in particular. If you can point me in the direction of folklore, I'll start there."

Satisfied that she had succeeded in overwhelming Eleanor with choice, Deirdre stood up and came round from behind her desk in the sky blue "Service Pod". "If you'll follow me."

"Oh, there's no need." It was hardly the British Library and she wasn't likely to get lost. "If you point me in the right direction I'm sure I'll find it."

"No, no – I insist. It's all part of the enhanced information experience we now offer to our clients."

The enhanced what? And since when did libraries have clients? Eleanor was obviously not going to win this one, so she meekly followed Deirdre's bony hips across the room and up some steps to a mezzanine area whose dull-green walls were lined with bookshelves.

Deirdre gave Eleanor a satisfied smile. "If you require any further research assistance or need help using the 'Read, Renew and Return Pods', do feel free to ask."

"Thanks," said Eleanor, sourly. She took off her jacket, hanging it over the back of a chair, and plonked her bag on the oval table. A man snoozing in an armchair at the other end of the mezzanine stirred at the sound, then closed his eyes and went back to sleep.

Wrinkling her nose at the musty smell rising from the corner, Eleanor went over to the shelves, pulled out half a dozen titles and carried them over to the table. It was strange, but library books had a scent of their own – of greasy fingers and other people's living rooms.

The book on folklore she picked up was from the late 1950s, but not much seemed to have changed in Combemouth and the year was still punctuated by wassails, summer regattas and harvest festivals. She jotted down a couple of notes, but there wasn't much here that wasn't already familiar to her.

The next book was a collection of essays on industry at the turn of the twentieth century and showed farmhands with immense bushy beards wearing smocks, holding pitchforks and standing next to melancholy mules.

Another chapter featured fishermen mending nets and preparing lobster pots. Turning the page she found a group of men on what she recognised as their harbour. Behind them was the Ship Inn where she and Daniel liked to sit and watch the activity in the bay over a drink. The fishermen were swarthy, any exposed skin tanned by the harsh weather they encountered out at sea, month after month. In the black and white photographs, the men's eyes shone out of their dark faces making them look startlingly alive.

For a moment, Eleanor felt a strange sensation wash over her: it was as though there was nothing between her and the men in the photo. No camera, no book, no time. The men's intense gazes seemed to flicker as she stared at their faces and she felt herself being sucked into the page. The sensation lasted for a fraction of a second then was gone. A blind flapped as a spring breeze blew through the open window behind her and she shivered. She shook herself, feeling slightly foolish, and closed the book.

The fishermen's sombre expressions brought to mind Maureen's story about the ghost ship and Eleanor shivered again. Was it possible to do a jolly window display about the town's seafaring heritage without mentioning death and drowning, she wondered? Probably not. But people loved pirates! Yes, that was it. She could have a window featuring fishermen, the *Santa Ana* and a few smugglers. She tapped the pen against her lips and frowned. That sounded like a bit of a muddle. And wouldn't a fishing theme be too close to her seaside window of the previous year? Perhaps she'd do best to restrict it to pirates and ghost ships. Eleanor smiled to herself, thinking of the children's books she could feature.

Happy to have some ideas to work on, she walked over to the shelves and carefully restacked the books apart from the one with the fishermen, a history of smuggling and a collection of marine myths and legends from the South West.

Mission accomplished. All that was left was to

sneak past the Keeper of the Books. Looking down from the mezzanine to the floor below, Eleanor could see that Deirdre had cornered some other poor woman in the crafts area and was loading her up with books about cross-stitch. Seeing a chance of escape, Eleanor trotted down the stairs, quickly checked out her books at a "Self-service Pod" and escaped into the sunny back street.

* * *

In bed that night Eleanor leafed through the books, making more notes of ideas as they came to her. "Wow – there's something here about the Combemouth ghost ship."

Daniel turned and leant on his elbow, looking at the book about marine myths propped up on Eleanor's lap. "What does it say?"

"It says pretty much what you told me the other day: that she is only seen every few years, often in late spring and usually in the days before or after a full moon. 'No one has yet come up with a scientific explanation for the vision,' blah, blah, 'but some superstitious folk believe a sighting of the *Santa Ana* heralds trouble.' Yikes, I don't much like the sound of that." Eleanor turned the page. "There's a rather nice illustration here, though," she said, tilting the page towards her husband.

"Let me see." Daniel ran a finger over the black and white print of a square-rigged galleon. "Yup, that looks like her," he said, smiling. "The artist was obviously at the beach at precisely the right moment with his etching kit."

"Very funny. It's spooky, though, don't you think? I might need to add some old ropes and cobwebs to the shop window. Or maybe sand and a treasure chest?"

"The garden centre will be pleased to sell you another ton of sand, I'm sure."

"Hmm, I might use a bit less this time," she said, laughing.

"Sounds sensible. Let's put these away, shall we?" Daniel took the book and notepad from Eleanor's hands and placed them by the side of the bed. "I don't want you having nightmares."

Eleanor snuggled up against him, relieved the tension between them had abated at last. "How could I possibly have nightmares when I'm safe in your arms?"

Daniel switched off the light. "I'm not sure you're terribly safe with me tonight."

"Goody," she said, lifting her face to meet her husband's kiss.

Chapter 10: Past Times

A day or so later, Daniel came home to find Eleanor kneeling on the floor of the living room surrounded by paper. "What have you got there?"

"I've been having a clear-out." Eleanor patted one of the battered cartons. "I expected them to be full of ancient invoices and shop paperwork from Frederick Williams' time, but a couple contain old newspapers and magazines and they're fascinating. Look – some of the Victorian ones are falling apart, but the papers from the 1920s are in good condition. The adverts are hilarious." She spread out the pages on the low coffee table. "I definitely need some of this magic soap that washes all the fat from your body leaving you slender as a flower." She pulled out another paper. "And I'm sure my puddings would benefit from the inclusion of evaporated milk. I might be able to use these adverts in the historical window display I'm planning."

Joining Eleanor on the carpet, Daniel leafed through the pile. "This paper is from the 1890s. Your predecessor clearly wasn't a man who ever threw anything away."

Eleanor smiled. "I remember when I bought the shop that Mr Williams told me he used to sell vintage newspapers. They were in with the stuff he left me but, to be honest, I'd forgotten I had them."

"I can see why he threw them in with the deal."

"Don't be mean," said Eleanor, playfully slapping

her husband's arm. "There are plenty of people who trade in old papers and magazines or they cut out and sell the illustrations separately and make a mint. Which, I guess, explains why some of the pages are missing. Anyway, I ought to ring Frederick and tell him what I've found in case he wants them back."

"I thought you bought them from him?"

"Technically yes, but I'd still prefer to double-check."

"That's very honourable of you, EI, but I doubt he'll even remember they exist – those boxes must have been in the office for a very long time." Daniel opened up one of the magazines. "There's an interesting story here about a runaway mule. It looks like the owner unhitched it from the cart and the animal took its chance of freedom and legged it, causing chaos in the market square. Oh," he frowned, "don't read the last bit it will upset you."

"I already have and it did. The unlucky beast was caught and 'soundly whipped'." Eleanor sighed. "They were harsh times and people weren't always treated more kindly than the animals." She began riffling through the newspapers. "I've been reading the news and features and there's a story that seems to have gripped the population here in the South West for some weeks."

"What's that?"

"It's in a section entitled '50 Years Ago' in a paper from 1922." Eleanor turned over a Bovril advert. "It's about a boy who was accused of stealing some jewellery. It clearly raised a lot of debate, with people arguing for and against the lad. The fact it was featured in a paper half a century after the event suggests it was quite a big deal."

"What happened to the little rascal? Did he end up being thrashed like that unfortunate animal?"

"I don't know. The page with the verdict on it is missing. Don't you think that's odd?"

"Not really – it may have had a particularly exciting advertisement on it," said Daniel. "Or perhaps it was used to wrap something like fish and chips."

"Ooh, fish and chips! I wish you hadn't said those words." Eleanor rubbed her tummy, which gurgled in response. "I'm ravenous and today is supposed to be one of my fasting days when all I can eat is lettuce and half a handful of blueberries."

Daniel stood up and pulled his wife to her feet. "I've said a hundred times you don't need to lose any weight – you're perfect as you are."

"Do you think so?" she asked, pinching the soft skin around her waist.

"I honestly do."

"Well, in that case Dan, cod and small chips for me, please. Hold the mushy peas."

"Would you like me to fetch them so we can have supper here in the comfort of our warm kitchen, or would you prefer to freeze your socks off by the sea?"

"Freezing by the sea, of course. It's the only way to eat fish and chips. I'll grab my coat."

Half an hour later they were huddled together on their favourite bench on the sea front munching their supper. It wasn't a particularly pleasant evening: the low clouds had a yellow tinge and there was the hint of a storm brewing over the horizon.

"I've been thinking about that story," said Eleanor, licking her salty fingers.

"About the donkey?"

"It was a mule, not a donkey. But no – not about that. About John Able, the boy who was arrested. He was only eleven and the snippet I read suggested he was likely to be sent to prison."

"So?"

"So, I'd quite like to find out what happened to him."

Daniel thought for a moment. "When did this all happen?"

"Sometime in the 1870s, I think."

"Were they deporting ne'er-do-wells to Australia then? He may have made a new life in the Antipodes or begun a long life of crime here."

"I hope the answer isn't the latter."

Daniel paused to wipe his mouth. "If he was stealing stuff as a nipper, I suspect he was a proper little villain."

Eleanor was shocked. "You can't say that without knowing the circumstances, Dan."

"Theft is theft."

"You sound like Erika! In any case, I can't believe a child of his age would steal for no reason."

Daniel shrugged. "I guess you'll never know what happened."

"But I could try to find out."

"And how are you going to do that?"

"I've no idea," said Eleanor, popping the crispy bits of her chips from the bottom of the bag into her mouth, "but I reckon Jim might be able to help."

"Your journalist friend?" Daniel nodded slowly. "Yes, I suppose he would be a good person to ask, but wouldn't it make more sense to visit the library first?"

"And put up with Dismal Deirdre droning on about

what a fabulous local history selection they have all over again? Nope." Eleanor shook her head. "I'm afraid that Combemouth Library will be absolutely my last resort until they bring in one of those bright young women from Waterborough."

The wind had changed direction, sending sand swirling around their feet, and the air had acquired a strange metallic tang that heralded a storm. From their bench on the promenade, they could see a dense clump of rain clouds heading straight for them.

Daniel took Eleanor's empty paper and scrunched it into a ball before deftly firing it into a nearby bin. "Goal!" Leaping to his feet he took her hand. "Ready to go?"

"I am!" she said, as they turned and ran back towards home, the rain at their backs.

* * *

While she was waiting for the kettle to boil, Eleanor decided to call Jim Rowe. Since marrying Dan, she'd neglected quite a few of her friends, especially the men she used to hang around with. There had also been a tricky period after Jim and Erika had broken up: they had gone out together for almost a year and Eleanor felt she couldn't see too much of Jim out of loyalty to her colleague. The fact the relationship hadn't endured had been hugely upsetting for Erika, and it wasn't until she and Jim had found a way to be civil again that Eleanor really felt able to socialise with him.

When Jim answered the phone, Eleanor asked if he would be free for a beer sometime. "It would be great to see you, but I also have a favour to ask."

"Sure, it's been a while since we had a drink together."

"You're right – I'm sorry about that, but I have been ridiculously busy." Eleanor pulled a face, aware of what a weak excuse it was and glad Jim couldn't see her cringing.

"It's okay," said Jim, kindly. "I understand. So when and where?"

"What are you doing tomorrow evening?"

"Nothing in particular."

"Fancy a pint at the King's Head? My treat."

"Sounds perfect."

"Great – I'll see you then."

"Oh, and what's the favour about?"

"I want your advice on how I might investigate some local history."

"Sounds intriguing!"

"It is, Jim, and I'll tell you about it tomorrow."

Chapter 11: Some Local Knowledge

When they were seated in the saloon bar at the pub, Eleanor told Jim what the favour was. "I want to follow up on a newspaper story I've come across, but I've no idea how to go about it. I thought you might be able to advise me where to start."

"Do you know the name of the paper and the approximate date?"

"It's the *North Devon Echo* and I know it happened in the early 1870s."

"That'll be easy enough," said Jim. "There are various options – you might want to check out the newspaper archives at the British Library."

"That's in London! Is there nothing closer?"

"The *Echo* merged with my own newspaper many years ago, but I know the *Gazette* keeps some old copies in binders and on microfiche in the office. If you can cope with their ancient technology, you might find what you need there."

Eleanor pulled out a notepad and pen. "Where are they based?"

"Behind the town hall in Waterborough. Or you could register with the British Newspaper Archives and search online."

"I ask myself what would a proper sleuth do and it's got to be the musty files behind the town hall."

"And what was the story you're interested in?"

"Oh, it was a snippet about a local lad who was arrested. I'm curious to know what happened to him, that's all."

Jim nodded, then swallowed the last of his beer. "Fancy another one of those?" he asked, indicating Eleanor's almost empty glass.

"Sure, why not."

As Jim went up to the bar, Eleanor's eyes drifted around the pub's cosy front room. Just above head height, the walls were covered with photographs and antique prints. On a shelf a foot or so below the ceiling was a collection of nautical paraphernalia from quadrants to glass buoys. In pride of place at the end of the bar was a brass bell and a fully rigged sailing ship in a bottle. It would, she thought, be a nice look to recreate in her seafaring window display.

Jim came back and set the drinks in front of her. "So what's this new interest in sleuthing all about, then?"

"Sleuthing and seafaring." Eleanor laughed. "I've lived here nearly seven years but I'm still ignorant about the place. I mean, Combemouth wouldn't exist without the sea but I know virtually nothing about the old fishing trade." She took a sip of her drink, which felt pleasantly cool against her throat. "As the local bookseller, I feel I should be more knowledge-able generally."

"I'm not sure how much there is to know. Combemouth was a traditional fishing town like lots of others along this stretch of coast."

"Just fishing? Did anything more exciting go on?"

"I guess shale and manufactured goods were trans-ported between Bristol and the rest of the world."

Eleanor thought for a moment. "I've also been

thinking about doing a display based around a ghost ship that Maureen and Daniel both say they've seen, which probably sounds a bit mad!"

"Not to me," said Jim, shaking his head. "Which ghost ship were you thinking of?"

Eleanor laughed. "You mean there's more than one?"

"There could be. Some people describe a vessel that sounds like a Tudor galleon – all high wooden sides and cannon like the famous *Mary Rose*. Others describe something more like a schooner."

"Which is? You see how ignorant I am!"

"Schooners are fast, high-masted sailing ships. They were very popular trading vessels in the eighteenth and nineteenth centuries. If you'd been sipping your pint of Old Wallop on the quay in 1890, that's what you might have seen sailing by. As well as these, of course." Jim half-turned and tapped at one of the photographs on the wall behind his head. "These guys were local fishermen and they went to sea in much smaller three-masted boats called luggers."

Eleanor studied the photograph of five men in oilskins gathered awkwardly around a pile of nets, as though aggrieved at being asked to pose for the photographer instead of getting on with their work. One man, who appeared to be in charge, stood to one side in a loosely fitted suit and a white shirt with a starched collar. He held a hat in his left hand while his right was placed jauntily on his hip.

Jim shifted along so Eleanor could move in closer. "It's very atmospheric. Do we know who these people were?"

"Probably not – names tend not to be recorded." Jim peered at the photo. "On the other hand, the photographer might have kept a record at his studio. I can't imagine the business is still going, though."

"Could you pass it to me? I'd love to get hold of a copy."

While the landlord wasn't looking, Jim unhooked the photograph from the wall and handed it to Eleanor who turned it over to read the label on the back. "Dipton Photographic Studios," she said, writing it down in her pad. "This could be the perfect thing to add a touch of authenticity to my shop." She smiled. "I'll look them up."

Chapter 12: Connie Brings News

Tuesday was not one of the days when Connie worked at the bookshop, but she and Harold often dropped in to The Reading Room to check up on things if they happened to be passing. Seeing that the shop was quiet, Connie was able to persuade her daughter to take a break. Over coffee in the shop's café area, Eleanor made the mistake of mentioning the issues she was still having with Dan about where they should live.

"I do think you're being unfair on the poor boy not letting him move in with you," said Connie, whose sympathies lay firmly with Daniel.

Eleanor took a deep breath. "It's not about being fair or not, it's about the practicalities. And I've never said he couldn't move in. The fact is the cottage is too small for me, Dan and Joe – plus Emily when she's visiting her father – and we haven't seen anywhere else we like enough to buy."

"I really don't see why you can't fit in the cottage – there would have been a family of ten and half a farmyard crammed in there in the olden days."

"That might be a bit of an exaggeration, Mother."

"But then you were just the same as a child," said Connie, ignoring her.

"I beg your pardon?"

"You'd never allow your sister into the Wendy

House because you wanted to have it all to yourself."

"That's not fair!" Eleanor was aware of squeaking like her seven-year-old self, but couldn't help it. "I was trying to save my dolls. Whenever I let Jenna in, she'd make them play at 'school' for hours. Poor Teddy always ended up in detention because he was like me and couldn't remember his twelve-times table."

"There you are, you see," said Connie, leaning towards her gentleman friend. "My younger daughter was never keen on sharing."

"I'm sure both your girls were delightful children," said Harold, keen to avert a row. "Now then," he said, rubbing his hands together, "has your mother told you the exciting news?"

"No," said Eleanor, frowning. "Let me guess. She's got a job as a lap-dancer? Taken up kite-surfing? Robbed a bank?" Since finding Harold, Connie had enjoyed a new lease of life and her daughters never knew quite what she was going to do next. Recent adventures included a thousand-mile overland trip to the South of France in Eleanor's antique camp-ervan to visit Harold's daughter.

"The news isn't about me," said Connie, sniffily.

"I'm very relieved to hear it. I'd rather not see your face splashed across the papers again for a while longer." The previous summer, Eleanor had found herself reluctantly heading up a campaign to block a marina, cliff-top aquarium and dodgy statuary – including a generously proportioned naked woman dubbed "Busty Bertha" – all planned by Freya for Bill Widget, then newly arrived in town. Eleanor and her mother had been thrust into the limelight – in

Connie's case that meant a profile of her on page three of the local newspaper.

"If you're referring to my part in the campaign, that was many months ago. And I wasn't 'splashed' – Jim did a nice in-depth feature about me for the *Chronicle*." Connie had caused quite a stir by lying down in the road during a protest march, which had provoked a spontaneous sit-down by her supporters, all of whom had to be persuaded to get up and leave by one long-suffering PC.

Although Eleanor could laugh about it now, the planning protest had caused a great deal of tension between her and Daniel who took the side of his ex-wife. The situation had become so bad at one stage that Eleanor had feared their relationship might not survive it.

Happily, things were eventually resolved and Freya had been allowed to design Bill the more restrained building on the moor where Eleanor walked the dogs.

"They still tease me down at the bowling club for stepping out with a 'page three' girl," said Harold with a chuckle.

"Oh, you are cheeky." Connie batted him playfully on the arm. "You know very well that my topless-modelling days are long gone."

"Enough, Mum. You'll be giving me nightmares." Eleanor cringed at the alarming picture forming in her head. "You were very lucky not to be arrested for threatening a police officer."

"You do exaggerate, dear. My foot didn't connect with the PC's shin and, anyway, I was wearing my wide-fitting moccasins. You can't do much damage with those."

"Your mother's quite right, they're very soft shoes," said Harold, thoughtfully. "Did you know that moccasin is a Native American word? Algonquin, I think it is."

"Is that so?" said Eleanor, before turning back to her mother. "Okay then Pocahontas, what is this exciting news Harold has promised us?"

"Did someone mention news?" Erika put down the box of books she was quietly unpacking and came over to join them from the back of the shop.

"It's still very hush-hush."

"Your secret's safe with me, Connie."

"I know you're not one to gossip, Erika, but I'm not sure about my daughter."

Eleanor rolled her eyes. "Are you going to tell us this news or not?"

"As I was about to say," said Connie, patting her curls, "while Beryl was doing my hair, she mentioned she'd heard from the vicar that Bill Widget has agreed to open the summer festival. There," said Connie looking pleased with herself, "what do you think about that?"

"I think it's splendid, so long as your friend promises not to sing."

"Don't be unkind, Eleanor. Bill has a lovely singing voice. It only sounds harsh and screechy because he has to shout over the noise of his band."

Having helped to defeat Bill Widget's original plans, Connie had become one of the singer's fiercest supporters and wouldn't hear a word said against him.

"And will his bandmates be making an appearance, too?" asked Eleanor. "I'm not sure how the good burghers of Combemouth would cope with their brand of ear-shattering rock music."

"No, I don't think Bill will have the rest of Tryll Spigot with him. They're taking a creative break and are unlikely to reform for a while yet." Connie picked up her handbag, preparing to leave. "And I'd say they were more thrash metal than rock."

Eleanor was always amazed by the random stuff her mother knew. "I'm sure you're right." Connie had become something of a rock music connoisseur since Bill's move to the area. "In any case, having 'Fingers' Widget involved is bound to bring in people to the event, which the vicar and his team will be pleased about."

Harold put his arm around Connie's shoulder. "I don't want to rush you, but we'd better be off now, love. I have a Skype date with the French grandchildren in an hour."

"How is Rachel?" asked Eleanor. "Is the guesthouse doing well?"

"The Tournesol Guesthouse seems to be flourishing, I'm pleased to say. Though I'm not so sure about my daughter's erratic love life," added Harold with a frown.

Connie squeezed his hand. "Rachel's a free woman again and she's having some fun."

Rachel was recently divorced and her father couldn't help worrying about her and the children. "I suppose so," said Harold, "though I'll feel better when she settles down with a nice man."

"Don't be such a spoilsport. In any case, your daughter has plenty of friends to look after her if anything goes wrong."

"As usual you're right, sweetheart," said Harold, beaming at Connie. "Shall we go?"

"Bless them," said Eleanor, watching the elderly pair leave the shop, hand in hand. "What you see there is true love."

Erika nodded a little wistfully. "Maybe there's hope for the rest of us."

* * *

Eleanor's mother had met Harold thanks to a silver surfers' computing course at the village hall. Having mastered email and online shopping, Connie quickly advanced to cruising dating sites and it wasn't long before the virtual Harold caught her eye.

Her daughters had been alarmed by this development. Buying your groceries online was one thing; hooking up with a strange man was not what they expected of their sensible, seventy-something parent. Connie had tried and rejected a few no-hopers along the way but, when she spied Harold, she declared that this was the man for her and they were off on a mini-break together.

Feeling she needed backup, Eleanor had dragged Jenna all the way from Islington to Devon to speak to Connie in person. Eleanor vividly remembered giving their mother a stern talking to over a pot of tea and a slice of lemon drizzle at Ye Olde Tea Shoppe while Maureen hovered in the background pretending not to listen.

"For once I agree with my little sister," said Jenna. "You can't go on holiday with a man you've never met in the flesh."

Connie folded her arms across her chest – a sure sign that her mind was made up and she wouldn't be shifted. "I distinctly remember your father and I letting Eleanor go off to stay with a pen pal in Germany – Brünhilde or whatever her name was – and I didn't complain about that."

Eleanor spluttered. "That was completely different. She was called Anna, she was a fourteen-year-old girl and I was staying with her family."

"The point," said Connie, stirring her tea, "is that Harold and I are pen pals and I don't see why we shouldn't have a little holiday together." Maureen caught her friend's eye and nodded surreptitiously.

"How do you know he's what he says he is?" asked Jenna, reading Harold's dating profile which she had printed out in preparation for the showdown. "I wouldn't be the least bit surprised if that mop of silver hair and those twinkly eyes were a front and you're actually exchanging billets-doux with a Gambian teenager in his bedroom. I've seen a documentary about these guys: soon he'll be coming out with a stream of hard-luck stories so he can get his mitts on your savings. He'll tell you he needs £5,000 for a new mobility scooter or a stair lift, when in fact the Gambian Harold will be using your cash to open a beach bar in Banjul."

"Really, Jenna, you do talk nonsense. Harold and I have exchanged emails and spoken on the telephone several times and he's plainly not an African gentleman. And I will meet him before our trip to check we are compatible – I'm not foolish enough to go away with someone without first checking their table manners." Aware that her daughters were still not convinced, Connie paused to reapply her lipstick then closed her compact with a snap. "Answer me this:

would someone from the Dark Continent suggest meeting for tea and an Eccles cake at Loxley Garden Centre?" Seeing that her daughters were too stunned to find words to counter this, Connie smiled. "I rest my case."

Not even Jenna could argue with the logic of trial by Eccles cake, so Connie was give permission to meet Harold – on condition that she promised to take a mobile phone (preferably switched on) and call them if the topic of beach bars arose.

After one garden centre, two stately homes and three nights at a B&B in the Cotswolds, Connie and Harold were most definitely an item and had been inseparable ever since.

Chapter 13: Dan Finds a Solution

Eleanor pressed her cheek against Daniel's warm skin, enjoying the sensation of the steady beat of his heart and the slow rise and fall of his chest as they dozed in bed. It was a Sunday morning at the beginning of May and Eleanor was sure there were subtle changes in the sounds outside their window. As she closed her eyes to listen, the seagulls' calls were as strident as ever but the blackbird's song was definitely more joyful, as though it could sense the approach of summer.

Daniel was propped up against a pillow, a hand behind his head, staring silently at the ceiling. Neither of them had said anything yet that morning, so it was a surprise when Dan spoke as though continuing a conversation. "I've come to a decision: if I can't persuade you to move, I guess we'll have to think about reorganising this place."

Eleanor sat up, suddenly wide awake, and turned to look at him. "Really?" she said, hardly believing what she'd heard. "Would you mind staying here?"

"I won't lie, El – I hoped we would start afresh somewhere that was completely new for both of us, but as we can't seem to agree on anywhere at the moment, I suppose we'll have to find a way to make it work."

She chewed her lip, guiltily. "I wish you loved the cottage as much as I do."

"I'm very fond of it, El, you know I am. We've had some wonderful times here. But it is a squash for two grown-ups – three if you count Joe – with a lifetime's worth of gear or what's left after losing half of it in a divorce." Dan shrugged. "But I love you and want you to be happy, and that's what matters most. And maybe, in a few years' time, you'll feel differently and be ready to move."

A smile lit up Eleanor's face. "Thank you, darling," she said, kissing her husband.

Daniel caught her hand in his, squeezing it for emphasis. "But, you will need to make a few changes – maybe swap rooms around and get rid of some books, clothes, furniture and other stuff to make space for the rest of my things."

"Of course," said Eleanor, nodding eagerly. "I'll do whatever needs to be done to make the cottage work for all of us." She beamed, taken by surprise by the sense of relief and happiness that washed over her. "I'm so happy at not having to move. I know you think I'm unduly fond of this place – and you're probably right – and I can't really explain why it means such a lot to me, but it does."

"I know." Daniel caught her in his arms and gently pulled her towards him. "Come here, woman, and show me how grateful you are!"

* * *

Eleanor didn't bother to ask what had made Daniel change his mind; she was simply delighted it had happened. If she had asked, Daniel might have been a tiny bit embarrassed to tell her.

The previous evening he had been out for a meal with friends in the same business as him, a group jokingly calling itself the AA or "Architects Anonymous". Eleanor had been to a couple of get-togethers at the beginning of her relationship with Daniel, but had soon come to the conclusion that she was happier at home with a fat paperback and a bar of chocolate. Dan's friends were charming and welcoming, but Eleanor had found the conversations about planning regulations, tenure-blind housing and energy targets hard to follow.

The subject of Daniel's living arrangements had come up the night before because his friends could see he was increasingly unhappy. Dan tended not to talk about personal things, but that evening he gave the group the low-down on the house-hunting trials and tribulations. "We've scoured the entire area and I've come to the conclusion that the perfect house doesn't exist," he said, gloomily. "We'll be stuck in separate homes forever."

His friend Michael tapped a fork against his glass and called everyone to attention. "Okay ladies and gents, our mission this evening is to solve the Pearce housing crisis."

So Daniel described his sea-front house and Eleanor's cottage while his friends made notes and scribbled drawings on napkins. Eventually, Michael's colleague Angela sat back in her seat and smiled. "At the risk of stating the bleeding obvious, couldn't you simply rearrange the rooms at the bookshop cottage? It's clearly in the ideal location and you could perhaps do something with the loft. I wouldn't be surprised if there wasn't potential for another bedroom up there."

"Of course!" said Daniel. The answer had been staring him in the face all the time. "Thank you," he said, raising his glass to them. "You guys are the best."

* * *

Having made up his mind that they would stay in the bookshop cottage, with typical efficiency Daniel set to work planning how to make the available space work for them. After breakfast, he went from room to room taking measurements, tapping on walls and jotting everything down in a notebook.

Downstairs was their kitchen, a pantry and the sitting room. Above was Eleanor's bedroom, two smaller bedrooms and cupboard space. On the landing, Daniel stopped and looked up at the ceiling. "What's in the attic, El?"

"Gosh, I really don't know."

"You've never been up there?"

She shook her head. "Not all the way inside. When I bought the house, the surveyor got out a stepladder for me and I popped my head through the gap and shone a torch around, but I didn't actually climb into the loft and explore."

"Right," said Daniel, shoving the notepad in his back pocket. "Where can I find this stepladder?"

"Follow me." Eleanor led the way back through the kitchen and into the garden. Along the side of the house was a small shed full of clutter.

When the stepladder was eventually disentangled from the hosepipe, garden tools and flowerpots, Dan frowned. "This is far too short. It's no wonder you weren't able to see anything. I'll pop next door and see if Graham can sell me a decent set from the hardware shop."

The shop was closed, but Anton was around and happy to help. Daniel gingerly carried the shiny new ladder back through Eleanor's cottage and up the narrow staircase, sending wobbly piles of books skidding down behind him.

Eleanor stayed on the landing while Daniel climbed into the loft space and disappeared from view. She watched the beam from his torch flicker across the square of roof visible from where she stood craning her neck upwards. Above her head she could hear her husband's tentative footsteps and some knocking sounds.

"What can you see? Is there anything interesting up there?"

"Lots!" Daniel's face reappeared in the gap, his cheeks now streaked with dust. "It's a big space and the floor has been boarded and the roof looks sound."

"Good." Eleanor nodded. "That's what the surveyor said when I bought it."

"Did he or she survey the shop as well?"

"No," she said, slowly. "I seem to remember someone else checking out the shop."

Daniel had switched off his torch and was climbing down the stepladder backwards. "I think we need to check out the attic next door."

Fortunately, the loft space at the shop was more easily accessed because Mr Williams had had proper drop-down ladders fitted some time in the past. Climbing inside, they switched on the light and Eleanor went ahead, followed by Daniel who again jotted down measurements on his pad. "Very good, yes." He muttered. "Just as I thought."

"What is it, Dan? You look pleased with yourself."

"I am pleased – very pleased!" He walked across to one end of the room. "This," he said, patting the rough stone, "is the end wall. Good and solid." He walked over to the other side. "And this is the division between the shop and the cottage. Knock here – can you hear it?"

Eleanor knocked and listened. "What am I supposed to be listening to?"

"The sound of nothing or, to be more precise, the sound of a wooden screen between this space and the next."

"Oh, very *Star Trek*. But what does it mean?"

Daniel came across and hugged her. "It means, my darling, that this must have been one building at some time in the past and no one bothered to divide up the loft spaces properly when the bookshop was created. There's no load-bearing wall to worry about, so we can take down the partition and open up the whole area." He put the pencil behind his ear and threw his arms wide. "This space goes right across the length of the shop and the cottage: it's huge." His enthusiasm had returned and he could see the design potential in the space. "We could put a window in that end and more windows along the back of the building overlooking the sea. It's going to be impressive. What do you think?"

Eleanor grinned, delighted to see her husband so excited about the project. "It sounds wonderful. But won't we need planning permission to do something like that?"

"Probably and it could take months to come through, but it'll be worth it in the end because you won't need to leave your beloved cottage."

"Months? How many months?"

"Well, it's almost May now so, if we get permission this summer, we'll be able to start work in the autumn and have it done by the end of the year."

"But that's not for ages!"

Daniel shrugged. "It's the way it works, I'm afraid. And until then, we'll keep doing what we're doing."

Eleanor's heart sank. The solution was perfect and she could see the new room in her mind's eye, so she was disappointed they might not be allowed to begin work for such a long time.

Seeing his wife's gloomy expression, Daniel smiled. "I could be wrong and it may come through much faster, but it's best to be cautious in my experience. Anyway, can you dig out the floor plans and the original surveys so I can double-check I've got this right?"

"Sure – once I've remembered where they are."

After lunch, Eleanor dug out the paperwork for the shop and the cottage and plonked four box files on the kitchen table. "Red's the shop and blue's the house. Enjoy!"

"Thanks," said Daniel. "I'll have fun checking them out tomorrow."

The next day, while Eleanor was busy in the shop, Daniel examined the floor plans for both properties: as he'd guessed, the attic space ran across the length of the building and there was no solid division between the two parts. Then he turned to the paperwork. "Well, what do you know!" Packing the papers into a folder, he jogged downstairs and went into the bookshop next door.

"Can you take a break, El? I've got something to show you."

Eleanor looked at Erika who nodded. "Go ahead."

Once they were sitting in the office, Daniel took out the papers and spread them over the desk in front of Eleanor. "This is perfect," he said, grinning. "Your Mr Williams already had permission in principal to adapt the loft space over the house."

"Did he? Gosh, I must have forgotten that."

"Well, I don't suppose it mattered when you originally bought the property and sorting out the shop was your main priority."

Eleanor picked up the official letter and studied it. "This is eight years old – will the permission still be valid?"

Daniel checked the date and shook his head. "I'm afraid not, but it does mean the penpushers are unlikely to object this time around. I expect there will be a bit of a delay, but I don't see why we can't get going soon."

"Perfect!" Eleanor clapped her hands together gleefully then frowned as the small matter of money came into her head. "Hang on, though – how will we pay for the work? I have zero capital."

Daniel shrugged. "I'll have to sell my place or maybe we could let it out. There's always a queue of people wanting to rent sea-front houses for the summer season."

"That's a much better idea – then if you grow tired of me and the cottage, you can move back to your place."

"As if I could ever grow tired of you, my darling," he said, gathering her in his arms with a kiss. "You'd have to be boring and ordinary, and I can't see that ever happening."

"In other words, I'm bonkers?"

Daniel pulled a face, thinking for a moment. "Not bonkers exactly, but I'm never entirely sure what's going on in your head."

"That's the way it should be," said Eleanor, laughing. "I'd much rather be a woman of mystery than someone totally predictable."

"You keep me on my toes, that's for sure." Daniel smiled. "Anyway, while we're waiting to sort out my house and double-check the permission, there's nothing to prevent us emptying the loft space. Then, once we've had the thumbs up from the council, we'll need to find someone reliable to help out with the building work. I'll do as much as I can myself to keep the costs down, but it'll be good to have somebody else around to lend a hand."

"You're an architect, you must know loads of people."

"I do, but quite a lot of them are busy at the moment." He happened to know that the best builders were currently working for Freya at Bill Widget's new property on the Top, but he thought it diplomatic not to mention the fact. "Anyway, all we need is some basic labouring at the moment, nothing specialist."

Eleanor thought for a moment. "I know who might be able to help."

"Who?"

"Anton. Graham's shop is pretty quiet at the moment and Maureen finds it hard to keep Anton occupied every day. And he'd probably enjoy a change from serving toasted sandwiches to hungry day-trippers."

"Just because he's from eastern Europe doesn't mean he's a builder."

"There's only one way to find out," said Eleanor, reaching for the phone. "I'll give Maureen a call and see if she can ask him."

Chapter 14: Digging in the Archives

With the excitement of the Big Attic Plan, it wasn't until a few days after her drink with Jim that Eleanor found time to visit the newspaper office to discover what had happened in the case against the boy accused of theft.

Once she'd explained what she was looking for, one of the friendly staff set her up at a desk and left her to it. Eleanor settled down in front of an ancient microfiche machine and scrolled through the pages until she found the report she was looking for.

She felt like a proper researcher as she carefully scribbled down the facts in her notebook. The article said that on 23 March 1872 an eleven-year-old boy called John Able had been arrested after trying to sell a ring to a jeweller who had become suspicious when the lad couldn't explain how he had come by it. The police had been summoned and John was dragged off to jail by his shirt collar.

The boy's mother, described as "a laundress and an honourable woman despite her profession", had fainted when she heard the news and remained shut up in the house speaking to no one during the trial. John's father was said to be away working on the construction of a new railway line and therefore not able to keep a steadying hand on the family, which included two further children.

The case had aroused local interest because, then as now, Combemouth was a small town where not very much happened and because the boy was previously known as being exceedingly pious and well behaved.

During the short time the trial lasted, the courtroom was full of supporters shocked by John's arrest. It seemed to Eleanor that the boy did himself no favours by refusing to explain where the ring had come from, which reinforced the views of many – including the two magistrates overseeing the trial – that he was guilty as charged.

Eleanor raised her eyes from the screen and stretched. Leaning back in her chair, she could see through the windows onto the street where mothers were pushing toddlers along in buggies and youngsters were chatting in groups. What a different life children enjoyed now compared to Victorian times. Frowning, she turned back to John Able's story.

It was plain that John's unwillingness to speak was interpreted as arrogance and contempt, which only encouraged the magistrates to deal with him severely.

On the second day of the trial, the audience was treated to the appearance of the vicar's thirteen-year-old daughter who, it was claimed, John had forced to conceal the ring until he was ready to sell it. According to the reporter covering the case at the time, "This pretty child, speaking in a whisper, denied any involvement in the crime, wrung her hands and wept, giving every appearance of sorrow at the sad situation into which she had been led by the vicious boy."

"I bet she was a right little madam," muttered Eleanor, under her breath. The girl – identified only as Miss B – was let off because of her youth and exemplary character, while John "being unable to satisfy the magistrates as to how the item came lawfully into his possession" was sentenced to one calendar month's hard labour. He was, said the magistrate, to be grateful for such leniency.

Eleanor sighed, wondering what happened to John after his prison sentence but doubting it would be anything good. Looking at the clock, she saw it was 12.30pm and she had arranged to meet Daniel in town for lunch. She quickly put away her things, thanked the archivist for her help and went out into the sunshine.

* * *

Once they were settled with two bowls of pasta, Daniel asked Eleanor how she'd got on. "Did you find the report?"

"I did. John Able was sentenced to be whipped then packed off to prison for one month's hard labour. Sending the child to work on a treadmill seems incredibly harsh, especially as there was no evidence he had actually stolen anything."

"I wonder how he came by the ring, then? And, more importantly, how did treadmills work?" Daniel grinned. "I imagine they were like gigantic hamster wheels, but probably less fun."

Eleanor put her fork down and frowned at her husband who was plainly not taking the story as seriously as she thought he should.

"Hamster wheels are light and at least Hammy can stop and have a nap and a nut when he wants to. These were massive things that powered machinery in the prison. Inmates had to walk inside them for ten minutes at a time for eight hours with short breaks in between. An entire day on a wheel!" Eleanor poked a breadstick in the air for emphasis. "Can you imagine how boring that must have been for an eleven-year-old? And, as if that wasn't enough, the magistrates recommended that John be sent to a reformatory school afterwards for a year. Don't you think that's harsh?"

Daniel tried to look serious, though he now had a vision of a massive hamster in his head. "Perhaps they wanted to make an example of him. Was there a crime wave at the time? Marauding hordes of under-twelves ransacking the town?"

"It's not funny, Dan. That boy's life was probably ruined."

"You're right – I'm sorry. I'm only concerned that you're taking this a little too much to heart. I know what a big softy you are when it comes to children and animals. I don't want you upsetting yourself," he said, spearing penne with his fork.

"I'm fine, really." Eleanor shook her head.

Daniel squeezed her hand across the table. "If you want to get to the bottom of it, maybe you should read around the John Able case and see what else was going on in the area at the time. That might help to explain why the magistrates were so tough on him."

"Perhaps I'll do that, although there probably isn't much more to discover."

* * *

In the dark hours before dawn, Eleanor awoke in a sweat, her heart pounding. She sat up in bed, waking Daniel who stroked her gently on the back. "Are you all right, darling? What's the matter?"

Eleanor wanted to speak but was half-locked in her dream and the words wouldn't come. Instead she turned from Daniel and soon fell into a heavy sleep, a sound like distant weeping in her ears.

The next morning, the dream was gone and when Daniel asked Eleanor at breakfast what had caused her to wake with a start at 3am, she had no answer, although a sense of unease remained. "Probably too much cheese before bed," she replied.

Dan looked at her thoughtfully. "I think it was more than cheese – you were in a panic about something. Are you worried about the shop? The attic conversion?"

"No, nothing like that."

Daniel frowned with concern. "There must be something if you're having nightmares."

Eleanor stirred her tea, fragments of the dream now swimming into her head. "You'll think I'm silly if I tell you."

"No I won't – and there's nothing wrong with being silly either. What's up?"

"I've had that boy on my mind – locked up and probably brutalised by the system. I guess that's what has upset me."

"Ha! I knew it would. Forget what I said about reading more about the case, El. It was a long time ago and there's nothing you can do about it. What you *can* do is concentrate on making kids' lives better in the here and now."

She nodded. "The bookshop brings lots of enjoyment to the local children and their worn-out mothers, I know that."

"Precisely – especially Harold's weekly *Jackanory* sessions with the little ankle-biters. So will you try to put the lad in the hamster wheel out of your mind?"

"Still not funny, Dan."

"Sorry," he said, turning to place his coffee mug in the dishwasher. "I'm off for a run, then I have a meeting with the managers of the school to finalise designs for their new classrooms."

Eleanor rose and kissed him. "Have a good day."

"You too. And try to put the crime report out of your mind."

"I will," she said, nodding. And so she would, but first she planned to do what Daniel had suggested and see what she could find out about the background to the case. If she was lucky, she might also discover how John's future turned out. She quickly texted Erika to say she'd be in late, asked Joe to cover for her, then drove to the newspaper office in Waterborough.

Once in the archives, she began to regret abandoning her staff and dashing over there. She didn't even know what she was looking for and was easily distracted from the densely printed news items by notices of "ripe fat cattle" up for auction, advertisements for Fry's Chocolate and details of "desirable residential properties" for sale on the coast. There was certainly nothing about a junior crime wave, the print was tiny and her eyes were stinging.

Deciding to take a break, she bought a muffin and a coffee and had elevenses sitting in the park where pink and white cherry blossom swirled around her like confetti. Squinting up at the bright blue sky, she determined to stay in the musty archives for an hour longer then give up and go back to the bookshop.

After half an hour, she had come to the conclusion that John Able's prison sentence was perfectly normal for the period and she was wasting her time expecting to find clues about what he did at the end of his sentence.

"How are you getting on?" The nice archivist who had helped Eleanor the previous day noticed her gloomy expression and came over.

"Not too well. I know what happened at John Able's trial, but not what he did when he left the reformatory school."

"You might want to search for him online using one of the family history websites."

Eleanor nodded at the young woman. "I'm beginning to realise I'll have to put in a few more hours' work if I'm going to get to the bottom of things."

"Exploring family histories can be a time-consuming hobby."

"And they're not even my own relatives." Smiling, Eleanor packed up her things and left.

As she was trotting down the stairs wondering how she would ever find time to pursue John's case further, she passed a familiar figure on the way up – it was Dismal Deirdre.

"Fancy seeing you here, Mrs Pearce," she said, narrowing her eyes. "What brings you to the newspaper archives?"

Eleanor hugged the bag with her notebook close to her chest, oddly unwilling to reveal her mission to the librarian. "Just doing a little research. What about you?"

"I've come to put up a poster for the summer festival. Would you like one?"

"Oh, the vicar has already sent one to the shop." Eleanor did her best to be agreeable; Deirdre was helping the vicar so she obviously had some good points when she wasn't being irritating. "Thanks anyway."

"You're welcome. I'm pleased to see you're pursuing your historical interests, although I am sorry you didn't find everything you required in Combemouth Library. If there's anything specific you still require I can easily put in a request for an inter-library loan."

"There's no need, really. I'm investigating something quite different at the moment and I'm glad to say I found what I was looking for right here."

"Did you now?" said Deirdre, clearly intrigued to know what Eleanor's new interest might be and what the archives had to offer that her well-stocked shelves didn't.

"Well, I must dash," said Eleanor, looking at the clock. "I can't keep my customers waiting."

Chapter 15: An Exciting Proposition

About once a month, Erika was asked to serve customers on her own while Eleanor got down on her hands and knees and rummaged through the shelves to check whether it was time for any of the second-hand books to go to the charity shop.

To Eleanor it made perfect sense in a proper, traditional bookshop to sell second-hand titles as well as the publishers' shiny new stock. To begin with, she'd kept the new and old books in different places. Then she'd tried putting them together and discovered that customers liked the combination of old and new. She now had regulars who preferred to buy a 1960s Penguin paperback with a moody line drawing on the cover rather than a modern edition with a lurid image from the TV tie-in. It was a fairly eccentric arrangement and it made stocktaking hell, but it added to the quirkiness of the shop and her customers loved it.

Eleanor was completely absorbed in her task when Erika put her head around the bookcase and whispered, "There's someone here to see you, boss."

Looking up, Eleanor was surprised to see a pale figure in a long black coat and dark glasses walking across the floor. It was their local celebrity himself.

"Mr Widget, what a surprise," she said, scrambling to her feet and brushing dust from her hands.

"Call me Bill, please." He removed the shades, his eyes crinkling into a smile.

"What can I do for you? Sorry – stupid question!" Eleanor laughed. She didn't know why Bill made her feel flustered. He had been around town for nearly a year and they knew each other reasonably well, but there was something about having a famous person in the shop that still made her nervous. "Are you looking for something special?" Since Bill had been spending more time in Combemouth, Eleanor had beefed up her selection of music titles and was quite proud of it. "I have copies of *Twang* if you're looking for biographies of fellow musicians."

"I'm not sure I would ever call Ivan Twang a musician," Bill rubbed his chin, thoughtfully, "though I might have borrowed one of his riffs in 1972. And I seem to recall he copped off with my lady after the Spigot's first Melbourne gig." He looked at Eleanor and shrugged. "Forgive and forget, eh? Actually, I'm not here to buy a book, duck." Bill took Eleanor's arm and drew her to one side. "I've popped in to ask you something."

"Ask away," she said, nervously, wondering what on earth it could be. She sat down on the comfy sofa she had set up at the front of the shop and Bill took the place next to her.

"You might have heard that I've written my autobiography. I didn't want to, but this chap from London made me an offer the manager couldn't refuse."

"Yes, I read about your book in the trade press. Well done you!" Eleanor was too polite to add that she'd read it in an article criticising publishers for paying millions for memoirs by "celebrities" barely out of their teens. Happily, Bill Widget did not fall into that category.

He looked sheepish. "Well, when I say I've written it, I talked into a machine for weeks on end and a grand young lass wrote it down. She asked me lots of probing questions about my dim and distant past then cleverly put the words in the right order."

Eleanor nodded. "You mean you had a ghost writer. That's quite common in celebrity books."

"So they tell me. And there I was thinking those young folk off the telly who seem as thick as two short planks could actually write! Seems like cheating to me, but I do what my manager tells me to do. Anyway, I've read the manuscript and it's really quite good, even if I do say so myself. There's all kinds of stuff in there I'd almost forgotten. You know: early gigs, old girlfriends, parties, fights, more girlfriends, tours, more fights."

Bill laughed nervously. "The present Mrs Widget won't approve of a few of the earlier chapters, but I'll deal with that problem when the book comes out. And I'm all Brenda's now," he added with a wink. "If I've learned one thing from my guru, it's that you must focus on the positive and not worry about the past – *que sera, sera* as they say."

Eleanor was thrown momentarily by the vision of "Fingers" Widget sitting cross-legged in an ashram with his spiritual healer. "Is your guru here in Combemouth?"

"No duck, not yet. He says he won't come over until the meditation centre is finished so I pop over and see him in Taunton when I'm in need of spiritual enlightenment and a break from the missus. Which reminds me, I must ask Freda to give the foreman a kick up the backside over at the new house."

"Freda? Do you mean Freya?" Eleanor tried her best to keep a straight face despite knowing how much Daniel's ex hated the fact that Bill always got her name wrong.

"That's the lass. Brenda can't stand her, but she seems to be doing a good job and the builders certainly jump to attention when she's around." He scratched his head. "Anyway, what was I saying?"

"You were telling me the exciting news about your book."

"That was it – the book."

"It's bound to be very popular locally, so I'll do a nice window display and make sure we have plenty of copies in. But you said there was something you wanted to ask me."

"Ah, yes. The launch. The publishers want me to have a launch party in some swanky London bookshop full of tosspots and I can't face it. They've been doing their best to bully me into it, but I've told them I'll only agree to a 'do' if we can invite my mates and have it at your shop. You are my local bookshop after all and I want to support you. So what do you say? Can we do it here?"

"Gosh, I don't know Bill. It's a kind thought but we don't have a lot of space."

"The smaller the better from my point of view. I don't want hundreds of people turning up."

Eleanor scanned the café and the children's area behind. "We can move the tables and chairs out of the way to open up this space and there's the upstairs room if it gets too crowded."

"That sounds grand."

She calculated the number of bodies they could fit in, thought about hiring posh glasses and wondered what snacks celebrity guests would need. "When's the book coming out?" she asked, going to fetch the diary.

"Can't remember – you'll have to ask the Boss. But it's not for a month or so yet."

"A month? Is that all?"

"Maybe a bit longer, duck. It's a week or so after the summer knees-up I'm opening for the vicar. There's no rest for me!" He grinned. "As I say, you'll have to speak to the keeper of the diary. But can I take that as a 'yes'?"

The chance to launch Bill's book in her shop was not something Eleanor could afford to pass over. He was a national treasure and the event would be great publicity for the shop, attracting new customers as well as locals who were rather proud of their very own rock star. She'd wanted a big name to fill the empty slot and she couldn't get much bigger than Bill. Okay, his launch wasn't going to be bang in the middle of the festival, but it was close enough. She nodded enthusiastically. "It's a definite 'yes'."

"Ah, that's excellent. I'll tell my manager to give the publishing folk a call so you can get everything set up." He stood up from the sofa, ready to leave. "I suppose I might as well buy a couple of books while I'm here."

"Is there anything in particular you fancy? Fiction, non-fiction?"

"I'm not well read, duck. You pick me out a nice fat thriller or two and something racy for the wife."

Eleanor smiled. "It'll be my pleasure."

When Bill had gone, Erika came over to join her colleague. "He looks like a happy customer."

"He is and I'm a happy bookseller. I was beginning to worry that I wouldn't find anyone. Worst case scenario, I was planning to drag in Daniel and Maureen to perform a double act on the theme of the Combemouth Ghost Ship."

"Sounds like a winner to me!"

"In my head it was perfect, but standing up and addressing a crowd is Dan's idea of hell. Maureen would have loved it, mind you."

"While we're on the subject of ancient history, I've been meaning to ask if you got any further with the Victorian case you were following."

"I did," said Eleanor, pleased to share the fruits of her investigations with a former copper. "I discovered that John Able was sentenced to one month's hard labour then sent to a reformatory school for a year. I'm all for kids behaving properly, but to be put away for twelve months for a minor theft – especially as no one could prove the boy had actually stolen anything – seems excessive. But after his punishment, I don't know what happened."

Erika shrugged. "It probably sorted out any criminal tendencies he might have had. Children were expected to behave properly in those days. I'd bring back flogging for shoplifters, personally."

Eleanor was shocked. "You're not serious?"

"Okay, I might draw the line at actual flogging, but a few hours in the stocks being pelted with rotten fruit might make some of the pests we get in the bookshop think twice before nicking the novelty pencils." Erika smiled. "A good clip around the ear never did anyone any harm."

"You're a hard woman."

"Me?" Erika pursed her lips. "Nah – I'm a pussy-cat. Anyway, given your new interest in Victorian crime I think you should set yourself up as 'The Bookshop Detective'. We could have a sign on the door in swirly Victorian script: 'Enquire Within Upon Everything. No Problem Too Large to Solve.'"

Eleanor laughed. "That's a interesting idea. And I'm sure your experience with the constabulary would come in very useful."

"Oh, my detecting days are a long time in the past, as you know."

"It might be some years since you put the cuffs on anyone, but you do have a nose like a bloodhound when it comes to crime. I've seen you identify a potential shoplifter a mile off." Eleanor knew that Erika had come into the world as Eric and for years had fought the feelings of being born in the wrong skin. As Eric Wilmott he'd entered the macho world of inner-city policing in a bid to suppress his feminine side, eventually working his way up to the rank of Chief Superintendent before retiring on a pension large enough that he didn't really need to work again.

With the money and the freedom from full-time employment came the freedom to change, and it was as Erika Wilmott that she now lived and worked in a peaceful corner of Devon where no one cared about her previous life.

"And my instincts are never wrong," said Erika, with a wink.

"True. Anyway," said Eleanor, "my investigations into the John Able case are on ice for the time being. My most urgent challenge now is to finalise arrangements for Bill Widget's launch party."

* * *

A few hours later, Eleanor received a very detailed email from Bill's publishers about the book with details of the launch, including posters, a press release and a guest list.

Looking at the names, Eleanor laughed. "Good grief. Even I've heard of this one. Wasn't he in the Rolling Stones?"

"Yup," said Erika, looking at the name, "and he still is as far as I know."

"I can't believe these people will take the time to visit our little shop."

Erika shrugged. "They might. You never know who's going to turn up at these celebrity bashes." She tapped on the calendar they had hanging on the wall behind the cash desk. "There are several big music festivals in the area next month, so some of the performers might come along to see their old friend Bill."

Eleanor ran a finger down the list and frowned. "I'm beginning to wonder whether I've done the right thing agreeing to have it here. We are going to be pushed for space."

At that moment her son Joe wandered through. "Does anyone fancy a cup of tea?"

Two hands shot up.

"Thanks, love," said Eleanor. "And when you've finished on tea duty, could you give Georgie a call? This is an emergency."

Chapter 16: Joyce is Coming

Daniel had a tricky design problem to solve in preparation for a meeting with a client the next morning, so he told Eleanor and Joe to go ahead and eat supper without him.

Joe was an enthusiastic, if untidy, cook and once in a while he enjoyed rustling up a chicken curry with all the trimmings for his mother. It made Eleanor feel guilty for complaining about him not leaving home, which she guessed was part of his plan.

She sat at the kitchen table with a cold beer, contentedly watching Joe slice onions and chop coriander. She didn't have a favourite twin – how could she? – but Joe was the child who resembled her the most. Whereas Phoebe was blonde like her father, Joe shared her own auburn hair and hazel eyes. Both kids were taller than either of their parents, which seemed to be the way with youngsters these days.

"Have you had chance to speak to Georgie yet about helping me with Bill's launch?" she asked.

"Yes, and she said she'd be happy to come if you need her to."

"Great. I'll have to clear it with Bill's team first, but it would be a huge relief to have a friendly publicist here."

They were tucking into their meal when there was

a knock on the kitchen door and Connie came in looking a tad flushed.

"Good evening, Mother. You're out late."

Connie kissed her daughter and grandson then sat herself down at the table. "I was on my way home from Tai Chi and thought I'd pop in." Her gaze wandered over to the stove.

"Have you eaten?" asked Eleanor, following the direction of her mother's eyes.

"I had a bit of quiche at five – I can't eat too much before a class or it throws off my balance and my 'white crane standing' goes wobbly and I turn into a dying swan." She chuckled, pleased with her witticism. "I wouldn't say no to a teeny bowl of curry."

Joe went to the stove and heaped food on a warm plate while Eleanor fetched some cutlery. "So what's up? You don't normally drop by of an evening."

Connie silently indicated that she needed a napkin. "That's delicious, Joe," she said, dabbing sauce from her lips. "I was going to tell you tomorrow, but I might as well tell you now – I've had a message from Joyce to say she's coming to visit."

Eleanor smiled. "Well, that's a surprise. I didn't think you spoke to each other often, apart from exchanging Christmas and birthday cards. How long is it since you two last saw each other?"

"It must be at least seven or eight years." Connie thought for a moment. "I remember she came to stay with us when she was visiting her daughter, but the last time I had the pleasure of Joyce's company was when she invited me to her villa in Spain after your father died. I've still got the scars."

Joe, who had been busy with his phone, looked

up. "Scars? What happened, Gran? You didn't have an accident, did you?"

Connie smiled and gently patted her grandson's hand. "I was speaking metaphysically, dear."

"I don't remember you telling me about any injuries at the time," said Eleanor, wrinkling her brow. "What happened?"

"They were invisible scars, if you must know. And I didn't want to worry you."

"Feel free to worry me now."

"If you're sure." Connie folded her napkin and leant towards her daughter. "Don't tell Harold, but I met a rather handsome gentleman at the yacht club while I was there – I was staying for six weeks you see." She turned to Joe, "I don't do one-night stands, dear. Once you're over seventy it becomes undignified." She continued, ignoring the look of horror on her grandson's face. "Well, this Reg clearly took a bit of a shine to me but as soon as I was home and safely out of the way, Joyce nabbed him."

"That's not very sisterly," said Eleanor.

"It certainly wasn't, but I can't be too cross because after a couple of years of wedded bliss Reg upped and died."

"What a shame. However did Joyce manage?"

"She managed very nicely, thank you. Reg didn't have children so Joyce inherited his money and his villa, sold her own place and is still living in the lap of luxury on the proceeds." Silence descended as mother and daughter mulled over the vagaries of fate and Joe fantasised about having a Spanish villa, a yacht and loads of spare cash. "Anyway, since I discovered the internet, we've been corresponding on Facebook."

"Have you seen photos of her?" asked Eleanor. "Is she looking well?"

"It depends what you consider 'well'. She's put on weight – it's all that rich food and sangria." Connie chuckled as she popped a final piece of poppadom into her mouth.

"If that's what you say about your friends, Gran, I'd hate to hear what you say about your enemies."

"Joyce is fine to be friends with at a distance, Joe. Unfortunately, I made the mistake of mentioning that Bill Widget was opening our summer festival and she said she'd fly right over to join us."

"Really? I wouldn't have had Joyce down as a Tryll Spigot groupie," Eleanor laughed.

"No, she's more of a Barry Manilow fan as it happens."

Joe winced. "I suppose someone has to be."

Connie slapped her grandson playfully. "She's interested in Bill's house, not his music, Joe. Apparently Mr and Mrs Widget have a villa along the coast from Joyce's place and she's been stalking them for months without success. She read about them in *¡Hola!* magazine and is mad keen for an invitation to their house so she can compare soft furnishings. She seems to think that if they can meet, she and Brenda will become bosom buddies and spend happy afternoons knocking back pina coladas together at the pool side."

"Well, whatever her reason for visiting, it'll be nice for you to see her again, won't it?"

"Yes, I suppose it will, Eleanor," said Connie, rearranging her chest. "But if she lays a finger on my Harold, I'll break her arm."

"Woah! Steady on, Granny. I thought you disapproved of violence?"

"I do, Joe. In principle. But that woman had better watch her step. She has rather a lot of what I believe is referred to in the vernacular as 'previous' when it comes to running off with other people's chaps."

Connie had picked up quite a lot of police slang, partly from watching crime dramas on the TV and partly from spending jolly times with Erika who loved to regale her with stories from her previous life in the police force.

Joe nodded. "Once a bad 'un, always a bad 'un."

"While we're swapping clichés, I think you should let bygones be bygones and simply enjoy having your old friend come to stay," said Eleanor. "How long will she be here for?"

"I wish I knew – Joyce never gives out details like that. She says she prefers to be 'spontaneous', which is another term for completely disorganised. It's most provoking not to have proper notice of when she's arriving. My spare room is in dire need of redecorating and she's bound to comment if everything isn't just so."

"If she's a good mate, she'll take you as you are," said Joe.

Connie laughed. "You clearly haven't met Joyce, sweetheart."

Eleanor smiled at her son. "He has, actually, but he was too little to remember. Anyway, I think it's nice you two are going to see each other again."

Grumbling, Connie ignored her. "And she's as spoilt as ever. I mean, she's already told me she expects to be met at the airport – she couldn't simply catch a bus to town like everyone else."

"I don't think that's unreasonable, Mother. I wouldn't expect you to take a bus all the way either."

Connie harrumphed, unwilling to accept defeat. "Anyway, I'd best go home," she said, looking at her watch. "I need to call Maureen and see if I can borrow Anton for a few hours to sort out my Anaglypta."

Eleanor rose and kissed her. "I'm sure Anton will have your house shipshape in no time."

"I hope so. I don't want the state of my spare room to be the talk of Torremolinos. Joyce was never known for her discretion."

After Connie had left, Joe joined his mother in the living room. "I was really surprised by Gran's reaction."

"How do you mean, love?"

"You'd think she'd be happy to see Aunty Joyce. I remember meeting her when we were little and she was fun."

"Gosh, fancy you remembering that. You and Phoebe must only have been about seven or eight when you met her."

"The bright pink hair made quite an impression on us."

Eleanor laughed. "I remember now – Phoebe tried to pull off a bit and eat it when Joyce bent down to kiss her because you'd told your sister it was made out of candyfloss. Joyce was very gracious about it."

"I know she's known in the family as Aunty Joyce, but whose aunt is she? I've never figured that out. Is she Gran's sister?"

Eleanor shook her head. "She and Gran aren't

actually blood relations, but they've known each other their whole lives. They have a love-hate relationship as you may have gathered. They love each other to bits, but something went on between the two of them when they were young. Gran won't say what it was. I did ask Dad once, but he said Mum would skin him alive if he told me so that was the end of the conversation."

"I still miss Granddad."

"So do I," said Eleanor, giving her son a hug. "And I know Gran misses him, too."

"Even though she has Harold now?"

"Oh yes. And I'm sure Harold misses his late wife just as much. That's the way it goes." She yawned. "Well, I'm off to bed. What are you doing?"

"I said I'd kip over at Greg's tonight." Joe frowned. "What time will Dan be back?"

"I'm not sure, love," said Eleanor. "But don't worry about me."

"If you say so, Ma." Joe grabbed his jacket, gave his mother a quick kiss and left.

In fact, it was nearly midnight when Daniel came home, quietly slipped out of his clothes and curled himself around Eleanor. She pulled his arm around her and clasped his hand against her stomach. "I'm glad you came home. I didn't know if you would," she murmured, sleepily.

"How could I not, when everything I love is here?" Dan gently kissed the tip of her shoulder.

"Love you."

"I love you, too. Now go back to sleep, darling."

Chapter 17: Ask the Expert

Eleanor was standing in the queue at the bakery, pondering the merits of white crusty over a seeded loaf, when the vicar – Philip White – nabbed her.

"I'm glad I've bumped into you," he smiled. "I wonder if I might have a word?"

"Of course, Vicar."

"Good! I have an hour before my next service, so perhaps I could walk you over to the bookshop and share some cake in your café?"

"Certainly." Walking back up the high street with a cleric by her side, Eleanor felt uncomfortable and could think of nothing to say. Whenever she met him, she always felt guilty for no reason. She supposed it was a Pavlovian reaction to the dog collar. As though reading Eleanor's thoughts, Philip pulled up the top of his fawn sweater in an attempt to conceal the white band.

Once in the bookshop, Eleanor showed him to a table and mouthed "cake" at Joe who was serving. "Have a seat, Reverend."

"Call me Phil, please."

It didn't seem right to address a member of the cloth by his first name, especially when it was such an unexceptional one. Philip was younger than his thinning hair suggested and had one lazy eye that seemed perpetually raised, as though fixed on heaven.

Eleanor sat opposite him and focused on the eye that was looking at her. "So, how can I help?"

"As you know, the summer festival is almost upon us and it comes in the middle of a major fundraising campaign to bring in some money for the church roof."

Eleanor's smile froze.

Philip noticed and laughed. "Don't worry, I'm not here to ask you for a financial contribution."

Eleanor relaxed a little. "That's good, as things are a bit tight at the moment."

"I understand perfectly. No, I'd like your help giving the event a final push. It's only a fortnight away and I'm keen to ensure we have a good turnout."

"We do have a poster up," she said, pointing towards the shop's noticeboard, "but I'd be happy to slip flyers into books, if that would help. Is that the kind of thing you mean?"

"Whatever you think best – you're the expert at involving the community in local campaigns after all."

"Oh, you mean the business with Bill Widget last year? The promotional side was down to Joe's girl-friend, Georgie – she works in publicity, you see." Eleanor smiled at her son who was approaching with mugs of tea and two slices of Victoria sponge.

Joe grinned. "I don't know about that, Mum. I think it was a team effort."

"You're right and your gran's input was probably what swung it in our favour." A vision of her mother lying in the road, her little legs kicking in the air as the police constable did his best to restore order passed through her mind. Philip appeared puzzled as Eleanor and her son chuckled at the memory. "I'll tell you about it one day, Vicar. In the meantime, I'm happy to do whatever I can to support you."

"And there was something else." Philip leant forward in his seat, brushing crumbs from his chin onto the floor where Bella happily hoovered them up. "The members of the committee have agreed to my suggestion that we hold our own version of the *Antiques Road Show* at the church."

"Really?" said, Eleanor, not quite knowing what it had to do with her. "How will that work, Vicar?"

"Phil."

"Phil." Repetition didn't make it any easier and she was still distracted by the vicar's roaming eye, which had alighted on the science fiction titles above her head.

"It will run along the lines of the BBC television programme, so people can bring along their treasures to be valued by experts in return for a small donation to the fund. I thought it would be a bit of fun. We'll have the usual bric-à-brac stall, too, of course, so if anyone finds interesting items there they can bring them to be valued. And if they discover their Ming vase is actually from Woolworths, they can take it home again or add it to the 'For Sale' pile. The chap who runs the auction house in Waterborough has agreed to come, but he says he'll need backup." Philip smiled hopefully. "So I wondered whether you might agree to be our second expert?"

Eleanor was startled. "Me? It's very flattering to be asked, but I don't know very much about anything. Except books, of course."

"Precisely! If people turn up with first editions or back copies of *Punch* that they've unearthed in the garage, you could do the valuation. What do you say? It would be jolly helpful to have you on the team and it would only take up a few hours of your time."

"Well, I couldn't give out accurate valuations there and then, but if something looked as though it might be valuable I suppose I could do some research and get back to the owner later on."

"That sounds perfect," said Philip, adding Eleanor's name to a slip of paper he pulled from his pocket.

"So, who else have you recruited?"

"Oh, everyone has been very kind in offering to help. Maureen will be taking charge of catering and has agreed to be the judge of the cake-decorating competition, and Graham from the hardware shop will be manning the bric-à-brac stall." Philip glanced across at Joe. "All I'm missing now are a couple of tall young men, preferably with a head for heights, to hang the bunting."

"I'll be happy to help," said Joe. "And I'll bring Anton."

Philip sat back in his chair, sighing with obvious relief. "I reckon that's everything covered."

To Eleanor it seemed as though one key figure was missing from the vicar's list. "I imagine you've asked Deirdre to be involved?"

"Oh, there was no need to ask. She's our Treasurer and has kindly taken it upon herself to be Head of Logistics." Philip scratched his head. "I'm not entirely sure what that entails, but I'm sure she will fill the role diligently."

"I'm sure she will."

"Well, I'd best be off. Thank you again, Eleanor."

Philip rose and took her hand, shaking it warmly in both of his. "Bless you."

Eleanor didn't know what the appropriate response was to a blessing, so she ended up doing a clumsy half-curtsey as she opened the door and waved Philip goodbye.

He'd only gone a few paces when she dashed after him. "Before you go, Vicar, could I ask you something?"

"Of course," he said, lowering his voice. "Would you like to pop around to the vicarage later for a chat? If it's something of a personal nature, I mean."

Eleanor laughed. "Oh, it's nothing like that. I wondered whether the name John Able meant anything to you?"

Philip thought for a moment then shook his head. "I can't say it rings any bells – should it?"

"Not necessarily. I've been digging into some local history and it's a name that has come up. I thought perhaps you might have some Ables buried at St Cuthbert's."

"I can't think of any offhand, but you're welcome to come and look around the churchyard. I'm afraid I haven't managed to commit the names of our permanent residents to memory yet." With that, he said his farewells and went on his way.

* * *

After work, Connie popped over to the cottage to report back on Anton's decorating. "He's made a start and I have to say he's making a lovely job of my walls – it's a proper picture in the back bedroom. In fact, he's doing such nice work I've asked him to spruce up my bedroom and the bathroom while he's at it. I'm determined Joyce won't find anything to complain about when she arrives."

"Your guest is very lucky to have a spruced-up house – not that it wasn't immaculate anyway," said Daniel.

"It's very nice of you to say so," said Connie. "I take that as a real compliment from someone who knows as much about houses as you do."

"Which reminds me," said Eleanor, turning to her husband, "according to Maureen, Anton trained as a bricklayer and plasterer before leaving Riga and he would be delighted to help out with some building work when the time comes."

"Great. I'll pop over and see him in the morning."

Connie frowned. "What are you two in need of a builder for?"

"Eleanor and I have come to an agreement over where to live and we could do with some help sorting it out."

"'Come to an agreement?' That sounds very formal."

"It wasn't intentional," said Daniel. "I'm not great with words." He smiled as Eleanor squeezed his hand.

"So, tell me what you've decided," said Connie, nervously. "You're not buying a house miles away and abandoning me, I hope?"

"We're not moving, Mum. Dan has had the brilliant idea of making use of the roof space."

"Oh." Connie was plainly underwhelmed by this. "You mean you're going to put a dormer window in the loft? Your father and I did that in the house in Chiswick back in 1973. I thought you were going to do something original."

Eleanor sighed and rolled her eyes wearily. "Well, I'm sorry we're not digging three floors down and installing a cinema and an Olympic-sized swimming pool."

"There's no call for sarcasm."

"It might not sound exciting to you, Mum, but it is to us and it means we don't have to move."

Daniel could see Eleanor and her mother starting to annoy each other and stepped in to keep the peace. "The thing is, Connie, we'll have a new space the entire length and breadth of both the house and the shop. It's not a massive change, but it will make quite a difference to how we live." He put an arm around his wife. "We'll finally be able to live together in the same place seven days a week and I can't wait."

"Well, I don't know," said Connie thoughtfully. "I think that posh Kirstie Allspot off the telly would have come up with something a little more inventive than a dormer bedroom, but at least you aren't moving away, which I am pleased about." She stood up. "I'd better go back and see how Anton's getting on. I left him putting a top coat of Mallorcan Sunrise on the walls."

"Nice choice – it should make Joyce feel right at home."

"You are comical, Daniel." Connie chuckled. "Well, *hasta la vista*." And with that she gave them both a peck on the cheek, gathered up her bag and coat, and headed off home to check everything was as it should be for her friend's arrival.

Chapter 18: Window Dressing

The festival was almost upon them and Combemouth was decked out in its finery, ready to welcome the world. The vicar, with help from Joe and Anton, had been busy with the bunting, and triangles in pastel shades now flapped in the summer breeze along the high street. Malcolm, a keen gardener, had taken charge of the floral displays and made sure that all the window boxes and planters along the road were looking their best.

By the beach, the promenade was decked out in red, white and blue ready for the sailing regatta and the "Bathing Beauty" competition. The latter was a popular event in which local chaps had to swim a quarter of a mile wearing Edwardian-style bathing costumes. There were prizes for Best Moustache, Saggiest Costume and Most Handsome Gentleman, and the winners were awarded cups by ladies from the local WI.

Looking at the preparations going on around her, Eleanor decided it was time to put into action Stage One of her plans for Bill Widget's launch. She had given the window display some thought and decided to use a musical theme.

Once the space was empty, she pulled a length of shiny black fabric from her bag and began pinning it in position inside the window. She had decided that a dark, silky background would help to give the display a heavy metal vibe. Bill had kindly agreed to lend her one of his less valuable guitars and a keyboard to use as props. As Tryll Spigot's on-stage gimmick in the 1980s had been lizards, Eleanor had also bought a few rubber reptiles from the pound shop which she scattered around.

She picked up a box of Bill's books and began arranging the fat paperbacks among the props. The black and white book covers looked great against the dark background and contrasted nicely with the ice-cream coloured bunting crisscrossing the street.

When Eleanor had finished, she called her husband to come and take a look. "What do you think?"

"Very striking," said Daniel. "I think you've excelled yourself."

They were standing on the pavement chuckling when Deirdre appeared beside them. "Well now, isn't that eye-catching."

"Thank you," said Eleanor, warily. "It's nice of you to say so." Could heavy metal really be to Deidre's taste?

Daniel wrapped an arm around Eleanor's waist and pulled her towards him. "You definitely have an artistic bent, darling."

It was Deirdre who spoke next. "I had a very nice coffee with the first Mrs Pearce the other morning," she said, addressing Daniel whose smile died on his face. "I expect she told you."

"No, she didn't."

"Oh, she probably forgot to mention it given how busy she always is. I'm so impressed Freya finds time to attend our book club when she's in town."

Eleanor felt Daniel tense beside her, the way he inevitably did when the subject of his ex-wife arose. "I'd better go back to work, El," he said, giving her a peck on the cheek and nodding a farewell to Deirdre.

"I must be going, too," she said, as the conversation had died. She began to walk away, then stopped and turned towards Eleanor. "By the way, I've discovered something that might interest you about John Able."

Eleanor froze. "How did you know I was investigating John Able?"

"You mentioned it when we ran into each other at the archives – don't you remember?"

"No, I don't. In fact I'm pretty sure I didn't mention his name at all."

"Really? Oh, perhaps it was your mother who told me." She tapped a skinny hand to her cheek. "Or was it Jim Rowe? The library has so many visitors, it is terribly hard to remember who told me what."

Eleanor was incensed, sure that neither Jim nor her mother would have said anything. There was only one possibility: the wretched woman must have quizzed the young archivist about her research.

"It is rather fascinating," said Deirdre, looking pleased with herself.

Despite her irritation, Eleanor was keen to know what the librarian had found out. "Go on."

"From my extensive research it would seem that your Mr Able was transported to Australia."

"Transported?" Eleanor was stunned. That would explain why she could find no records of him coming back to Combemouth. "How do you know that?"

Smug was the only word to describe the expression on Deirdre's face. "As a librarian I have access to a great many online journals and international sources. I did a little digging and came across a Devon man called John Able who had been transported and died in Perth in 1910. I'll print out the details and drop them off if you wish?"

Nodding, Eleanor said thanks, but her head was in a spin. This was her case to solve – how dare Deirdre meddle in it?

Chapter 19: Festival Time

The Combemouth Summer Festival and Country Fair kicked off on Saturday and the vicar's hard work and prayers were rewarded by dry sunny weather. Most of the activity was scheduled to take place in marquees on the large green in front of St Cuthbert's Church. Every bit of wall was decked out with bunting and someone had added a few Union Jack flags left over from the Queen's birthday celebrations.

By mid-morning a small crowd had gathered around a temporary stage ready for the grand opening. Eventually, the vicar jogged up the steps onto the wooden platform in chinos and a bright shirt that almost concealed his dog collar.

Philip White hadn't been in town very long and some of the traditionalists – including Eleanor's father-in-law – had yet to grow used to his modern ways. He had already caused consternation amongst the Sunday morning regulars by introducing a screen onto which he projected uplifting images of smiling children gathered around wells in a scorched landscape.

When there were hymns to be sung, these were alarmingly modern and unfamiliar. The parishioners found it no comfort that the words bobbed jauntily along the bottom of the screen, which Philip had placed directly in front of the altar. The change led to some rather un-Christian comments from sections of the congregation, including Malcolm who couldn't help complaining about the vicar to his son who stood beside him on the green.

"I know it's an unfashionable view, Daniel, but the whole point of religion is to make you suffer. At least, that's how it was in my day. And here's this young chap trying to make it – well – entertaining." He shook his head crossly. "It's not right, you know." Malcolm's own parents had been Scottish Presbyterians and "fun" had never played any part in their worship.

Daniel laughed. "It sounds as though Philip is making you suffer plenty, Dad."

"I suppose so. And I don't mean to be unkind – he's a good man and I know he's trying his best to involve more youngsters, and lots of people do enjoy the 'happy-clappy' approach. It's not my cup of tea, that's all."

Right on cue, Philip clapped his hands together and addressed the crowd.

"Welcome, everyone, to the Combemouth Summer Festival! Here to pronounce us officially open is our very own rock god . . ." He crossed himself theatrically then put his hands together in a gesture of prayer. "Begging your pardon, oh Lord," he said, raising a few embarrassed titters from the crowd. "Here is rock star and showman extraordinaire, the legend that is our very own Mr Bill 'Fingers' Widget, a man whose music has brought joy to generations of fans across the globe."

The assembled crowd cheered and clapped as Bill came forward, smiling and waving. In the background, the sound system was playing a CD of Tryll Spigot's *Greatest Hits* and the youngsters near the front of the stage began to bounce around, strumming air guitars and headbanging to the music.

Since coming out of retirement (with some local encouragement), Bill was once again flavour of the month and was often to be found on TV quiz shows. Philip had done well to book Bill to open the festival – free of charge – as his manager liked to keep him busy.

Bill made a short speech saying how happy he was to be in Combemouth then sang a verse from one of his hits, which the crowd joined in with enthusiastically. Once his official duties were over, he rejoined Brenda then went across the grass to seek out Daniel and Eleanor.

"Hello duck, how are the arrangements going for my launch?"

"Not too bad at all," said Eleanor. "I think Georgie has everything under control."

"Hello Brenda," said Connie, coming up to join them with Joyce in tow. "I see you've been keeping busy, Bill. Harold and I went to see your show with our salsa group and we thought you were marvellous."

"Thank you, Connie. It's very decent of you to say so." Joyce stood there slightly starstruck, waiting to be introduced. "And who's this here?" asked Bill. "Your twin sister?"

"Certainly not! This is my old friend, Joyce."

"I've come all the way from Spain to see you," said Joyce, simpering. She had arrived in town a couple of days before and was resplendent in shocking pink.

"Spain, eh? As it happens, me and the wife have a little place on the Costa del Sol, just up the coast from Torremolinos."

"What a coincidence." Joyce put a hand to her chest in mock surprise. "So do I."

Brenda's eyes narrowed. "Have we met before? I've a feeling I've seen you somewhere."

"At the yacht club, perhaps? My husband and I always enjoy an evening by the marina."

The mention of a husband seemed to reassure Brenda that Joyce wasn't likely to be a threat and she relaxed a bit.

"Ay, the wife likes it there though I think it's over-priced. Anyway, we'd best get on. *Adiós.*"

"*Adiós* Bill, Brenda." Joyce smiled, flushed with success. "What a nice man. And isn't Mrs Widget stylish?"

"Orange is a bold choice at her age and all that crumpled linen is not to my taste, but I'm sure it hides a multitude of sins." Connie looked around. "Where's your father, Daniel? I'd like him to meet Joyce."

"I last saw him in the cake tent with Maureen, admiring the apple pies."

"Come along, Joyce. There's no time to waste."

Eleanor smiled as she watched Connie drag her friend across the green. "You'd better keep an eye on your dad, Dan. Mum's keen to distract Joyce from Harold, so Malcolm could end up as the tethered goat."

Daniel grinned. "Dad's old enough to make his own mistakes. And it would be nice for him to have a companion."

"I'm not sure Joyce would be much of a companion – she lives in Spain for half the year and disappears off to a bungalow in mid-Wales for the rest of it."

"Dad likes a woman who has been about a bit . . ."

"From what Mother says, that describes Joyce to a T."

Daniel laughed. "What I mean is a woman who has travelled – lived abroad, that kind of thing. Dad spent many years in the Middle East and North Africa before he settled down with my mother, don't forget."

"I had forgotten that. So you might be right. And we could do with some romance in our lives."

"Aren't I romantic enough for you?" asked Daniel, leaning over to kiss her.

"You can never have too much romance, I'd say," she said, returning his kiss. "Shall we go and see what's happening over there?" Eleanor pointed towards a tent strewn in green, purple and gold shawls with a huge rainbow banner by the door. Outside sat a woman with dyed red hair and so many bangles on each plump arm it was a wonder she could lift them. Eleanor smiled as she recognised one of the bookshop's bestselling local authors, Lavinia Threlfall.

"Hello Lavinia. I see the vicar has roped you in, too."

"I like to help where I can."

"What are you up to here?" Eleanor popped her head through the flap and breathed in the scent of joss sticks. "Let me guess – either you have a crystal ball in there or you're reading palms."

Lavinia didn't laugh. Instead she pursed her lips and pointed to a small sign pinned to the side of her tent which read "Authentic Tarot Card Readings £5".

"As you can see, I'm offering to read the cards – I don't do palmistry and my crystal ball never leaves my bedroom. It's far too precious to travel."

Eleanor's smile transformed itself into a rictus grin as she took Daniel's hand and backed away, nodding. "Marvellous. What fun."

Lavinia's eyebrows shot up at the word "fun". "Tarot is a serious method of divination that has been used for centuries, as you should know."

"Of course. Well, it was nice to see you. Bye." She turned and whispered to her husband. "I think I put my foot in it there. Let's see what else we can find."

"This is always entertaining," said Daniel, pointing towards three ladies separated by screens, each with a bowl of fruit. "It's the human fruit machine."

He raised his hand to wave at Joe and Georgie. Georgie had arrived from London the day before to spend some time with her boyfriend before Bill's launch. They had met when Georgie handled Lavinia Threlfall's book launch at The Reading Room some years before. Georgie had since become Joe's sort-of girlfriend but, as she lived in London and Joe was in the South West, it wasn't always easy. However, Georgie had recently begun working freelance, so she and Joe hoped to see each other more than once a month. With them were Crumpet and Bella who was wearing a rosette, having come first in the Waggiest Tail category at the dog show.

"I have no idea what's going on here," said Georgie, looking bemused.

Eleanor laughed. "It's a game of chance like roulette, but with slightly worse odds. Joe, show Georgie how it works."

"Do I have to?"

"Yes – it's for charity. Don't be such a skinflint."

Sighing, Joe sloped over and gave the man in charge of the game 50p then pulled the wooden arm that activated the "fruit machine". As he did so, each of the ladies selected a piece of fruit from her bowl and held it up.

"Ah, bad luck Joe," said Daniel.

From left to right, the three ladies had chosen a banana, an apple and an orange.

Joe sulked. "I have never won at this game – I'm sure it's rigged."

"It's not rigged," said Eleanor, "the ladies can't see each other. Don't be such a bad loser."

"I think this is brilliant," said Georgie. "I must have a go." She went across and handed over her money. "Okay now, ladies, I'd like you to concentrate, please." She rubbed her palms together and closed her eyes. The wooden arm went down and the ladies made their choices: left to right, orange, orange, orange.

"You've won!" said Eleanor.

"How exciting," said Georgie, laughing. "But what have I won?"

The chap at the desk pointed at the motley selection of items on display. "Take your pick, my dear. I'm afraid the best prizes have already been taken, but I hope you'll be able to find something."

"Tough call," said Joe, his hand on Georgie's shoulder as they considered the display. "I think it has to be the bedsocks or the bottle of Blue Nun."

"Blue Nun? Is that wine?"

"Allegedly. But if you don't want it, I'm sure my gran will be happy to take it off your hands."

* * *

Connie and Harold had gone to join their friends from the dance group. This was led by Alfonso, a skinny, moustachioed gent in his seventies who had arrived in Combemouth after a career on cruise ships and in various holiday camps. The local men had been doubtful when their wives developed a sudden interest in Latin moves, but their anxieties were calmed when Alfonso took up with Linda from the greengrocer's.

Alfonso's troop had one of the open-sided tents on the green, and were showing off their paso dobles to the locals.

Joyce was a nifty mover and more than happy to join in. Daniel had to laugh at the look of pure horror on Malcolm's face as he was pulled onto the dance floor and twirled around.

Chapter 20: All the Fun of the Fair

Bill was in his element shaking hands and signing a few autographs, but Brenda looked pained as she wandered around the green, the heels of her Jimmy Choos sinking dangerously into the grass.

As Bill's manager, Brenda disapproved of too much smiling, arguing that it went against the bad-boy image she had spent so many years building up. To counteract the impression that Bill had gone soft, Vince – his chauffeur, ex-roadie and best mate – accompanied them to events. Now he hung around in a black suit doing his best to scowl and look menacing.

Bill smiled at his wife. "You'll have to take those shoes off or the vicar will be after you for damaging his croquet lawn."

"He'll have to put up with a few holes because I don't intend to walk around in flat shoes for anybody."

"Take 'em off altogether and enjoy the sensation of fresh grass between your toes!" Bill was used to Brenda being grumpy and generally ignored her or teased her out of it.

His wife gave him a look as though he'd suggested she strip off completely. "Don't be ridiculous."

"Shame. You've got pretty little toes," he said, patting her on the rump.

Brenda grabbed his offending hand in hers. "Behave, will you? There could be paparazzi in the shrubbery."

"I doubt it, duck. Let's have a bit of a wander around and see what's happening." He studied the pages of the festival guide then looked up at the church clock. "I think we're in time for the ferret racing."

"I'm not going anywhere near those horrible creatures. Everyone knows they're vicious and smell to high heaven."

"That's a myth. They're lovely animals." A misty smile lit up Bill's eyes. "My dad kept ferrets and they were very nice, affectionate things. Stinky, I grant you, but so would you be if you lived in a cage inside a shed."

Brenda sighed heavily. "Is there anything less rustic going on?"

"There's an arts and crafts tent, my sweet. Shall we have a gander?"

"I suppose we ought to take a look while we're here."

As they entered the tent, Brenda wrinkled her nose – as far as the Botox would allow – at the handmade crafts while Bill and Vince seemed entranced.

"Look at this, Boss – it's a bog dolly," said Vince, picking up a pink crocheted toilet-roll holder. "My mother always insisted on covering up loo rolls with these."

"Your house always was the poshest in the street," said Bill. "We had to make do with that shiny toilet paper at ours."

Brenda's hands were placed firmly over her jet-black bob, screening her ears from the offending words. "Will you two shut up about lavatories!"

"Sorry sweetheart. Are we embarrassing you?" Bill knew well that his wife preferred to forget the ordinary working-class backgrounds they all shared. "Let's look at the art, shall we?"

"It's not much better than the handicrafts." Brenda sighed at the array of amateur watercolours depicting kittens, wonky landscapes and peculiar abstracts.

"Well now, but that's rather good, don't you think? The artist has captured me in my prime there. Who painted it, duck?" At the end of the tent, set apart from the other artwork, was a large canvas. On it was a portrait of Bill skilfully drawn in black ink with energetic splashes of tangerine and blue bursting out around his head.

Brenda perused the list of paintings. "It's by somebody called A. Kulda." She tipped her head from side to side, tapping the list against her hands. "It is quite striking and it would fill a space in the new house."

"If you want it my sweet, I'll buy it for you."

Brenda turned and gently stroked Bill's face. "You're a good, generous husband."

"Generous? Oh dear," he said smiling, "is it very expensive?"

"No, not at all."

Bill waved at Vince, who carried his boss's wallet for him. He extracted it now from an inside pocket and handed it over. "In that case," said Bill, "let's have them wrap it up for you."

Brenda stopped his hand. "I'd like to think about it for a while first."

Bill shook his head at Vince who quietly put the money safely back into his jacket.

* * *

After wandering around the various stalls, Eleanor and Daniel bumped into Frederick Williams, the previous owner of The Reading Room.

They exchanged greetings then Eleanor remembered something she had been meaning to tell him. "I found some newspapers and magazines of yours at the shop and I wondered whether you wanted them back."

"My dear, the last thing I need is more clutter – you're very welcome to the lot. All the interesting editions were sold years ago, so I can't imagine they're even worth keeping."

"There are some quite amusing advertisements I might cut out and frame. And the Victorian crime reports are fascinating, too."

"Is that so? I'm afraid I never had the patience to read the tiny type," said Frederick.

Eleanor smiled. "I don't mind the tiny type if the story's gripping."

Daniel saw Mr Williams' puzzled expression. "My wife has become obsessed with a Victorian theft."

Eleanor dug him in the ribs. "I'm not obsessed – I'm developing an interest in local history, that's all." She thought for a moment. "But I don't suppose the name John Able rings any bells, does it Mr Williams?"

Frederick thought for a moment then shook his head. "No, I can't say it does."

"Never mind," said Eleanor. "I'm enjoying doing the research."

"Well, that's the main thing." Mr Williams smiled and took his wife's hand. "We're off to Bat the Rat."

"Good luck."

At that moment, Dismal Deirdre hove into view carrying a red clipboard and making straight for them. "Oh no, spare me," said Eleanor under her breath. "The Head of Logistics is heading this way."

"Hello Deirdre. How's it going?" asked Daniel, stepping forward to screen his wife from her foe.

"It's going splendidly, thank you. I have something for you, Eleanor," she said, unclipping an envelope from the clipboard and reaching behind Daniel to hand it over. "It's John Able's transportation records."

Eleanor muttered her thanks, but was saved from having to respond more fully by the vicar who came bounding over.

"Sorry to interrupt, but would you mind terribly taking your place on the bookstall? There's already quite a queue of literature lovers forming!" He smiled at her encouragingly. "I'll take you over there if you're ready."

Suddenly, Eleanor felt rather nervous at the thought of appearing in front of everyone as an expert. "Okay," she said, following the vicar.

Daniel squeezed his wife's hand encouragingly. "You'll be fine."

Chapter 21: An Interesting Encounter

Philip led Eleanor across the green to a quiet area where a rather dapper gentleman in a white suit and Panama hat was seated under a blue and white striped awning by the side of the church.

"That's Mr Cheetham from the Waterborough Auction House." Philip waved a hand in greeting. "He's on furniture and objets d'art."

Eleanor covered her mouth, doing her best not to giggle at the auctioneer's unfortunate name.

"This is your spot over here," said Philip, indicating a table where three people were already waiting patiently with books in their hands. "You'll be needing this for the takings," he said, handing Eleanor a large biscuit tin. "Good luck!"

"I'll do my best," she said, grasping the tin and walking over to her table.

It was mid-afternoon and the sun was blazing down but the huge umbrellas erected by the organisers in case of rain did equally good service as parasols, so Eleanor had a nice cool spot for her valuations.

Soon her nerves calmed and she began to enjoy looking at people's books. She had dads bringing in their *Beano* albums, elderly ladies with much-used copies of Mrs Beeton's cookbooks, and endless streams of youngsters with battered copies of *Harry Potter*. She oohed and aahed over everything and took notes of interesting editions, promising to advise the owners of values later in the week.

After an hour or so the rush was over and Daniel came across with a cup of tea and some of Maureen's shortbread. "How's it going? Found any treasures, yet?"

"Lots! Though only treasures that are worth something to their owners."

"How much longer are you on duty? I'd like to have another stroll with my wife at some point."

"I'm supposed to stay at my post until half past – can you manage without me until then?"

"I suppose I'll have to." Shading his eyes against the sun, Dan searched the green. "In any case, I need to find Dad and see how he's coping with Joyce."

"She doesn't still have him locked in a tango, does she?"

"Nope – I think Maureen rescued him from the dance tent but Joyce was in hot pursuit."

"A tug of love – how thrilling! Come back and tell me if there's any romance going on, won't you?"

"I will," said Dan, with a wink.

* * *

Half an hour later, Eleanor had valued a set of *Mr Men* stories, an original *Jackie* magazine and had promised to research the price of a signed 1906 edition of *The Mayor of Casterbridge*. It was time to put away her notepad and find her family. Peeking inside the cash box, she reckoned her "customers" had added about £30 to the vicar's appeal fund, which she hoped he'd be pleased with.

She was about to call it a day when she heard wheezing and saw a new customer heading her way.

"Am I too late? I do hope not."

Trundling towards her across the grass was an elderly gentleman tugging a tartan shopping trolley. Eleanor vaguely recognised the man as one of the old boys who sat together by the bandstand, leaning on their sticks as they watched the world go by. Joshua, she thought his name was. Breathlessly, he sat down opposite Eleanor and looked her up and down. By his feet was a Yorkshire terrier – not much bigger than your average guinea pig – whose ears twitched nervously. Given that the dog was dressed in a fluffy pink coat, the twitching could have been due to embarrassment.

Bending down, Joshua dug around in the trolley, then placed a faded plastic carrier bag on the table in front of Eleanor.

"I'd like to know what you make of this."

Eleanor carefully opened the bag. Inside was another carrier bag and inside that was a heavy object wrapped in brown paper tied up with string. Removing all the layers, Eleanor was slightly disappointed by what she found.

"Oh, it's a Bible," she said.

Joshua leant back in the rickety plastic chair. "Well, I can see that, my dear. But what's it worth?" He'd picked up the tiny dog that had begun to whine and was now anxiously scanning the green for predators.

Eleanor smoothed her hands over the dark-green leather binding then carefully opened the cover, releasing the musty scent of old paper.

"I'll have to check, but I think this could be quite valuable."

"Hundreds, thousands?"

"That depends on its age and condition," she smiled. "As I say, I'll have to check but at least £50." She leafed through the pages, gazing at the illustrations. "It is beautiful," she said, quietly.

"Give me £20 and it's yours."

"I can't do that – it might be worth much more to a collector."

"I don't have anywhere to keep it and £20 will be plenty. If you don't want it, I'll take it to the bric-à-brac stall across the way and see what they'll give me for it."

The thought of such a handsome volume ending up on Graham's bric-à-brac stall with cracked teapots and incomplete jigsaws was too painful to contemplate. "Okay – I'll buy it." How could she not?

Joshua grinned a toothless grin. "I've got a whole house full of the damned things and I want rid of them. Hold this, will you?" He thrust the quivering dog into Eleanor's hands and bent over the trolley again. "Here, look. What d'you think of these?" He put another pile of books on the table. "This lot will be interesting to you, I dare say. Printed by Williams & Makepeace, they were."

Eleanor looked at him blankly. "I'm sorry, I haven't heard of them . . ."

Joshua scratched himself vigorously under the armpit. "Well, you should've – you're living in their building."

"Of course! How could I forget?"

When she bought what was now The Reading Room from Young Mr Williams six years before he told her the place had been a publishing company part-owned by his father – imaginatively known as Old Mr Williams. The front of the present shop was where the books were sold. The rest of the building and part of her cottage were dedicated to the press: printing downstairs, proofing and hand-binding upstairs. There was still a connecting door between the two properties behind the Welsh dresser in the kitchen.

When she moved in, Eleanor had found catalogues dating from when the business was set up and had been amused by the eccentric selection of titles for sale. Now half a dozen of these were placed in front of her. She picked up and examined an Edwardian lady's guide to composing letters for every occasion, a survey of local waterfowl dated 1931 and an illustrated collection of *Seafaring Tales for Children* from 1900.

"Again, I'll have to check the prices for you," she frowned, "but I don't expect these will be terribly valuable."

"Let's say £50 for the lot then, shall we?"

Eleanor opened and closed her mouth, feeling as though she'd been outmanoeuvred. "Okay then. I'll have to send you a cheque because I don't have that much cash on me."

Joshua shook his head. "I don't need the money – put it in the reverend's pot."

"You want me to put £50 in the church fund?"

"That's what I said, isn't it? I'll take that off you, shall I?" He nodded towards the fur ball that had curled itself up in Eleanor's lap and was snoring contentedly.

"Sure," she said, handing over the dog to Joshua who took the creature gently in one gnarled hand.

Then something came over her that she would later regret. "If you'd like me to visit and go through the rest of your library, I'd be happy to take a look. If you wanted to know what your books might be worth, I mean."

Joshua started and examined her through his rheumy eyes. "Library? How do you know about my library?"

Eleanor could have kicked herself. What a nuisance to end the day with a tricky old man, with most of his teeth missing and slightly whiffy trousers. It was time to backtrack. "I don't know anything about a particular library – it's a turn of phrase. I was trying to be helpful, that's all." She took a deep breath and silently counted to ten. He was an elderly gentleman and there was no need to be cross with him. "I should have explained that The Reading Room is well known for its second-hand stock and customers sometimes sell us books they no longer want or have room for." Or the owners have died, but she decided not to mention that to Joshua who must have been about a hundred and ten. He harrumphed and turned away.

"Maybe," he muttered, before placing the dog on the ground and heading off in the direction of the cider tent, the empty shopping trolley bouncing along behind him.

Daniel, who had been watching the proceedings from under a nearby tree, came over to Eleanor's table, an amused look on his face. "I see you've had a visit from our local tycoon."

"Very funny – that old chap looks as though he doesn't have two pennies to rub together."

"Appearances can be deceptive." Daniel picked up one of the books and began leafing through it. "I'm not kidding, you know. They say he's a millionaire twice over."

"Who's 'they'?"

"People." Daniel shrugged. "It's one of those things everyone around here knows about."

"A bit like the ghost ship, then?" Eleanor smiled. "In other words, the story about Joshua's wealth is a rumour with no basis in fact?"

"Not at all. It's a fact he inherited pots of cash from his parents and never had children of his own, so he's not had much cause to spend it. Ergo, he's a squillionaire."

"That's sad," said Eleanor, thoughtfully. "To have tons of money but no one to enjoy it with."

Across the green, they watched as Joshua reappeared from the cider tent with a gleaming pint in his hand. Once settled on a bench in the shade, he lowered the glass to the ground so the dog could take a sip.

"You're right though – no one would guess he was a wealthy man from looking at him," said Daniel, shaking his head at the sight.

"He looks like a tramp in those battered clothes, not to mention the state of his hands." Eleanor couldn't help noticing that Joshua's fingernails were in need of a scrub. "And I reckon he's shaving with a blunt knife, bless him. He's obviously not spending his money on male grooming products."

"He doesn't spend it on anything – he's notoriously mean. His house is falling down and he doesn't possess a car." Daniel thought for a moment. "I think his one and only extravagance is silly coats for that dog of his."

"Where does he live? I can't think of many places around here suitable for millionaires." Apart from the new house Freya was building for Bill, but neither of them wanted to discuss that.

"He lives at Combemouth Manor, which is hidden down a long drive a little way off the Dunster road. It's the oldest house in this part of Devon, I believe."

"It sounds intriguing."

"I don't know about intriguing, but it's a Tudor building with some unsympathetic Victorian additions: crenellations, turrets, that kind of thing. As well as being ugly, a building like Combemouth Manor is a money pit: its stone walls are held together on the outside by wisteria and ivy and inside by cobwebs. You can guarantee it will be freezing cold in winter and not much warmer in summer."

"I don't think it sounds ugly." A dreamy look came over Eleanor's face. "I think it sounds charming."

Daniel laughed. "I suppose if you were willing and able to spend a couple of hundred thousand on it, the house could be made quite attractive."

"What a pity we don't have a few hundred thousand knocking around," said Eleanor, smiling. "For a house like that, I might just give up the cottage."

Sighing, Daniel put his hands on his hips. "Forget it, El. It's not going to happen."

"I'd love to take a peek inside though, wouldn't you?"

"Nope. Anyway, it's not for sale."

"Shame. You know I can't resist an old ruin."

"I hope you're not referring to me?"

Eleanor put her arms around Daniel's waist and hugged him tightly. "As if! You're in excellent condition for your age."

"Correct answer," he said, bending down to kiss her. "Anyway, I wouldn't be at all surprised if Clarence inherited the lot one day."

"Clarence?"

"The mouse hound."

"Poor little mite. It must be terrifying being that small." Eleanor had a vision of the dog being carried off by a passing jackdaw, four tiny paws poking out from the sleeves of its pink fun-fur sweater as it disappeared overhead. "But Joshua can't be all that mean," she said, holding up two of the books for Daniel to see. "He let me have this lot for far less than they are probably worth. In fact, he seemed very keen to be rid of them. And he refused to take the money and told me to put it in the vicar's collection box instead."

"Really? That doesn't sound like Joshua Pinkham to me. So, you've bought more books?"

"Only a few," she said, sheepishly. "I had to have them because they were printed by Williams & Makepeace at what is now The Reading Room. And I know I don't need any more books, especially now I'm supposed to be making space . . ."

Daniel sighed. "But when did 'need' ever come into book buying?"

"True. And the Bible really is a beauty. Let me show you . . ."

Daniel stopped her, keen to get on. "You can show me at home, but first you have to see the specimens in the fruit and veg tent. Graham's gooseberries are stunning, if you're easily impressed by small hairy fruit."

Eleanor pinched his side. "Don't be horrid – I think it's lovely."

"I'm not being horrid, but the festival is relatively new to you. I've had giant marrows and crocheted tea cosies inflicted on me since birth."

"I thought you loved these traditional events?"

He shrugged, leafing through the guidebook Philip had put together for the show. "You're right, I do. So what would you like to see next? Cake decoration? Miniature gardens? Crafts?"

"Tough call." Eleanor tapped her chin as she mulled over the options. "But I think top of my list for this afternoon has to be the vegetable sculpture category."

"An excellent choice if I may say so. Let's start there."

Chapter 22: Philip Has Visitors

Eleanor had arranged to drop off her takings at Philip White's house a day or so after the festival. She was hoping he might live in the vicarage, then remembered that the fine old house had been sold off and was now the offices for a team of solicitors. Instead, the vicar of Combemouth lived in an ordinary pebble-dashed bungalow in a quiet cul-de-sac.

In front of the house was a neat square of lawn edged with marigolds and salvias in serried ranks, and a concrete birdbath on a stand in the centre. How annoying it must be having to pass the beautiful vicarage every day to return home to this rather dull place. I'm getting obsessed with houses, she thought, as she walked up to the front door and rang the bell. Through the frosted panel she could see Philip approach.

"Eleanor – welcome. Come through to the office."

She followed the vicar down the short corridor to a room at the back of the house overlooking a long garden that swooped down towards the sea. "Wow, what a view!" Perhaps this place wasn't so dull after all. Even more impressive than the vista were the photographs that lined the walls: Philip in a West African country wearing loud shirts surrounded by smiling youngsters. Another of him standing in front of a school building helping to dish out food from cooking pots, large ladies in brightly coloured wraps and head gear on either side of him waving ladles in the air. Philip in a desert landscape with a family, the smallest child holding one skinny cow on the end of a rope under a baobab tree and beaming at the camera.

The vicar saw Eleanor admiring the images and walked over to join her. "Such noble people," he said. "They have so little and yet they are so generous and filled with such a sincere faith."

"Were you doing missionary work out there?"

"No, that would be a blessing. I was teaching for a Christian charity, which is where I found my true calling." He pointed at an imposing woman in red and orange Kente cloth. "That's my colleague, Myrtle. I'm hoping she'll be able to visit us one of these days." His voice softened and Eleanor was sure she detected a note of wistfulness.

"Gosh." Eleanor was lost for words at the discovery of the vicar's exciting past. "Working there must have been fascinating."

"Fascinating and humbling, yes." He smiled. "Make yourself at home while I fetch us a drink. Tea okay?"

"Perfect, yes." Eleanor sat down on a sofa completely covered in patterned cloth and let her eyes roam around the room, which she now saw was packed with memorabilia from wooden sculptures to African animals in polished stone. She was admiring a very fine hippopotamus carved out of soapstone when Philip returned with floral cups, mismatched saucers, a beige teapot and a plate of sensible-looking biscuits.

He set the tray down on a table and poured out

the tea before handing Eleanor a teacup on a chipped saucer. "So what have you got for me? Your table seemed to be very busy with bookworms!"

"I think it went fairly well," said Eleanor, handing him the biscuit tin she'd been using as a cash box but hadn't yet emptied. "But I doubt it's enough for more than a couple of roof tiles."

Philip held the tin in both his hands for a moment and closed his eyes, as though trying to guess the value of the contents from its weight. When he opened his eyes, he caught Eleanor looking at him curiously. "I was saying a silent prayer to thank all those kind people who donated."

He really was a good and holy man, Eleanor thought, now wishing she'd managed to persuade her "customers" to part with a bit more cash.

Philip took the top off the tin and tipped the contents onto the tray next to the plate of Rich Tea biscuits. "This is super," he said, prodding the pounds and pennies into separate piles and adding up the meagre offering. "You have done jolly well: there's £37.42 in the tin and a cheque for £50 from your good self. That is very generous, Eleanor."

"Don't thank me, Reverend. The £50 was for books I bought off one of your parishioners. He refused to take a penny for himself, instead insisting that the money should go to the church fund."

Philip beamed. "You must tell me who our benefactor is so I can thank him or her personally – unless the money was given anonymously, of course."

Eleanor shook her head. "No, I don't think it was meant to be a secret. I didn't know the gentleman's surname, but my husband tells me it's Pinkham."

"Joshua Pinkham donated £50 of his own money to St Cuthbert's? Good heavens," said Philip, crossing himself. "Well, well. Our Lord truly does work in mysterious ways."

"He's not a regular worshipper, then?"

The vicar laughed. "No, he keeps well clear of the church as a rule. Although he did come and see me the other day about something, as it happens."

* * *

Philip had been surprised to hear a knock at the vestry door a week or so before. It wasn't often he had callers in the middle of the day and it was one of the many things he missed from West Africa. There, life was lived outdoors and people were constantly in and out of each other's homes. It was quite normal for families to look after friends' children and it took him quite a while to figure out who were blood relations and who were simply neighbours. He had grown used to people coming and going all day and using his kitchen as an unofficial meeting room or somewhere to complete homework. In Combemouth, he was always delighted when his parishioners called on him, but he was quite taken aback to find Joshua Pinkham on his doorstep.

"Mr Pinkham! Well, this is a pleasant surprise. Come in and make yourself comfortable." Philip ushered Joshua to a seat and sat down opposite him on a peeling wooden chair.

Joshua looked around at the dark wood of the walls. The lower shelves were packed with books but the top one held a motley selection of hats, spectacles, odd gloves and scarfs, all abandoned in the church. He frowned, thinking they appeared like so many relics.

On the other side of the room was a collection of West African art, including a stilt man wearing a horsehair headdress and a skirt made from raffia. On the wall was a photograph of the latest bishop in his regalia, who looked out across this display as though perplexed to find himself in such exotic company. It was an incongruous collection of things to find in an English country church.

When his guest seemed reluctant to speak, Philip rose to his feet. "Let me put the kettle on."

"No need. I shan't stay long." Joshua was not a man to waste words and when he was ready to speak he came straight to the point. "Vicar, I shall be three score years and twenty next month, which means my time on this earth will be well and truly up."

Philip leant across and gently stroked Clarence's head where it emerged from the gap in its owner's bobbly brown cardigan. "I think you are taking the words of the psalmists a little too literally Joshua, if you don't mind me saying so."

"I know what I know, and I've lived ten years longer than I should have done." Joshua shook his head vigorously. "My father, his father and his father before that all dropped dead on their eightieth birthdays." He emphasised the words by tapping the vicar's desk firmly with one gnarled finger. "Now, tell me why I should be any different?"

"But eighty is the new sixty, isn't that what they say?" Philip smiled, hoping to lighten Joshua's mood, but the old gentleman's mouth stayed set in a downward curl. The vicar decided to take a different tack. "There are numerous reasons why you should enjoy many more years of life yet. We live in different times to our fathers and grandfathers. Think about it: there's no typhoid. We have smallpox vaccinations, better nutrition, the NHS, comfortable homes – lots of things. I suggest you put these negative thoughts out of your mind and enjoy every day as it comes."

Ignoring him, Mr Pinkham extracted a large brown envelope from inside his cardigan. "I have my instructions here, Reverend, and I'd be grateful if you'd follow them. Don't worry about the costs – my solicitor has been told to hand over the readies."

Seeing that Mr Pinkham was not going to be shifted in his views, Philip took the proffered envelope, which carried with it the distinctive aroma of old dog, albeit one in a rather snazzy coat.

"Very well, Joshua, if that's what you want. I'll put this in a safe place and hopefully there won't be any need to open it for many years yet."

Mr Pinkham harrumphed, seemingly taking the suggestion that he might not be about to die as an insult. As he stood, ready to leave the room, Philip offered his hand. "I hope to see you again."

Joshua made a grumbling noise and snorted. "Don't you worry – you'll be seeing me in a box very soon indeed. I've had it on good authority that the *Santa Ana* has been sighted three times this month, which is a sure sign the grim reaper is on his way."

"That's superstitious nonsense."

"I'm surprised to hear you say such a thing, Vicar – you a man who has spent time in Africa, a place full of powerful spirits."

Philip had to concede that was a good point.

"I would never say there weren't unknown forces at work in the world, Joshua, but I'm certain a ghostly vessel is not likely to see you off before your time."

"Well, we'll see."

"Try to put it from your mind. And remember – my door here or at home is always open if there's ever anything you would like to talk to me about," he said, grasping the old man's hand firmly in both of his. "I play a mean game of Scrabble, too, if you ever fancy some entertainment."

Joshua harrumphed again, readjusted Clarence, who had crept along one baggy sleeve and settled himself under his owner's armpit, and left.

* * *

Visiting the young, pasty-faced vicar had been a nec-essary evil as far as Joshua was concerned. He really wanted to be chucked on the compost heap once he expired, but had been told it wasn't possible because of council bylaws or some such nonsense. Hence his visit to St Cuthbert's. The Pinkhams had a family plot in the graveyard that was all paid for, so this was where Joshua intended to be interred in a few weeks' time. "You're lucky," he said, addressing the dog, "I've got a special place already set aside for you in the orchard. Much nicer than a darned churchyard." Clarence did not look reassured.

Chapter 23: Combemouth Manor

A couple of days later, Eleanor was surprised to find a note pushed through the door from Joshua Pinkham asking her to contact him about his books. She gave him a call and agreed to visit and give him her opinion the following day.

As arranged, Eleanor turned up in her lime-green van with a notepad, a camera and a Welsh spaniel. She didn't know whether Joshua simply wanted to chat about options or whether he would ask her to assess his entire collection then and there. Having done plenty of house clearances in the past she knew it could be dusty work, so she went along in old jeans and had a scarf ready to cover her hair.

Combemouth Manor was as eccentric as Daniel had described it. Reached down an overgrown drive that seemed to go on forever, the house was a mishmash of styles in pale stone and red brick. As well as the main house, which was a couple of storeys high, there was a separate wing with a tower. It was all higgledy-piggledy and Eleanor found it enchanting.

The windows were grubby and covered in cobwebs and, if she hadn't known any different, she would have thought the place was abandoned. The steps up to the imposing front door were almost completely overgrown with purple columbine and dense clumps of foxgloves so Eleanor decided to walk around the house to see if she could find another way in.

Halfway along a side wall, a door opened and Clarence shot out then began barking frenziedly at Bella who ignored him and carried on sniffing the lawn.

"You're here, then?" In the doorway stood Joshua looking, if possible, even shabbier than he had when Eleanor had met him at the fair.

"Yes, I'm here," she said, trying not to stare too hard at the stains down the front of his threadbare sweater.

"You'd best come in."

Eleanor followed Joshua as he shuffled down a cool flagstoned corridor and around the corner through a door that seemed to mark the boundary between what would have been the servants' area and the main house. Eventually, he took her into a reception room where the floor was covered with Afghan rugs and the walls were painted in a deep, rich red. Every surface seemed to be covered with knick-knacks of one sort or another and there were animal heads and painted landscapes hanging on the walls. One side of the room had wall-to-ceiling windows framed by heavy velvet curtains, but the two longest sides were completely covered in books.

Eleanor gasped. "This is beautiful," she said, the room reminding her of the sun-filled place where she'd married Daniel a few months before. Yes, it was a bit tatty and the stuffed boar's head baring its teeth on the wall might not be to everyone's taste, but the place had potential. "You could hold weddings here, you know? Brides would love it."

The look of horror on Joshua's face was enough

to stop her in her tracks. "I'll fetch tea," he said, and disappeared.

As she hadn't been invited to sit down, Eleanor decided to check out the bookshelves instead. She chewed her lip, wondering what she'd taken on. At a rough guess, the small area of shelves she was looking at must have held about three hundred books: she was going to be there for some time.

If Joshua wanted her to catalogue everything accurately, she would have to remove each book from the shelf and photograph the binding and imprint page. She puffed out her cheeks, wishing she'd brought Joe along to help instead of Bella, who now came running into the room, hotly pursued by Clarence. At least the little dog seemed to appreciate their company.

Behind the dogs came Joshua with a porcelain teapot, silver sugar bowl and two battered mugs on a tray. "Right then, missus," he said, moving a heap of paper out of the way to make space on the fine old table.

"Thank you," said Eleanor, pleased to see the mugs were clean at least. Surreptitiously, she sniffed the milk before adding it. "What is it you'd like me to do?"

"I want you to help me get rid of that lot," he said, sweeping his arm across the back wall.

"All those books?"

"All of those on that wall there – I shan't bother with the others. The mice are welcome to those."

Eleanor smiled nervously. "I have to be honest and tell you this isn't my area, Mr Pinkham. What you need is a specialist who knows about antiquarian books. I can put you in touch with an expert if you would like me to."

Joshua frowned. "I don't want to deal with strangers."

"I'll come with them, if that helps?"

"No. You'll do for me." Eleanor wasn't sure whether she should be flattered or not by Joshua's decision. "Now, can you help – yes or no?"

"I can," she said, "though it may take a little time."

"That's all right, so long as it isn't too long. I've got to be somewhere next month."

"Okay. Well, I'd better make a start."

"I suggest you begin at the top and work down."

There were sliding library ladders that could be moved around the room and Joshua brought them over to one end of the back wall so Eleanor could reach the high shelves. These were thick with dust and assorted mummified insects, so she was relieved she'd brought something to cover her hair.

During the morning, Eleanor gradually moved across the shelves, extracting books, caressing their bindings and carefully lifting fine sheets of paper to admire the illustrations. In the few gaps between books she found a motley array of objects. Once she had the strange sensation of being watched and found herself eye to glass eye with a stuffed stoat bearing a distinct resemblance to Clarence. She turned away from the creature's melancholy gaze with a start. Someone in the family had clearly had a thing for taxidermy: on the mantelpiece was a glass case containing a number of baby rabbits in Victorian costume arranged around a tea table.

Below her, Joshua had come back into the room and was sitting in a leather armchair watching her with interest. "Well?"

It was harder work than Eleanor had anticipated, climbing up and down the ladders to take photographs and make notes, but she was enjoying herself despite the cobwebs. "You have some lovely books here, Joshua – even some first editions. I can tell you now this lot will be worth a few thousand pounds, but I'm making a separate list of the books I think you might want to keep in the family."

Joshua made a grumbling noise that sounded rather like "bah-humbug". "Never mind family."

"I expect you have nephews and nieces who would love to have these children's books, for example?" When there was no response, Eleanor came down the ladder, took off her gloves and wiped a hand across her grubby brow. "Well, I have to go now, but I'll be back tomorrow to carry on."

"Very well. And don't be late."

* * *

The next day, Eleanor reached the middle section of the bookcase. She had cleared a long length of books about local flora and fauna, carrying them down to the table where she could take better photographs. It was when she went back to check out the bare patch of wall that she noticed something peculiar. She called Joshua as she backed down off the ladder, rubbing her dusty hands on her trousers. "I think you should come and look at this."

Joshua, who had been sitting reading, stood up and approached, his face serious. Grasping the ladder, he slowly climbed up two steps until he was at eye level with the empty shelf.

"What is it, missus? I don't see nothing."

Eleanor dragged over a heavy mahogany chair,

slipped off her shoes and stood on it. "There," she said, pointing at the wall. "What's that?"

In front of them, a small patch of bookcase was empty. It was only the glint of hinges on the left-hand side and an indentation on the right that revealed the wall was not solid. "I think it's a door."

Joshua's eyes opened wide with surprise then he put a finger into the indentation and pulled. It was indeed a door. Opening it, he reached into a cupboard and withdrew a red leather briefcase, which he handed to Eleanor to put on the table. Next, Joshua brought out a wooden box which he carried down the ladder and put next to the briefcase.

"Well, goodness me! What a surprise." Eleanor grinned broadly, expecting Joshua to be as excited as she was by their finds, but he said nothing. She stood watching him in silence for what seemed like an age until the grandfather clock struck 4pm and Joshua looked down at Clarence, who was sitting on one frayed slipper pawing his master's ankle. "Teatime." Without another word, Joshua went off to the scullery to feed the dog.

Chapter 24: Skeletons in the Cupboard?

Eleanor couldn't wait to get home to tell Daniel about her day.

"Joshua seemed as taken aback to see the secret compartment as I was. Don't you think it's odd that someone would have such a thing and not tell their children or grandchildren about it?"

"Not necessarily," said Daniel. "I expect plenty of wealthy Victorians had places where they could hide their belongings from thieves and disgruntled employees." He thought for a moment. "What was in the briefcase, anyway?"

"No idea and we won't know until Joshua finds the key, which could be anywhere."

"Or he breaks the lock."

Eleanor shook her head, remembering how Joshua had walked away from both the case and the box as though they were of no interest. "He won't do that. In fact, I had the distinct impression he didn't want to open either of our finds. I'd have been tearing them open straight away, but he's an odd chap."

"That's the general consensus." Daniel smiled.

"Says who?"

"Everyone who's ever had dealings with him. Of course, if you'd like to know more about Joshua

Pinkham, you should speak to Harold. They're around the same age and probably knew each other as kids."

"Never! Harold looks much younger."

Dan laughed. "He'll be pleased to hear you say that."

Eleanor opened her diary. "It's 'Storytime with Harold' in the bookshop tomorrow. I might have chance to quiz him then."

* * *

"Storytime with Harold" had been running for nearly a year and was a huge hit with the local children and their parents, some of whom clearly enjoyed being read to as much as their offspring. When Harold had finished the day's session and was relaxing with a cup of Earl Grey, Eleanor sat beside him in the children's corner and asked about Joshua. "Dan said you might know him."

Harold laughed. "I've known him since we were five – we went to the same primary school, you see."

"Do you remember much about him as a boy?"

"I remember rather a lot, actually. He lived in the manor house, same as he does now, but it was very rare for other boys to be invited to play there." Harold frowned. "Pity really, as we were keen to explore the turrets and towers, even though the place was rather creepy."

Eleanor thought back to the stuffed animals and lugubrious family portraits lining the dark corridors. "I can see you might have found the place daunting as a child."

"I always had the impression Joshua was quite lonely. His mother was distant and undemonstrative and his father seemed terribly fierce."

"Do you mean aggressive?" Eleanor hated to think the young Joshua might have been mistreated.

"Oh, Joshua was never beaten or anything like that. His father was simply a serious chap – I don't remember ever seeing him smile." Harold thought for a moment. "Of course you have to bear in mind that fathers were authority figures in those days – they didn't play with their children or show much affection the way dads do today."

"No, I suppose not. But he must have been extremely serious if you noticed it."

"That's true, I suppose." Harold nodded. "There was also the fact that Joshua's parents didn't get involved in the local community, which immediately earned them a reputation for being standoffish."

"And where did their money come from? Dan said they were a wealthy family."

Harold shrugged. "That's a good question. I believe Joshua's grandfather built up a fortune in shipping and passed the business down to his son who expanded it into a huge international concern."

"Does Joshua have siblings?"

"I seem to remember there was a sister who died in infancy – many children did in those days, you know – and an older brother."

Eleanor felt sorry for the lonely boy in the big house with no one to play with. "And does Joshua have children, Harold?"

"He was married to a lovely girl. She died some years back and they weren't blessed with children."

"Poor chap. No wonder he's miserable."

"Well, they say what goes around comes around."

"Sorry, I don't follow what you mean."

Harold looked at his feet. "Forgive me – I shouldn't have said anything. It is only rumour after all." He began to rise from his seat, but Eleanor caught his arm.

"Hang on – you can't stop there! Tell me what you mean."

Harold sighed. "It's only ancient gossip but the story goes that some of Pinkham's forebears were wreckers, a career choice which doesn't make you many friends around here."

Eleanor leant forward. "I was wondering about including wrecking in my ghost ship window display, but I'm not clear what wreckers actually did."

"They were the worst kind of devils." Eleanor had never heard Harold use such strong language and was surprised to see the fierce expression that crossed his usually serene face. "Wreckers deliberately lured ships onto the rocks or sandbars where they were broken up by the sea so their contents could be stolen away."

"That's not very nice – but they rescued the passengers, surely?"

"That's the worst part of it – in days gone by they would save the cargo but let the men drown." He grimaced. "Can you imagine what it must have felt like? To see people on the beach who could save you and to know they were only waiting to push you down beneath the waves?" Harold shook his head sadly. "What a terrible way to die."

"How awful." Eleanor was shocked. "That's – well, it's tantamount to murder." She thought about the *Santa Ana* and remembered the story Daniel had told her of ghostly voices being heard calling out over the water. "Is there any suggestion wreckers were involved in grounding the *Santa Ana* all those centuries ago?"

Harold nodded. "I'm afraid so. She was a Spanish galleon, probably loaded with precious cargo for the King of Spain. A ship like that would be a tempting prize for an impoverished fishing community."

"What a dreadful thought."

"Indeed, but wrecking happened, I'm afraid. A ship's cargo was seen as another harvest from the ocean."

"Perhaps it was, but I would hate to think of Joshua's forebears being involved in something so terrible."

"You're right and I shouldn't even have mentioned it. Though Pinkham is a Cornish name." Harold, a Devon man, couldn't help adding this detail under his breath.

"Are you saying all Cornish people were wreckers?" asked Eleanor, quite taken aback.

"Goodness me, no." Harold looked chastened. "It's a practice that went on right around the British coast – we were famous for it. Or infamous, I should say."

"Well, I don't know what to say, but it is rather gloomy." Eleanor uncurled herself from the bean bag she had collapsed onto in the children's area and stretched. "Which reminds me – I haven't showed you Deirdre's notes about John Able's transportation to Australia." Harold was a genuine history buff and Eleanor knew he'd be keen to see them.

"Ah, yes. I mentioned the convict records to Georgie – as she comes from that part of the world – and she was most intrigued."

"She wasn't offended when you mentioned them, Harold?"

"Good heavens, no. Why should she be?"

Eleanor shrugged, feeling a little embarrassed. "I thought Australians were as bored of us Brits banging on about the convict business as Germans are about WWII."

"Not our Georgie."

"Let's show her, then."

They found Georgie at the front of the shop. "I was asking your manager about her memoirs." She turned to Erika, smiling. "I know you've been working on them for two years now and I'm sure people would be fascinated to read your history."

"Yes, it's very 'on trend' to be trans – everybody's at it, rather like going gluten-free. Actually, I'm having second thoughts about writing a straight history – if you'll pardon the pun. I might make it into a fiction-alised account of my life thus far, so I can include some racy stuff and be really rude about my former colleagues in the police force without being sued."

"Sounds like a bestseller to me." Eleanor grinned. "In the meantime, I have something to show you." She took Deirdre's printed sheet out of its envelope and laid it next to her notebook on the counter.

"As you can see, my annoying librarian friend has found records that show John Able was put on a convict ship and transported to Western Australia for stealing jewellery. He was in and out of prison his entire life and died in Fremantle Jail in 1910."

"Gosh, the poor chap was only forty-nine when he died." Harold shook his head sympathetically. "He must have had a jolly hard time."

"Most of those guys had pretty terrible times," said Georgie. "My nan lives in Fremantle right behind the jail – it's a great museum now, by the way. Me and my brother used to visit a lot and I was quite into convict history in my teens."

Harold nodded. "I remember the museum. My wife and I visited many years ago when we were staying with relatives in Bunbury." He picked up Deirdre's printout and frowned. "If you know about convict history, Georgie, I think you will agree with me there's something here that doesn't fit."

"Let's see." Harold passed Georgie the printout. "And may we see your notes from the newspaper archive, Eleanor?" he asked.

"Of course," she said, handing them over.

Harold put on his spectacles as he and Georgie studied Eleanor's scribbles.

"You've made a note here that John was convicted in 1872. Is that right?"

"That's right, yes. Just after he had turned twelve."

"Meaning he was born in 1860 . . ."

Georgie nodded. "So he can't have been transported because the last shipload of convicts from the UK arrived in 1868 when your John Able would have been eight years old."

"Which, in any case, is four years before he went on trial in Combemouth," added Harold.

Eleanor was stunned. "Are you sure?"

"Totally one hundred per cent certain," said Georgie, emphatically. "It's something my nan drummed into me from an early age. The last ship to bring convicts to Western Australia was the *Hougoument*. She set sail in October 1867 and arrived in January the following year." She tapped the page. "Your librarian's guy must be another John Able altogether."

"Excellent detective work, team." Erika nudged her boss in the ribs. "I bet you can't wait to tell Deirdre she got her facts wrong?"

Eleanor smiled. "I shall enjoy that immensely." She was pleased that John hadn't died in prison thousands of miles from home, but what had happened to him remained a mystery.

Chapter 25: The Briefcase

The next day, Eleanor returned to Combemouth Manor to continue going through Joshua's books. When she rang the bell, there was no answer so she walked around to the kitchen door, peeking in through the dusty windows as she went.

The door was unlocked so she opened it and called out. "Hello. Is there anybody home?" There was no response so she yanked on the bell pull and listened to the clank of bells echoing through the house. Still nothing. She was beginning to worry about the lack of response when eventually she heard the skittering of paws as Clarence ran across the flagstones of the hall-way and began barking in excitement. Having greeted Eleanor, the dog turned and ran away. Bella took off after him towards a different part of the house.

The dogs led Eleanor to a large sitting room where she found Joshua at his desk surrounded by all kinds of writing paraphernalia from fountain pens and bottles of ink, to piles of yellowed envelopes, rock-hard erasers and heaps of paperclips whose primary colours looked out of place among the Victoriana. In the centre of it, Joshua had made a space now filled by the red briefcase they had taken from the hidden cupboard the day before.

"Morning missus." Joshua turned to greet her, waving the grey handkerchief he'd been using to wipe grime from the closed lid of the case. He stuffed the handkerchief inside his shirt then withdrew a side drawer from the Victorian writing desk and picked up a cardboard shoebox full of keys.

Eleanor smiled. "Have you found the key to the briefcase?"

"Perhaps. I've found lots of keys but none of them is right, so now I'll have to try the rest." He cradled one hand in the other. "Trouble is, I can't hold them properly, what with my arthritis."

"Could I help?" Without waiting for a reply, Eleanor threw her handbag onto a maroon Chesterfield and took the box from him.

"Not them, they don't work." He pointed at another, bigger box. "Try that lot."

"Okay," said Eleanor, pulling up a seat while Joshua moved away from the desk so she could reach the case. "Let me see now." She bent over and fitted the first key into the lock. Nothing. She tried a second, then added it to the "doesn't work" pile.

"I'm thinking that Father might have hidden the key somewhere more cunning," said Joshua, thoughtfully rubbing his stubble.

Eleanor looked across at him. "I think a box of keys is about as cunning as you can get. But I'm sure it must be here – it's simply a matter of being thorough." She tried two more keys with no luck. Sighing, she picked up the box and jiggled it around, then closed her eyes and circled her fingers over it. "Eeny, meeny, miney, moe," she said, before selecting a key at random and inserting it into the lock. "I have a good feeling about this one," she said with a grin. It was nonsense, but she wanted to keep Joshua's spirits up.

Joshua was mumbling something about "hocus-pocus" as Eleanor turned the key and the lock snapped open. "Ta-dah! There you are, you see – a little bit of magic always does the trick." She knotted a piece of string around the briefcase key so it would be easy to identify and handed it over. "There you go." She smiled at Joshua, who sat in silence. "So . . . shall I open up the case for you before I carry on with the books?"

"No." Joshua stood and opened the French doors that gave onto the garden at the back of the house. "I'd best see to the broad beans and you should carry on with what you came here to do." He had been relatively jovial up to that point, so Eleanor was suprised by the sudden change in his tone.

"Right, okay then," she said, standing. Eleanor couldn't help feeling disappointed that her curiosity wasn't going to be satisfied, especially as she'd been the one to discover the secret compartment in the first place. "Are you sure you don't you want to see what's inside the briefcase?" she asked as Joshua shuffled past her into the garden.

Joshua paused, his eyes fixed on a lavender bush by his feet. "There's no need to open it. I know perfectly well what I shall find in there."

* * *

"And what was in it?"

Over dinner that evening, Eleanor was telling Daniel about her day. "I still don't know. After I'd unlocked the briefcase, Joshua left it on the desk and that was that. I was there all morning and it wasn't mentioned again."

"Perhaps he was going to open the case this afternoon after you'd gone."

"Maybe." Eleanor frowned. "There was something about the discovery that seemed to worry him. We've become quite friendly over the past few days and, though he never chats, we do exchange the odd word. But today he barely spoke to me once I'd unlocked the case."

"What I don't understand," said Daniel, selecting a grape from the fruit bowl, "is why he wanted to open it if he knew what was in there and had no intention of looking anyway."

"I've no idea, but I expect he'll tell me when he's ready."

"Weren't you tempted to lift the lid when Joshua wasn't looking and take a quick peek?"

"No, I wasn't!"

"Really not?"

"You know me so well." Eleanor grinned at her husband. "Okay, so I was tempted, but I hope you know I would never do anything of the kind. It would be an abuse of trust."

"I know, I'm only teasing."

"I am madly curious, mind you." Eleanor popped a small chunk of cheese into her mouth and chewed thoughtfully. "I'm due over there one final time, so perhaps all will be revealed then."

Chapter 26: Unexpected Gifts

When Eleanor went back to Combemouth Manor a few days later, she found Joshua in a more positive frame of mind. She was barely through the door before he greeted her and took her into the sitting room. "Here now," he said, handing her something wrapped in a plastic bag and sealed with rubber bands, "I have something for you."

"Thank you," she said, taking the bag and going to open it. "But really, you don't need to give me a present."

Joshua held up his hands. "Don't open it here and give me no thanks. Take it away and never ask me anything about what's in there. Is that clear?"

Eleanor's head was full of questions, but the look on Joshua's face told her he was serious so she went into the library to carry on with her work.

By teatime, the business of photographing the books had come to an end. Eleanor went outside to tell Joshua, who she found in the kitchen garden tying up the sweet peas. "I'm done," she said. "The next step is for me to go online and find out the values for you. Then, when you're ready, I can put the books up for sale – the ones you decide not to keep, that is."

Joshua grumbled. "The sooner the whole lot is gone the better."

"But there must be some you'd like to keep, to give to friends and family? I'm sure you have plenty of relatives who would be delighted to have these books."

Ignoring her, Joshua scooped up Clarence and headed for the kitchen. "Teatime, Clarence."

Realising this was to be Joshua's last word on the subject, Eleanor shook her head sadly. "Well, I'll be off then," she shouted in the direction of Joshua's retreating figure. "And thank you for the gift."

* * *

When Eleanor arrived at the cottage, she found Daniel sitting on the sunny patio drinking tea with Malcolm who stood up to greet her.

"And how's my favourite daughter-in-law today?" he asked, kissing her lightly on both cheeks. "I gather Joshua has been a little trying."

"Oh, he's not that bad. Just socially inept." She smiled. "But all is forgiven because today he gave me a present."

"Let me grab you a cup of tea, then you can tell us about it," said Daniel, going into the kitchen to fetch Eleanor a drink.

"Hurry up," she said, laughing, "I'm gasping."

"I'm agog to find out what Joshua has given you," said Malcolm.

"So am I! He told me I wasn't allowed to open the bag until I was at home. It's very mysterious." She looked at her companions. "Ready?"

"We are," said Daniel, handing her the tea. "Go for it."

Eleanor put the package on the garden table then removed the rubber bands that were tightly wound around the plastic bag. Inside was a shoebox and inside that was her gift. "Oh! It's the wooden box we found in the safe with the briefcase." She pulled each side without success. "I can't figure out how to open it!"

"It looks like a Victorian tea caddy. May I see?"

"Be my guest, Malcolm," she said, handing it over.

"It's locked. Has Joshua given you the key?"

"I hope so." Eleanor picked up the shoebox and noticed a slip of cardboard at the bottom. Picking it up, she saw there was a tiny key taped to one side which she handed to her father-in-law. "Phew, I nearly threw it away."

Malcolm inserted the key, turned it and the top unlocked with a click. "Now what have we here?" Eleanor was straining to see. "As it's yours, I think you should open it."

Lifting the lid, Eleanor saw a small silk bag in a green and gold paisley pattern. She gently pulled apart the silk drawstring running around the top edge and looked inside the bag. "It's a pendant." She held up a silver oval dangling on a chain then ran a thumb over the raised image on the front. The engraving was shallow, making it hard to read, but it seemed to represent a man standing with a tall staff in his hand. "I wonder who the figure is?"

"I'd say it was a St Christopher," said Daniel. "Patron saint of travellers."

"Ah, what a thoughtful gift." Eleanor was quite moved by it. "Perhaps Joshua chose it because he knew I'd travelled to Devon from London."

"That's assuming he knew the pendant was in there, darling."

Malcolm had gone back to examining the wooden box. "I've done a little woodwork in my time and this is a very fine piece." As a former engineer, he liked to know how things worked. "There must be a reason why the base is so deep. Aha," he said, turning it over in his hands, "just as I thought. There's another compartment. Do you have a pin, Eleanor?"

"There'll be one in my needlework basket, I'm sure."

Daniel smiled. "You have a needlework basket? I never knew that."

"They say couples should have secrets from each other to retain the excitement. Anyway, I do, though I haven't sewn anything in years. I'll fetch it."

Eleanor dashed upstairs, opened the drawer at the bottom of her wardrobe and extracted the faded yellow basket she'd had since secondary school. She carried it down to the patio, then dug around among the cotton reels, ribbons and odd buttons before eventually pulling out a stout pin. "Will this do?"

"Perfect." Malcolm took the pin and prodded it into a hole that was carefully concealed in the side of the box. This released the side panel which then slid up and a drawer immediately sprang open to reveal a small envelope.

"Well, what do you know?" said Daniel. "I think you have a secret message!"

"How exciting." Eleanor reached out to take the envelope then hesitated. "Actually, I think your father should do it. I'm so clumsy and I wouldn't want to tear it."

Malcolm gently lifted the envelope from the drawer and laid it on the table. "Are you sure you'd like me to open it?"

"Yes please."

Peeling back the flap, Malcolm withdrew a sheet of paper that he carefully unfolded before handing it to Eleanor.

"What does it say?" asked Daniel.

Eleanor peered at the letters written in small, ornate handwriting. "I don't have my reading glasses and the writing style is so old-fashioned I can't make out all the words. It's a poem of some description." She screwed up her eyes, reading aloud. "'Seeker . . . bosom . . . God.' I'll have to find someone to help me decipher it."

"May I see?" asked Malcolm, putting on his glasses. "I'm old enough to decipher this kind of script."

"Be my guest," said Eleanor.

Ah, yes. It's a poem, but not one I recognise." Malcolm slowly read out the words.

"Seeker bold, ye who travelled from afar
Think but on this —
Blessed is he who finds
Repose in the bosom of the
Everlasting Lord, which dwells on earth and in Heaven.
No more shall he breach the lusty waves but
Divine peace shall be his who
Abides in God's tender care,
No more to fret upon life's travails."

Malcolm looked up. "Well, whoever wrote this was no Wordsworth but it's competent enough."

Eleanor took up the paper and studied it,

rereadingtheverse. "It'smorelikeaprayerthanapoem. I'd love to know who the poet was."

"My guess is Joshua Pinkham," said Daniel.

"Of course! What a clever husband I have!"

Malcolm patted his son on the shoulder. "That's the obvious answer, Dan, but I wouldn't be so sure. Joshua may be even more ancient than me, but the writing and the paper look much too old to be his work."

Eleanor was silent, gazing unseeing at a pot of geraniums.

"What's the matter, El?" asked Daniel. "You look very serious."

"I was thinking that Joshua will probably bite my head off, but I have to return everything to him. The pendant and poem must be important heirlooms and they should stay in his family, not be given to me. I'm not sure I should have bought his Bible at the festival either, now I come to think of it."

"If you hadn't bought the Bible," said Malcolm, thoughtfully, "Joshua might simply have thrown it away, which would have been much worse."

"True, but I'm sure I've short-changed him – well, the vicar actually, because the money went into the church fund."

"Why don't you speak to Philip White before you visit Joshua?" said Daniel. "It might set your mind at rest about the Bible at least?"

Eleanor nodded. "Yes, I think will."

Chapter 27: A Date with the Vicar

The next day, Eleanor put Joshua's Bible into a bag and lugged it through town to St Cuthbert's Church. It was a welcoming place, where people often popped in to grab a few moments of peace, but today it seemed completely empty.

She eventually found the vicar on his hands and knees in the children's corner surrounded by piles of Lego, wooden toys and books, one of which he was reading intently. He smiled as Eleanor approached.

"I hope I'm not disturbing you," she said.

"Not at all," said Philip. "I was just tidying up." He closed the brightly coloured pages and put the book on a shelf. "So what can I do for you on this fine day?"

"I'd like to ask your opinion about something, if I may."

Philip stood up and rubbed his hands together. This was what he'd entered the Church for: to examine the finer points of theology, to argue for the power of prayer as a force for good, to debate the nature of evil – he was ready for anything. "I'm always delighted to help where I can," he said, leading her to the vestry.

Eleanor spoke first. "You remember I bought some books from Joshua at the *Antiques Road Show* thingy?"

"I certainly do, because the money went into the church funds."

"That's right. Well now I'm wondering whether I

did the right thing by taking – buying – the Bible off him. I was going to put it on the shelves in my shop and sell it, but perhaps you could find a better use for it – send it off to Africa, maybe?"

Philip was secretly disappointed that the question was not more intellectually challenging, but determined not to show it. "It's a generous offer, but our church has special funds for Bibles. Frankly, our base in the Gambia is awash with them!"

"I doubt they have many like this one, though." Eleanor took the heavy volume out of her bag for the vicar to see. Philip's slight annoyance at not being invited to debate a tricky religious point faded when he saw the handsome volume. Taking the heavy book in both hands, he ran his fingers reverently over the gold embossing of the cover.

"What a pity Joshua doesn't want to keep it or hand it down to his relatives – I assume he has family?"

Eleanor shook her head sadly. "His wife died and he doesn't have children. I've tried to ask about nieces and nephews, but he won't be drawn on the subject."

Philip turned the pages, alighting on one of the black and white engravings. "These prints were created by the French artist Gustave Doré, you know, so it will date from the late nineteenth century."

"Really? Gosh, no I didn't know that. Lordy, I am ignorant – oops, sorry to blaspheme Father, er, Phil." Eleanor was aware of getting into a tangle, not knowing how to address a vicar and taking the Lord's name in vain.

Philip's expression turned saintly as he wafted his hand in the air. "I don't think He would mind too much under the circumstances and would perhaps agree that this Bible should stay in Joshua's family where it belongs."

"I could try to persuade him to take it back, but what if he refuses?"

"In that case, you might consider donating it to your local parish church." The vicar smiled, continuing to turn the pages, admiring the prints and smoothing each one down with his hand. The book was heavy so he leant it up against two other books to make it easier to turn the pages. "Now, what have we here?"

Inside the back cover was an envelope.

"Oh, I wanted to ask your opinion about this as well," said Eleanor, taking the envelope and carefully withdrawing the poem. "Joshua gave me a St Christopher pendant in a Victorian tea caddy and this was in with it. My father-in-law thought it might be a prayer and I wondered whether you might recognise it, what with being in the prayer business." Eleanor laughed nervously, wondering why being with a man of the cloth made her talk rubbish.

Philip unfolded the flimsy sheet and began reading aloud the words written there. "'Seeker bold, ye who travelled from afar, Think but on this . . . ' Well, well. How interesting."

"Is it familiar to you?"

Philip stroked his chin thoughtfully. "Funnily enough I do recognise the words, although this isn't a traditional prayer as such. Come with me."

Standing, he led the way out of the vestry with its African memorabilia into the church. Eleanor followed him down the nave to the rear of the building. "There, do you see?" He pointed at a dark wooden panel with words etched on it and outlined in gold.

Eleanor crouched down to read. "They're the same words!" She read the words again, but there was no name of an author or a date. "Do you know how long the panel has been here?"

"To my shame I don't remember, but it will be in our records. I'll look it up and let you know."

"Thank you, Vicar. I'd be grateful."

* * *

Later that day, Eleanor received a phone call from Philip.

"I have some information about your poem. Can you come over to the church?"

"Sure." She checked her diary. "I can pop over tomorrow if you're free."

"I've got the mums and toddlers at twelve, but any time before that would be fine. Oh, and bring the pendant Joshua gave you."

"You mean the St Christopher?"

She was sure she could hear Philip chuckling down the line. "Yes, that's the one."

When Eleanor arrived at the church the next morning, the vicar was outside pulling up dandelions. "I know they're all part of God's creation, but they are rather a nuisance." Philip got to his feet, brushing soil from his hands. "Come on in."

Eleanor followed Philip out of the sunshine into the building's dimly lit interior where the cleric's sandals made a flapping sound on the cool terracotta floor. He stopped by the inscribed panel and turned to her. "We Anglicans don't pay much attention to the saints, as you know, so I've had to do a little bit of homework. May I see your pendant?"

"Of course," said Eleanor, handing it over.

"Aha. Just as I thought." He smiled, weighing it in his hand. "I'll come to this in a moment but, first, what do you make of the stained-glass figure?"

Eleanor lifted her eyes from the inscribed words in the direction of where Philip was pointing: in the window above the panel was a tall bearded figure in a blue cloak holding a staff.

"Oh, it's St Christopher."

"Are you sure? Look again and tell me what's missing." The vicar was enjoying himself now.

Eleanor racked her brains for what she remembered about how the saint was generally depicted. "Isn't he normally shown with a child on his shoulder?"

"Exactly! But there's no child here. Do you see what he's carrying instead?"

She stepped forward to examine the saint more carefully. "He seems to be holding a ship. And he's standing on a sea monster."

"It's a whale actually, but well done!" Eleanor knew she should be annoyed at being treated like a child, but Philip was so pleased with himself she couldn't help being pulled along by his enthusiasm. "Now look again at your pendant. Oh, you may need this." He extracted a small magnifying glass from his shirt pocket and handed it to Eleanor.

Holding the glass over the silver oval she could see every detail of the figure moulded into the metal. "It's the same – the saint has a ship tucked under his arm and there's a fish – I mean whale – under his feet."

"So . . .?"

"So if it's not a St Christopher, what is it?"

"It's a St Brendan medal," said Philip triumphantly. "And he was?"

"St Brendan the Navigator, patron saint of sailors. Which makes perfect sense in an ocean-going community like our own."

"Yes, I suppose it does." Eleanor bent down to study the verse under the window again.

"And the inscription is a prayer for sailors, do you see?" Philip read out the last lines, tracing each word with his finger. "'No more shall he breach the lusty waves but Divine peace shall be his who Abides in God's tender care, No more to fret upon life's travails.'"

"That's pretty – and clever, too," said Eleanor, pleased with herself for having noticed something Malcolm and now Philip had missed. "It's an acrostic poem."

"Sorry?"

"Look at the initial letters of each line."

Philip read them out. "S, T, B, R, E . . . oh, they spell St Brendan!"

"Right – but who wrote it?"

"Oh, I have information about the inscription here." Philip picked up a musty book from the pew and opened it at a spot he had marked with a piece of card. "The stained-glass window and the panel were both donated to the church in September 1900."

"By?"

"The window was made by Gideon Smith, a leading stained-glass artist of his time, and the prayer was etched and gilded by a Mr Philips."

"But who wrote the poem and paid for the stained glass and the panel to be erected? Is that recorded?"

"I'm afraid not. All it says in our records is that both pieces were gifted to the church by an anonymous benefactor."

"Anonymous? Is that normal?"

"Actually it's quite unusual. Generally when a local bigwig makes a sizeable donation of this kind, they want to make sure everyone in town knows about it." Philip put the bookmark back into the record book and closed its yellowing pages. "I'm sorry, but it looks as though we'll never know who that kind person was or, indeed, why they commissioned such a fine decoration for St Cuthbert's."

Eleanor chewed her lip thoughtfully. There might not be a written record, but a theory was beginning to form itself in her mind.

Chapter 28: An Exciting Discovery

Eleanor decided to run her ideas past Erika over coffee the next morning, before the bookshop opened for business.

"What do you think of my theory about the identity of the mysterious benefactor?" she asked, offering a plate of biscuits to Erika.

"Let me get this straight: the church contains an engraved panel and a stained-glass window of St Brendan the Navigator, but there's no record of who commissioned and paid for them?" Erika jotted down the facts on a scrap of paper.

"Correct. And there's no dedication either, which Phil tells me is unusual."

"And the epigraph inscribed on the wall is the same as the poem written on the piece of paper you found in the tea caddy given to you by Joshua Pinkham?"

"Yes, in a hidden compartment underneath the silver pendant that just happens to have the same saint engraved on it as the chap in the church window. All of which leads me to conclude that the mystery donor must have been someone in Joshua's family, wouldn't you agree?"

Erika frowned. "The evidence does seem to be pointing in that direction, but you need to consider other options before coming to a conclusion."

"What other options?"

"You're doing the sleuthing, boss, so you tell me!"

As Eleanor thought about it now, it seemed quite obvious. "Well, I suppose whoever wrote down the verse on the piece of paper and put it in the tea caddy might have copied it from the church wall. There's no reason to think they were the author of the poem or the donor."

"Precisely."

"Darn."

"Which doesn't mean that's the answer, but it's something to bear in mind."

"You're good at this," said Eleanor. "I bet Eric was an ace copper."

"He was."

They sat in silence sipping their drinks, the subject of Erika's past life hanging in the air. After a moment, Eleanor spoke again. "Of course, it might be that the donor was indeed a Pinkham but Joshua doesn't know about it because the person was so modest he . . ."

"Or she – who's to say the person who paid for the window wasn't a woman?"

"Fair point." Eleanor nodded. "That he or she didn't even tell their nearest and dearest, so Joshua isn't aware of the connection."

Erika tapped the rim of her coffee cup thoughtfully. "On the other hand, if the benefactor was a Pinkham and Joshua *does* know about it, you'd think he'd be proud to tell everyone. And he'd want to hang on to the pendant and handwritten verse if they were linked to the donation in some way."

"I agree."

"I'd like to see the pendant sometime."

"That can be arranged." Eleanor went across to the counter to fetch her handbag and brought out the paisley silk bag. "Here you go," she said, handing it to her colleague.

"That's nice." Erika took the pendant out of its bag and peered at it through her reading glasses. "Have you opened it yet?"

"Opened it? What do you mean?"

Erika raised an eyebrow. "There's a hinge at the top so I'm guessing it's a locket."

"Is there? None of us noticed that!"

"Not much gets past me." Erika handed it back. "You open it – I don't want to tear a nail when I've just had them done."

Eleanor slipped the tip of her thumbnail under the catch and carefully prised open the locket. She smiled at her colleague. "There's a photograph." In the oval frame was a studio photograph of a young woman. Her hair was waved and tied up at the back but wisps had escaped and were gathered around her brow. Her eyes appeared bright and thoughtful as they gazed out from under dark eyebrows in her heart-shaped face. "She was very pretty, whoever she was. And all without the magic of Photoshop."

As Eleanor opened the locket fully, a curl of paper slipped out from beneath a second cover and wafted gently down to the floor. Erika bent to pick it up then went to hand it to her boss who nodded at her to uncurl and read it. "It says 'I did you a great harm, for which I am truly sorry. Your melancholy friend, V.'."

"Wow. This is fascinating – who was V?" Eleanor was walking up and down excitedly. "First I uncover a mysterious hidden cupboard at the back of one of the bookcases and a briefcase that Joshua is reluctant to open, then this. Things are becoming very interesting indeed."

Their conversation was interrupted by the shop's brass bell jingling as the door opened and one of their regular delivery drivers came in carrying two cartons of books.

"Right," said Erika, "I'd better get on with some proper work."

"Me too," said Eleanor, drinking the last of her coffee. She then carefully smoothed out the slip of paper from "V." and put it in an envelope next to the locket in a desk drawer.

"I've had a thought," said Erika, some minutes later. "Didn't you say Joshua sold you a Bible?"

"He did, yes, and told me to give the money to the vicar for his roof."

"Have you had a good look at it? In days gone by, people often kept family records in Bibles – births, deaths, marriages, that kind of thing. If the gifts to St Cuthbert's Church were made by one of Pinkham's forebears, you might find a note about them in there."

"That's a brilliant idea," said Eleanor, who was kneeling on the floor restacking the children's storybooks. "I haven't spotted anything, but it might be worth taking another look. Thanks for the tip!"

* * *

Back at the cottage, Eleanor decided to follow up Erika's suggestion and search the Bible for proof that it was a Pinkham who had paid for the church window. There was nothing like a family tree and no other records inside the front cover so she began laboriously leafing through every page.

When Daniel came in from his run, he paused to kiss his wife before heading upstairs for a shower. "Have you suddenly found religion?" he asked, his brow shiny from his exertions. "I don't think I've ever seen you read the Bible before."

"It's nothing quite as holy as that." Smiling, Eleanor told Daniel the reason for her search. "I've been sitting here for hours and I've only checked through this much," she said, indicating a small span with a finger and thumb. "I've still got about an inch and a half to go through yet."

"Would a nice glass of cold white wine make it easier?"

"Definitely, darling," said Eleanor, tipping back her head so Dan could kiss her lips.

"Give me five minutes and I'll fetch us one."

Eleanor carried on leafing through the book, listening to the ancient plumbing clank above her head. It wasn't long before Daniel reappeared in fresh clothes, his dark hair clean and damp. Eleanor wolf whistled as he walked past her to the fridge to fetch the wine. "D'you know, I really quite fancy you?"

"I'm glad to hear it," he said, his lips forming the lazy smile that always made Eleanor's heart flip. "Cheers Miss Marple."

"Cheers." Eleanor sipped her drink. "I'll spend another few minutes on this then I'll think about supper. Is pizza and salad okay?"

"Perfect," said Dan, drawing up a chair on the opposite side of the table to his wife and stretching out his long legs. "What's that?" he asked, nodding towards the book.

"What's what?"

"It looks like there's something going down into the spine."

Eleanor tilted the heavy book up towards her so she could see what her husband was pointing at. "This? Oh, it's a ribbon bookmark. It should be resting between the pages but it seems to have been folded back on itself and pushed down the spine instead. How odd."

She tried and failed to pull it out with her fingers. "It seems to be well and truly stuck."

"You need to reach underneath it with something. Hold on a second," said Daniel, rummaging through the kitchen drawers. "Try this."

"A chopstick? That's not very reverential."

"It was either this or a meat skewer, which might do more damage."

"Okay. Hand it over." Eleanor took the chopstick, spun the book around and carefully slid the end under the ribbon. "I think it's coming." Daniel watched as his wife gradually withdrew the length of black silk from the spine. After a moment it stopped. "It's caught on something."

"Hang on, I'll fetch a torch so we can see what's going on." Dan picked up his car keys and shone the mini torch down the gap between the pages and the book's spine. "There's something tied to the end of the ribbon, El. Give it another pull."

Eleanor put down the chopstick and gently tugged on the ribbon, jiggling it from side to side. "Got it," she said, as the fabric came out. "Gosh, look at this." Dangling from the length of silk was a gold ring.

Daniel whistled. "You've found hidden treasure."

"Blimey. I wasn't expecting that."

* * *

After supper they curled up on the sofa, the Bible on the coffee table at their feet. Eleanor was looking at the ribbon she'd laid on the cover, still attached to the binding. "It's an odd shape for a ring, don't you think?"

"It looks pretty ring-like to me. What do you mean?"

"Well, it's big and has a very rounded edge. I think it could be a curtain ring rather than a piece of jewellery you'd wear on a finger."

Daniel laughed. "Why would anyone bother to keep one curtain ring? And why put it on the end of a ribbon and shove it inside a Bible?"

"I've been asking myself the same questions and have come to the conclusion that a ring on a piece of ribbon actually makes a jolly useful bookmark." Eleanor picked up the ribbon from the book, watching the gold circle spin in the warm evening light that streamed in through the window. "I might make some to sell in the shop."

Daniel frowned. "But why was it pushed down the spine where it couldn't be used?"

"Who knows." Eleanor sipped on her coffee thoughtfully. "If it's not a curtain ring perhaps it's an earring – you know, like the hooped ones gypsies and fortune-tellers always wore in Hollywood movies from the 1940s."

"That's possible, I suppose. But I still don't see why someone would keep a single earring."

"Perhaps they hoped they'd find the left-hand one down the back of the sofa one day." Eleanor put the ribbon back on the book cover and curled up against her husband.

"You have left- and right-hand earrings?"

"Joke alert."

"Very funny." Daniel gave Eleanor a squeeze. "Or it could have come from the nose of a piglet."

Eleanor prodded her husband in the ribs. "You may mock, but Erika says it's important to consider all possibilities when assessing evidence to avoid leaping to false conclusions."

"Your colleague is a wise old bird." Daniel thought for a moment. "Perhaps you should call the auction-eer chappie who was at the festival. You never know, your curtain ring might turn out to be really valuable and pay off our attic conversion."

"Sure, or it could raise some more dough for the vicar's fund."

Daniel laughed. "Or you could send it to one of those companies that advertise in the tabloids: 'Send us your unwanted gold'. As if gold was ever unwanted."

Eleanor sighed. "A, it's probably worth tuppence and B, it isn't mine to sell."

"Which means you'll have to face the wrath of Joshua and tell him you've found something else he ought to hold on to." Daniel smiled. "Best of luck."

"Thanks, I may need it."

"Is he coming to Bill's launch party, by the way?"

"I've invited him, but I think it's unlikely he'll come. I have the impression he's not terribly comfortable with strangers, poor old bugger." She yawned and stretched. "Speaking of parties, I need my beauty sleep. I have loads to do tomorrow."

Daniel stood and took both of Eleanor's hands in his, gently pulling her to her feet. "Come on, sleepyhead. Let's get you to bed so you can dream of rock bands."

"And treasure." On the way, Eleanor picked up a book from a chair at the bottom of the staircase.

"What have you got there?"

"It's another of the books I bought from Joshua."

Daniel tipped his head to see the cover illustration, which showed three pink-cheeked, fair-haired youngsters on a sailing dinghy. "*Seafaring Tales for Children* – that looks like my kind of thing. Can I borrow it when you've finished?"

"Of course. The stories are fairly jolly, though the one I'm reading at the moment does seem to be rather 'improving'." Eleanor opened the book and stroked the heavy cream paper, running her fingers over the inky black type.

"Who's the author? Anyone we've heard of?"

"The name's VE Bennett. I've no idea who he was." Eleanor yawned again. "And I'm not sure how much I'll manage to read tonight. I'm bushed."

Chapter 29: Seafaring Tales

Although Eleanor felt tired when she went up to bed, it was Daniel who fell asleep first, leaving her to read in a pool of light. She was entranced by the brightly coloured illustrations scattered throughout *Seafaring Tales for Children* of rock pools and of children enjoying jolly japes. The colour plates were concealed between the pages, making their jewel-like hues even more striking. The stories themselves were well told, even if the language was a little stilted. She opened the pages to a story set in Victorian times called "A Boy Led Astray".

A Boy Led Astray

Jack was out hunting for crabs when he saw a flash of gold in the rock pool. Pulling the thing from the chilly water, Jack whooped for joy. What luck! He tucked the treasure inside the lining of his cloth cap and ran back along the beach to his home, all the while keeping an eye out for vagabonds. Jack was not quite ten years old and small for his age, so did not want to be set upon by older boys and lose his prize.

He knew the common law among fisherfolk was "finders keepers" and there was not a house in the bay without roof beams that were once part of a ship's hull. Villagers might also enjoy a barrel of fine French brandy if some should accidentally come their way.

Jack felt jubilant when he arrived at the neat cottage that was his home so the look of horror on his dear mother's face when he took out the treasure from his cap caught him by surprise.

"Will you not take it, Mother?"

Instead of catching Jack in her arms and embracing him as he expected her to do, Martha grabbed a broom and shooed her son back towards the door.

"Take that thing out of my kitchen, wicked boy. I'll not have you bringing bad fortune into this house."

Jack looked at the prize he held in his hand. "Why would gold bring us misfortune?"

Seeing her son's bewildered face, Martha softened her tone. "Because, child, what you have there is a ring purchased by a sailor to save him from drowning. That gold was meant for the sea, not the land." Martha had put down the broom but was still standing well away from her son whose blue eyes examined her quizzically.

"I don't understand, Mother."

"When a man goes to sea, he purchases a pair of gold earrings – one he wears in his ear, the other he throws over the larboard side of his ship with the words 'Protect me, O Davy Jones'."

Jack trembled at the mention of the mythical Davy Jones who ruled the oceans deep. "Then, where is the other earring?"

"God willing it will be shining brightly in the

ear of the man who bought it. But if anything should happen to the sailor," the good woman crossed herself, "if he should drown, the ring will pay for him to have a good Christian burial."

Jack was quiet now, studying the earring in his palm. "If it is an unlucky thing, should I take it to the Reverend Brown?"

"No!" Martha laughed, sourly. "The church has no need of gold."

The rector was a proud, haughty man who lived in a fine house and looked down his nose at the folk who lived in the cottages, especially the women who struggled alone while their husbands were away, seeking work in the city. It was also whispered that the rector was in league with the customs' men and – if the gossip was correct – was happy to share a portion of whatever they recovered before handing it over to Her Majesty's government.

Martha rubbed her arms vigorously as if chilled. "That ring should be in the sea not on land and certainly not in the pocket of the priest. You must take it away now, do you hear?"

"But if I'm not to take it to the church, where shall I take it? Should we sell it, Ma?"

"Sell it? Fie, child! Who would choose to buy something perchance fallen from a dead man's ear? No, indeed. You must hasten down to the beach and throw it as far into the sea as you can."

"And will this undo any harm that has been done by taking it from the water, Mother?"

Martha crossed herself again and nodded slowly. "We must hope so." Everyone knew the tales of men who feared to save a drowning man in case they were taken instead. "Go now, son, and take care no one sees you."

So Jack clasped the ring tightly in his small hand and ran from the house, down the lane to the beach as the sun was setting. As he ran, he thought about the whereabouts of the other earring. What would he do if he arrived at the shore and found the other earring caught in the flesh of a dead man? Jack shivered at the thought of it and was relieved to find there were no grey corpses to be seen, just a pair of stray cats fighting over a fish head, and seagulls gobbling up minnows cut off by the retreating tide.

The sea was already a fair distance out, so Jack decided to clamber up to a higher point from where he could swing his arm wide and send the ring spinning a goodly distance away.

The safest approach to the headland was from the footpath, but night was falling and the sea was retreating fast so Jack decided to scramble up from the beach. The ascent was perilous because the rocks were wet with sea spray and the gulls harried the lad whenever he came too close to their nests.

Gradually Jack pulled himself hand over hand to the top, then stood with his heart pounding, reluctant now to send his treasure spinning into the void. Must he really part with it? He supposed he must as his mother would not have the ring in the house and he was forbidden from giving it to the rector or from selling it.

Jack sat on the cliff edge, his back to the land

as the wind whipped up locks of his hair and the
setting sun grazed his eyes. He slipped the ring
over his thumb and twirled it around, thoughtfully. What he held was gold – gold! Mother said
it belonged to the jealous rascal who ruled the sea.
But if Jack cast it back into the water, might it
not be eaten up by a fish? What then if someone
caught the fish and sold it to a gentleman who
found it there in the creature's belly? The gentleman would benefit, which would not be fair. It
was his, Jack's treasure – he had found it.

The boy had a pure heart and his conscience
quaked at the word "treasure". He clasped his
hands over his eyes to shut out visions of pale
young sailors wandering forever around Davy
Jones' watery kingdom.

But there were no dead sailors and Jack felt sure
that the man to whom his ring belonged was safe
and well. Perhaps he had left the sea altogether
and was now a prosperous landowner in America?

Jack pulled a ragged kerchief from the pocket
of his britches, placed the earring in the middle
and carefully tied the cloth into a knot. He then
tucked the bundle inside his shirt beneath his
grubby linen where it felt cool against his warm
skin.

The decision was made: Jack would not throw
away his prize. Instead he would keep it safe. It
meant he would be forced to lie to his dear mother,
but so it must be. He would hide the earring, but
he would always think of the fishermen at peril on
the sea. Jack puffed out his chest as it came to him
that he would include those sailors who perished

in his prayers each night before bed and pray for them twice on Sundays.

Running for home, his head bent against the wind as he , Jack n the darkening slope, he made a solemn promise that the earring would turn him into a virtuous man. He would never sell it, but would work hard at his schooling and become a learned and wealthy gentleman. Then, when he had made his fortune – after purchasing for his mother and sisters a fine house, silk frocks and a carriage – he would give his money to the needy.

Eleanor's head was full of visions of the sea as she closed the book and turned off the bedside light. It seemed there was to be no escape from gold rings for the time being.

Chapter 30: Fact or Fiction?

The next day was Sunday so there was no need to leap out of bed, but Eleanor still awoke at her usual time. She lay there for ten minutes, listening to Daniel's steady breath beside her and the soft pitter-patter of rain on the windowpanes. Closing her eyes she tried to go back to sleep, but to no avail. It was not quite 7am when she eventually crept out of bed, tucked the storybook under her arm and tiptoed downstairs. She made a cup of tea, fed the dogs, then curled up in an armchair to continue reading VE Bennett's story.

Folk said the ghostly outline of the *Santa Maria* had been seen in the dying embers of the day, a sure sign of trouble to come. When a great storm came and tore up two fishing vessels, the people crossed themselves and said it was a miracle none of the crew was lost.

Jack had never confessed to his mother that the ring was in a leather pouch under a floorboard in the room he shared with his sisters. No one blamed him and yet he felt the guilt on his young shoulders. Every time he stepped on the beach, Jack was reminded of the earring. Every time he went in search of crabs for their supper, he couldn't help but see flashes of gold in the rock pools. It was as though Davy Jones was playing games, punishing Jack for cheating him of the ring and perhaps of a soul. And yet Jack knew it was too late to throw the thing back into the sea so it remained hidden and lay heavy on his conscience.

True to his word, Jack prayed for lost sailors each night and went to church twice on Sundays, vowing that one day he would make amends for his misdeeds. Sometimes he thought that if he could use the ring for good, this might put everything right again: the opportunity came sooner than expected and from an unexpected quarter.

The rector of the church was a vain greedy man beneath whose sombre clothing lay a cold heart. The rector had a wife who was sickly, worn away by her husband's harsh looks and harsher words. This poor lady fell ill, but the rector would not let the doctor come near her, saying "It is God and God alone who decides which of us shall be healthy and which sick; which of us shall live and which die. Who are we to go against the wishes of the Almighty?"

Between them the rector and his wife had one child, a daughter named Lily, who was as fair as the flower whose name she bore. She knew Jack loved her and this fondness was the boy's downfall.

One day Jack came upon Lily weeping in the churchyard and shyly asked what was amiss. "My mother is sick and dying," she answered, "but Papa will not bring the doctor and I have no money for medicine."

As soon as the girl's words were out, Jack knew

what he must do. Here was the answer to his prayers: a way to use the cursed ring for good. "I will bring you money, Lily, so you can buy medicine and your mother will not die."

"How, Jack?" Lily knew the boy's family was not wealthy. "You know it is a sin to steal."

"Indeed it is." And without another word Jack ran back to the cottage and took out the ring from where it had lain beneath the floorboards for nigh on two years.

Before dawn the next day, Jack walked the many miles to town and entered the jeweller's shop. This man, looking at the boy's ragged clothing, suspected that he had before him a common thief – or worse.

"An earring? Now then, boy. Whose ear did you take this from?"

"No living man's ear."

"So you stole it from the dead?"

"No indeed, sir."

"Answer me then how it came into your possession, boy?"

"I cannot say, sir." Jack knew that if he confessed to keeping the ring, his mother would know he had disobeyed her and not thrown it into the sea as he had promised to do. And if he told the jeweller he needed the money for his friend's sick mother, it was certain that Lily would be beaten by her father and Jack could not let such a thing happen. He must remain silent and accept his punishment. And so, when the jeweller caught him by the ear and dragged him onto the street to find the policeman, Jack made not a murmur.

"Dan!" Eleanor closed the book and ran upstairs to wake her husband. "You'll never guess what."

"Morning." Daniel gazed at her blearily. "What is it, darling?"

"I know what happened to John Able." She waved the book in the air. "It's all in here."

Daniel scratched his face and yawned, his brain not yet fully in gear. "What? Who?"

"The story I've been reading – 'A Boy Led Astray' – it must be based on the newspaper case that I've been following because there are too many similarities for it not to be. There's even a ghost ship like ours." Eleanor quickly ran through the plot and described the setting while Daniel did his best to concentrate.

Eleanor was pacing up and down at the end of the bed now. "I knew it. I knew John was innocent. He didn't steal the ring, he found it and – okay, he shouldn't have kept it – but there was no one he could give it to . . ."

"Woah – hang on a minute," said Daniel, catching Eleanor's hand and pulling her down onto the bed beside him. "You're telling me this is what you've read in a children's story?"

"Yes, in Joshua's book."

"But it's a work of fiction, El, so the author could easily have changed the facts to make it more appropriate for children."

"You may be right, Dan, but I have a strong feeling there's more to it than that."

"Okay, so if we do accept the story is about John Able and he really was innocent of theft, how did the author know about it? If John never told anybody the truth and it wasn't recorded at the time, who was the author's source?"

Eleanor sat bolt upright. "What if VE Bennett was actually John Able and he decided to write his own version of events?"

"That's possible, I suppose, but if the point was to clear his name, why use a false identity? Why not write the book as himself?"

"Good question. I need to Google the author." Eleanor jumped off the bed. "Where's my iPad?"

"Last seen on the kitchen table underneath the usual mountain of magazines and random stuff for the recycling bin."

"Right," said Eleanor, charging out of the bedroom. "Let's see what we can find out about Mr Bennett."

"Okay," said Daniel, yawning. "I'm right behind you."

When he came down to the kitchen in his bathrobe some minutes later, Eleanor handed him a big mug of tea. "Look at this," she said, pointing at the screen.

Daniel leant over to read what was written there. "So the author wasn't John Able under another name. That's a shame."

"Not necessarily. The author might not have been John, but this is equally intriguing." Eleanor scrolled down the page. "It's all here – 'VE Bennett: the pseudonym for Violet Elizabeth Makepeace, children's author of the early twentieth century.' It says that Violet was known for her children's stories and she was married to the publisher, Reginald Makepeace."

"Who?"

"You know – as in Williams & Makepeace? Don't you see, Dan? The author of Joshua's storybook was married to one of the guys who owned the publishers that used to be at The Reading Room."

"Well, well. That is quite a coincidence."

"Just think – Violet might even have worked on her stories right in our cottage!"

"Fascinating, but why would she base a story on John Able?"

"Not sure." Eleanor chewed her lip. "Any suggestions?"

Daniel thought for a moment. "Well, if Violet lived and worked in Combemouth, perhaps she had heard about the case and decided it would make an interesting tale. Remind me of the dates again."

Eleanor fished out the notepad in which she'd recorded the details of the court case from the newspapers. "John was arrested in 1872 aged nearly twelve, and this book was published in 1900 when he would have been forty."

"So it was written a long time after the event. Doesn't that seem a bit odd to you?"

Eleanor nodded. "Maybe, but don't forget I only heard about John's alleged crime because it was retold in a 1920s newspaper, so it must have been quite well known."

"That's true. And how does it all end in Violet's story?"

"I don't know – I was so stunned by the similarities that I stopped reading to come and tell you about it."

"It could be your answer lies in those pages."

"You're right, darling!"

And with that, Eleanor kissed her husband, grabbed the storybook and padded off in her slippers to continue reading.

* * *

In the bookshop the next morning, Eleanor was excited to share her discovery. Connie liked a good murder story and was disappointed that her daughter had found nothing more thrilling to pursue than a minor theft. Erika listened more attentively to what her boss had to say. "So what's this about the book then, Eleanor?"

"The tale in the storybook is exactly like it was in the newspapers: Jack is convicted of stealing the ring because he can't account for how he came by it and is sent off to prison. He then spends months in a reformatory school for boys where he's taught reading, writing and arithmetic. It has to be based on the John Able case."

"Perhaps," said Erika, cautiously. "And what happens when Jack gets out of the reformatory?"

"In Violet's story, he works hard and becomes a 'prosperous gentleman' as he had planned to do when he first decided to ignore his mother and keep the ring. He moves to the city, marries an heiress, has a host of angelic children and dies peacefully in his bed, loved and admired by all who knew him."

"The happy ending doesn't sound very realistic," said Connie.

"I think your mother's right, Eleanor. I would have thought a lad in John Able's situation would end up in a bad way. I bet Violet picked out some facts from the case to write a morality tale: you can do wrong but still have a good end if you pray a lot and work hard. I'm not sure it should be read as an accurate account of what really happened."

Eleanor was deflated. "When I read the story I

thought it might hold the answers, but now I seem to have hit a brick wall. It doesn't help that John appears to have disappeared altogether."

"Perhaps he was bumped off by one of the other prisoners," said Connie, helpfully.

"What a ghoulish imagination you have, Mother."

"Not at all – I'm simply exploring other possibilities as Erika told us we should. And when you say 'disappeared', have you actually tried looking for him?"

"Of course, I have," said Eleanor defensively, aware that her mother's question was very sensible and she hadn't done much poking around yet. "I've done a bit, anyway."

"A bit as in . . . ?"

"As in I scanned the newspapers that came out two years after John was packed off to jail to see if he turned up in Combemouth when he was released but I couldn't spot any mentions of him."

Connie shrugged. "Well, either he was a goner or he was too ashamed to come home after his name had been blackened, so decided to move to a big city where nobody knew him."

"That's an excellent point, Connie," said Erika, before turning to Eleanor. "Have you checked the census returns yet?"

"Gosh, I hadn't even thought of those." Eleanor chewed her lip thoughtfully. "Although, thanks to Deirdre, we know he wasn't transported. I'm not much use at this detecting lark."

"It's not as quick and easy as they make it look on the telly." Erika laughed. "Why not dig around and see what you can find out about Violet Makepeace?

You might be in luck and discover something that takes you directly to John Able."

"Good idea, and I know the perfect person to ask about Violet."

Chapter 31: The Secret Author

The next day, Eleanor called Frederick Williams and arranged to pop round to see him. He wasn't used to Eleanor dropping by for a chat so he feared there must be problems at the shop.

"Is everything going well at The Reading Room? You're not having any difficulties, I trust?" he asked, shakily handing her the cup of tea his wife had poured before leaving them to their meeting in the sunny conservatory.

"No, everything at the bookshop is absolutely fine," said Eleanor, balancing the delicate cup and saucer on her knees. "The reason I wanted to see you was because I had a couple of questions about Williams & Makepeace, actually."

"My specialist subject! Ask away," he said, with a smile.

"I've been reading a book by an author called VE Bennett published by Williams & Makepeace at the beginning of the last century."

"VE Bennett? Well, goodness me – that's not a name I've heard for a while! Which book is it you're reading?"

Eleanor had brought the volume with her. "It's a collection of seafaring tales for children, first published around 1900."

"Ah, yes." Frederick took the book and began

leafing through the pages. "This album had some rather exciting tales in it, I seem to recall." He stroked the thick cover with its image of youngsters in a sailboat on a choppy sea, the waves crested in white. The illustrator had painted plump grey donkeys on the beach and put a red and white lighthouse on the cliffs against an azure sky. Smiling, Mr Williams opened the book and checked the contents list. "Gosh, what a lot of stories there are here. Mind you, old Violet didn't half churn them out."

"Violet? So you knew VE Bennett was really Violet Makepeace? That was going to be my first question!"

"According to my father, she was rather a *grande dame*. She had a very high opinion of herself and expected to be admired by everyone, especially small children." Frederick chuckled. "Violet was a large lady who used to bustle into the printing area and completely disrupt things by demanding that her books be proofed first, and such like. My dear grandfather was a mild-mannered man and he became very agitated when he saw her approaching the shop with her green silk umbrella thrust out in front of her like a sword."

Eleanor leant forward eagerly. "Do you know why she didn't write as Violet Makepeace, if that was her name?"

"I suspect she didn't want readers to think her books were published simply because she happened to be married to the publisher. And perhaps in those days young boys were less likely to read a book of jolly adventure stories if they believed they were written by a woman rather than a man." Frederick thought for a moment. "Of course, everyone in Combemouth knew who she was, not least because she used to include so many local landmarks in her stories."

"Yes, I spotted that." Eleanor nodded, thoughtfully. "Is there anything more you can tell me about her?"

"Let me think now." Mr Williams lifted his watery eyes, searching his memory. "She was a local girl and had been very pretty in her youth, so I'm told. She was much sought after by all accounts and could have had her pick of the young men, as she never ceased to remind poor old Reginald Makepeace."

Eleanor laughed. "She sounds like a difficult woman."

"Yes, indeed. Now what else?" Frederick gazed out of the window as he trawled his memory for traces of Violet. "Oh, and her father had been the rector here in town, I believe, so she grew up in the vicarage."

"That's it!" Eleanor set down her teacup with a start, making the saucer clatter. "She's 'Lily'."

"'Lily'?" Mr Williams looked puzzled. "I'm not following you, dear."

Eleanor quickly filled him in on what she knew of the John Able court case and the similarities she'd detected in the plot of "A Boy Led Astray", in particular the part played by a young girl. "In the story, Jack tries to sell a gold ring to help Lily, whose father is the vicar. The writer describes the girl as being 'as fair as the flower whose name she bore'. But she also tells us Lily was a weak, selfish character who let the boy who loved her go to prison by not speaking up and telling people what had really happened."

"Well, isn't that interesting?" Frederick Williams picked up the book again, admiring the line drawings of young Jack pulling the ring from the rock pool and later being dragged off to jail. The artist had also done a very atmospheric drawing of sailors collapsed on the beach and a picture of a young girl in a shawl weeping in front of a fierce-looking judge. "If you're correct and Lily really was based on Violet Makepeace's own experiences as a child, perhaps it was guilt that led her to write the story all those years later. To apologise to the John Able chap, do you see?"

Eleanor nodded. "Yes, it would make sense. Unless she was completely heartless, as an adult she must have come to recognise the damage done to the lad's reputation." She stopped and thought for a moment. "But how could she possibly know whether Jack or John or whoever it was would read the book?"

Smiling, Frederick flipped back to the beginning. "Perhaps she gave him a copy," he said, tapping the page.

Eleanor took the book and read what was written under Mr Williams' finger. "Oh my goodness! I completely missed that," she said, laughing. What she now saw was the printed Dedication "For J.A." Underneath, handwritten in lavender ink, someone had added "Yours ever, V."

"You're a genius, Frederick."

"Well, I wouldn't go quite so far. I'm rather interested in those bits of a book that other people tend to ignore – imprint pages, acknowledgements, dedications, indexes and so forth." He scratched his chin. "It's force of habit, I suppose, having grown up in the book trade. So what will you do now, Eleanor?"

"I would like to dig around a little bit more and see if I can discover what happened to John." She tapped her watch. "But first I have an errand to run in Waterborough, so if you'll forgive me I must dash. Thanks so much for the tea." She put the storybook into her bag and stood up.

"You're most welcome and I did enjoy our chat." Frederick rose to his feet to embrace her. "Do come back any time, and promise you'll let me know if you discover any more thrilling information about Violet."

"I certainly shall!"

Chapter 32: Seaside Snappers

Eleanor's next mission had been lurking on the "to do" list since her drink at the King's Head with Jim Rowe some weeks before. Hoping to buy a copy of the photograph of fishermen she'd seen at the pub, she had trawled the internet and discovered that Dipton Photographic Studios still existed although they had changed their name to Seaside Snappers. The company's main business was now weddings, but the present owner had a catalogue of old photographs he sold to tourists and collectors. As the shop was on the way back from Frederick Williams' house, Eleanor decided to kill two birds with one stone and call in.

She left the car and walked through the park and past Waterborough Abbey to find the narrow cobbled street where the Dipton family had run a shop for over a hundred years. At some point, somebody had evidently decided to modernise the place. The beautiful bay window she'd seen in old pictures had been replaced by a single large pane of glass covered in posters urging passers-by to "Get Snappy!".

On entering, Eleanor was pleased to see that the shop was still quite traditional on the inside despite its lurid exterior and silly name. A middle-aged man in a figure-hugging Seaside Snappers T-shirt came forward to greet her, extending his hand. "Kevin

Dipton at your service. How may I help? Passport photograph? Graduation? Golden wedding? Not for you, obviously – you're much too young!"

Eleanor did her best to smile at the witticism. "Actually, I'd like to buy a copy of a photograph I saw on the wall of the King's Head in Combemouth."

"Splendid, splendid – I get quite a lot of custom from visitors to that pub. I should put the landlord on commission." Kevin rubbed his hands together. "Do you happen to have the number of the photo?"

"Yes, I copied it down from the back of the frame."

Eleanor handed a slip of paper to Kevin who nodded. "Oh yes, this is one of our bestsellers. The ladies do like those handsome fishermen," he added with a wink, then went behind the counter and began to leaf though a large box filled with photographs in crinkly plastic covers. "Here you are," he said, passing Eleanor the photograph, which had a label identifying it as "Fishermen tending their nets, Combemouth harbour, 1898".

Eleanor stared at the men in their broad-brimmed soft hats, all paused in their work to look at the camera. Three were squinting into the light, clay pipes clamped between their lips; two others were looking out of the frame, as though unwilling to engage directly with the photographer.

"Do you know who these men were? That gent is clearly not an ordinary sailor." She pointed at the tall man in a suit and tie who was standing slightly apart from the group.

"I'll have to look elsewhere for that information."

"If you could find it for me, I'd be very grateful." Eleanor smiled obsequiously, keen to know more about these long-dead men, especially the gentleman whose face now seemed oddly familiar.

"Anything to oblige our customers," said the shop owner, as he unlocked a tall metal filing cabinet and pulled open a squeaky drawer. "Although I don't expect they'll be identified."

"Really? And why's that?"

"Because these were photographs of 'picturesque types', not portraits as such."

Eleanor waited patiently as Kevin sank down to his knees and extracted a file. "Well, this is interesting," he said, reading a card. "It says here the fishermen were residents at the St Brendan hostel."

Eleanor thought she knew Waterborough well but, as she scanned its layout in her mind's eye, she couldn't place the hostel. "Can you tell me where the hostel is?"

"It was up by the town hall, but I'm afraid it isn't there any more."

"How come? What happened to it?"

Kevin rubbed his chin, trying to remember. "I seem to recall the council demolished the place in the early 1970s to build the bus station. Progress, don't you know? Shame, because it gave plenty of the old salts a decent place to live when they'd fallen on hard times."

"That is a pity." The card was still in Kevin's hand and Eleanor was trying and failing to read the faded text upside down. "Does it say anything more about the men in the picture?"

"Not really – oh, hang on a second. This might interest you." He turned the card and read the other side. "It does mention that the gentleman on the right-hand side of the picture was the founder of the hostel."

"And what was his name?"

"Alfred Pinkham, Esquire."

The name took Eleanor completely by surprise and she couldn't help laughing out loud. "Pinkham? As in the local Pinkhams?"

Kevin looked at her oddly. "I should expect so. The family has been living in the area for many years now."

Eleanor took the photograph and peered at the faces, her head whirling. If the photograph was taken in 1898, the man in the suit could be Joshua Pinkham's grandfather. Why had he never mentioned his illustrious ancestor, a man who had opened a hostel for poor sailors? "Could I ask you one more thing?"

"You may."

"Did the original Mr Dipton also take studio portraits at the time?"

"He certainly did. That was the mainstay of the business." A look of immense pride and nostalgia passed over Kevin's face. "We had the most varied selection of backdrops in the county – folk came from far and wide to have their pictures taken in front of the pyramids or the Alps."

"How marvellous! You wouldn't happen to have portraits of a John Able or a Violet Makepeace would you?"

Kevin's eyes alighted on the clock, which showed nearly 5pm. "We're about to close, I'm afraid. Perhaps you could come back another time?"

Eleanor's face dropped. "I'm not sure when I'll be able to come back. Couldn't you take a very quick look at your records? I can tell from how easily you found my photograph how efficient your filing systems are. Please?" With that she clasped her hands together in supplication, gave Kevin her warmest smile and hoped for the best.

It worked. "Very well, but if I can't find anything in the next ten minutes I'm afraid you will have to come back."

"Sure," said Eleanor, nodding eagerly. "And I can help you look, if you like."

"That won't be necessary." Kevin opened a cupboard beneath the counter and brought out a number of index card boxes. Slowly, he flicked through the cards while Eleanor tried to hide her impatience. "Well, I can tell you now there's nothing under A for Able."

"How disappointing," said Eleanor, drumming her fingers on the counter as Kevin slowly opened and closed the other boxes until he found M–O. She had her heart in her mouth as Kevin dug out a card.

"However, you're in better luck here. It seems that a Mrs Violet Makepeace (née Bennett) did have several portraits done with us over a period of many years."

"Would I be able to see them, do you think?" Recognising that Mr Seaside Snapper was clearly in a hurry to shut up shop and go home, Eleanor tried bribery. "I'll buy lots of copies, of course."

Kevin looked wearily at the clock once more, then turned the sign on the shop door to "Closed". "You'd better come through to the office," he said, showing Eleanor into a room at the back of the shop. "If you'd like to sit there one moment, I'll see what I can find."

Eleanor watched impatiently from a hard plastic

chair as Kevin lifted down two large boxes from a row of packed shelves, placing the index card with Violet's details on the table in front of him. He then pulled out a selection of photographs, carefully placing a tick beside each number on the card.

When Kevin had finished, he called Eleanor over. "These are all the photographs we have of your lady, taken before and after she married."

"Fabulous – thank you so much!"

On the table were over a dozen photographs of Violet taken during her long life and showing a change from a slight child to the rather buxom author described by Frederick Williams. In one or two, she stood next to a thin-faced man who must have been her husband. In another, she sat with a dimpled child on her lap. Eleanor eagerly scanned the pictures then gasped and brought her hand to her lips as she picked up a small photograph in an oval cardboard frame.

Kevin spoke kindly. "You've found the one you were looking for, I gather?"

All Eleanor could do for a moment was nod, too overwhelmed to speak. "Yes, I think I have."

* * *

By the time Eleanor arrived home, she was buzzing and thrilled by her successful day.

Daniel poured his wife a glass of wine and listened as she told him what she'd learned from Kevin Dipton about the fishermen photo. "And I'll have to call Mr Williams in the morning and tell him about the photographs Kevin found of Violet Makepeace."

"Speaking of calls," said Daniel, "the vicar left a message for you to ring him."

"Did he say what it was about?"

"No, but it didn't sound urgent."

"I'm pooped from all the running around, but I'll definitely call him tomorrow." Eleanor smiled at her husband and grasped his hand. "But that's enough about my day, what have you been doing?"

"As it happens, I've had rather a good day, too."

"Tell me more."

"I have been speaking to my contacts in the planning department and guess what?"

"What?"

"They're going to give our attic conversion the thumbs up, so we'll be able to start work on it properly very soon."

"At last! That's great news, Dan." Eleanor threw herself into his arms. "This is turning out to be a very positive day indeed.

* * *

At lunchtime the next day, Eleanor dashed round to St Cuthbert's to tell the vicar what she'd discovered from Frederick Williams and Kevin Dipton.

"There was a hostel set up by one Alfred Pinkham, Esquire?" Philip laughed. "That is very interesting. Meanwhile, I've been doing some detective work of my own and I think you'll be pleased with what I've discovered."

"Tell me, I'm agog!"

"Well, I was disappointed not to find proper records for the stained-glass window and the inscription, so I got in touch with my boss to see whether he had any bright ideas on how we might trace the donor."

Eleanor smiled. "Your boss?"

Philip chuckled. "Not the Almighty. I think He has

more important things on his plate at the moment. No, I went to see the bishop – he owes me a favour. Anyway, he couldn't help specifically with our window, but he was able to lend me a book about the work of Gideon Smith."

"And he was . . . ?"

"Smith was the artist who made our St Brendan, remember?"

"Ah, I remember now. And what did you find out?"

"Only this," said Philip, opening the book and turning it towards Eleanor.

"Ooh, there's a photo of the window in our church. What does the text say?"

"It says quite a lot – Mr Smith was clearly not a man to trust with your secrets. The donor wanted to remain anonymous, as we know, but Gideon told the author of the book everything about the commission. Here, I think you should read it for yourself."

"Now I'm intrigued." As she read, a contented smile spread over her face. "Well, what do you know?" And, although Eleanor thought it probably wasn't the done thing to exchange a "high five" with a vicar, she did it anyway.

Chapter 33: A Difficult Meeting

It seemed to Eleanor that all roads led to Combemouth Manor, so the next day she went to see Joshua Pinkham, hoping he could answer the many questions she had swirling around in her head.

Eleanor found him in one of the sitting rooms, Clarence lying in a patch of sunlight by his feet. Having already experienced Joshua's reluctance to talk about his family or anything to do with the past, Eleanor decided to begin with what she hoped would be the easy stuff.

"I've checked the valuation of the Bible and the other books you sold me and I've definitely underpaid you." Smiling, she handed Joshua an envelope with the extra cash in it. "I didn't know whether you would like this or whether I should give it to the vicar."

"Vicar."

"Although, if you have changed your mind and would like to keep the Bible, I'd be delighted to return it to you."

Joshua drummed the arms of his chair impatiently. "I thought I'd made it plain that I don't want it back."

"Okay then, if you're sure." Now Eleanor had to move on to more difficult ground. "I also wanted to thank you for the beautiful tea caddy." Joshua harrumphed, but said nothing. Emboldened by this,

Eleanor went on. "I love it, but I don't think I can accept the beautiful pendant or the handwritten verse my father-in-law found in there with it." She took the paisley silk bag containing the locket from her handbag and presented it with the envelope.

Joshua hesitated for a moment before shaking his head. "I don't take back things I've sold and I don't take back gifts neither."

Eleanor spoke gently, convinced more than ever that Joshua couldn't have known what was in the tea caddy. "But, Joshua, surely the locket is an important family heirloom? There's a photograph of a girl inside, do you see?" She carefully prised open the locket to show him the picture, but he barely glanced at the image before looking away.

"I don't know nothing about no girl."

"Well, I think I can help you there." Eleanor grinned, pleased with her discoveries. "She is Violet Makepeace – you know, the lady who wrote children's books as VE Bennett? She was married to one of the publishers who owned my bookshop."

Joshua frowned as though trying to recall Violet's name but said nothing, so Eleanor went on. "The thing is, I think she might have written a story based on a court case I've been following about a local lad called John Able, who was royally stitched up by Lily – who was really Violet – back in the 1870s. I may be completely wrong, but there are loads of similarities and the book is dedicated to 'J. A.', which I'm guessing stands for John Able." Eleanor smiled. "Sorry, I'm gabbling." Joshua didn't return her smile, instead staring fixedly at the ground as the grandfather clock noisily chimed the quarter.

Eleanor took a deep breath and continued. "Because the locket came from the cupboard hidden behind your bookcase, I thought you might be able to tell me if there was a link between Violet, John Able and your ancestors." When Joshua didn't answer, Eleanor thought he might not have understood. "What I mean is, I don't suppose your forebears would have kept a photograph of Violet locked away in a special place if she wasn't important to them. Do you see? And there's more."

Eleanor moved her chair closer to Joshua, eager to share what else she'd found out. "The vicar has discovered that your grandfather, Alfred Pinkham, paid for one of the stained-glass windows at St Cuthbert's. Isn't that exciting? And the verse in the tea caddy is the same as an inscription under the window, but I haven't figured out the reason for that yet."

Joshua still didn't respond, instead gathering Clarence into his lap and silently stroking the dog, so Eleanor continued. "Your grandfather was such a modest man he didn't want his name recorded, but Philip managed to find a reference to him in a book. Oh, and Alfred also established a hostel for sailors in need of help. You must be very proud of him."

At this, Joshua turned towards Eleanor. "I have nothing to say on the matter." He then closed his eyes, signalling very clearly that their one-sided conversation was over.

"Never mind." Eleanor sighed, surprised and quite disappointed not to receive any help unscrambling the puzzle. As she stood up to leave, she remembered one last thing. "Oh, I nearly forgot. There was something else." She drew the gold ring from her pocket and held it out for Joshua to see. "This was on a ribbon pushed down the spine of your Bible where it was being used as a bookmark, I think. It may be an earring, but I'm not sure. It certainly seems an odd size and shape for a wedding ring. In any case, it's yours."

Eleanor had been turning the ring in her palm so, when she looked up, she was alarmed to see the change that had come over Joshua's face. His normally florid complexion had taken on a grey tinge and she feared he was having a heart attack. "Good heavens! What's the matter Joshua? Don't try to stand," she said, rushing towards him.

"First the ship and now this. I knew I was right," he grumbled, getting to his feet. "I shall be dead in a fortnight."

"Dead? Whatever do you mean?"

"Eighty. I shall never see eighty. All this worry you're bringing to my door – you'll be the death of me." And with that he crashed out of the room with Clarence at his heels.

Flustered, Eleanor remained open-mouthed for a moment then ran after them along a wide corridor into the study where Joshua stood shaking by the window. "I'm so sorry to have upset you," she said, laying a hand on his arm.

Joshua shook it off roughly. "Leave me be."

"Are you sure you'll be okay? Can I bring you some tea? Shall I call a doctor?"

Joshua banged the desk with the flat of his hand, making Clarence's ears twitch in alarm. "In heaven's name, woman. Why will you not do as I ask?" With that, he turned and strode out of the room with surprising vigour, leaving Eleanor feeling embarrassed and cross with herself for angering her new friend.

* * *

Back at Dan's house, she plonked herself down at the kitchen table with a sigh. "Well that went well – not."

"What happened?"

"Pour me a stiff gin and I'll tell you."

Daniel made two G&Ts then carried them up the steps to the high garden behind his house to which Eleanor had retreated. "So tell all."

Eleanor puffed out her cheeks wearily as she watched people on the distant promenade taking an evening stroll. "God, it was awful. It started badly and gradually got worse and worse." She swirled around the ice and lemon in her glass then licked her cold finger. "Joshua was not happy when I suggested he'd made a mistake in giving me the locket and poem then went completely nuts when I showed him the ring."

"What do you mean by 'nuts'?"

"Nuts as in he changed colour, accused me of attempted murder, then basically threw me out."

"Oh dear. That does sound bad."

"You can say that again." Eleanor sighed wearily.

Dan gently nudged her knee with his. "Don't look so glum, El. You tried your best."

"I'm worse than glum! Joshua's convinced I'm going to kill him." She took a large swig of gin. "I've made such a mess of things and I want to put them right, but I don't know how to go about it."

Daniel squeezed her hand encouragingly. "It's not all bad though, is it?"

"Isn't it? How do you make that out?"

"Well, it seems to me that Joshua's extreme reaction proves your theory's right: there *is* something that links Violet, John Able and the Pinkhams."

"True." Eleanor perked up immediately. "But how do I persuade Joshua to tell me what the connection is when he now hates me?"

"And is about to turn up his toes."

"Not funny."

"Sorry!" Daniel raised his hands in submission. "I was only trying to cheer you up." He smiled. "Perhaps Harold could have a word. After all, they were friends in their youth."

"Ha! Our lovely Harold is convinced the Pinkhams of yesteryear were pirates and murderers who would drown a man for a farthing, so I'm not sure he's the right man for a mercy dash."

"Maybe you should send in the vicar to talk to Joshua."

"I think that's guaranteed to finish him off."

Daniel sighed. "Well, my darling, those are my best suggestions. Other than that, you can always go back and face his wrath or . . ."

"Or I leave him to die, with only a Yorkshire terrier in a leopard-skin onesie for company."

"Joshua is not going to die, you silly thing."

Eleanor brushed away a tear. "You didn't see him, Dan. When he saw the ring he went so pale, it was as if he'd seen a ghost." She dabbed her nose with a napkin. "There's nothing for it – I've caused the damage so I'll have to go back and put it right." Sniffing, she set down her empty glass and rose to her feet.

"I honestly don't think it's a good idea to go back now – especially after a large G&T." Dan took her hands. "Let's have supper. You can always go and see him in a day or so."

"But he might be dead by then!"

"Trust me." Daniel lifted her chin gently with his fingers. "He might still be cross, but I can guarantee he won't be dead."

Eleanor chewed her lip nervously. "Okay. I'll leave him in peace for a while, but then I must go and apologise even if I'm not entirely sure what I've done wrong."

"Perhaps you rattled a few skeletons that Joshua believed were firmly buried."

"Or perhaps he didn't know about Violet, John and the rest of it." Eleanor thought back to the afternoon. "From the look on his face, I'm not convinced Joshua knew the St Brendan window was his grandfather's gift."

"But why would an act of charity upset him so much?"

"Your guess is as good as mine."

* * *

After Eleanor had driven away from Combemouth Manor, Joshua went into his study and picked up the red briefcase that had been lying untouched on the desk since it was unlocked a week before.

Putting the bulky case under his arm, Joshua opened the French doors and stepped out into the walled garden. He pushed away the roses and peonies that fell across the path, threatening to trip him up, and settled on a bench at the far end among the lavender. It was always known in the family as Grandpa's thinking bench, and Joshua had carried on the tradition of seeking out its faded blue seat whenever he had anything serious to contemplate.

He laid the briefcase on the bench and bowed his head in thought. Clarence sat trembling on the ground, his head tipped to one side as though waiting to see what his master would do next.

Joshua turned and scratched the dog's tiny head with two rough fingers. "Well then, young sir, I reckon now's as good a time to do this as any, don't you?" He picked up the tiny animal and put him on the seat beside him then, with a heavy heart, he unfastened the clasp and opened the briefcase.

Chapter 34: Big Preparations

Eleanor didn't go back to see Joshua the next day or the day after because things were too busy at the shop and she felt guilty due to the amount of time she had taken off. Although Erika, Connie and Joe were more than capable of keeping the show on the road, Eleanor was usually at the shop six days a week. Recently, however, she had been nipping out rather a lot to pursue the John Able case and see Joshua. Now, though, it was all hands on deck.

It was the day of Bill's launch and the bookshop was a hive of activity. Erika was taking care of customers while Eleanor and the others concentrated on making sure everything was ready for the party.

By mid-afternoon there was still a lot to be done, including giving the place a good clean. Work had started on converting the attic and Daniel's small team of helpers were constantly trooping through the house and shop so there was a thin layer of dust everywhere, which Eleanor was doing her best to ignore.

"Do you want me to come back later with my Marigolds, dear?" asked Connie.

"That's a kind offer, Mum, but I've decided to take the Quentin Crisp approach to dusting."

"Which is?"

"That the dust doesn't get any worse after the first four years."

Connie tutted. "You might be happy to live in squalor, but we can't expect Bill and his party to sit around in a grubby shop."

"Fine. If you want to whizz around the shop with the Pledge, be my guest. By the way, where's your house guest?"

"Joyce has gone off to buy a frock for this evening," said Connie. "She said she wanted to look her best for the party."

"Does she still have her sights set on Dan's father?"

"I couldn't say, but if pursuing Malcolm keeps her away from Harold that's fine by me." And with that she went off to the office to find the cleaning kit.

Eleanor looked around the shop. The books had arrived from the publishers and Georgie had sent out the official invitations and been busy on social media advertising the event. "I've been running a competition to give away tickets and signed copies of the book to ten lucky people."

Eleanor was rather alarmed by this, given the size of the shop, but Georgie told her not to worry. "It's about raising the shop's profile, that's all."

"As long as it's only an extra ten bodies, we can probably fit them in."

"Georgie has everything under control, Ma, don't worry," said Joe, looking adoringly at his girlfriend as she twisted her blonde hair up into a knot to keep it out of her face as she worked.

"What do you think of this then, Eleanor?" Georgie stepped back, indicating the display board she had set up. Behind the table where Bill was going to sign copies was a massive photograph of the man himself doing something violent to a double-neck guitar.

"It's very striking," said Eleanor, laughing. "I'm not sure we've had anything quite so terrifying here before." The photograph had been taken when Bill was in his prime and showed him gurning at the camera, sweaty and bare-chested in tight leather trousers.

"Wait till you see the display board I've had made to go outside." Georgie had also arranged for a gigantic cut-out of Bill to be placed on the pavement, in case anybody was in doubt about who that evening's guest was going to be. Eleanor's heavy metal window display had already caused a shudder of alarm among some of her more conservative customers, even though she had included books about Beethoven and Rachmaninoff for musical purists.

Eleanor clapped her hands together with glee. "I think it's brilliant," she said, immensely pleased to have Georgie there. When she had spoken to Bill about her, she had emphasised the young woman's abilities and played down the fact that Georgie had been a key player in the protest to stop his silly theme park and marina being built. The London publicist was relieved not to have to trek down to Devon and only too happy to hand over the job to a perky Australian freelancer, especially one who knew the territory so well. "It's really nice having you in charge."

"No worries, Eleanor. It's going to be a great event and what could be nicer than being paid to hang out with you guys?"

"It's true – we don't see you often enough."

"Hopefully, we'll see a bit more of each other from now on."

Happy to see that the display side of things was

under control, Eleanor dug out her list to make sure she hadn't forgotten anything. Just then, Anton appeared in the shop in his overalls having come down from the attic space where he'd been working with Daniel.

Anton had recently taken to wearing his droopy hair in a "man bun" on the top of his head, a style Eleanor thought rather ridiculous. Unfortunately, Joe disagreed and sometimes tied up his dark curls too. According to Connie they looked like salt and pepper pots, but when the boys walked down the high street together all the local girls swooned.

"Will we see you at the launch, Anton?" asked Eleanor, partly to be polite and partly because she wasn't sure what kind of social life the young man had. He seemed to spend most of his time with oldsters like Maureen and Graham. "Though I don't suppose you've heard of Bill Widget and his band," she added.

"Sure thing, Eleanor. Tryll Spigot are super huge in Latvia – my friends at home will be so jealous, you know?"

"Goodness, really? I had no idea Bill's band had a Latvian following."

"Why yes," said Anton, scratching his dusty beard. "Super huge. This is why I was inspired to paint Bill's portrait," he added sheepishly.

"Oh yes, the portrait." Eleanor thought back to the enormous painting she'd seen at the country fair. "That was great – such, er, lively colours."

Anton smiled. "I must thank your mother for the paints. She let me use some of the colours from the house when I'd finished the decorating."

Eleanor was amused to discover that the bright blue splashes exploding around Bill's wrinkly features came from her mother's boudoir. "It was a masterpiece!"

Anton shrugged a little sadly. "Is a shame no one bought it."

"Plenty of artists don't sell their early work," said Eleanor, patting him gently on the arm. "Forget about it and come along to the party later."

"Sure thing. And first I will go back to Graham's house and take a shower, so there will be no dust on me." He flashed another dazzling smile at Eleanor, who gave herself a severe telling-off for thinking how attractive he was.

Anton was almost at the shop door when something occurred to her and she stopped him. "Anton, could I ask you something. Do you know what this is?"

The young man saw what Eleanor had dug out of a pocket and now held in the palm of her hand. "Of course. I have the same." Lifting his hand he touched his right earlobe where he wore a single gold earring. "It's okay to wear this to the party?"

"Yes, of course. Sorry, it reminded me of something, that's all."

She had been right: it was an earring. Eleanor had intended to leave it with Joshua but when he'd chased her out of the house she'd put it back in her pocket.

Once the launch was over, she was determined to go back to Combemouth Manor to try to repair their friendship – and make sure he wasn't dead.

* * *

The books were in place, the white wine was chilling and the canapés had been delivered. The last thing to sort out was what to wear, but Eleanor had that under control, too. She didn't often wear dresses but she did have an authentic 1950s black dress bought many years before at a vintage fair and which she pulled out for smart occasions. With its crossover top, cinched waist and starched skirts, it suited her figure perfectly. The dress had smelt a bit musty when she'd exhumed it from the depths of her wardrobe, but it came back from the dry-cleaner's looking and smelling as good as new.

It wasn't until an hour before the party that she dashed back to the cottage to put it on.

"The dry-cleaning has done something funny to my dress."

Daniel came over and ran an admiring hand over her curves. "It looks bloody marvellous to me," he said, kissing her gently on the neck.

"I don't know," Eleanor examined herself in the mirror. "I'm sure it never used to be quite this tight around the chest." Eleanor had never been slender like her sister, Jenna; instead she had inherited her mother's softer, rounded build. And since marriage to Daniel she had definitely piled on the pounds – partly because she was happy and partly because she no longer skipped meals or made do with a packet soup and an apple of an evening. Dan was as thin and wiry as he'd been in his twenties, which was somewhat unfair given that he ate like a horse. "Do you honestly think I look all right? I can barely breathe."

"You look beautiful, but if you're not comfortable change."

Eleanor smiled, thinking how good Dan was at saying the right thing. "I guess I'll be okay so long as no one makes me laugh. Anyway," she said, looking at her watch, "there's no time to change. Everyone will be arriving any minute now."

She ran a brush through her auburn locks and slicked on some lipstick, assessing the finished result in the mirror as her husband stood behind her.

"I look forward to helping you out of the dress later tonight, El."

"Steady on, tiger. I need to stay inside it for a few hours yet."

"Shame," said Dan, kissing her.

"Don't squeeze me or I might pop," she said, laughingly moving Daniel's hands from her waist.

He sighed. "Come on, then. Let's go and see how the team's getting on next door."

Chapter 35: Let's Party!

One of the first people to arrive was Jim Rowe, who had been sent by the *Chronicle* to interview Bill and take a few photographs of the event. His eyes lit up when he saw Eleanor. "Wow – you should wear dresses more often. You look, erm, very nice."

"Thanks," she said shyly, smoothing down the broad skirts that shot out over her hips. Across the room she could tell that Erika was deliberately turned away from them; she and Jim were on speaking terms again, but their friendship had never fully recovered from the breakdown of their affair. "So how are you, Jim? Is there anything exciting happening in Combemouth I should know about?"

He thought for a moment. "I guess the most exciting thing to happen recently was an accusation of match-fixing at the summer festival."

Eleanor frowned. "I don't remember there being any athletics. I must have missed it."

"I'm talking about the ferret racing, actually. The owner of the front runner is suspected of giving it performance-enhancing drugs before the race."

"Blimey, it's all going on out there."

"But never mind that," Jim bent over to whisper in Eleanor's ear, "my sources tell me you've been spending an awful lot of time over at Joshua Pinkham's house recently."

"Yes, we're having a torrid affair," she whispered back, pouring red wine into Jim's glass. Seeing his horrified expression, she laughed. "That was a joke, by the way."

"Thank goodness," said Jim, looking at his feet. "It was a rather alarming thought." He smiled his crooked smile and Eleanor remembered that she had once found Jim rather attractive and had even toyed with the idea of going out with him. But that was a long time ago.

"Apart from having the torrid affair, I've been cataloguing Joshua's books. I told him he needed an antiquarian bookseller to value the collection, but he insisted he wanted me."

"He wanted the best person for the job. I hope he's paying for your time?"

"We have an arrangement." Eleanor winked. "Anyway, I've finished now. It was slow work, but it was fascinating to be in the manor house." She made sure there was no one around listening to their conversation before speaking. "We discovered a hidden cupboard at the back of one of the bookcases. That's top secret information, by the way."

"Of course," said Jim, nodding and pulling a serious face.

Eleanor reached up for the glass she'd left on one of the poetry shelves at the beginning of the event and took a sip of her wine. "It got me thinking: if the family has secret compartments concealed in bookcases, might it not also have a few skeletons stashed in cupboards?"

"Such as?"

"Oh, I have a theory that the John Able case – the

one I asked for your help with – is somehow connected to the Pinkham family. I've found one or two clues but no concrete evidence. Anyway, the question keeps niggling away at me."

Jim laughed. "This is where I recall you're a big Agatha Christie fan."

"Well remembered. But don't you think it's odd that Joshua is so unwilling to talk about things?"

"Not especially. Joshua is of a generation that doesn't like to talk about the past. He's a man used to keeping his affairs private."

"That's what Dan said." Eleanor was quiet for a moment, thinking. "But I'd love to dig into Pinkham's family history a little bit."

"To learn what?"

"Oh, lots of things!"

"Such as?"

"Well, Joshua's grandfather seems to have been a local benefactor, but kept his generosity a secret from everyone. Why would he do that?"

"Humility?"

"I suppose so, Jim." Eleanor sighed. "In any case, it would be great to discover something positive to cheer up Joshua and prevent him thinking he's going to die any day now."

"Why does he think that?"

"The *Santa Ana* turning up has upset him, but it's mostly my fault."

"What on earth did you do to him?"

She laughed. "Nothing! All I did was ask him about connections between the Makepeace family and the Pinkhams. Oh, and about a locket. But what really tipped him over the edge was when I showed him a ring I'd discovered hidden in his Bible." Eleanor took another tiny sip of wine, aware that she needed to stay focused tonight. "So there you have it."

"Lots of detecting still to be done, by the sounds of it. And you'll deserve a medal if you manage to cheer up the most miserable man in town."

"Bless him. He's not a bad old stick under that faded corduroy exterior."

"I think you're needed." Jim nodded towards the back of the room where Erika was banging empty glasses down on the table and pretending not to look their way.

"Oops. Someone looks unhappy. See you later."

* * *

Bill Widget was enjoying being the centre of attention, signing books and chatting to ardent fans. Much to Eleanor's amazement, most of the "celebrity" guests from Bill's original list had turned up, although there was no one there who was familiar to her.

Joe and Anton, meanwhile, were standing open-mouthed as one ancient rock musician after another came into the shop and slapped Bill warmly on the back. Eleanor went over to the boys to ask for information about who was who.

"Who's the chap in the purple trousers with the piercings, Joe? The wizened-looking geezer who looks about ninety?"

"That is only Ivan Twang, one of the most influential bass players in the entire universe. Here in our shop." A faraway look came over Joe's face. "If I die now, I'll be a happy man."

Anton, who was standing beside him, was clutching an envelope. "I, too, will die a happy man." He lifted the envelope to his mouth and kissed it. "Eleanor, that man is a saint."

"Ivan Twang is a saint?"

"No," said Anton, shaking his head. "Bill Widget is a saint." Eleanor could see genuine tears of emotion forming in the young man's eyes. "Tonight he tells me he wishes to buy my painting from the fair. The lady in charge of the art tent . . ."

"Beryl?"

"Yes, Mrs Beryl – she says no one buys cheap art. 'Anton,' she says to me, 'think big – we will sell it for £250', like a joke, you see?"

"Sort of," said Eleanor.

Anton smiled across at Bill. "But tonight, Mr Widget came across and said £250 must be a mistake." Anton opened the envelope for them to see. "I think, okay, so he'll give me £25, which is fine. But no – he gave me £1,250 and says he wants to buy all of my work."

Eleanor watched as two happy tears leaked out of Anton's green eyes and disappeared into his beard as he pressed the damp envelope to his lips once again. "That's great, but perhaps I should put the money in the safe for you." She couldn't bear the thought of the boy wandering drunkenly down the high street and losing the money at a kebab stall.

Anton nodded. "Thank you, Eleanor," he said. "I am most grateful."

"I'll put it in the office. Can you keep an eye on things out here, Joe?"

"Sure, Mum," said Joe, his attention still on Bill and his mates.

Smiling, Eleanor tucked the envelope into her cleavage and wriggled her way through the crowd to the drinks table to see how her colleagues were getting on.

"It's going well," said Georgie, "though I'd no idea we'd get through so much sparkling elderflower. This could be the first launch where I've actually had booze left at the end of the evening. Totally unheard of at a publishing event," she said, shaking her head in disbelief.

"I think a lot of Bill's mates have turned teetotal in their twilight years," said Eleanor surveying the room. "Some of them do look as though they've been pickled in alcohol for forty years or so. Thank goodness there's another box of the alcohol-free stuff in the back. We wouldn't want them rioting and throwing their false teeth at us."

Georgie giggled. "I'll go and fetch some more cordial."

"Don't worry, I'll go. I have something to put in the safe as it happens – Bill bought Anton's painting and handed over the readies this evening."

"What great news!"

"It is and I want to prevent the lad from going into town and losing the lot tonight. I won't be long." Eleanor trotted off to the office, where she put Anton's cash in a locked drawer.

It wasn't until she bent down to pick up the bottles of elderflower cordial that she heard the sound of metal parting from metal and realised the zip running down the side of her dress had burst at its lowest point and now revealed two inches of her black underwear. "Damn. There must be a safety pin somewhere." Searching the office drawers she found nothing. She emptied out every pot on the desk, but all she found were paperclips, rubber bands, fluff and the tops of long-dead biros. When she had tipped out every possible container, she gave up and returned to the shop, which was now filled to the gunnels.

After handing over the cordial to Erika, who had taken over from Georgie, Eleanor squeezed her way over to her son who was now singing along to a Tryll Spigot track with Anton.

"Joe," she hissed, "can you pop next door and find me a couple of safety pins?"

"Safety pins? What for?"

"Never mind what they're for. Just do it will you, love. And hurry."

"Er, where do you keep them?"

"Who has a place where they 'keep' safety pins? You'll have to search around a bit – try the kitchen cupboards or my bedroom drawers."

"Okay."

Eleanor turned around and smiled at the packed room, her hand clamped to her hip in a jaunty pose. With any luck no one would even notice the teeny gap in her dress. She stood watching Bill sign books and chat to fans for what seemed like an age before Joe returned.

"Got them."

"Well done, love," said Eleanor. "Hand them over."

Joe dropped two tiny safety pins into his mother's hand and shrugged. "That's the best I could do."

They were minute, but beggars can't be choosers so Eleanor smiled grimly and ducked back into the office where she placed one pin at the bottom of the zip and the other midway up for good measure. "It's not going to hold," she muttered to herself. "Damn it."

Looking desperately around, she spied the stapler on the desk. "That's it!" She knew it was fairly dark in the shop and the dress could always be mended later. Grasping the fabric seam between her thumb and finger she stapled over the zip, effectively sealing herself into the dress. She had to laugh at the idea of it and was pleased with herself for thinking so creatively. She tried a tentative wiggle: the zip held. "I'm a genius," she whispered to herself as she left the office and returned to the serious business of schmoozing rock stars and selling books.

Over the heads of their guests, Daniel noticed Eleanor re-enter the shop and went over to see her. "Is everything okay, darling. You're walking a little oddly."

"No, no. Everything's fine. Oh, or it was," she said, as Joyce waltzed into the shop in what could only be described as a kaftan. "Tell Malcolm he's welcome to hide in the office if he wants to make himself scarce."

Daniel shook his head. "I'm not putting myself between Joyce and any man she has set her heart on, even if it is my father. That woman is scary."

"Coward. Meanwhile, where's my mother got to?"

"Last seen in Crime Fiction with Ivan Twang."

"I'd better go and rescue the poor man."

"It looked as though he was having fun, so I wouldn't worry. And here they come."

Eleanor turned to see Connie arm in arm with Ivan. As they approached, Ivan gave Connie a peck on the cheek and went off to speak to some other old rockers.

"Are you making new friends, Mum? It's a good job Harold isn't here to see you flirting with older men."

Harold had graciously declined Eleanor's invitation to the launch saying his musical tastes tended more towards the classical.

"What an interesting man Mr Twang is," said Connie, her cheeks slightly flushed. "He's been telling me about his three wives and his years on the road. Now he's given up the high life and farms in a lovely Somerset village. He says it's wonderfully quiet and calm except in June when there's a big music festival in the fields next to his. He has a herd of Dexter cattle and they don't like the racket one bit, apparently."

"You must have had him trapped for ages, Mum, he's given you his entire life story."

"Not all of it, just the last dozen years or so. Anyway, I said I would recommend his autobiography to my bookclub. The girls enjoy something spicy every once in a while."

"When you've finished mingling with the stars, could you check what Aunty Joyce is up to? Daniel hasn't seen his father for a while and I'm afraid she might have him in a headlock somewhere."

"Oh, Malcolm's made his escape," said Connie. "Joyce is chatting to Vince now. It turns out they bump into each other regularly in their local Gigante supermarket. She didn't recognise him at the festival the other day because she's used to seeing Bill's minder in shorts and a Hawaiian shirt, not dressed as a hit man."

"It's nice she's found somebody to talk to." Eleanor gazed tipsily at the throng of people. Apart from the minor hiccup with the dress, everything was going swimmingly.

Bill Widget was enjoying himself chatting to

customers who remembered his glory days and to younger fans who had recently discovered Tryll Spigot's music. Eleanor was feeling relaxed and happy because books were being sold and the end of the party was in sight. She had found her glass and was enjoying another sip of wine when Ivan Twang sidled up to her.

"Very nice do," he said, raising his glass of mineral water to her in greeting. "If I ever write volume two of my life story, I'll follow Bill's lead and insist we have the launch here."

"Thanks, Ivan. It's kind of you to say so." Eleanor smiled. "We do make an effort."

"I can tell," said Ivan, looking her up and down. "And I'm impressed you dressed for the occasion. Very nice – definitely my era."

"Oh, I like vintage style." Eleanor was pleased – if a little surprised – by the reaction her 1950s dress was getting. She had received a couple of winks from the old guys during the evening and even an approving nod from the town's two young Goths who'd left their usual hanging-out spot in the shopping precinct to see their guitar heroes.

"Bold," said Ivan, thoughtfully, as he walked away. "Very bold."

Bold? Whatever did he mean? It seemed to Eleanor that a little black dress was about as uncontroversial as you could get and she was relieved it had grown more comfortable over the evening.

Which was a bit odd . . . That's when she glanced down and saw a row of silver sparkles on either side of the black fabric where the staples had come adrift. Worse still, the zip had split and peeled open to reveal several inches of pale flesh. As if that wasn't enough, the safety pins were still in place.

At that moment, Bill came over to say goodbye. "It's been a grand night, duck. Thank you for organising everything."

In horror, Eleanor clasped a hand to her waist and hoped against hope that Bill wouldn't notice her wardrobe malfunction. "You're welcome – it's been fun," she said, between gritted teeth.

"Wearing Versace tonight, I see," he said, cheerily. "It looks a lot better on you than it did on Liz Hurley. Where did you leave Hugh Grant?" At this Bill laughed, clearly pleased with his joke.

"If you'll excuse me one moment," said Eleanor, turning on her heels and fleeing from the shop and to the cottage.

* * *

"Stupid dress," she said, throwing herself on the bed. She was crying with frustration now. "I looked bloody ridiculous." She pulled at the safety pins and stray staples, one of which caught her finger, releasing a pinprick of blood. "Ow!"

Daniel, who had followed her to the cottage, strode over to where she sat on the bed and took her hand gently in his. She gazed up at him through eyes streaming with tears. "I made such a fool of myself."

"No one would ever think you were foolish." Daniel kissed his wife's injured finger then smoothed her hair back from her damp cheek. "The evening was a huge success. Bill was delighted with it, the guests had fun," he kissed her again, "and you looked gorgeous and sexy and I love you."

Eleanor wailed. "I don't believe you."

Daniel kissed her gently on the lips. "Let's extract you from this dangerous garment and I'll do my best to convince you."

Chapter 36: Secrets Revealed

The next morning everyone at the bookshop was feeling a tad groggy, although the general consensus was that the launch had been a triumph. What's more, Daniel had almost managed to convince Eleanor to see the funny side of her exploding dress.

Mid-morning, Georgie came in to help tidy up, although most of the work had been done after Eleanor fled to the cottage. "I'm sorry for leaving you and Erika to do the clearing up last night," she said, guiltily.

"It's part of the job," said Georgie, cheerfully. "And there wasn't much to do, anyway. The books were all sold, the snacks were eaten and Joe helped Erika to sort out the empty bottles and put the sofa back."

"Well, I appreciate it," said Eleanor. "I see 'Bill' has gone." The large poster Georgie had put behind the signing table had disappeared.

"Yes, I hope you don't mind but Anton begged and pleaded to have it. Joe was a little disappointed, but I said you might let him have the cut-out 'Bill' from outside the shop."

"Fine, though I'm not sure it will fit in the back bedroom."

Georgie screwed up her face. "And I'm not sure I want to share a room with that thing either. I guess we'll have to turn him to face the wall when I'm staying over."

"Good plan. Now I'd better carry on with the paperwork. There's nothing I enjoy more than totting up the takings from a successful event." Eleanor rubbed her hands together and headed over to the counter.

Soon, the shop was busy with customers. Some had been attracted by the cut-out and the window display, others by the news on social media about Bill's party. As it was Saturday, there was also the habitual mixture of walkers and tourists enjoying a sunny day at the seaside as well as people in town for the Combemouth Festival.

Erika and Joe were doing most of the serving, leaving Eleanor free to use the computer. She was immersed in the figures and didn't look up immediately when a man approached.

"Good morning, missus. I hear your frock was quite a hit last evening."

It took Eleanor's brain several seconds to put together the familiar voice and unfamiliar vision and to make sense of what she saw. "Joshua! You look so, so . . ." What was the word she was looking for? She groped in her mind for the perfect description, but there was only one word that would do. "So clean!"

Joshua smiled, smoothing a hand over the lapel of his sky-blue suit. "Seersucker. I haven't worn it for a while and it's a bit tight around the midriff, but it's my favourite."

Eleanor was aware that her mouth was hanging open as she gaped at the apparition standing in front of her. "And you've had a shave." Gone was the grey stubble and Joshua's hair was newly trimmed and slicked back in neat waves.

"Been to the barber's," said Joshua, running a hand over his chin, which was now as smooth and pink as a baby's bottom. "They did my eyebrows, my nose, my ears and everything," he added proudly. "And a young lass did my nails, too, see?" He clearly hadn't been to the dentist yet, but it was still a remarkable transformation.

"That's marvellous," stuttered Eleanor. "I'm . . ." What was she? She was pleased, amazed and taken aback, not least by the citrus scent that now wafted towards her. Joshua was wearing cologne. "I'm speechless."

Joshua chuckled. "If we've managed to rob her of words for a few minutes, I'd say that was money well spent, wouldn't you Clarence?"

Eleanor peeked over the counter to the floor where the dog sat wagging his tiny tail and looking happy for the first time she could remember. He, too, had clearly had a much-needed wash and was naked apart from a new blue collar and lead.

Eleanor came out from behind the counter. "May I give you a hug?"

"You may," said Joshua. "But mind the suit."

"I think we need tea."

"You'd best make three cups – I've told the vicar to meet us here."

Eleanor sat Joshua down in the café area and went to fetch the drinks. By the time she had made the tea and come back to sit opposite him, Philip had arrived. He had clearly run all the way from St Cuthbert's and the shock on his face was a picture to behold. By now,

Eleanor's amazement at Joshua's transformation was beginning to fade, but not so her curiosity.

Joshua leant back in his chair, ready to address his audience. "I expect you'd like to know why I brought you here today."

"Yes please. If that's all right," said Eleanor. Philip, who was still speechless with surprise, simply nodded.

And so Joshua explained. "When I was a boy, there was a lot of bad talk about the Pinkhams – that we were Cornish and notorious wreckers. It was a taint that lay over the family for years." Joshua frowned. "My mother and father never discussed or denied it, so I grew up believing I was descended from rogues and murderers."

Eleanor's heart sank as she listened, distressed at the thought that perhaps the rumours Harold had shared with her were true. Then she watched as Joshua's expression changed into one of happiness.

"You've done me a favour, missus," he said, patting Eleanor's hand. "If you'd not come busy-bodying around, I'd never have opened the briefcase and would have gone to my grave thinking I came from a family of cut-throats."

Eleanor and Philip looked at each other. "What was in the case, Joshua? When we originally found it, you said you knew what it contained."

The old man swallowed a mouthful of tea and delicately patted his lips. "I knew I'd find my grand-father's papers and I did. Lots of them. What I didn't expect to find was his journal and letters from Violet Makepeace."

Eleanor gasped. "So there was a connection."

"There was. Alfred loved Violet and she loved him back, but not until it was too late."

"Oh no," said Eleanor. "Did one of them die?"

"It was a little more complicated than that."

"Let me guess: Alfred Pinkham loved Violet but she married Reginald Makepeace, is that it?" Eleanor frowned. "But where does John Able fit in? If he does."

Joshua looked at her. "Now I've read the journal I can tell you that John Able was my grandfather but he changed his name to Alfred Pinkham. Violet was the girl he tried to help by selling that damned earring. As it said in the newspapers – and in Violet's story – Alfred was arrested and sent to prison, and the only person who knew he was innocent and could have saved him from almost two years of hell was Violet." Joshua's expression darkened with anger. "That girl knew Alfred – or John as he was back then – had found the ring at the beach and never stolen nothing in his life."

"Exactly like Jack in the story," said Eleanor.

"Yes," Joshua nodded. "And I didn't know about it until I opened the briefcase."

"What happened when your grandfather came out of the reformatory school?" asked Philip, who had now regained the power speech.

"He was fortunate indeed and was taken on as an apprentice by an engineer in Bristol where he lived for seven years." Joshua shook his head sadly. "He could have travelled the world afterwards, but he missed his home and his family so he came back to Combemouth." He laughed. "By then the foolish boy was going under his mother's maiden name, which was Pinkham. Ironical really, wouldn't you say?"

Philip frowned. "So you're saying that your grand-father, John Able, didn't steal the ring but chose a name associated with Cornish wreckers?"

"Precisely. He was not yet fourteen when he left the reformatory school and hadn't had any education to speak of." Joshua shrugged. "I suppose he picked out a name he was familiar with and liked."

"Where does the locket fit in?" asked Eleanor.

"When Alfred turned up in Combemouth aged twenty-one, Violet recognised him as John Able and sent him letters apologising for what she'd done and saying she loved him – all nonsense, of course, as she'd not seen him since he was a child. It seems that Grandfather didn't respond, which is when she sent him the locket."

"With the apology – 'I did you a great harm, for which I am truly sorry'." Eleanor remembered the words very clearly. "But John – Alfred – must still have felt something for her if he kept it?"

"I daresay he did." Joshua scratched his chin, seeming surprised to find the stubble was gone. "In her letters, Violet urges John to tell people who he is and to clear his name, but he refuses." Joshua turned to Philip. "He worked hard and become a prosper-ous man, Vicar. And he was devout, too. He kept his promise to help poor sailors, but he never wanted thanks for it because he never forgave himself for lying to his mother and hiding the ring."

"Which is why his name isn't recorded at St Cuthbert's." Philip nodded. "And can you tell us any-thing about the verse?"

"I can. Any chance of another tea first, missus?"

"Sure," said Eleanor, pouring him another cup.

Joshua sipped the tea thoughtfully. "Now, where had I got to?"

"You were going to tell us about the verse," said Philip, helpfully.

"Ah, yes. Well, according to John's journal it was Violet who wrote the poem and sent it to him. He had founded the St Brendan Hostel by then, you see, and I think it was another nudge from Violet to encourage him to tell people about his good deeds. John must have liked the poem because he later had it inscribed on your wall under the window."

"Perhaps he also wanted to show to Violet that he forgave her for what she had done as a girl. And the ring in the Bible," asked Eleanor, "is that the one John found in the rock pool when he was a lad?"

Joshua shivered. "You gave me a terrible shock when you showed me that. Who but a wrecker would keep a dead man's earring hidden in a Bible?" He sighed. "But now I know different. I read in Grandfather's journal that the original ring was confiscated when he was arrested, but as soon as he'd saved enough money he bought another pair of earrings. Then, when he returned to Combemouth, he did what he told his mother he'd done all those years before – he climbed up onto the Top and threw one ring into the sea. The other he kept in his Bible to remind him of the fishermen who had perished."

Philip smiled gently. "So all those years you thought your ancestors were wreckers, your grandfather was in fact an angel."

"I wouldn't go that far, but it seems like he did his bit. There wasn't only the hostel, you see. He also put money into building the new lighthouse and starting a school for poor boys." Joshua looked down at his hands, clearly moved by the secrets he'd uncovered. "I only wish my dear father could have known the truth."

"I feel sure he did." Philip leant over and squeezed Joshua's arm warmly. "And now is perhaps the time to tell everyone that your grandfather's money saved the lives of countless seamen, gave poor sailors a roof over their heads and educated hundreds of lads. We might wish John Able had shared his good deeds so your family could revel in them, but he was humble and modest. I think we must forgive him that."

"Amen, Vicar."

Eleanor and Philip sat silently for a moment, thinking about the events of the past, while Joshua tipped the last of his tea into a saucer and placed it on the ground for Clarence.

When the slurping had finished, Joshua turned to the vicar. "Did you bring my letter as I requested?"

Philip nodded. "Here it is." He handed over the brown envelope Joshua had brought to him some weeks before.

Joshua took it and tore it into pieces. "I shall be writing another one, but not for a while yet as I've changed my mind about dying. First I'm going on holiday. If that old rogue Harold Greaves can find himself a lady friend, a handsome chap like me won't have any difficulties." He smiled, an expression as unexpected as it was joyful.

Joshua got to his feet and handed a large house key, a lead and a bag full of dog paraphernalia to Philip. "Look after Clarence for me, will you? He's had a bath." He bent down to pat the dog. "I'm off on a cruise, young sir, and I'm afraid you're not allowed to come." There were tears in Joshua's eyes when he straightened up. "That there's my only friend."

"Nonsense," said Eleanor, welling up. "I'm your friend. And so is Philip here. And so is Harold," she added, with a little less conviction.

"Eleanor's right," said Philip. "And I think you'll find there are lots of folk who want to be friends with you. In fact, I'll prove it."

"And how are you going to do that then?"

"Just you wait and see."

Chapter 37: Two Weeks Later . . .

It was one hour to party time and everything was almost ready. The event was going to be held outdoors, so Graham and Malcolm had been around the garden tidying up the weeds, deadheading and generally sprucing the place up.

Tables were set up across the lawn, each one with a crisp white tablecloth and a jam jar filled with summer flowers in the centre. Eleanor and Connie – with a modicum of help from Joyce – had done the best they could with the lived-in part of the house, and the kitchen had been scrubbed to within an inch of its life. Now the beautiful old crockery and silver cutlery shone in the sunlight.

"Where do you want this lot?" asked Joe, carrying a tray of glasses across the lawn.

"Take them over to the marquee, love," said Eleanor. "The bubbly should be nicely chilled by now."

Daniel, who was setting out chairs, came over to his wife. "Have you seen the cake? Maureen has done a fantastic job."

"I have," said Eleanor, chewing her lip. "I hope we've done the right thing asking her to make it in the shape of a ship, given his thoughts on the matter."

"Don't worry. I'm sure he'll love it."

* * *

When the taxi drew up outside Combemouth Manor, the driver laughed. "Are you having a party?"

"No, I'm not." Joshua frowned as he climbed out of the cab. "What's going on here then?"

From the driveway he could see the vicar's pastel-coloured bunting crisscrossing the lawn and draped across the front of the house. A dozen café tables were set out and small bunches of flowers had been tied to the back of each chair. "The blasted vicar is using my garden for a wedding reception, the cheeky bugger!"

"I've always said they're rascals in Combemouth," said the taxi driver, a Waterborough man.

"Whoever the bride and groom are, they're in for a nasty surprise if they think they're going to get away with this," said Joshua, turning puce with indignation.

"They've chosen a nice day for it, mind you." With that the driver spun the car around on the gravel and left, leaving Joshua to take in the perplexing sight. Grumbling, he picked up his case and began stomping down the side of the house towards the kitchen, then stopped dead in his tracks when he noticed the front door was wide open. Not only that, but the weeds had been cut back and someone had placed a bay tree either side of the steps.

"What the heck . . . ?"

At that moment, Clarence came hurtling across the grass towards his master, delirious with joy. Joshua picked him up, making the dog squeak with happiness. "Where's that vicar then, young sir?"

"I'm over here with your friends."

When Joshua turned around, Philip and a host of smiling faces appeared from behind the shrubbery where everyone had been hiding.

"Welcome home, Joshua," said Eleanor, stepping forward to hug her grumpy friend. "And Happy Birthday."

"Well, I'll be . . ." Joshua's emotion went from surprise to happiness as he took in the small crowd around him.

Joe, Georgie and Anton began handing out glasses of champagne as people Joshua hadn't seen for years came up to greet him and wish him well.

"I hope you like what I've made for you, Joshua," said Maureen nervously, as Eleanor led everyone over to the marquee.

Inside, Joshua bent over to examine Maureen's creation more closely, then scratched his head thoughtfully. The cake was constructed in three layers and decorated with a beautifully crafted figurehead, two rows of cannon and sugar paste sailors scrubbing the decks and shinning up masts. "I reckon if we cut off the main mast, that will be the *Santa Ana* gone for good." Joshua picked up a sailor from the foredeck and gobbled him up. "All that stuff about the ghost ship being a harbinger of doom and death is poppycock. As you can see, I'm fit as a fiddle and twice as sprightly." He winked flirtatiously, turning Maureen's cheeks quite pink.

Just then Harold stepped forward, a solemn expression on his face. "I must apologise for believing those terrible rumours about the Pinkhams," he said quietly. "It was unforgivable and I am truly sorry."

Joshua grasped his old schoolfellow by the hand and shook it warmly. "You were not to know any different, Harry."

"But we know the truth now," said Philip, "so let's

raise our glasses to wish Joshua a very happy eighti-eth birthday and to say thank you to his grandfather, John Able, for his generous gifts to this town."

Joshua smiled, tears coming to his eyes as he took Eleanor's hand in his. "And thank you, missus, for everything."

"It's my pleasure," she said, as everyone drank a toast to Joshua's health, happiness and new life.

THE END

ON HIS WAY
BACK TO ME

BRITTANY BACINSKI

To the lovers I lost and the lovers who lost me

Foreword

"I look down into the water as I imagine him being carried by that instead. Envy grew as I pictured Paul enrobed by anything or anyone else other than me. Without effort, tears stream down my cheeks. I rub his ashes over my arms, my neck, and my face, feeling the bumpy bits of him over my lips.

"I will never let you go," I whisper with my eyes staring up into the endless blue sky. "I will carry you with me forever."

—On His Way Back To Me

✧   ✧   ✧

I wrote this scene after I saw a photo of his ashes floating on water posted to my Facebook feed in real time. It was the first picture I would ever see of him where he wasn't "him" at all. He was glitter on water.

Watching him take on another form, one without those golden-brown eyes that could make me do anything... it did something to me. And I was never the same after it. So, I did what any writer would do. I turned my pain into art. And then I told the world about it.

When I was in the pit of my grief, I craved a book (or even a movie for that matter) that would *fearlessly* take me on the same turbulent journey; one of maddening grief and pure love. I wanted so deeply to be validated in my experience and to feel seen. I couldn't find one that went to the depths I was searching for, so I wrote one myself.

Thank you all so much for letting share bits of my tragic love story through the journey of Jade and Paul. It's one of the most healing things I've ever written and it's my hope that someone else out there can find solace in this book, too.

Sending all my love and gratitude, especially to the grieving souls holding this in your hands right now. I'm honored beyond words to be on your journey. Thank you for being here, I love you.

BOOK ONE

PROLOGUE

COULD A PERSON feel worse than I do right now? That's what I'm asking myself every few minutes as I trudge my numb, heavy legs uphill. The love of my life is dead, and there is a great possibility that I'm being hunted by my husband. If I don't make it to the top of this ice-cold mountain before dark, I will die here. Nothing could feel worse. Maybe being burned alive, but even the heat of fire sounds better than this. I'd do anything to feel a flicker of warmth again.

My eyes dart around the foggy forest, scanning the trunks of the trees as I search for another sign of life hiding behind them. *What if I wasn't alone? What if he finds me before I reach it?* I try not to let the thoughts consume me, but the sound of gunshots still ricochets through my mind with each painful step forward. Anyone who say hiking the Appalachian Trail is easy, hasn't done it frozen and nearly dead.

If Sam is tracking me again, I can guarantee it's at a faster pace than I can walk. The fatigue and the rapidly dropping temperatures have slowed me down more than I'd like to admit. Sam's a runner with stamina, and I'm certain there is nothing that could slow him down, especially if he has a goal. And since the goal would be me back in his possession, I can only bet he's moving at lightning speed. If I don't make it to the Phone of the Wind soon, I will have risked everything for nothing.

I notice my vision fading and out as my breathing begins to

shallow. I know this feeling. It's the feeling I get before a fainting spell. If I'm honest, I know I'm due for a fainting spell, and I know it's because I haven't eaten anything today, other than choking down the last of the dried-out beef sticks hours ago. If I don't get off my feet immediately, I will collapse. And if I do pass out, who knows if I'll wake up. The exhaustion has enveloped my hunger, and I've been too broken to feel anything else at all. My numbness has covered me like an icy blanket. I'd be fine with dying if dying meant that I'd see him again, but staying alive is the only way I will. I'm too close to him to give up now.

Regardless of how terrible I feel, I manage to continue fumbling forward with my frozen toes, my stiff legs feeling desperate, and my eyes glazed over with a haunted grief. Everything feels heavier and off balance, my body wobbles to stand upright. I can't stop now, but I can't keep going like this.

Daylight has started to slide behind the trees while darkness slowly creeps in. I roll the pack off my back, lean against a mossy log, and close my eyes for a quick second, knowing to be careful not to keep them closed for too long. As it turns out, riding the line of death is harder than I thought. One wrong move and it's game over.

My vision stops flickering and all the breath in my lungs returns with a burst of adrenaline when I open my eyes to see it. *Is that... what I think it is?* My dry lips part, hanging open in disbelief. I walk closer at a pace I can be proud of, peeling away branches left and right as I inch closer, crunching leaves and sticks beneath me. *Am I hallucinating? Or have I finally arrived?* I rub my fists over my eyes, making sure that what I see is what is there. A surge of energy pulses through my body hard and fast, as if I have been resuscitated upon its discovery. I cover my mouth with my frozen hands and fall to my knees, the hard ground supports my collapse. Tears attempt to make their way out but freeze on my cheeks on the way down.

I made it. I am here.

As I walk closer to catch a better look, I stare for a minute, examining it cautiously. The old rotary phone is attached to nothing, but this wet, towering tree. A cool, opaque mist surrounds it. Bright, green moss travels the way up the phone post with not a power line in sight. It's then that I remember a phone connected to the dead wouldn't need an electrical connection. I laugh at myself for even considering that it might. I inch closer to the phone in a jubilant daze. It doesn't look supernatural or appear to have any sort of portal magic to me, but what did I have to lose? What if it worked? Nearly dying on this journey just to look foolish in front of an empty forest full of trees for any chance at hearing his voice again would be worth it. My throat clenches and tightens as I struggle to fight back a dry, heaving sob. *God, I have missed him.*

I pull back my dark, frozen hair stuck to my neck and begin to inch my fingers towards the phone. When I'm close enough to touch it, I trace my fingers down its spiral cord, running my stiff hand over the hard plastic before I pick it up. The tips of my nails are purple, and the tops of my hands sting from the wind chill.

What was supposed to happen when I touched it? Would I see him? Would I only hear his voice? What do I say? What might he say to me? My curiosity pulls my body closer. Slowly, I press the receiver against my cheek, as I close my eyes slowly and imagine his face. The face my entire body craves, his stubble resting against my palms, his smile melting the bitter cold from my body. Those golden eyes, the ones that still make me ache from the inside out.

I take a deep breath in and wait. When nothing happens, a shattering wave of heartbreak and disappointment roll over me. As I'm about to remove the receiver from my face, I begin to feel something. A subtle warmth envelops me. A strange sensation of bees buzzing around and swirling madly inside of my skull takes over. Heavy weight falls over my eye lids, much too heavy to keep them open and by some force, I feel hands grab the fabric from my coat, pulling my frozen body into an even warmer space. Orbs of light sparkle all around me. I can feel myself somewhere else, but I'm afraid to look.

"You can open your eyes," a woman's voice spoke softly. "He is waiting for you."

CHAPTER ONE

IT'S THE FIRST varsity game of the season. I'm sitting in the bleachers wrapped tightly in a fleece blanket with my two best friends that I'd had since the fifth grade. The chill of the fall night air has started to make my hands ache and I realize now that I probably should've worn gloves. Of course, at fifteen, I'm too cool for them anyway. I'm too cool for a coat, too, and it's one of the main fights I have with my mother before ever leaving the house. The goal was to show off the outfit: low rise jeans, layered shirts with lace lining the top and tiny buttons down the center. The star of the show, however, was the faux diamond necklace that plunged down into my newly grown breasts. I was a sophomore, and I wanted to look like it. I had highlights and doubled pierced ears to prove it. If anything was going to shine under these Friday night lights, it was going to be me and my new boobs.

I'm shivering next to my friends, stealing their blankets, wishing I had a coat on, when I notice him. Two rows above me there is a boy I've never seen before. At first, I wonder if maybe he is new in town or if he is from a different school. From where I am sitting, the sun is setting above him, his golden hair and golden eyes glitter from the distance. He is surrounded by a couple people I know already, so it only makes sense to me that I need to investigate this new guy. I have a terrible habit of growing quiet and awkward around boys I'm attracted to, so my plan to approach him needs to be indirect and nonchalant. I consider flashing him a cool smile or a soft head nod and hopefully catch his name without being obvious that I am interested.

And when I realized that wasn't going to work, I knew I needed to act on things myself. *There is just something about this boy.* So, I ask my friend Jessica to do the scoping out for me. Shoving her shoulders froward with my palms, I beg, "Please, go see who that is. Aren't you, curious, too?"

She gives me an evil glare, pulls her lip in tight and shakes her head. "No, he's not my type. My type is on the field playing football."

I smile at her and give her a look as I remember the last favor I did for her when she had a crush. "Come on. You owe me."

She huffs and grabs my cheeks with her hands, smooshing them together. "Fine." She rips the blanket off me and wraps it around her. "You're annoying, but I love you."

With my back turned, pretending to watch the game I stuff handfuls of popcorn in my mouth, anxiously waiting for her to return with all the juicy details. Within a minute or two, she plops back down next to me.

"He said you're going to have to ask him yourself," Jessica says, breathlessly.

"Who said that? The new guy or Ryan?" Ryan was in our grade, and he was kind of a jerk.

"Both."

"Ugh. Why are they being so difficult?" I cross my arms and stuffed another fistful of popcorn in my mouth.

"Probably because you won't be *his* girlfriend. You know Ryan is probably jealous, he's liked you forever."

"Well, it's not my fault he can't spell... I like to write letters back and forth with someone who can read and write. And he's also mean which makes him ugly, too." Jessica covers her mouth and giggles.

"Are you going to go talk to him?" she asks.

I shake my head. "No, never mind. I don't want to. Forget it."

"Yes, you do. Go," she says, pushing me off the seat. "Go!"

When I look back, she's giving me a thumbs up, and I thought right then I might puke on my shoes. I walk slowly, carefully watching my feet march up the bleachers. The last thing I want to do is fall between them. When I look up, my stomach flips.

"Hi," I say, my voice sounding much too nervous and shaky. Ryan is smiling like an idiot that I wish I could slap. I hate playing this game, but I don't just want to know who this guy is, I need to know.

"Jess said you were asking about my friend," Ryan says, crossing his arms.

I nod, trying not to be awkward but failing miserably.

"This is Paul," Ryan adds. I can't keep my eyes off him as I get closer. I try. "He's Donny's little cousin. We took him under our wing all summer. He's one of us now," he says, slugging his arm playfully. I nod, this time making eye contact with Paul.

"Nice to meet you," he says, his voice deeper and warmer than I expected.

"Same," I say, playing it cool as if I wasn't at all interested. Because according to the magazines, that's what you do. You act uninterested when you're interested.

"Do you go here?" I ask.

He smirks. "Do *you* go here?"

"Yes, I'm a sophomore." I push my hair behind my ears. "You?"

"Freshman."

I laugh and instantly feel more comfortable knowing now

that I was older than him.

"Oh, you're just a little guy," I say. "Welcome to high school."

He chuckles. "Is it your high school? Do you own the school or are you the principal?"

Oh, he's funny. I cover my mouth and teeth with my hand as I attempt to hide my real monstrous laugh. I can't do my cute girly laugh when someone is genuinely funny.

"I'm your elder, you should be respectful you know." I nudge his arm and giggle.

Then I felt it. That spark.

"Alright. I'll respect you, but only because you're smaller than me. I'll look out for you, okay? If anyone picks on you, come find me."

"You're funny." And he's cute. The perfect combination.

"What's your name?" He leans closer to me.

"Jade."

"Nice to meet you, elder Jade." He extends his warm hand for me to shake. He looks at me and smiles. I notice this adorable freckle that rests above his lip, and I realize just then how badly I want to kiss him.

"I guess it's nice to meet you, Paul." My stomach flutters in and out of nervous twists while standing next to him.

"I'm going to get a hot cocoa from the concession stand, I'll see you—" I say, turning away from him.

"Want me to come with you?" he interrupts, extending his hand out to my shoulder softly, breaking away from Ryan and the boys. "You know, to keep you safe. You're so small, I don't want you to get lost in the crowd or something." He laughs as I nudge him with my elbow and catch myself falling against his chest. There's this sudden comfort with him like I have known him for years in only a matter of moments.

Then it happens. I find myself leaving my friends that I have known for years behind to hang out with a boy I barely know.

We walk to the concession booth together and stand in the long line.

"Hot cocoa is the worst," he says. "It's just chocolate milk all warmed up. I'm getting a coffee."

"I didn't know you were such an old man. Do you have a wife and kids, sir?" I tease. He laughs and leans his body into mine playfully.

"I don't, just three baby sisters. I need coffee to stay awake sometimes. I help my grandma out a lot, my grandpa is always working on the farm. I'm basically the man of the house, so I stay caffeinated."

I consider asking about his parents, but get the feeling I'd rather not want to know.

"That sounds like a lot of work. I have one baby sister, and she's exhausting."

"You should try coffee."

"Won't it keep me up all night?"

"Not if you have a little sister. You'll be tired no matter what."

"My sister is three, so maybe I should start drinking coffee."

"My youngest sister is three, too."

I shiver and squeeze my shoulders tight, blowing warm air into my hands with my mouth. The sky is dark, and the air is cool and thin. Paul takes off his hooded sweatshirt.

"You want to wear this?"

"Oh no, that's alright. You wear it. It's cold."

"No. Here, you take it." He pushes the sweatshirt into my cradled arms.

"Thanks." I pull it over my head, the soft, over washed fabric feels like butter on my skin. I breathe in his scent—clean laundry, wood, and earth.

"It's clean, I did laundry yesterday," he says, clutching his strong arms for a second before letting them hang exposed. I try not to notice how strong he looks, but it's too late. It's all I can see now.

"You do your own laundry?" I tip my chin in disbelief.

"Didn't I tell you I'm one of five kids?" he laughs. "Yeah, well, I do laundry to help out. Grandma Lo is busy enough, between working at the store and raising us. My grandpa works nights at the factory. If I didn't do my own laundry, I wouldn't look this good." He winks.

"Or smell this good. Wow, I could live in this sweater forever."

"Then keep it. It's yours."

"Seriously? Wouldn't you miss it?" I run my hands over the soft, gray fabric.

"Nah, I think I'd regret not seeing a pretty girl happy more."

The rest of the football game, I find myself snuggled up under a knit blanket next to him and away from our friends in the bleachers close together. Under the blanket, I feel his hand reach for mine. Somehow, I know this is just the beginning.

CHAPTER TWO

A FEW DAYS later, I see him on a run. He must've seen me in the front yard getting off the school bus. We just moved into a new home and unbeknownst to me, Paul was my new neighbor. Not exactly next door, but close enough to walk to. He didn't have a phone yet when we met, so he first put handwritten letters in my mailbox. And since I knew where he lived, I put letters back in his mailbox, too. I was too lazy to walk all that way and hated getting my shoes muddy down the dirt road, so I would steal a stamp from my mom and mail them. The good news is, he had great grammar and he knew how to spell. The bad news is all the anticipation I feel waiting for his replies.

We wrote back and forth about our favorite music, what movies we were watching and what school was like for each other. On his last note, he asked for my phone number. Since we weren't in the same grade, I didn't see him at school much, even though we went to the same campus. The next day I had a call on the house phone, luckily, I answer and not my parents.

"Don't have a cell phone yet, but my hands are tired from all these love letters I've been writing you." His voice, deep and mature for his age, makes my knees wobbly when it hits my ears. I start spiraling the phone cord with my finger around and around. If I could see my own goofy smiling face right now, I would want to smack myself. I'm too happy for my own good.

"Love letters? That's what these are, huh?" I say, smiling even bigger into the phone, clutching the latest letter to my chest with my chipped, purple nails.

"Well, yeah… I mean, I'm not writing them to anyone else."

"Me either…" I say. I know where this is going. And if I have any way to make it just right, this can't happen. Not yet.

"You know, you're too young to be my boyfriend. You're only 14." It feels harsh, but I don't know any other way to put it.

"Well, good thing you said it first, because I was worried that you're too old of a lady to be my girl anyway. Much, much too old," he laughs. Thankfully, he isn't hurt. And if he is, he is very good at hiding it.

"It's cool if you were to date an older girl, that makes you cool. Me? Not so much."

"Since when? See many men dating older women? I don't think so."

I glance over my shoulder, holding the phone tight to my face and spin around to make sure no one is around me.

"It's not like we're years apart—just one," I say, convincing myself into saying yes to the feelings I can longer control.

"Exactly. I'm glad you said it first." I can picture his face, that sarcastic smile. The little freckle above his lip.

"So, we aren't dating then. It's settled. You're not my boyfriend, because I'm too old for you." A piece of me crumbles inside, though it's hard to decide where it's located, I can feel it from my head to my toes.

"I've been enjoying practicing my good handwriting, made the muscles in my hands stronger, too," he faintly laughs. "It would be a shame to give it all up now…"

"I'll still write you back, silly." The cord twirls again in my fingers as I picture his hands weaved through mine.

"I only want to write letters to my girl."

"Really? Well, I'm not anyone else's girl if that helps."

"It might."

"How about I wait until you're a little older to officially be your girl?"

"And what are you right now then if you aren't my girl?"

"Hmm," I say, thinking of what I might be. "Your girl... in waiting."

"My girl in waiting. Alright. Can I still see you and can we still be friends?"

"Yes and yes. Everything will be the same. We just can't...fall in the L word, and you can't officially be my boyfriend until you're 15... and a half. That way, we only have six months of me doing all the driving around."

"Do we have any other rules, elder Jade?" Paul laughs.

"We can't kiss anyone else." I don't want Paul to think I haven't kissed anyone, and I wasn't sure if he has either, so I make sure to mention it just in case.

"Anyone else? That's a long time without kissing anyone. We haven't even kissed."

I stay silent, thinking of what I might say. Thinking of nothing other than kissing him for the first time.

"So, it's pretty much like you are going to be my girl, even if we don't say that's what it is out loud." He laughs again, knowing this is obviously ridiculous, but he never says it.

A stirring, unraveling sensation consumes me, and a wave of confidence takes over.

"Can you do me favor? Meet me at the stop sign?" I say. The stop sign on our street is the halfway point between our houses. My heart starts pounding. The unraveling turns into a sea-sick feeling.

"Why?"

"I have something to give you," I say, shoving my feet as quickly as I can into my tennis shoes. The door opens, it's my mom with my baby sister on her hip.

"I'll be there in 15 minutes. Ten if I run," he says.

"Can you run?" I say, already breathless.

I lace up my tennis shoes, throw on a jean jacket and head toward the door.

"Where are you going, Jade? Dinner is in twenty minutes, I brought home Lonnie's Pizza."

"I'll be back by dinner. I'm going to run. Need some fresh air."

Once outside and down the road a bit past my house, I start to run. My breath is pulling in the cool fall air faster and faster. The gravel is crushing hard beneath my feet, and sure enough, it had rained this week, and the road is mucking up my shoes. A couple times I feel like stopping to catch my breath, but I keep running with the intense motivation of seeing Paul's face. I throw both elbows back faster and faster behind me. When I hit the point in the road just over the hill, Paul's body is running towards me. At the same time, I also see a car behind him, and I run faster.

"Paul!" I yell out. "Paul!" He must hear the car behind him as he runs toward the shoulder of the road. He starts walking while I keep running. Paul bends over at his knees to catch his breath and then stands there with his hands over his head, pacing side to side. When I get close enough to the stop sign, I start slowing down, taking my jacket off to tie it around my waist.

"Hey," he says, smiling.

"I have something for you," I say, swallowing down any fear I had until this moment.

"What is it?"

"This," I say, closing my eyes, pulling his cold face into mine for our first kiss. His lips felt soft, and he put his arms around me. I felt it then. The feeling of warm honey flowing around inside of my stomach. My breath slowed and my shoulders fell forward into his chest. Without effort, I sink into a full body surrender as we melt together. From this moment and every moment after I knew it would be different—the first taste of him was just the beginning.

"I almost got hit by a car." He laughs as I pull away from him. "But it was worth it for this. I would definitely almost get hit by a car again for it." He leans in to kiss me again and my body tingles from my head to my toes.

"I realized we hadn't kissed. So, I figured if maybe we had, you wouldn't want to kiss anyone else."

"Can I tell you a secret?" he says.

I nod.

"I wouldn't have kissed anyone else anyway. I would've happily waited to kiss you." He pulls his hands from his pockets and grabs mine.

I smile. "Really?"

He smiles and shrugs. "You're the only one I want to kiss."

Paul isn't like most teenage boys his age—he was wholesome, patient, and sweet.

I believe him. And then, he kisses me again.

ONCE A WEEK, we met for a kiss at the stop sign. We run like lunatics into each other's arms, with no one watching but the birds and an open corn field. After all the running, I was forced to tell my parents that I was trying out for the track and field team in the spring. Told them all the running I had been doing was practice. They even bought me new shoes to support my new running habit. Of course, it was a lie. I had no real interest in running on a team or winning a medal. I just wanted to see Paul. All it would take was a phone call after school for him to say,

"Race you there?" and the next thing we knew, we are locking lips breathlessly after the ten-minute run.

"How many winded kisses will it take for you to be my girl?" he asks, holding me against his chest, kissing the side of my forehead.

"How many kisses do you think you'll keep running for?"

"As many as it takes."

WINTER CAME AND running to the stop sign became more difficult. It snows a lot in Ohio and even when it doesn't, it's too cold to go on a run outside. Even the letters became sparse. I didn't turn sixteen until August, and the only way for Paul and me to see each other is if our family knew that we were spending time together. If they knew, they could drive us to each other's houses or even to the movies for a date, even though Paul didn't think his grandparents would like the idea of him hanging out with a girl, especially an older girl going into her junior year.

"They probably would think you would be pressuring me for... you know," he whispers into the phone.

"No, I don't. What?" I know, I just want to hear him say the word. Sex.

"To have sex... with me." When he says it, a part of me tingles in a place that no one else knows about.

"Well, I'd never do that, so..."

"Have sex?" he whispers.

"No, of course I will have sex, genius." I laugh. "I mean with you. I mean... pressure you to with me." I am fumbling over my words as I picture it in my head. "That's not something girls do."

"So, you're saying you would have sex me?" he laughs, whispering the word sex into the phone.

"You're so dumb. I'm hanging up," I tease.

"Have you ever, you know?" he asks me quietly.

"Have you?" I ask instead of answering no.

"No. I haven't."

"Well, me either. That settles that."

"I think they might let us hang out. I think we should tell them."

"What do we tell them?"

"That we're—friends."

"We are friends. It won't technically be lying."

"If they ask how I know you since you're older, what do I say?"

"Just say you met me at a football game, duh. Still not a lie."

"Okay. Good plan. We just won't lie. We are just friends anyway."

"Friends who sometimes kiss." He laughs, and I do, too. "My girl in waiting."

"No one needs to know that part."

A WEEK LATER, I am invited to Paul's for an after-church brunch at his house. I am also invited to church but make an excuse about needing to babysit my little sister so I couldn't attend. I was terrified of church. I imagined myself sitting there, thinking of all the sinful acts I wanted to do to Paul. Somehow, I thought my dirtiness would be all over my face, like I couldn't hide from the preacher or Jesus. It was bad enough my diary had to witness what was inside of my head, God didn't need to know, too.

We didn't grow up religious, so I had no idea what to do at church and I wasn't ready to find out on my first official date with Paul. If that's even what it was. Paul called when they got home from church and told me I could walk down fifteen minutes to noon. I didn't want to look stupid when everyone else was likely in church clothes, so I decided to wear a pale gray, short-sleeved dress with tiny white daisies on it that hit just below the knee and slip-on shoes I wore for special occasions like weddings and parties. I didn't want to wear jeans because people like to dress up for church. I also know I needed to make a good first impression, so instead of walking on the dirt road and ruining my outfit, I have my mom drop me off to save me the long walk. Lord knows I'm not running today.

When I walk in the door, the smell of fresh bacon and eggs greeted me. Coffee, buttered biscuits, honey, and blackberry jam dressed the table. Old, country style plates are set on the table for all eight of us. I feel shy at first. As I picked at my fingernails, I notice I have the hardest time bringing my head up or looking his grandfather in the eyes. Something about the old Southern man in a suit terrifies me. His face is cold and stern looking, flecked with gray, just-shaven stubble on his bold jawline. He tries to be friendly, which makes it even scarier, because being friendly isn't his natural state, especially after all Paul has told me about him.

He's a man I don't want to like, and therefore, don't care if he likes me either. I just want to be likeable enough to spend more time with Paul. I can't misstep or misspeak, and I must be careful of my every move. I know he is watching, judging, and scoring me.

The farmhouse is old but sturdy and large. Tidy and clean, yet everything looks worn down and cozy, just like a grandparent's house should be. From the big windows you can see cows in the pastures, baby sheep trailing after mama sheep, an old white barn, chickens wandering around the yard, and a big, rusty green tractor resting in the grass. I imagine Paul shirtless and sweaty riding the tractor and baking in the sun. I catch myself blushing at the thought and then look around, wondering if anyone could sense what I felt inside. Good thing I didn't go to church.

His grandma calls me from the kitchen, "You ever make homemade biscuits, Jade?" Amazed she's talking to me, I clear my throat and walk into the kitchen.

"No, ma'am," I say. "My mom isn't much of a cook. Well, she cooks but not from scratch. Not like this. Everything looks and smells so good." She puts her apron on, ties it around her wide waist.

"I see," she says, raising her eyebrows a bit in concern. "It's that whole generation, sweetie. They ain't making much if it don't come from a box or baggie." She turns around, taking a good look at me as she smiles—her plump, rosy cheeks push her big glasses up. "Oh, Paul. He always knows something good when he sees it." She pulls me into her round, doughy body, still in her church dress and pearls. "If Paul approves, then so do I." Her perfume coats my mouth, and I try not to cough. The smell is so strong, I hold my breath until she lets go.

"I have another batch of biscuits to make, I forgot you were coming, and I wanted to make sure you get enough to eat." She hands me an apron. "You could use a bit more meat on your bones. And I'll be sure to send you home with some to take to your parents. You'll be a baker before I'm done with you."

She moves around the kitchen as if she were gliding on water, effortless and in her element. She reaches for the flour and hands it to me.

"I don't think we even have flour in our house," I say holding the heavy container of flour. With her body now half in the fridge, she pulls out a Mason jar and a glass bottle of milk.

"Today, we're going to fix that. You'll know how to make your own biscuits. And once I teach you how easy that is, you'll want to make everything else yourself." She puts the glass in my hand. "Buttermilk, sweetheart. From our cows out back. Not the grocery store, these biscuits come straight from the farm to our table. We aren't putting money back into people's wallets who don't need the paycheck more than we do. We don't rely on nobody in this house other than the land and the Lord."

Paul peeks in from the dining room, pouring orange juice into the glasses, trying to keep his eyes off me in an apron.

"If there is ever another Great Depression or if, God forbid, times get tough like that ever again, we will be prepared on this homestead and so will every generation that lives in this house after me."

I always thought of her generation to be one to unnecessarily panic, even if they did have a good reason to feel the way they did. I tried but could never imagine a world that would be as complicated as the one she knew at my age. So much has changed for the better, I don't think I need to take that bit to heart, but I am curious how to make these biscuits, so I make sure to pay close attention.

The first batch looks and smells so good, I can't believe I helped make them. Imagining having them any time I want, so long as I make them myself, makes me feel a sense of confidence and independence I've never felt. My stomach begins to rumble as I wash my hands in the sink. I haven't eaten yet because I am too nervous to. I've never been more anxious in my life to learn a new skill with my number one motivation being to eat as many of these biscuits as I possibly can. I imagine the melted butter and the cool jam on the flakey top. My mouth starts to water.

"Mrs. Thompson, where do you want the buttermilk?" I ask, washing my hands in the sink.

"Call me Grandma Lo. And once your hands are dry, head over to this wooden block next to the rolling pin and I'll take it from here."

With her big, wrinkled palms, she guides me around each ingredient, letting me pour them into the large glass bowl one by one. After mixing, we roll the gummy dough onto the board with a flour coated rolling pin. After we place them in the oven and set the timer, she pats me on the back.

"See? Not so hard, was it?" She smiles.

"It's all you," I say. "You make it easy. Can Paul make these, too?"

She laughs. "Only me, my mamaw and God know this recipe, and now you. Someday, I'll share it with his sisters when they're older. I only share it with women who have the heart to be in the kitchen. I could see it in your eyes, the sparkle you got when you saw the table. The same one I had when my mamaw taught me."

I untie my apron and place it back in her hands. "I'm honored. I'll guard this recipe with my life now." I smile as she busies around the kitchen putting things back in their place. Paul's sisters squeal and play with toys in the background from the living room.

"That's good, honey. If Paul has a future on this farm like his granddaddy, he's going to need a lady someday to whip him up these biscuits after a hard day's work." She chuckles and puts a few dirty dishes into soapy water.

"Oh, we aren't… well, I don't think I am his…"

"If you're here, you are." She looks at me and winks. "But don't worry. We won't tell his Pop-Pop. He's the one with the biggest opinions." I nod. "Paul is a young man that is sure of himself, always has been," she says. "If he likes something or someone, you know it. But he's careful with his heart, too, and he doesn't trust just anyone with it. He's only allowed a handful of his friends over for a sleepover as a child and doesn't get too close with many people. Especially after what happened with his parents."

She unties her apron and hangs it on a nail near the pantry. She closes the pantry door. "And who could blame him?" she quietly adds. "Poor kid lost his mom and dad in the same day when he was only four."

"What happened?" Surprised I even asked, I feel a twinge of guilt – maybe I have asked too much too soon and maybe it isn't any of my business. She leans to peek into the dining room and then back into my shoulder to whisper.

"They passed on in a house fire. It was all over the news back in ninety-seven." She tightens her lips and clears her throat. "Meth lab explosion." My eyes widen, and my hungry gut sours. "Luckily, we had the kids already. CPS had been called three months prior. It's not a story we tell often, especially because we raised his daddy in the church. We expected better out of him. He was a God-fearing man that got wrapped up with the wrong crowd, pulling his beautiful wife and their kids into that whole mess."

"I'm so sorry. I can't imagine…"

"Thirty-two. He was only thirty-two." She wipes a tear from her eye with a handkerchief. "It's alright." She blows a breath of air out and pats her hair. "We did the best we could."

Not knowing what to say or how to say it, I nod and find my hand embracing her shoulder.

"Addiction doesn't care that we did our best as parents. It didn't care that he was a kind and loving man with a bad problem." She swallows, clears her throat, and collects herself. "Anyway," she says and dabs the corner of her eye again, "Paul's heart is big, but he's careful with it. You be careful with it too, you hear?" I nod again.

Knowing this secret about Paul during our first date makes it hard to forget. Not only is it the first time I am in his house, the first time I meet his family, and the first time I ever made biscuits, it's also the first time I feel myself falling in love so deeply with someone in a way I wasn't prepared for. From this moment forward, I know there will be a force inside of me that wants to keep his heart safe and carry it with me forever, no matter what the future holds. Paul's story has become engrained in my own. His scars feel like mine. His pain, his sadness, his past, all became something I want so badly to love into wholeness again. I couldn't erase what happened to him, but I would if I could. And that's a feeling I never felt for anyone else.

While we sat at the table, I felt I knew Paul on a deeper level. When he locked his eyes with mine and grabbed my hand under the table during prayer, it was the moment I felt it. I love this boy, and I wanted everyone to know about it, including Paul. Which means I now have two secrets.

CHAPTER THREE

THE INEVITABLE HAPPENS.

Though I tried to wait a full year and half, we are officially dating, and everyone knows about it. I've been non-stop teased for dating a boy younger than me, and not only that, he's also a poor farmer boy. Not that anyone in Tiffin was exceptionally well to do; but there were some kids who certainly had more than others. And Paul wasn't that kid.

"You could be dating Josh or Alex, but you chose Paul?!" my friends scoff. What they meant was the boys that played sports, had more money, were more popular. People didn't understand why I chose Paul. No one sees what I see in him. No one. Even my mom laughs when I place a picture of him by my bedside.

"Him?!" she exclaims, pointing to his school picture where he's wearing glasses and an admittedly nerdy-looking cardigan. He has since gotten contacts after the school photo. He had to save enough money to get them, since his grandparents wouldn't get them for him—because they were too expensive. That's the thing about Paul, if he wants something, he's determined to make it happen.

"Yeah," I smile, straightening the photo upright against a few books. "Him."

Yes, he's younger, but he's also more mature than most boys I know. He's younger, but he is so intelligent that he's two grades above his math and science level, making him smarter than I am.

He is also taller and fuller than the boys in my grade, too. He's a corn-fed country boy as my mom would say. When he was even younger, he was so gifted that the elementary school had to take him by bus to the middle school for math class. He is different. And I realized quickly that I'm attracted to that. I like that he knows more than I do. I always felt like it would be boring to be with someone who didn't teach me anything or challenge me, and that's exactly what Paul does. Paul teaches me about everything. He teaches me how to ice skate, skip rocks, shoot a gun, make homemade mac and cheese from scratch, do laundry, slice a watermelon, rehearse all the U.S capitals with me.

Today after school, we take a walk in the woods behind his house, just past the farm. We follow a path Paul made with the tractor, holding hands until we stop to sit beside a creek, just far enough back for us to kiss without anyone seeing or his sisters asking to come with us. Next to the babbling water, we sit down on a fallen log, and I feel words that have been buried too long begin to bubble up.

"I've been keeping a couple secrets, Paul," I admit. His face turns white; I can tell he's afraid of what I might say next. It comes out fast, much faster than I was hoping it would. "Grandma Lo told me what happened to your parents. The first day I met her, when we were making biscuits." I look down at my hands. "I'm really sorry I kept that from you, but I didn't know how to talk about it. I can't imagine how hard that must've been for you. I hate thinking about it, actually."

I don't know whether I should say it out loud or leave it unspoken, but now it is too late. I feel his sorrow in my bones, and from this moment forward, I will carry his pain with me like it is my own. I could feel it begging for a witness, and I want to carry this together. He shouldn't have to carry this alone.

Paul sits there quietly for a minute with his head down.

"I bet it's still hard to believe at times." I say, picking at my jean pocket.

"Yeah," he says, collecting his words as he stares at the ground.

"Even though it has been eleven, almost twelve years now, it's still...." he swallows and bites his lip. "Thankfully, we were staying with my grandparents already or else... I would've been dead, too."

"I'm glad you're alive," I say, grabbing his hand in mine. He squeezes mine back tighter.

"Me too." He looks away and mumbles under his breath. "I'm glad they're dead."

"That's a little harsh. You don't mean that, do you?"

"So is doing meth and abandoning your children who needed you."

"You have a solid point." If he hates his parents, then so do I. Even though I don't need convincing to be angry at them for what they did to him, I am well on my way on my own.

We sit there silently for a bit. Words feel heavy. I put my arm around his shoulders, pull him into a hug, and rest my head on his shoulder.

"You know, I think it's pretty incredible that even after all that you've been through, you are still this amazing person."

He turns his head and locks eyes with mine, drawing his lips in to kiss me. This time when he does, it feels different. Better. I feel it from the inside out.

"Jade." He looks away at the creek. The sun is starting to set already, and the air is cold on my cheeks.

"Yeah?" I say, turning to him. I notice a few freckles on his nose light up under the sun.

"I love you." He turns and looks at me now.

"How do you know?" I ask. Inside I am screaming, *I love you, too.*

"I just know."

"Are you sure? What if it's just *really like* and not really love." I fumble around with my restless hands, the same hands that beg to touch him in places that I haven't yet. Places only my diary knows about.

"I do really like you, but I know it's love." He smirks at me then.

"And you're sure?" A small part of me feels resistant to his confession, like it's too good to be true. That maybe I didn't deserve it.

"It's not really something I can explain." He stands up then, tossing a rock into the creek. "It's something I feel. Something I have been feeling. When I'm not with you, you're on my mind all day, every day. The only thing I can think about is seeing you again. When I wake up, it's you. Before I sleep, it's you. Even when I'm with you, it's still not enough."

I pause, not because I don't agree with, but because everything he's saying is exactly how I have been feeling.

"I know," I finally say. "I feel it, too."

"You do?" His shoulders sag in relief as he turns to look at me now.

"That was my second secret," I say. "Of course. If that's what love is, then I think I really do love you, Paul."

"Can I tell you something else?"

I nod, catching his eyes.

"I've never told anyone that before. It wasn't easy to do—"

He covers his mouth for a second with his hand. When he removes it, he's smiling at me. He gives me those eyes.

"I haven't either."

"Can you say it again? It sounds so nice coming from your mouth." His voice sounds like sex, and for the first time, it makes me so painfully aroused that I start to throb in new places.

"I love you."

"Maybe a little louder." He laughs. "So, the cows can hear you."

"You're ridiculous," I tease and shake my head. "Fine. I'll do it." I stand up and shout so the whole county road and all the cows, chickens, sheep, and their babies can hear. "I love you, Paul!" I look at him, my cheeks red and my throat tender, "Happy now?"

"That was good." He scratches his chin and makes a face. "I think you can do better. This time so the worms underground can hear." He laughs again, his smile dimpling into his cheeks.

"I love you, Paul, forever and ever!" I shout so loud my throat burns a little as it comes out. That last part came out without effort and unplanned.

He kisses me then.

"How was that?" I ask, breathless.

"Forever, huh?" He smiles, brushing my arm with his hand.

"Forever." I face him, wrap my arms around his neck. "I will love you forever and beyond."

We stand there, watching the sun settle under tired, golden clouds, our shadows holding hands underneath us. The scent of a new season is just under our noses.

"And beyond," he agrees.

CHAPTER FOUR

I T'S RAINING TODAY. And rain has kind of become "our thing." When it rains, Paul likes to pull the car into an empty parking lot, blast a cheesy country love song and dance with me outside until we're soaked.

"You know the drill. Turn it up as loud as it goes, open the door, and run out with me on the count of three," he says, nodding at the car stereo as he unbuckles his seat belt in the dark, high school parking lot. The place we go to disappear and fade into each other. A small town doesn't offer much for entertainment outside of a smoky bowling alley or a movie theatre. When we're bored of our options, we find ourselves here.

It's warm for a spring night in Tiffin, so I agree to this. I twist the knob to full blast; the crooning twangy voices and guitar strings fill the openness of the outside air. It's just me and Paul.

"Okay ready? One... two... three." We ran out together and into each other's arms, swaying our happy, dancing bodies in front of the car, the dim lights shining onto us.

"Damn. How did I get so lucky?" He says after kissing my wet forehead. He pulls me in closer to him. "This cool, older girl gave me a chance and now here we are."

"Older girl." I laugh and look up at him. "I forget that I'm your elder. Maybe that's why you like me so much."

"Nah," he says, running his hands through my wet hair. "It's hard to put my finger on what it is exactly. Because honestly, it's everything." He kisses me hard, the passion flowing through his lips is strong and intense. My body fires up on all cylinders, and I grab tightly onto his back, pulling him closer and closer. I've never wanted him so close. He pulls away and looks at me. I look back and we both say it without saying it at all.

"That's enough rain. Let's dry off, shall we?" he says, picking me up and carrying me to the car. He opens the back seat door and helps me in. Paul keeps towels in his car for our spontaneous rainy dances, it's adorable. He starts to dry me off when I pull his body close to mine again. Something in me needs him closer than ever.

"I think I'd dry faster without my clothes," I say. He looks at me and swallows.

"Yeah, I think so, too." He's seen my bare chest before. We've gotten up to second base, but never more than that. Not yet. I remove everything except for my underwear.

"I think I should take mine off, too. To dry faster," he says, sliding his wet pants off first.

I nod at him; my mouth falling open as I watch him undress. He leans over my body, drying off my legs and kissing them all with each upward movement. Something comes over me, and I rip the towel from him and put his hand inside of underwear.

"Take them off, please," I say, still locking his eyes. With lips onto mine, breathing into me, he slides them off.

He traces the inside of my legs with his hands before moving them higher and higher. He looks at me as if he's asking for my approval. I nod again and let his fingers explore the inside of me as I moan with my mouth on his neck.

Feeling nearly possessed by him, I whisper in his ear, "Do you have a condom?"

He pulls away and looks at me.

"Are you sure?" he asks, kissing my lips again. He breathes me in deeply with his forehead resting on mine.

"Yeah."

He fumbles into his wallet and pulls out a wrinkled condom. I wonder how long he's had it in there and how long he's been waiting to do this with me. If he was ever feeling impatient, I never knew about it. I wasn't sure when I'd be ready, but I knew I wanted to lose it to Paul. I had been telling my diary about it for months, and tonight I feel ready. I feel safe.

He rolls the condom down slowly, and my stomach sinks a little. *This is really happening.*

With his body leaning over mine, I kiss his shoulder.

"Jade," he says.

"What?" I swallow and take a deep breath in as his scent fills every bit of emptiness that has ever existed inside of me.

"I love you. I just wanted you to know again."

With Paul resting at the base of me, I lean my head back, close my eyes, and smile as he enters me slowly.

"I love you, too."

WHEN YOU LOVE someone, you crave them. And since that night, I found myself always craving Paul.

Before I am on my knees with Paul in my mouth this morning, I was flipping him pancakes. Rarely are we left alone, but when we are, we don't waste any time anymore. We know we only have an hour and half to do what we've been dying for each other from the last moment we were together, which was just a week ago. Paul's grandparents are at church and then they're stopping at the feed and mill store for the farm on their way home. We calculated it will give us at least two hours. Paul faked being sick, and I rode my bike there as fast as I could. When we aren't together, days feels like weeks. Weeks like months. Time is an illusion that moves much too quickly when we are.

"You're such a good cook," Paul says as he kisses my cheek. I'm mixing the flour, buttermilk, eggs to make batter for the pancakes. When we're alone, we like to play house. We don't initially try to play it though; it just comes natural for us. Often, he has no idea we're playing, but I do. I pretend this farmhouse is all mine. Well, ours. I pretend we live here with no one else. The whole five-bedroom, wooden home, ours. Of course, I'd decorate it differently. The antiques and creepy knickknacks would have to go. His grandmother's rooster figurine collection, gone. The moth-ball scented quilts spread over the tops of the sofas, gone. And I would make sure we had a bigger television. And internet, we'd definitely need internet. I'd upgrade the old antique stove to something easier to use, a stove with buttons to press. I hate using these old clicking knobs. Every time we use it, I'm afraid it'll burst into flames and burn the house down.

Since Paul lives with his grandparents, it has always felt like he lives in a time capsule, and when I visit, I'm transported to an older, simpler time in life. There is a sort of peaceful presence in this home, but one too many Jesus paintings for me. Before doing an ungodly premarital act on Paul, I try to turn my head away from Jesus. The judgment is too much for us both, I think. It doesn't stop me though. I slide down slowly to my knees, handing Paul the spatula.

"Can I trust you to not burn our breakfast?" Unbuttoning his jeans, he nods. "Though, it will be very, very hard," he laughs, winking down at me.

"Good one," I say with a grin.

Pleasing him has become as normal as breathing. I'm bleeding this week, and instead of the mess and clean up, I surprise him with another one of his delights.

The last time I was bleeding when we were alone, we took a

bath together and he swam inside of me in the clawfoot tub. It wasn't as messy as I thought it would be, and it was more pleasant than we both expected. I thought he would've been freaked out, but he assured me that watching cows give birth and having sisters of his own made him more in touch with females in general. He knew too much for his age, and because of it, I have never felt safer.

Because we don't have time to run the bath and we're also short on time, I know oral is a quick way to make myself linger on him until the next time we can be together. Not to mention, I love having him in my mouth. We don't always need to have sex, but we always want to. We can't get close enough. Even when he's inside of me, it still doesn't feel close enough.

I use some techniques I read in my mother's Cosmopolitan magazine. I take the shaft firmly in my hands, lick around the fleshy veiny parts like I'm enjoying a warm meaty ice cream cone. I try to remember which is most important, the sucking or the licking. I can't remember, so I try to do equal parts of both. Paul seems to enjoy it, while still managing to flip the pancakes in between moans. I stop for a second to tell him to keep his eyes open or they will burn. When he comes, I clean up and wash off in the kitchen sink. For a second, a wave of sinful shame comes over my body as I imagine his old grandmother washing dishes in this sink later today. I'm glad this house doesn't talk.

Getting the sexy parts over with in the beginning usually means we spend the rest of the time together more present and emotionally connected. If we hadn't, the tension would've consumed us until we did. I prefer doing it first, talking after, but sometimes, we aren't always that lucky. We spend hours secretly tracing the lines of our underwear with our fingers. Every private corner we turn, he slips a quick finger inside of me and sucks on my mouth. His passion for me and my body burn into my brain until we are able to find a way to release. And once released, it's as if we can step back into our bodies and exist as humans again. Because when we aren't human, we're animals. All who are madly in love are.

Paul zips his pants and looks at the kitchen clock.

"We only have about forty-five minutes left," he says, his voice pained.

"It's never enough time," I say, wrapping my arms around his neck.

"I know." He kisses my forehead. "I don't think it ever will be enough time. Even forever doesn't feel long enough."

I nod and swallow any sad thoughts of our morbidity down. I don't even want to picture it for a second. In this moment, I wish I could freeze time and be sixteen forever.

We sit down to eat breakfast together quickly and spend the last twenty minutes cuddled into each other's arms on the rocking chair on the front wrap-around porch. The cows are laying in the heat of the sun, the chickens are calm, and everything feels at peace. Even with all that peace, something restless bubbles up inside of me. I love this, but I always want more. I hate myself when this feeling finds me and ruins a good moment.

"Someday I'm going to leave this town. Move to a big city. Do something big with my life," I say, looking at the muddy farm. "What do you want to be when you're older?"

"Paul. I hope I can be him as long as possible," he laughs and I find myself frustrated with him for the first time, though I don't show it. He must be able to feel it because he responds quickly after that.

"Stay here and take care of my grandparents like they took care of me. Return the favor," he says, his voice content. I feel it then. My insides spin around a little uneasy. I can hardly contain this feeling stirring inside of me.

"Don't you want more?" I ask, confused.

"I don't think I was raised wanting more, just happy to have what I've already got." He looks at me then, a little fear grows in his eyes.

"I know, but still." I grab his hand, hoping that maybe he'd see the world the same way I do if he could feel my skin as I spoke.

"If you didn't feel like you owed anyone anything, where would you want to be? What would you do?"

Paul looked out into the farm, scanned the field and the barn with his golden eyes. He takes a while to respond and shakes his head.

"I don't know. Never let my thoughts wander farther than the Painsville river." He smiles then. It was hard to tell if that was really what he wanted or if it was all his mind would allow.

"That's only 30 minutes away."

"I know."

"I can't imagine staying here forever. I hate this town." His face looks hurt as the words leave my mouth, as if I just insulted someone he loved dearly. I can't hold it in, the rest came out with force and much faster than I would have liked.

"It's—boring. No one does anything great here. There's nothing to do." My voice becomes more aggravated, and Paul's smile fades from his face before it turns stoic, protective.

"That's what I like about it. There's nothing to prove, you have what you need. It's quiet, simple, peaceful."

I pull away and turn to face him. "Would you come with me? If I moved away to the big city? To start a brand-new life, make some big dreams come true. Could you do it?"

"Let me ask you a better question." He grabs my hand then, his face softens. "Could you stay here with me? Marry me and make all my dreams come true, give me four children to raise on this farm, and let me show you what dreams are made of?"

I lay my head back down onto his chest and stare up into the sky.

"What happens when two stubborn people are in love?"

"That's easy. Compromise. We find a solution we both love."

"And if we don't?"

"Let's not get ahead of ourselves," he says, looking back at the clock hanging in the kitchen window behind us. "Right now, is all that matters."

CHAPTER FIVE

I T WASN'T SUPPOSED to end.

If you asked us before this day, we would've said we'd be together forever. It's silly to say that at sixteen, but even if we couldn't look that far into the future, even if we didn't know how we'd spend the weekend together, we knew how we'd spend the next year, and the year after that. We had tunnel vision for only each other, that's all that mattered then.

The day that broke us started out perfectly. My parents had already left for work, so it was just me at home, my little sister is at daycare. Paul drove to my house to pick me up for school, as he started to do since he got his license four months ago. I hear him open the door and let himself in.

"Hey," he shouts from the kitchen. "I'm here a little early, brought you something." He sets down the warm cups of gas station coffee and cocoa, opening the lid up to pour in a couple packets of creamer, stirring it in with a spoon.

"Oh, hi! Just a minute, I just—I don't have any make up on," I yell, grabbing a tube of mascara and a hairbrush as I run down the hall in a hurry before he sees my bare face.

His keys rattle against the counter, and I hear his footsteps press down on the squeaky staircase. For a minute, I picture it. Our future. Our home. Us waking up together in the same place, every day, forever. He comes into the bathroom where I'm clumsily throwing my clothes into a ball on the floor as I jab an eyeliner pencil around my eye lid with my mouth open.

Not looking at him, I ask, "What time is it?"

He walks up behind me and grabs my waist. The heat of his hands radiates through my damp towel.

"Don't worry, we have time," he whispers in my ear. His breath on my neck sends my head back into his chest and my lips onto his. My body melts into his arms and it isn't long before the towel falls to the floor. I've been aching for this since the last time I saw him, and I can feel myself opening between my legs at the mere thought of him inside of me again. Paul and I started having sex a couple months ago, and though we've sneakily done this many times, it never felt so at home. Literally. It is just the two of us in this empty house. For a moment, an image of future flashes through my mind. I imagine Paul in his 30's late for work just to be inside me, to hold me against his warm body. I daydream about it all the time, but in this moment, I can almost feel the reality of it. A home, a life, a future with Paul.

"You look so beautiful like this. I never see you without make up. You look perfect." He runs his hands through my wet hair before he picks me up with both arms. He doesn't play football, but he could if he wanted to. His arms are strong, and his body is athletic from working and bailing hay at his grandparents' farm for years.

I wrap both of my legs around him and start unbuckling his pants, our mouths still glued together. Each breath heavier than the next with his tongue tangled in mine as we grow lost in a world of our own.

The door slams from downstairs. Paul pulls away quickly, and my heart begins to beat so fast it feels like it might explode.

"Jade?" I hear my dad yell from the kitchen. His voice sounds panicked and angry. "Is Paul here, too?" His footsteps quickly trot up the stairs. We both stand up, desperately trying to get clothes on, but the door swings open, and dad catches us half-clothed. He turns away.

"Goddammit it, Paul!" His voice growls loud and hostile. "You need to leave," he screams with his head turned. "Now! Immediately. Go!"

A father's worst night also became my own worst nightmare. We were caught having sex, and there is nothing worse that could ever happen to me in my life, I am sure of it. This is the worst-case scenario, and I am watching it unfold before my eyes. Paul scrambles to pull his pants up, the fear and panic settle into his face. I pull my top over my head so fast that it's backwards, and I don't have enough time to switch it around. Paul rushes downstairs, swipes his keys off the counter so quickly that he forgets his coffee on the way out. It's just dad and I now.

I procrastinate getting ready, hoping that will delay facing anything down there that I'm not ready to face. Looking my father in the eyes after he had just seen Paul insert himself into me. I want to puke and disappear simultaneously all at once when I think about it. I scan the mirror before facing my fears head on downstairs; my hair is still damp from the shower and my face red hot. Before I make it down, dad shouts up to me. "Call me before you leave. I have to go to work." He slams the door shut.

The house feels colder and emptier in a new way. I cover my face with my hands and drop to the floor in the kitchen. *How could this happen?* The worst thought and nightmare of all jumps to the front of my mind: *if Paul's grandparents find out, I will never see Paul again, and it will be over.* My heart begins to ache in places I didn't know existed. Shame, guilt, sadness, anger at myself for letting this happen, fear, disappointment, each emotion finds a place to settle into my body.

THAT WAS IT. My worst fear had arrived just as I imagined it would. My father told his grandfather what happened. He felt the moral responsibility to call him up, and after they each argued back and forth for hours about whose fault it was that this had happened, it was decided that we could no longer be together and no longer see one another. That was the last day Paul was my boyfriend. But it wasn't the last day he was inside of me. Or the last day we'd be together. We fog up my car in alleyways every chance we get, and he climbs out the window once his grandparents are asleep and I come to the rescue for us. That only ended once they saw the tracks from his muddy shoes coming from his bedroom window. Each time, we get more creative. It is like sneaking out is some sort of maze game to find our way back to each other again somehow. We are determined. It is not over until it is over.

THE FIRST SNEAK out was the most intense. We met at his grandparent's barn in the middle of the night. The crop farm was about a half mile down from the farmhouse where they lived, and sometimes he stays overnight in the barn house so he could sleep in longer. I loved hay bailing season because it would tan his body and make his muscles swell. The sun would bleach his hair brighter, and his tanned skin made his amber brown eyes nearly glow.

That night we met in the barn, it was lit by a lonely old light bulb hanging by a string, Paul was still in his work clothes, worn and tattered overalls and dirty farmer boots.

"I can't be up too late; we bail early in the morning and my Pop's will know if I'm tired, it's because of a girl. He'll know I'm seeing you again."

I huff. "I hate this. How could one thing, a thing that most teenagers do, be the thing that makes them hate me and forbid us from being together."

"He doesn't hate you, he just likes God more," he says. "I think he's convinced I'll be hell-bound if I keep seeing you, or worse, end up like my parents." He adjusts a wool patterned blanket on his bunk. I look at him with beggars' eyes. He slides down his pants and kisses my neck. His pulse against mine felt holy, his lips were the puzzle piece missing to mine. He was my other half, and nothing felt complete while we were apart.

I'd began to grow angry at Paul, even if it isn't his fault. I want him to fight for me, to fight for us. The sneaking around is fun, even sexy at times. But I miss what we had before—a real relationship. One that felt so natural and easy that it felt like we were already married—his family became my own. And now they hate me. I've never been hated before, especially by people that I love. The feeling turns my stomach when I think about it. *If it wasn't for that day, everything would still be perfect.*

Paul looks at me. "What's with that face?" he asks. "Looks like you want to hit me."

I picture it for a second, hitting something, but not him. I want to break something in half just to watch it become destroyed. I wonder how he knows.

"I'm just thinking, is all," I say.

"About what?" He slides his shirt off over his head and smiles.

I walk over to him, rage-filled and aroused. I push his chest down onto the bunk and grab his jaw tightly before sliding my tongue into his mouth and forcefully inserting him into me.

He pulls his head away, "Wow. You were really ready for this, huh?" he says. I ride him angrily, intensely, so hard that it nearly hurts, but I want to feel him so deeply. Maybe if he's closer to me from the inside, I won't be so upset. Maybe I'll forget about everything else.

"Jade. Jade. Slow down," he says.

"What, isn't it good like this? Don't you like it rough sometimes?" I read that once in Cosmo, too.

"I mean… sure, I guess. But this isn't you." He looks at me. "What's the matter?"

Even if I want to, I can't hold the tears in. They pour out and so does everything inside of my heart. I am bursting, and there's no stopping it now.

"I'm nothing but a slut and everyone hates me." The whole town knows by now. Word has gotten out that we broke up because we were caught having sex. "You look like the hero who got laid, and I'm the whore who ruins lives. It's not fair."

"You're mad at me?" he sputters.

"No," I say, wiping a handful of tears from my cheeks. "I'm mad at everything and everyone else but you. I wish I was mad at you. I wish I could hate you."

"Why would you wish to hate me?"

"Because loving you hurts, especially when I can't have you."

He is silent then and nods. "You should go," he says. "It gets harder and harder every time we keep doing this. Pretending it's not over, even when…"

He doesn't finish saying it, because he doesn't have to.

I WAITED ANOTHER week after that and drove to his house. After weeks of obeying his grandparents' rules, they even had to change his phone number as they had been suspecting us of still seeing each other. It had been too long since I'd even heard his voice, and I knew that if I just showed up, he couldn't say no. His room was on the first floor, so I parked my car and walked over and knocked on his window. It took a couple knocks before he opened. His face looked frightened.

"Jade, what are you doing? You know we aren't supposed to see each other."

"I need to talk to you," I say, forcing the window open further and shoving my body inside.

He looks behind him, checking his door. He opens the window and puts his finger to his tender lips making a shushing sound.

"Come in. Just please, be extra quiet." I nod. "And you know you can't stay long. My Pop's will literally kill me."

The ex-marine quite literally would kill him in some capacity, he's right. If he isn't making him do 100 military push-ups, or 5 AM mile runs before school, it is something equivalently brutal. Even I'm afraid of his grandfather, but my fear isn't as strong as my desire for Paul. I need his love and I need it now. And I need to know if he needs me, too. I feel like I can't go on another day, carrying this pain in my chest, this void in my life. The physical distance has begun to wear on me. It begins to ache in places from outside of my mind and into my body—my stomach is empty, and my heart feels cold and carved out.

"I know, thank you for letting me in. I'll be quiet."

In his moonlit room, I stare at him for a moment. His face full of fear, he can hardly settle his tense body. I sit a couple feet apart from him on his bed, the bed that would tell our secrets if it could ever speak, like how this is not the first time I was on top of it.

"I had to see you, I'm sorry." I grab his blanket tightly with my fist and close my eyes. Images of his body on top of mine fill my thoughts. I try to hold back, I try not to touch him, I pretend he's a breakable collector's item needing to be handled with care.

"I wanted to see you, too."

"You did?" I say, my voice elevated above a whisper. He puts his finger to his mouth again and shushes me quietly. I cover my mouth tightly.

"Of course, I did. I didn't want this. This wasn't my choice." He looks away, as if looking at me would make him break, too. He tries to be firm and direct as he tries to speak without emotion. He tries to make it easier. This makes my cold body start to shiver, I can almost feel my teeth chatter.

"Are you cold? Why are you shivering?"

"I do this sometimes when things feel emotionally pained. It's almost like my body forgets to pump blood throughout my veins, like it's trying to kill me instead of keeping me alive. Like I'd rather be dead than feel this way."

"Don't say that, Jade. That's a stupid thing to say."

"What, that I'd rather be dead?"

"That's not how you feel, is it?" he asks, his face concerned.

"Sometimes, yes." I pause. "I think I'd rather be dead than be without you."

"I don't know how to be without you. Or maybe it's just that I don't want to." He grows quieter, his stiff body softening. He looks at me, his face excruciatingly beautiful.

"The teachers, my friends, my parents—everyone is worried about me." I shake my head afraid to say the next part. "I have literally died inside without you, Paul. I can't do this without you anymore."

His eyes lit up by the glow of the moon. He grabs my hands, and the warmth pulses through me instantly. My hands tremble, and my legs grow restless as lumps collect in my throat. My eyes are so heavy with tears that I'm afraid to blink and set off the waterfall from my face. I am afraid once I start, it won't stop.

"I'm sorry," I say as collect my face in my hands.

Without effort, a tear falls from my eye like an accident, but I don't look at him. He wipes it away and runs his fingers through my hair. He leans in for one small kiss, before he pulls away, only for me to pull him back into me to devour him. I've never craved him more.

He forces himself to stop and pulls me off him so intensely, it jars my neck.

"Look, I can't. We can't. This is a horrible idea. You should just go. We can't keep doing this." I pull back even further, afraid of what he might say next, holding my breath without realizing it. My head feels a bit dizzy from it all.

"But that doesn't mean I won't spend my whole life loving you." Those words make me catch my breath.

"Then stop this." I stand up. "I won't let you give up on us. Come with me. Let's go on a drive." I smile, grabbing his hands and squeezing them into mine. "Please…"

"Jade, I can't."

Everything in Paul is programmed to be good, to not end up like his dad. One mistake and he's afraid he'll ruin his whole life. In this moment, I fear that Paul thinks I'm the biggest he ever made—when all I wanted was to be the best thing that ever happened to him.

"Paul. It's me," I say with conviction, to remind him in case he somehow has been so brainwashed that he forgot how much he loved me. "Don't you remember us? Have you already forgotten? I feel like I don't even know who you're being right now." I grab both of his shoulders and shake him a little. "Who are you? Are you in there?" He grabs my hands and shushes me again.

"No, I haven't forgotten, and I'll never forget." He kisses my hand regretfully. "But I also can't change this. What's done is done, even if it wasn't supposed to be, or will never feel done." He chokes up. "It has to be over."

I crawl out of his window more broken hearted than I was when we first ended it. I turn back around to ask him one last burning question.

"Do you still love me?"

He helps me out of the window, and with his hands sliding the window down he responds, "Does it really matter? It has to be over."

He closes the window and turns out the light. His words leave me breathless again, yet this time I'm not sure how long I can breathe without him.

CHAPTER SIX
(Two weeks later)

A NUMBER I don't recognize calls my cell phone. I answer reluctantly.

"Hello?"

"If you were in a room full of everyone you've ever met, who would you be looking for?" I smile and fall back onto my bed—his voice takes my feet from under me. "You. You know it would be you, Paul."

It's true, and he knows I'll be looking for him, and he will be looking for me, too.

"Meet me in the barn again tonight, I need to see you."

"I thought last week you said—"

"I know what I said, and I changed my mind. I just feel like—I feel like I need you."

Of course, I'm nervous. Rarely am I nervous about seeing Paul, as he's the most familiar feeling and person I've ever known. But tonight, I know it will be different. I know it's because I have one last chance to convince him that we're worth fighting for. The pressure feels almost too much. I can hardly eat all day; my stomach is too twisted up inside. Every bite I take is harder to swallow than the one before. My hands shake as I slip a dress on. The same dress I wore on our first date and haven't worn since. It's a little shorter than it was on me then, but I think maybe I look older, sexier in it and maybe he will find it all too hard to say no to. Maybe then he'll remember me. Remember us and never look back.

Paul is leaning against the barn, waving me in quickly under the dull glow of the barn light. The crickets and cicadas chirp so loudly, I can hardly hear him say, "hurry up," but I can see his mouth move in the distance. He brushes his hands through his hair and shakes his head smiling.

Close enough to him now, he says, "I like the dress."

I grab the hem of it and look down at my tan knees. "Thank you. It the same dress—"

"I know," he says, slowly pulling me in at my waist and onto his lips. I breathe him in, his signature Paul scent turns me inside out. I grab his strong bicep, and as I do, I feel myself melting and opening under my dress.

We're together another perfect night, a blanket under the stars and a couple cans of his grandpa's beer, which felt like an extremely bold move. I realize then he's just as nervous as I am. I hate the taste but love the way it makes me forget about how sick I'm still feeling about everything that has happened between us. Paul isn't much of a drinker, but what teenage boy hasn't sipped on a beer every now and then? I try not to overthink it too much, which is likely the point of the beer anyway.

I put his open palm softly on my throat, "Do you feel that?" I ask.

"Feel what? Your little neck?" He laughs a little, and sips his beer.

"No. I move his hand over my pulse. "My heartbeat."

"Here, how about this." I put his hand up my dress and under my bra onto my warm chest.

"Do you feel that?"

"Yes. I feel that." He kisses my neck, his warm, yeasty breath clouding over me. "I feel something else, too." He leans his body into mine and places my hand down his pants to feel his rock-hard excitement. He starts to breathe deeply in my ear.

"You're my second heart beat. I swear I didn't have two until I met you," I say to him. He doesn't say anything, he doesn't have to. With his body, he says everything words can't. He needs me right now. He loves me deeply. He misses me more than anything. He doesn't say it, but I can feel it.

We make love in the field next to the barn, and even though it began sprinkling a little and our clothes are damp, we can't stop. We do it again moments after. It's clear, we still can't get enough of each other. When we finish, we run into the barn and get dressed in our soggy clothes.

"Just kill me now," he says smiling, pulling his legs into his pants.

"What do you mean? Why would you say that?" I ask, feeling bothered and confused. I hope he isn't feeling regret. He pulls me into his arms.

"Because if this was what my last day looked like, I'd die happy. This is exactly how I'd like my last day to be. Next to you. It can't get any better than this."

He feels like a part of me that would always be there, like I had grown a second heart that only beats when we were together, as if it's somehow activated by his breath, his smell, his touch.

If he can die happy today, I can, too.

CHAPTER SEVEN

THIS EXCITEMENT BETWEEN us only lasts so long, especially as the weather grows colder and he spends less time at the farm, which is one of our only safe places to meet up. The inevitable happens slowly. Spending less time together pushes us apart, our conversations growing shorter and emptier. As time passes without seeing each other, we have seemed to run out of things to talk about. Nothing is what it used to be.

Being physically disconnected was pulling the plug on every other kind connection we still had. Eventually, we stopped seeing each other regularly and the time between hearing from him grew more distant. Rumor had it that he even had a couple girlfriends, ones he took to homecoming and prom dances with. He was trying to move on and so was I. And though deep down we were forced apart, I still wanted him to choose me. To fight a bit harder. And when he didn't, I knew I would have to walk away in a different direction too—even if it was never the path I had intended to take. Even if I still craved him like a forbidden fruit—he wasn't mine anymore and there was nothing else I could do to keep him.

My best friend Jessica always said, "The best way to get over someone, is to get under someone else." She meant sex. And so, sex is all I tried to find. I wasn't looking for love. I had found that once already and it hurt like hell. I wasn't falling for that or anyone else again.

"What's your body count, girl?" Jessica asks me as we are getting ready for another party. She zips her thick thighs into a mini skirt and tucks her shirt in.

"Body count?" I ask.

She freezes and stares at me seriously. "How many people have you killed?" She laughs. "Oh my God, you are dense." She rolls her eyes, "How many guys have you slept with since Paul?"

"I don't know, one or two?"

"You're lying."

"How do you know?"

"Because we all know how many people we've been with. Unless you're a prostitute, then maybe you'd lose track. But you're not." She puckers her mouth and takes another drink. "And I know you've only been with Paul."

I roll my eyes at her as I take a drink of some weird vodka she found somewhere she mixed with a sickening sweet lemonade.

"We're getting your body count up before college, alright?" she says. "Besides, how many girls do you think Paul's been with?"

"Monique said she saw him around town, and I guess she said he's gotten even cuter. Said she hardly recognized him."

"Oh, really?" I say, rolling my eyes pretending to be unamused. To convince her that I don't care.

"I hate to say it, because I know it's a sore subject." She unwraps a protein bar she took from her mother's purse and takes a bite, chewing with a face that tells me she hates the taste. She grabs her doughy belly with one hand and snarls at it in the mirror before sucking it in as much as she can, turning side to side to analyze the false sense of weight loss. "He was just okay looking when you dated, but now, I hear he is some real eye candy. Monique says he looks like he's eighteen already. Maybe nineteen. But isn't he younger than you?"

Hearing her call him eye candy makes me both sick and angry, but also, a little excited at the thought. I can hardly imagine him looking any better. I thought he was perfect as it was. I didn't say that to Jess though. I take another bitter drink of my boozy lemonade and stay quiet.

"Oh, I know that face."

"What face?"

"The one you make when you're mad."

"Don't get mad, Jade," she says, putting her arm over my shoulder as she checks her breasts in the mirror. "Get even." She smiles at me convincingly.

"When you're in college, you'll meet someone even better and completely forget about him," she says.

I wonder then if Paul will go to college and what will become of him.

Jess puts her arm around me, pushing my drink to my lips.

"And then you'll be like, *Paul, who?* And you'll live happily ever after."

CHAPTER EIGHT
(Three and a half years later)

I SEE PAUL again one night in college. I invited him to this St. Patrick's Day party on campus. He didn't end up in college, he stayed back on the farm, and Jess was right. I am now dating Sam—a rich, successful older guy who appeared to have life figured out. I told myself Paul and I were just kids back then and that it didn't mean anything. I even tried forgetting him as much as I could and most days, I was convinced I had. Still, I didn't tell Sam about Paul. He couldn't know that I had wanted to see him, too. Knowing him, he would have too many questions and analyze us too deeply and ruin everything. I had to be swift, so I had it all laid out in my head. If he asked who he was or how I knew him, I would say he was a friend I used to know and that would be that.

Paul knows Sam will be there though, I told him ahead of time. It wasn't like Paul to act like he cared either way, I imagined he just wanted to see me. I didn't care either that he knew I'd be with Sam, I just wanted to see him. I wondered if Paul only saw me as a friend he used to know or if he still felt the deep, burning desire we once felt as I did. I want to feel the heat of his skin, even if only a handshake. I want to see if my second heart was still there. And if it is, would it still beat for him? I had to know.

Sam is leaning against the stairs and notices me fidgeting

around nervously.

"You alright?" he asks, knitting his eyebrows together.

I nod, smile, and take a drink from my green beer, running my tongue over my teeth to keep them from getting stained. He touches my thigh and gives it a squeeze.

"Good," he says before jumping back into conversation with his friends.

Sitting on the arm of a beer-stained chair near the doorway, I check my phone to re-read Paul's text.

Paul: *Sounds like a plan. See you soon.*

This is actually happening. After years of being apart, I will see him again tonight. At this point, all the butterflies are obnoxiously doing that flapping thing they do in my stomach.

We are still sitting near the door when Paul walks in. When I see his face, my heart does a backflip as soon as our eyes meet. He looks so good it makes me feel nauseous. It has been years since I've seen him. Of course, we texted here and there, but I haven't seen how much he's grown into his own body. It made me angry. First at myself, and then angry at him. *Why didn't we try to work this out again? Where would we be if we hadn't gone our separate ways?*

Instantly, my head goes down a rabbit hole of thought. I wonder if maybe I'll bump into him and touch his arm as he walked upstairs. If maybe I'll see him in the hallway and then he will stop, and our eyes will meet, and we will *know*. And then maybe he'll push me up against the wall and kiss me passionately. My mind takes me to daydreams about Paul on occasion, but this one is starting to feel as if it could be real.

Paul makes small talk with our group of friends and then with Sam. He looks at me then and laughs a little. I laugh, too, I can't help it. Since when is he so charming? The boy I once knew is a little shy, but watching him come out of his shell is like watching a caterpillar turn into a butterfly. He's different now.

"Hi Jade." His voice melts me the same way it always has.

"Oh, you two know each other?" Sam says, pointing at me with his thumb. I want Paul to feel jealous of Sam for reasons that I know don't fully make sense. If he saw me with an older, attractive boyfriend, would he regret not trying harder when we were younger?

"Yes, we do. I knew him back when—"

"Back in high school," Paul interrupts. "Believe it or not, this used to be my girl." He put his arm around my shoulder and winked at Sam playfully. His touch ignites an immediate warmth into my stomach.

"But it's okay though, don't worry, that was a long time ago. We were so young then. Babies, practically." Sam looks at me and takes a drink of his beer. I can tell he's analyzing Paul.

My cheeks turn hot and red. Paul takes a drink of his green beer and smirks at me like I am still his girl. In the moment, I forget that I'm not. I still harbor a desire for this boy that defies all logic and time. Was it years since I'd seen him? It feels like days, maybe weeks. There's no way nearly three and a half years had passed since we were together. The hair on my arms lights up like a Christmas tree, and the corners of my eyes hold back tears so hard that my eyesight starts to blur. It's clear my body is holding on to feelings I didn't know I had.

I turn my head for a moment, tip a beer back and drink as fast as I can, trying to roll the water back into my eyes. I remember my mom once telling me it is impossible to drink something and cry at the same time. When I turn my head back, Paul is looking at me. It was like he knew what was happening inside of me.

The night is running out, and I find myself waiting for an opportunity to see Paul alone. Sam is in a very involved game of flip cup with some other drunk guys at the party, and it's then that I see my opportunity to escape.

Throughout the night, I've kept a close eye on Paul discreetly, visually scanning him around the room. He is deflecting every sloppy female that throws herself at him. I don't want Paul to know that I am trying to run into him. I want it to be casual, serendipitous even. But all that honestly went out the window when I first texted him to come to this party. It's clear it isn't romantic fate; we both have a plan to see each other and talk. But what we didn't have was a good strategy on how to make that plan work. From outside, I can see Paul through the window. He has some new, festive green beads around his neck, and it makes my stomach turn imagining how he acquired them. I want him all to myself.

Paul looks bored, though he is making small talk with a few people around him. I wonder if he is waiting for me or if he will leave soon out of lack of interest. Maybe he thinks I've grown less attractive and that he can do better. He's leaning up against the kitchen island. The lights are off, but strobe lights flashed every few seconds to the music. I wonder if they have the lights and the speakers synced up to move together, or if I had so much beer that I just think they are. I decide to make my way to the sliding glass door, filling my cup with more green beer at the keg beside it and gulping down half the cup before stepping inside. The closer I get to him, the more I feel it—my second heartbeat. This time beating twice as fast. Thud-thumping more than it has ever thud-thumped.

I walk past the kitchen and head upstairs to the bathroom to check my makeup before heading down to talk to him. I investigate my face in the mirror and notice my hair now looks significantly worse than it looked when we first arrived, frizz in places frizz shouldn't be. I try to smooth it out with my hands, but it hardly helps. My eyes appear more sleepy and drunk looking, too. Almost like they were drawn on to look extra round. I wipe the corners of them where the tears leaked earlier. I do a strange smile to check my teeth. Everything about my face seems so unappealing that I consider locking myself inside until the party ends.

There's a couple of loud knocks at the door that are trying to force me out, I yell through the door, "Just a minute!"

I wash my hands quickly, and before I'm able to dry them the door opens. With my back turned, I yell, "Seriously, what the hell! I said just a minute."

I turn around to see Paul. He opens the door and closes it behind him.

"Here we are again. A bathroom, believe it or not." He looks around, laughing, and scoots his body in front of me, pressing me into the sink as he squares himself with me.

"We don't have much luck in bathrooms, do we?" I say, though I wished I hadn't.

He makes a face that says "true", but he doesn't say it out loud.

"It's quieter in here. Don't you think?" he says, his voice gentle and deep all at once. Before I can think or open my mouth for words to come out, my body throws itself into his arms. His shoulders feel stronger, and his hands are rougher, hardworking, and mature now. Before we know it, our lips lock. Kissing him now feels more intense than it ever has. It is clear, Paul's kiss is the best one I've ever had. Electric and inviting. My body shudders as it realizes I've been kissing the wrong men all this time, because kissing Paul feels too right.

I love us in this moment just as I've loved us in every moment. I slide my tacky green St. Patty's Day shirt off, and jump into his arms, wrapping my legs around him. His goofy, four-leaf clover beads press into my chest. I squeeze my legs around his waist as he sets me up on the bathroom sink and he begins to unzip them. He slides his warm hand in my underwear, and I begin to moan a little. He puts a finger inside of me, and memories rush back of the first time he explored me. This time, it feels better, like he's had more practice. I don't let my mind wander far enough to imagine him with anyone else, or it would ruin the moment.

We kiss each other so heavily that I haven't even seen his face up close. I stop for a moment and pull my face back.

"I just want to see you," I say. With both hands, I touch his cheeks, and light stubble tickles against my hands. He feels so much more like a man now. His eyes somehow seem lighter, and his hair is a little darker than I remember.

"You." I say, throwing my arms around his neck and hugging him so tightly that I'm sure it hurts him.

"You," he says, kissing my shoulder. My body melts into his. "You're more beautiful now than you were the last I saw you." He takes his hand and runs it through my hair. "Your hair is darker, longer, too."

We sit like that for a minute before he says, "This is kind of right where we left off." Those words somehow split my second heart wide open, and I started to feel pain in my chest quite literally.

"Yeah," I say, hanging my head down.

"Want to finish what we started all those years ago?" I pull back and concentrate on his face and smile again, trying not to think of Sam in the heat of this moment. Trying not to worry about it, which somehow, strangely makes me feel worse. I put my forehead against Paul's and start unbuckling his pants. In this moment, it's just us. The rest of the world doesn't exist.

"I mean, that works, too." He laughs a little. "But I was talking about us." He smiles, and his lips look almost pouty, so I kiss them again.

"Don't you feel it?" he whispers into my ear. "Something is still very much here." He kisses my forehead. "I don't think it ever left."

A few large knocks pound at the door. A couple of drunk girls giggling, and slurring are outside of it, "Hurry up, we have to pee! I don't want to pee in my shoe," another squeaky girl yells and the other girls howl in laughter.

"What are we going to do?" I whisper. "I don't want anyone to see us together."

"Why not?" he says, pulling my hips into his.

"Because technically, I'm with Sam."

"No, *technically* right now, you're *with* me. And I don't want to let you go again."

I panic and jump in the shower, pulling the curtain closed. If I am lucky, the drunk girls won't notice I am in there and Paul can escape without me, and no one will know what a disaster I've made.

"What are you doing? Just come out with me and let's leave. I'll take you home," he says, his voice sounding frustrated yet calm and convincing.

"What about Sam?" I ask, covering my mouth immediately after I say it.

"What about him?" he says, buckling his pants, making a confused face. As if I should forget Sam ever existed. As if I were still his. Even though that's exactly what I feel like doing, I question whether that's the right thing to do.

"Shhh. Just go," I whisper and wave him out the door. I sink my body deep into the tub and pull the curtain tighter. "I'll see you downstairs in a minute," I whisper to him. I can hear him open the door to leave.

"Oh heyyyy!" the girls say to him. He ignores them, and the door closes.

The girls didn't notice me, but they take longer than I expect to leave the bathroom. Once they leave, I make my exit and start to look for Paul. Instead, I find Sam.

"Oh, there you are, I just won another game. Was on a pretty big winning streak." He laughs and slurs. "Are you having fun?" he asks as he leans in to kiss my cheek. I pull away and pray he can't smell Paul.

"Yeah, I just need to find... my...drink." I scan the room, looking for Paul. "I set it down, and now I can't find it."

I lie. And he was gone. I can't find Paul the rest of the night. Shortly after, Sam and I leave. We walk home, and Sam drunkenly confesses his love for me. Part of me wonders if I also love Sam, and hearing him tell me loves me in his cute, drunk voice does make me feel gooey inside, but at the same time, I know that what happened with Paul tonight would change everything, even if Sam never found out about our kiss. I knew about it, and not only did I know, but I also feel something I hadn't felt in a long time. A feeling for Paul that I was sure would never come back. Until I saw him, until I touched him again and made it real all over again.

When we get back home, I intend on waiting for Sam to fall asleep before texting Paul. Instead, I pass out next to Sam.

THE NEXT MORNING, I roll over and open a text from Paul.

> **Paul:** I thought you'd choose me...

I reply: *You left last night. And that wasn't the first time that you left... I thought you'd choose me back then. That you'd fight for us... but you didn't. It's all so complicated now. You know that.*

Paul: *It doesn't have to be.*

He replied quickly. Another text follows immediately after.

Paul: *Not anymore. We can make it work again. I know we can...*

Sam rolls over. "Good morning, babe." He kisses the back of my neck. "Let's get breakfast."

I put my phone face down and try to forget it exists. It's easier that way.

CHAPTER NINE

THE SUN IS starting to set and the sky is turning sleepy shades of orange in some parts and smokey gray in others. All day, I go through all the same motions with Sam, only to be completely distracted by what the hell I'm going to say to Paul. All day I've wondered where Paul is, what's he doing, what's he thinking, what he's wearing. I want to know more about Paul now than I ever have. I didn't get to ask what's going on in his life. Now I feel curious and strangely empty not being connected all those years. The little taste of him last night has me full on craving him today, and I know that's a big problem, for all of us.

"What's wrong, today?" Sam asks. "You aren't being yourself." He picks at his fingernails. "You're being very quiet and distant. Was it what I said last night?"

I sigh. "No, I'm just tired. It was a long night last night. I'm good," I say and grab his hand affirmatively. Lying to us both. "Never been better." I walk to the bathroom and once the door is closed, I pull my phone from my pocket to text Paul. What I want to say is how he never fought hard enough to choose me after all this time, either. How he can't just show up and expect me to set fire to the world I've built without him. Like nothing else mattered but him and I. And in that same breath, I feel so weak for him that I'd agree with those feelings, that I should set the rest of my world on fire, that nothing else did matter but him and I. Instead, I try to focus on the angry parts of my heart over the one that deeply longs for him, it's always been easier that way.

Paul, I love you. I will always love you. I write it and delete it. Feeling guilt for Sam now, who just gushed his love for me last night, I would hate to feel heartbreak all over again. I remember now that this is exactly why I wasn't supposed to fall for anyone else ever again after Paul. Too many complicated feelings. Falling hurts.

I'm sorry, Paul. I write it again and delete it. For the life of me, I can't think of the right words, and I don't have it in me to see one of us hurt again. Or worse, I wonder if I threw it all away with Sam, the guy who has his life mapped out with a bright future for Paul, who still was walking around life aimlessly, just living day by day without a solid future. I knew he wanted to stay in Tiffin, and I knew Sam wanted what I wanted, a big life in a big city.

Sam is only a semester away from graduating the university. Paul had dropped out only after a few months once his grandfather fell ill to help run the family farm. I wondered where I'd end up if I chose Paul and not Sam. Would the feelings I had for Paul fade once the rush and intensity fizzled out? What if over time, we ended up becoming that bored couple brushing our teeth together at night with blank stress in the mirror, and what if nothing felt like lighting anymore? Would Paul live up to my fantasy of him in my head, or would it break my heart to see him fail to be the man I dreamt he was? These were the questions that kept me up at night. What I need is a fortune teller, but what I have is a blank canvas, two sets of paint and only one portrait to display in real time.

And then there was the one thought that made me ache all over—what If it was a simple life with love like Paul's is all I ever wanted? And yes, we would live completely different life, one far different than the upscale life that I saw for myself with Sam, owning my very own bakery in Chicago. What would happen if I stayed here in Ohio forever? What if we lived in the same house on the farm like he did growing up? What if we never became anything significant, but all we had was this awe-inspiring love that did nothing for my dream and everything for my soul. I couldn't bear the what if's and it all felt like too much to decide on. Still foggy from the hangover, I decide in this moment to pretend like the night never happened. I don't need to make this decision right now. I put my phone back in my pocket, leaving the text unanswered and get ready for bed. Paul will be there tomorrow, and the next day after. I still have time.

"YOU DIDN'T SAY it back," Sam says immediately as I walk back into his room. It takes a minute to remember what he's talking about. He's right I have been distracted because Paul has consumed my entire brain and body since last night.

When I remember his I love you confession, I take a deep breath and exhale slowly as I find the right words. "I know, I'm sorry. I just wanted to make sure you weren't just drunk and that you meant it. You know?"

He nods. "Well, I meant it." I pull him into my arms and kiss his forehead.

"I love you, too," I say quietly. In the moment I feel like I might. *Don't I?* What is love, anyway? I care about him. I like spending time with him. We have good sex, and he is funny. I couldn't always compare every man I met to what Paul. And I had, if I did, I'd never find anyone. No one compares. What Paul and I had ended, and I wondered if that's how it was supposed to go. I wondered what would happen if you tried to revive a dead love. Or worse, what to do with a love that you thought was dead but isn't and would likely never be.

I wish I can say that the next day I had some beautiful message to send back to Paul, but I don't. In fact, that was the last message I have from Paul for about a year. A week later, I begin feeling prickly for what I did behind Sam's back, mostly because I sense that he felt my pull away from him, and somehow that brought him closer to me.

Sam loves me and I'm happy enough.

CHAPTER TEN

S AM STANDS THERE next to the priest, tall and shining. His smooth, clean-shaven face smiles at the guests in the church pews and then back at me. The smile that both costs and earns him a fortune. The shine of his golden watch catches my eye as he pats at his coiffed, dark brown hair. Those pale blue eyes, the ones that could make me do anything, meet mine as I walk down the long aisle towards him.

My long, silk gown shimmers and trails behind me, gathering up white rose petals with each step. My hair is tied neatly into an elegant knot, holding up the flowing organza veil that covers my face. As I inch closer, an unusual pang settles into my stomach that makes me turn my head back towards the door. A thought pops into my head, one where I run from this moment instead of taking a single step further. My father squeezes my hand and nods his final seal of approval as he hands me off to my new husband.

Church bells chime several times from the belltowers. Sam kisses me, his new bride. A tight clenching sensation takes over my face and jaw, as if my teeth are holding back the things I wish I could say but can't.

The reception hall overflows with the fragrant smell of expensive perfume and the sounds of a live string quartet. Our favorite people dance happily with each other, fill their glasses with Dom Perignon and stuff their faces with bacon wrapped chestnuts.

Champagne bubbles continue to fill my mouth, covering my body in its warmth.

Until Paul's voice hollows through my head from last night, chilling me from the inside out.

✧　✧　✧

"JADE, DON'T. PLEASE don't marry him," he says, his voice pained and desperate.

In the middle of shaving my legs in the tub, I drop the razor into a pile of bubbles. I was trying to pamper myself to relax my nerves before the wedding. Sam is staying at the Towne Plaza hotel with his parents to sleep apart the night before, as old traditions warned us to do.

"Shit." Paul's voice wasn't the one I needed to hear today of all days. The day before I marry Sam.

"What?"

"I cut my leg." A bit of fresh blood drips slowly down my shin. I try to wash it off with water, but it keeps on bleeding.

"Oh, I thought maybe... I don't know. Well, are you okay?"

"Paul." All these years I have had him in the back of my head and in the biggest part of my heart. I try to use my strong voice because there's no reason to start this conversation now. It's too late. "You know tomorrow is my wedding day, right?" I say, holding my thumb over the cut underwater now.

"Yes. Obviously, that's why I'm calling now."

"Okay—and why now?" I ask, my voice crosses before exhaling an obnoxious sigh. "Would you rather me show up to the wedding... slam open the church doors and say 'Stop this wedding! I'm in love with this girl.'"

Yes, I wish you would. I didn't say it, but I wanted to.

"I don't know, Jade. I guess I just thought you'd make your

way back to me by now."

A fire burns inside of me, passionate and rage filled. Equal parts of me would love the grand gesture of him storming the church, demanding his undying love for me and equal parts of me wished for him to come to his senses, to let me move on.

Let me go. For real this time.

"But why didn't you say this month or years ago. Even days ago. I've been with Sam for four years."

Paul was quiet, but his breath is heavy, I can tell he's searching for the right words.

"You're right. And I have been waiting patiently. All this time," he says. "But you left, and you kept on leaving. I have always been right here."

"I had to." My voice struggled to get that out, a whisper comes out instead.

It's not fair for him to say and he knows it.

"And—it's not called waiting just because you never left town," I say, shocked at how evil and awful that must sound. The thought of hurting him makes the acidic blend of carbonara and Pinot Gris from rehearsal dinner creep up my throat. Forcing anger made this easier than being sweet.

"I'm getting married tomorrow. To Sam," I said, swallowing it down again. "We have to let this go." I close my eyes, put my hand over my mouth and hold my breath.

I hate myself. I love Paul. I can't.

"I can't make any promises. But if you change your mind—" he paused. "I'll be here. Waiting."

"Goodnight, Paul." I hang up and rolled my eyes, trying to convince myself that I really didn't want to hear his voice when every ounce of me comes alive again when I do.

"I love you, too," I whisper back to the blank silent phone. The center of my chest feels torn apart as my heart slips down into a pit of misery. Even if it didn't want to admit it, my body knows the truth. In the bath I start to shiver as I realize what I've just done.

All these years I have been without Paul, I'd been aching to put back the pieces we'd been forced to shatter, and now, my last chance to be with him again has finally come and gone.

I didn't choose Paul.

An emptiness consumes me as I realize I will likely always be this way without him. I run my hands through my stringy, wet hair. Droplets drip down my face as I put the phone down, only to pick it back up again.

Hands shaking, I dial quickly.

"Mom, Paul called."

"Oh, god. Paul, *Paul.*" Her voice sounds painfully irritated.

"Yes, Paul. The Paul I dated most of high school, Paul."

"What did he want?" she says.

I hesitate for a moment before sputtering it out like hot water from a tea kettle.

"For me not to marry Sam."

She laughs loudly into the phone. I swirl my hand around in the bubbles, pull the drain up with my toes, the water rushes beneath me quickly.

"Gosh, the nerve some boys have." I could just picture her with her hand on her hip in that way that moms do when they're really putting pressure on a subject. "What did you say?"

"I said I'm marrying Sam."

"Good. Sam has a great job, good family, and stability. I like Sam." She sounded relieved.

"You'd regret it if you didn't. Men aren't like him, you know. He's hardworking and smart. Wealthy and charming. It's hard to find an *and* man."

"An *and* man?"

"A man who is more than one thing. Sam is an *and* man. Paul—isn't. Could never be. What does he do for a living anyway? Last I heard he was still at the farm, living with his grandparents."

I pause, my eyes begin to fill up as I try to hold back tears again, my stomach feels like it wants to fold itself in half and disappear.

"Mom, I feel like crying."

The tub is empty now and so am I. I sit inside, my naked body rubbery against the cold porcelain, the phone in one hand and my chest in the other.

"Then cry, sweetheart. But not too much, you don't want your eyes all puffy and red for pictures tomorrow." She chuckles as if she wishes she had not had this discussion with me at all. As if we could go back in time and forget Paul ever existed, like he didn't at one time mean everything to me. Like he should somehow be erased from my brain.

"See you at the wedding, my beautiful bride. When you wake up, you'll be Mrs. Samuel Fuerst."

I POUR CHAMPAGNE until Paul's voice in my head becomes more of a quiet muffle. I dip my finger into my Swarovski crystal flute, spinning it around in circles to make it sing, to drown out the haunting sound of his "I love you."

The day is beautiful, really. Sunny in early October. Warm, but the leaves are still adorned with their stunning fall display. Pops of yellow gold, bright oranges and burgundy reds dress the trees surrounding us. The bridesmaids twirl for golden hour photography in their chocolate brown satin dresses that shimmers like copper when the sun hits them just right. Everything is immaculate. Everyone looks perfect. It's exactly what I pictured when I imagined my wedding day with Sam. My cheeks begin to twitch by the end of the night from all the forced smiling, for the cameras, for the people. For my husband.

I am happy, I remind myself. I picked Sam forever. And I am happy.

CHAPTER ELEVEN
(One year later)

THE FIRST SIX months of marriage are the best ones. We rarely fought. We baked fresh bread together. I made him lemon tartlets and souffles and he'd kiss my lips and compliment me as a thank you often. We rarely left bed. We had so sex often, we hardly got to anything else. When we laughed, we laughed so hard it hurt. We ate charcuterie and sipped Italian wine and laughed and made love like love was still involved. Everything was perfect.

This was exactly what I had been longing for. A classy, modern life with my hunky, successful husband, and our dream life. The only thing missing was a white picket fence, golden retriever, and a baby. If you asked me then, I'd tell you life was good. I'd say, isn't the magic in the mundane? Can't you find it with the same partner, the routine of it? I'd say, isn't there supposed to be peace in comfort? I wondered how long most days the peace would last.

Some months are longer than others. And there are days of peace, I like to remind myself of them often.

Then there were days when I'm loading the dish washer with Sam over my shoulders, scolding the way I'm putting them in.

"No, no, no. That's not how they go in," he said, pushing me off to the side. "I'll just do it. I don't want it done wrong." Or when I first folded his laundry only for him to throw the entire folded piles back into the laundry after screaming in my face about not snapping his shirts and pressing them first.

"I'm a professional, Jade, not Bozo. I can't be looking crazy in shirts folded this way." And after a while, my meals started to lose their flavor according to him, too.

"Did you use any salt on this roasted chicken? And how high did you cook it? It tastes like rubber." It appears as if everything I did suddenly was all wrong. I wondered if marriage had made me clumsy, forgetful, foolish, or if maybe Sam was the one who changed. When I ask about it, he tells me I am too sensitive. That I am always trying to pick a fight, or that I just want to make a big deal out of nothing.

But for some reason, everything was getting worse. It was the first time we lived together, and I tried to remind myself that this must be an adjustment phase. And that maybe it was my fault somehow. There was no way I would've known about his incumbent needs before moving in. There was no way to know that I'd feel like quitting after only a few months. In the dark, lonely moments, I text Paul. I have a rule for myself to keep things casual. If I couldn't see Paul or touch Paul, I was safe from making a mistake I might regret. But that didn't stop me from texting him.

Me: Hey. How have you been?

Realizing he may have a different phone number by now, or he may have grown sick of me stringing him along. Or worse, maybe he found someone else, too. And that would confirm just how stupid I am. I regretted sending it almost immediately, it felt easier to let the last conversation we had dissolve into thin air like it never happened. Especially now that I'm so close to having it all, I can't leave even if it wanted to. Instead, my phone lit up with a quick reply and vibrates in my pocket. I wait until Sam leaves the room before pulling my phone out. I swipe the screen to read Paul's text.

Paul: *Hey. Wow, it's been a while. I was wondering if you forgot about me. I'm good. I'm still in Ohio for a little bit longer, Grandma Lo has seen better days.*

Me: *Oh no. Is she going to be okay?*

Paul: *Hard to say. She's a tough old bird, she's holding on as best as she can.*

Me: *Aww, I'm so sorry. She always made us the best grilled cheeses.* I send a frowny face and make one in real life.

Paul: *Ha, yeah, she did. She's made me a couple since I've lived here the last year, but I will admit she has lost her touch recently. Luckily, she's taught me her tricks, so the legend will live on.*

Me: *Thank God. The world could use more of Grandma Lo's cooking.*

Paul: *How are you and Sam?* He sends a wink face.

I take a big sigh in. I didn't want to answer it.

Me: *We're alright.*

I change the subject, kind of.

Me: *Did you find miss perfect yet?*

Paul: *Yes.*

My heart sinks. Of course, he has. I waited too long. I close my eyes tight and let out another sigh before responding.

Me: *Oh yeah?*

Paul: *Yeah*

Punch to the gut. I put my phone down until it vibrates

again.

Paul: *You*

I can't hold back my smile of sweet relief. But also, another punch to the gut. *What can I say to avoid conflict but keep him interested?* Be a little flirty.

Me: *Oh, the one that got away, huh?*

Paul: *Something like that...*

I imagine his smile, running my fingers over his beard. I close my eyes and smile too. I wait twenty minutes before I respond. Sam walks into the room and distracts me. I head to the bathroom, close the door, and text Paul back. My heart races from the thrill of hiding. Or was it my second heartbeat? The confusion makes my stomach feel sick.

Me: *Keep me updated with your grandma. And with you from time to time. I like knowing how you've been.*

Five minutes go by. Sam knocks on the door. "You alright in there?"

"Yeah, I'm fine. I think I had bad sushi at lunch."

"Gross." I hear his footsteps walk away quickly.

Paul: *I will, I feel the same.*

Paul: *It's nice to hear from you...*

I flush the toilet, playing along with my sushi story and walk into the kitchen.

"Have you decided what you want for dinner?" I ask, looking at Sam as he clicks away at his laptop at the dinner table.

"Lost my appetite," he says.

"Me too," I say, cradling myself in my arms.

CHAPTER TWELVE

AN ARGUMENT GONE wrong on our honeymoon was when I first realized this was something more than incompatibility. A heated conversation about wine pairings had shapeshifted into an ugliness I'd never seen from Sam before, like having some precious metal band on this left finger gave him this freedom to suddenly be terrible. Power and control by way of a small golden ring. It didn't make sense, but then again, nothing did anymore.

"Oh, I think I'll pick this one!" I leaned over the wine menu and squint my eyes to read the tiny print. Between this buzz, being newly married, and being in Paris, I couldn't be happier. "I'll have the—how do you say this in French?" I giggle a bit and cover my mouth. I had one glass of wine and I realize now that I have started growing chattier than normal, which is usually the cue that I'm officially having a good time.

"Are you sure?" Sam looked at me, confused.

"I've only one glass, what do you mean?"

"It's what you picked. That's not the wine I'd pick while in Paris. You can drink a blend like that in the Midwest. Get this," he said, pointing at another option aggressively.

"Nah. This one has a fun name," I said it slowly to the waiter, and he giggles. "I'll have this one."

Sam looks at me with an erupt-at-any-moment face. But he didn't. Instead, he sits there silently after the waiter had left. It was clear, he is ignoring me on purpose. He is fuming.

"Sam? What's wrong?" I lean into him, stroking his arm. He shoves me to the side, moving his chair further away from me.

I am confused in this moment. *Was it me? What did I do wrong?* I had an opinion about the wine, and not even a bold one, but when I looked at Sam, his eyes look different. His body grew tense, he crossed his arms and avoided eye contact with me as I was speaking.

When our waiter comes back to our table to bring our meal and refill our glasses, Sam perks up, smiling again, showing off his perfect white teeth. He goes out of his way to be exceedingly polite to this man, which was usually a quality I admired about him. He knows how to treat everyone, how to make them feel important and was kind to everyone he met. Sam knows how to garner attention and swoon everyone around him, and because of it, everyone has always loved him. But tonight, it feels like an act. An act I had never seen before.

When the waiter left our table again, Sam slipped his hand under the table and pinched the back of my arm. At first, I thought it was sort of funny. It was like us to tease and poke fun at each other. Love taps, he calls them. However, I couldn't recall that he had ever pinched me before, and he'd never done it angrily, until our honeymoon.

"Ow, that hurt," I said. "What was that for?" I rub my hand over the back of my arm where it stings.

"Why are you acting so *stupid*?" He leans into my ear and whispers. "We're at a nice restaurant."

"Stupid?" I shift my body away. He's never called me stupid before. "Why are you being so mean?"

"No, you're being childish. All I'm saying is—just let me pick the wine next time. You know you don't know wine like I do."

"That doesn't mean I don't know how to order or do things for myself."

"Yes. That's exactly what it means. You grew up in Ohio for God's sake, don't embarrass yourself—"

The waiter arrived again, opening the bottle of wine before pouring us more. Sam swirls the wine, sinks his nose down into his glass with his eyes closed, and takes a deep breath in.

"This is the perfect blend. Just like us." When he opens his eyes, he winks at me and smiles at the waiter as if nothing has happened at all.

"It's our honeymoon." He grinned and grabbed my hand, squeezing it tight. Too tight.

"Congratulations! Cheers to the perfect blend indeed," the waiter says before walking away. I gulp down the bitter, sour wine. Paul's voice hums through my mind. *I'll be waiting.*

Thoughts began to consume me every day after. *Did I marry the wrong man?*

✧   ✧   ✧

THIS MORNING, WE have brunch plans with Sam's mother, Genevieve, and his sister, Mary. Mary picked a new spot that's within walking distance from our condo. As a foodie, she knew I would be excited about the menu: Earl Grey pancakes with a lemon ricotta compote, exotic breakfast hashes and an extensive craft cocktail list. Mary sends a screenshot of the Blue Heron menu to the family group chat.

> **Mary:** *Anything with blood orange on the menu means they serve top shelf liquor. It's like a thing I've learned.*

Mary is a painful twenty-two years young, and though we're only seven years apart, it feels like fifteen. Her eyes are large and seem to take in the world with every blink.

She's trendy, tall, narrow, and blonde. The exact opposite of me. She wears her hair in a blunt cut just under her chin, parted down the middle, with shiny make up and shoes with heels. She's always dressed in a high fashion ensemble with some sort of ruffle, ripple, pouf, bow or flow. Mary always knows the celebrity gossip, upbeat pop tunes and is a social media star with a rather large following online, giving her more entitlement than she needs.

She's often posing online in luxury bikinis with her tan and toned model body stretched out in some way that makes her legs look three miles long, wearing a designer brand of expensive sunglasses. "Sometimes they fly me out somewhere warm to shoot in their swimwear. I get paid money to go to escape the Chicago winters and lay on the beach. I can't believe this is my life," she said at the last family Christmas.

"Mary's 'an influencer'," her mom says in air quotes with her fingers.

"It's like a real job, but more fun," Mary chimes in, showing off her free $1700 watch a brand had sent her for their winter promotion.

Our walk to the restaurant is short, but I find myself exhausted by the time we sit down due to the humidity of the July sun. I blot my forehead with a handful of napkins when no one is looking. My damp shirt clings to my lower back. Sipping my glass of water down, I scan the menu quickly and order the scallion potato waffle with a truffle egg and an Americano with a splash of soy. Sam orders me a mimosa. "To lighten you up." He nudges into my ribs with his elbow and makes a sideways smile.

"Jade's had a hard year. It's a big adjustment living in the city," Sam announces.

"Is that why you're dressed like you still live in Ohio?" Mary says, pressing lipstick over her mouth.

I look down at my outfit—jeans, gray tee shirt, sneakers, and then back at Mary. She smiles a very I told you so smile as she watches me examine myself.

"Maybe I should borrow something more glam from your closet next time…" I force a laugh.

"You'd have to hit the gym with me first. Not to be mean, but I'm at least a size or two smaller than you. And not to mention, my legs are twice the length." She's right but it still burns a little when she says it. Okay, it burns it a lot.

Sam's mother refuses to call me by my name, always referring to me as Sam's wife or a cutesy nickname. As if by her giving me a name means she had to keep me around.

"Well, Dorothy, you're no longer in Kansas anymore. Chicago is nothing like Ohio." His mother presses her lips tight around her cocktail and takes a sip. Bright pink lipstick stains the rim of her glass. Mary clicks away at her phone as if she'd rather be anywhere but the place she begged us to go. In between taps on her phone, she'll glance at me and then at Sam. She makes a face at me and turns her head as if she's observing us.

"Have you thought about Botox?" she asks. I shake my head as I realize that thought has yet to cross my mind.

"Mary, what the hell…." Sam says, pressing his fingers into his eyelids shamefully.

"What? She's almost thirty. It's time." She sips her cocktail. "She's like six years behind the average Botox consumer. I've been getting it the last six months. It's a game changer."

"She's not your average Botox consumer. I quite like that about her, Mary. She's a real person with real expressions."

"Is that…empathy?" she says coyly. "No, it couldn't be."

Sam rolls his eyes and puts his napkin down on his lap.

"I'm not suggesting filler or anything." she says. "Just a little juice for her elevens."

"My elevens?"

"Yes, girl, those awful deep lines in-between the brows." She rubs her polished, pointy nail between her eyes. "You're too young to be looking old. I know a guy, hang on." She digs in her purse for her phone but realized quickly it was already in her hand. The phone whooshed over her Botox clinics office number.

"I see Dr. Stephen. Tell him I sent you."

"It wouldn't hurt. Sam, maybe she should." His mother chimes in, picking at her shirt. "Nothing wrong with a wife who cares about her appearance. You're a big shot, you know? Your dad never let me walk around looking like I'm—" She laughs a little too hard before settling herself down. "Like I'm from Ohio." She looks at me. "Sorry—I couldn't help it." She wasn't sorry, and even the words leaving her mouth sounding foreign.

Sam looks at his mother, at Mary, and then at me.

"I mean, you could if you want to—I won't mind. I mean, appearance does matter in my industry—"

"And this family, apparently," Mary adds as she takes her first sip of water.

I nod and excuse myself to the restroom. If I didn't get right up when I did, I would say something I'd regret or start to cry. I didn't want to be weak enough to do either.

I WONDER HOW much my face aged from the loneliness and despair of being married to Sam. Whose fault was it for my decline? His or mine? In the bathroom mirror, I notice my cheekbones had lost their bounce, like if I were to smile it would slide right down my face. I hadn't had a real smile in a while, and I wondered if my face had lost the muscles to hold one up if I did. I rub my hand on my warm cheek, plucking around at my skin with my fingers. My almond eyes are sadder than they've been and my lips poutier, more puppy-dog like. Even my dark hair that was once notoriously wavy has flattened out as if it was giving up on being happy, too. I don't even wear my hair natural anymore anyway. It's always pressed straight. Sam likes it better that way. It's more elegant, he says. I push my hair behind my ears as I stare back at this girl I hardly recognize. What happened to her? And what would it take for her to come back?

As I walk out of the bathroom, I feel my phone vibrate. Mary had texted me. That's weird. She was just being a jerk to me.

> **Mary:** Look, I'm sorry I was just being a bit intense, but it's just how my family is. Sam can't know I have a soft side, especially towards you. Around him and mom, I've got to be different. They can't know I've got your back.
>
> **Mary:** If marrying my brother has made you my sister…. the sister I literally prayed many years for…. I'd tell my sister she deserves more.
>
> **Me:** I promise, I'm fine. But thank you.
>
> **Mary:** You look like shit. Go be happy, girl.

I thought about what that meant. Better. What better might look like. Then, without trying, I thought of Paul.

I don't respond, put my phone in my pocket and pretend I didn't see it.

It vibrates again. Mary's tapping away texting me across the table. I pull my phone out of my pocket and read her text.

> **Mary:** If marrying my brother has made you my sister…. the sister I literally prayed many years for…. I'd tell my sister she deserves better.
>
> **Me:** I promise, I'm fine. But thank you.
>
> **Mary:** You look like shit. Go be happy, girl.

What I couldn't tell her was the truth. That she was right, but I didn't know what to do about it yet. And I was sure leaving him would make my life a million times worse. She's young, she doesn't know what divorce really does to a person. In her mind it's just breaking up. Marriage doesn't end in a breakup; it ends in war. And Sam is the last person I want to go to war against.

We continued brunch, and I drank mimosa's until I felt like laughing instead.

"Jade, you okay? Like *really* okay?" His sister leans over the table, folds her hands under her chin.

"Good lord, Mary. Can you stop prying?" Sam says, placing his sunglasses on top of his head.

"Something seems to be eating you up. Is it Sam? Is he being his true asshole perfectionist self?"

In the moment, I feel both validated and betrayed. Sam is difficult, and everyone had known it but me. I was blind. Or maybe it was there all along and I chose to ignore it.

Sam laughs. "Don't be ridiculous, Mary. I'm not a perfectionist. I just have standards, unlike you. And stop being so nosey. She's fine." Sam glares at his sister Mary.

"Sam, Mary. Play nice," his mother chimes in, tearing a croissant roll in half, smearing butter inside.

"What?" She makes an over-the-top surprised face as if to prove a point. "Jesus, don't look at me like I'm the bad guy. I'm just making sure his poor wife is surviving being married to him." She rolls her eyes and takes a sip of her blood orange cocktail. "No one else survived as his girlfriend, I'm just curious what magic Jade has up her sleeve. Maybe Jade has really changed him."

"You're an idiot, you should focus on your grades and passing a test for once in your life instead of worrying about my love life." An awkward silence takes over, my fork screeching between my jammy egg and the porcelain plate as I cut into it. The sun beats down onto the umbrella, sweat collects above my lip. Sam kicks my leg under the table to signal me to speak up and defend him. It hurt, but I don't show it. I've shut off any indication of pain long ago. My desire to give and receive has become somewhat of a distant memory.

"It's true. I'm fine." I nod, agreeing to the words coming out of my mouth, but inside, I wonder if it's obvious. How I feel about Sam.

"Really?"

"She's more than fine. Wait until she sees what's she's getting for her birthday," Sam flashes a proud, toothy grin.

"You have to spoil her with gifts. If you didn't, she'd probably leave." Mary giggles again, slurring her words a bit as she flags the waitress for another round.

A smile appears on my face without trying. Before it spreads too wide, I reel it back in, curling my lips under my teeth.

"Oh, that's not true. Sam is wonderful to me," I say. I realize by now, Sam and I have played Mr. and Mrs. perfect for far too long. And if anything is off cue, we'll both look like liars and fools. It's easier to play along this way, for everyone. If anyone knew that deep in my heart I wanted to leave, our perfection would come crashing down and everyone would know it was all for show. People would feel sad for me instead of overjoyed and proud. I'm the girl who has it all, and I intend on keeping it all, even if it kills me.

"Blink twice if you need help." Mary laughs again.

I wonder what Sam is getting me for my birthday. That's six months away.

I try not to blink.

CHAPTER THIRTEEN

A T THIS POINT, it has been a couple months since we'd even seen each other naked, but tonight we tried.

"It was awkward, and I know it's been a long time, so it might've been clunky," he says to me, pulling his boxers up over his waist. I tell him I'm sorry, that it was likely my fault, and asks if he wanted to split a Xanax. Sam falls asleep holding me and me crying. I haven't enjoyed sex with Sam since after we got married.

A part of me harbors a bit of guilt. *What kind of wife didn't enjoy pleasing her husband? What kind of wife doesn't love to be pleased by her husband, either?* Even the thought of his hands on me or his heavy breathing on top of me makes me want to curl and die a little. I think some of this is normal in a marriage, but the last time I had good sex, it was not with Sam. That makes me feel guilty, too. I know what this means, even if I'm afraid to say it out loud.

"I don't think I love you, Sam," I whisper soft enough that he couldn't hear. "I think—" I swallow the dreaded lump in my throat. "I think I hate you." Sam was already asleep, snoring away. He always snores when he drinks.

SOMETIMES I DAYDREAM about a divorce like it is some sort of "Make a Wish" foundation dream cruise I couldn't wait to board, even if that meant knowing at the end of cruise, I'd be at the end of my rope. It doesn't change the fact that the cruise still sounded like a fantasy to me. A divorce sounds nice, but at the same time, it sounds scary and complicated. Overwhelming. Deadly.

With Sam, I have a beautiful condo with million-dollar, stunning views on the gold coast overlooking the Chicago skyline, a pristine neighborhood, security guards, elite community, rooftop parties. I have wealth and safety, things I didn't think I'd ever find, not at my age when most people under thirty are still stumbling through student loan debt and online dating fails. I "have it all" and yet, I feel empty. And sometimes, I don't hate him. It's just that my body has somehow shut off and it wants nothing to do with Sam anymore, which shouldn't make sense because Sam is an incredibly handsome man. Women seems to fall over him everywhere we go. Somedays, I can still hardly believe he picked me. Women always stop to tell him how pretty his eyes are, even when I'm next to him.

"Wow, your eyes. I've never seen such a pretty, light, ocean blue color. They are beautiful," said the lady at the bread shop. Never minding the fact that I am standing right next to him.

"Oh, I hope you aren't offended," she said. "Your eyes are pretty, too," she said out of sympathy. I know she really didn't mean that, and no one has ever said anything about my exceptionally average brown eyes unless they were half-shot and trying to get a lay.

"No, I'm not. I get it. His eyes are spectacular." They really are. He's quiet and calculated. He's introspective and analytical. He's intelligent and comes from a wealthy family. Went to a private school and had a picture-perfect childhood. He has a wildly successful career in the family commercial real estate business. He seemingly fit the bill of the man of my dreams, it was a no-brainer. I would marry him, and my dreams would come true. I would be happy, fulfilled and have it all, including my biggest dream—the upscale bakery located in the heart of the city. It would be all mine. And I would be far away from Tiffin and the Painesville River without a single cow or field of hay insight.

Sometimes, I can't tell if he hates me, too, or if it's just one-sided hate. I can't tell if he treats me so horribly because he doesn't love me, or because he loves me so much, he doesn't want to lose me. I've noticed our relationship runs on cycles. We can have a wonderful couple weeks where we get along and life is great, enjoyable even. Then the wheel turns, and we're back to screaming and arguing and me hating every minute of being his wife.

"I WONDER IF this is normal in a marriage or if this is how it goes?" I ask my mom, phone pressed against my shoulder and cheek, pouring the box of linguine into boiling water. "Does love run on cycles? Are we supposed to hate each other sometimes and be obsessed with each other the next?"

"Honey, I don't have the best examples to draw from, either." She huffs air into the phone in a forced laugh. Mom is on her second marriage after the first ended with a toaster thrown at her head. My father is her current husband, is on the straight and narrow after a few hiccups with the law over a couple DUI years ago, and my mom is still resentful for having to drive him around for ten years without a license, though she never left because in her words, she would be dammed to go through a divorce again. She'd rather carry him like a tether than leave.

"The other day, Mom, he told me that I was chewing like a Neanderthal." I push a section of hair back behind my ear. "While we were with his colleagues at a nice restaurant. It was mortifying."

"Oh Jesus, Jade." She laughs. "You know he was joking. You have always been so sensitive."

"It wasn't funny. It was mean," I say. "I would never do that to him."

"And don't use all your big fancy words from Chicago. Mortifying," she mocks. "Just say embarrassing like a normal person."

"A normal person? Am I not a normal person?" My mother means well, but she's never been the gentlest on conversational delivery.

"You've always tried to be someone you're not. I love you more than the world, but you know it's the truth." Struggling to open the jar of pasta sauce, I let out an angry noise.

"Don't be upset. It's not always bad thing, I just wish you were more grateful for what you have. Nothing has ever been enough for you."

I pause to think about that for a moment and can remember being a teen and making my parents feel bad for not having enough money. We didn't have the least amount of money, but I wasn't the richest girl in school. The Guirtz twins were. Their stepfather owned several dairy farms and an ice creamery that had a national fan base. "Blue Moo's" it was called. They claimed to have invented the blue moon flavored ice cream cone, but everyone in town said it was conspiracy and that their stepdad, Jonny Webster, stole it. The twins drove shiny red convertibles to school, and there was nothing more I wanted than to be them. To have a cool car, nice clothes, and not have to do chores for the measly ten bucks to pay for bowling or the movies with my friends. I did always desire a simpler, easier life in that way. Everything that I enjoyed involved working hard for it first, earning it. I was tired of earning when other people I knew were just seemingly attracting the things they desired effortlessly.

"Mr. Webster ain't an honest man, Jade. He's a crook. He

just got out of jail five years ago for tax fraud. Those aren't honest possessions," my father would say. "I'd rather work hard for what I've got and have it be honest and owned. I don't want to owe the bank or anyone nothin." Whether it was honest or not, I wanted a life of luxury and ease. And if the twins had it, so could I someday.

I finally get the pasta sauce open and say, "Thank God," in relief.

"For what, honey?" my mom replies, I can tell she's no longer paying attention. Her TV is blasting in the background. "Sorry, baby, my show is on. I forgot what I was sayin."

"I'll just let you go. I'm making dinner."

"Honey, I just want to remind you one thing before I head off. Don't expect success from doing something you love. No one ever got rich making cookies. That's called a hobby. Why don't you just be a good housewife and bake cookies for him for a change? What man wouldn't love that? Pour some love into him, and maybe you'll get more in return. I bet that is all Sam is saying. That should be plenty enough. He has given you enough."

"Right—" I say, refusing to fight. I can never win with her, so I don't even try. Instead, I've learned to surrender silently.

"When are you and Sam coming back down to visit? We miss you. It has been months since I've seen you two."

"Hopefully soon. Alright? Sam has been working a lot,"

She mumbles something I can't understand. "I better see you by Thanksgiving," she says.

"Does Paul still live in town?" I blurt out without meaning to. She takes her time to respond, which makes my palms sweat a little.

"What does that mean? Why do you want to know?" Her tone sounds suspicious.

"I don't know. Just curious. I haven't talked to him since…"

"The day before your wedding?"

I pause quietly, reflecting on the last words he spoke to me over a year ago. *I'll be waiting.*

She clears her throat. "He's still here. In town, with his grandparents."

"Do you ever see him?"

I can tell she's not enjoying me asking about him, her tone has shifted from content to concerned.

"He's pretty hard to avoid, you know? With him living down the same county road and all. Tiffin is a small town, you know that."

"Huh," I say. I imagine Paul bailing hay, his strong arms, his wide chest filling out dirty overalls. Him. Washing dishes in the farmhouse sink, his thick strong forearms wet and covered in suds. Him, helping his grandparents in their old age. Giving himself selflessly out of love. Paul being Paul.

"If it makes you feel any better, I think he's still alone. Single, I mean. He's not married," she says.

It doesn't make me feel better, it makes me feel worse. Sick, even. Paul is still available, and for some reason, I find that harder to come to terms with than if he wasn't. If he wasn't, then he wouldn't even be an option for me to consider, and all my daydreaming would come to an end. It was simple math. But the fact that he is alone, possibly still waiting, painfully takes its hold on me. A feeling that melts down from my chest into my toes. A longing that has grown legs.

"All the good ones like Sam get snatched up early. Makes you wonder why he hasn't found someone else. That used to be a red flag back in my day. If you weren't married by twenty-five, it meant something was wrong with you." She laughs a little.

"Paul isn't one to rush into anything, I'm sure he'll find

someone at the right time," I say, knowing that was half-true. The truth was likely that Paul's heart still belonged to me, and he didn't know how else to pass the time. Thinking about that only made me feel more sick.

"Anyway, don't worry your head about some boy from forever ago. You've got a good life," she says as if she' reminding me why I picked Sam. "And send me another sunset picture from that rooftop. I can't believe that view. You sure are one lucky girl."

She ends the conversation guilt tripping me to come back home with Sam to celebrate Thanksgiving in Ohio this year with my family. I hang up the phone wondering if I'd run into Paul if we did.

CHAPTER FOURTEEN

S AM IS LATE. Again.

I sit at our kitchen island alone, swinging the barstool side to side slowly with my hips. The squeak of the metal echoes in the vastness of the wide-open space. The open floor plan Sam couldn't wait to own. I twirl my spaghetti as I think about marriage again. What it is versus what I thought it would be. The longer I think, the more I realize I have never seen a marriage I envied.

Sam doesn't cheat and he's never hit me, not really. He's grabbed my wrist a little tight, he's shoved me into a wall a time or two. I probably deserved it. I maybe had too much to drink, and my smart mouth caught up with me, I'm sure. Sometimes, I look around at my life, and I'm grateful it's all mine. I'm proud, even. But often, it doesn't feel like mine. It feels like it belongs to Sam, and I'm just borrowing it.

When Sam gets home much later that night, he ruffles through the covers and slides into his side of the bed. I'm rolled to one side, back turned away from him, scrolling through pictures of cakes and desserts. My face presses into my memory foam pillow, my hair still wet from showering. This is what I do every night; dream of the small bakery I long to open in the Gold Coast nearly tasting the buttercream on my fingers already. I scroll and screenshot the ones I admire for inspiration.

I open a social media account and pull up Paul's profile.

Normally he never posts, all his photos are still from five years ago when he didn't have a beard, his hair was shorter, and his face was younger.

Except now, I notice there's a new one. A photo of him and a long-legged girl, her blonde hair frozen in time as he twirls her on a beach in Florida. I felt both relieved and pained to see him in a relationship, but I would tell no one that, not even him.

By the looks of it, she is what my mother would call "trashy," and the longer I looked at her profile, it was confirmed. Each photo convinces me he must be on drugs to choose someone like her. I might be "Ohio average" looking, but at least I have class. I scroll down to what she does for a living as I collect as much information to hate about her on her page. She works at a Game Stop, has a tramp stamp on her lower back and faded, orangey blonde, box-dyed hair. Some of her photos show her smoking cigarettes. *Paul, what the hell?* He despises smoking, and always has. As if all of this wasn't bad enough, her profile photo is her in a puppy dog filter with glitter sparkles and hearts, kissing Paul on the cheek. My stomach sours. A girl like this is not even Paul's type, I shake my head in disbelief before slamming my phone down onto my nightstand.

"You're mad?" Sam says, rolling his body over to mine. Yes, I'm mad, but I can't tell him all the actual reasons why. I say nothing.

"Look, it was a late night again. I'm sorry, but I promise it'll all pay off. I'm working hard for *us*. I hope you know that."

I nod. "Did you see the dinner in the fridge?" I ask, back still turned.

"I did, looked delicious. What was it? Spaghetti? We had dinner at the office. Take-out—" he says disappointed, rolling his body into my back, wrapping his arms over me. "Yours looked better."

"You can take the leftovers to work."

"And I'll brag to everyone about my chef of a wife."

"The chef who isn't really a chef. Just the girl who took a few culinary classes, never finished, doesn't really bake anymore, but works for her husband's company from home as a virtual assistant. That chef?"

"We aren't doing his right now, are we?" Sam says.

I blow a frustrated puff of air from my mouth.

"Jade. Come on. You know this is temporary. I'm going to make so much money this year we won't even know what to do with it all. And once that happens, you can have everything you've ever wanted. Please—" he says, his arms grabbing me tighter.

"Good night, Sam," I say, patting his arm before rolling back over away from him.

"I love you, Jade."

I swallow and press my eyes shut. "I love you, too."

Once he's rolled back over onto his phone again, I pick mine back up to make sense of what I just saw before Sam mistook my anger towards him. Now, I'm upset about two things at once. *Who has Paul become? What did my wedding day do to him?* Paul doesn't ever routinely update his social media, which make this post more off-putting and unlike the guy I once knew. I wondered in this moment if he was just settling for any old girl with all her teeth still left in town, or if he was doing this to get my attention. If that was the case, it's working.

For a minute, regardless of what I thought about her, I found myself increasingly jealous of her. Then, I considered doing something I know I'd immediately regret. I decided to click 'like' on the photo even though I didn't like it. I didn't like it one bit. I did it just to convince other people it didn't bother me. And yes, to get his attention. After closer inspection, I notice these were engagement photos. *Paul is engaged.*

The ring is small, hardly a diamond, especially if you were to compare it to mine. I hold my left hand out and admired my rock for a moment, tilting it left and right to watch it sparkle. I will give Paul this, she looked like a porn star. Her body was tanned and snatched tight, her lips plump and oversized. It was impossible to look at her and not think of sex, which made me hate her more, because I imagined her perfect body and her stupid face all over him without even trying. I hate her and her big bimbo tits and I didn't even know her. I rolled my eyes after I hit "like," and wanted to gag after. Moments later, a text pings on my phone. It's Paul. It's been over a year since our last communication.

Paul: *Thanks for the approval.*

I know he's talking about the engagement.

Me: *Who said I approve?*

I send an emoji that makes a questionable face.

Paul: *I figured the 'like' meant you were happy for me.*
Me: *I am happy for you.*

I lied.

Paul: *So, you do approve?*

He sent an emoji that makes a sideways smirk.

Me: *Do you want me to approve?*
Paul: *I want you to feel how you feel.*
Me: *How do you think I feel?*

Paul always felt like mine because I had him first. Even when he wasn't mine, he still was. I owned something of his could that he could never get back and a place in his heart that I took first. His first love and his virginity. This girl never knew it, but she never stood a chance. I smiled; the confidence of that fact felt warm enough to put me to sleep. In the morning, I keep myself busy enough tidying the kitchen, so I won't feel like checking for his text every five seconds. Having the phone in my hands makes me anxious, so I put it on the table face down. I pour myself a cup of coffee and open my work laptop. I tell myself I'll only pick it up when it vibrates. Just then, it does.

Paul: *If I knew maybe I wouldn't be engaged to someone else.*

Damn. He said it.

Me: *Well, you are now. So, congrats…*

I try to say this convincingly, but I've never been a good liar. Usually when I lie, I go silent. It's easier for me to be quiet than to lie.

Paul: *Will I ever know how Jade feels?*
Me: *Jade feels happy that you're happy*
Paul: *You know I'd be a lot happier if it were you*
Me: *I don't know what you want me to say, Paul*
Paul: *I don't know either, I guess*
Paul: *Never mind, sorry*
Me: *You're marrying… what's her face now. Shelby, is it? I think that's great.*

I lie again.

What I want to say is how I really felt. Which is that I felt terribly bitter and angry that he was engaged. I wanted to tell him that I think his new fiancé Shelby is ugly and that he could do better. And by better, I mean me.

Paul: *You're mad. It's cute...*

Damn it. He knows me.

Me: *I guess I haven't changed a bit. Still cute, all these years later.*

Am I flirting? What am I doing? My heart races a little.

Paul: *Wouldn't know. Haven't seen you in forever.*

Me: *Maybe we should change that...*

And just like that, I have opened the floodgates.

CHAPTER FIFTEEN
Thanksgiving (two months later)

I AM SCURRYING through the only run-down grocery store in town when I see him. My mom calls Sam and me halfway into town to ask us to make a stop to grab a bag of frozen peas for my niece who had bumped her head on the coffee table.

"We could also eat them, too, once they're thawed. With a spoonful butter or something. Won't go to waste," Mom said.

"Jade?" His voice takes the breath from my lungs for a moment. I hold in whatever air that's left inside of me before remembering how to breathe again. I turn from the freezer aisle, my hand growing numb from holding the frozen door open too long.

As I turn around towards him, my heart sinks into my stomach and flips upside down. There he is, standing in front of me, wearing his Carhart overalls and boots. He's carrying a case of beer, a gallon of milk, and a loaf of bread. His face is covered in an overgrown golden beard, and his eyes, shining like a million pieces of broken amber under the glow of the fluorescent lights.

My cheeks caught fire, bright red and burning, which is hard to do standing inside of a freezer. But if anyone could make me feel warm inside regardless, it's him.

"Oh, Paul. Wow, so good to see you." I close the door, clutching the peas in the corner of one arm as I opened the other to hug him. The hug feels like it lasted for twice as long as it needs to. He still smells the same, his signature earthy scent of farm mixed with the clean, fragrant smell of detergent and dryer sheets. The same "him" smell I remember.

"Yeah, wow. Look at you."

He takes my hand and makes me do a slow spin.

"This coat looks very fancy on you." He brushes the wool sleeve with his hand. I know he means expensive when he says fancy.

"You look great, though." He smiles big and shakes his head a little.

I laugh. "It's Thanksgiving, you know my mom is big into personal appearance. She had me wearing a full face of make up at twelve."

"I remember. I always told you to take it off. Liked you better without it." He looks down at his boots caked with dried mud.

"How've you been?" I ask, staring at his face, studying it like a map.

"Good. Yeah, I'm still here," he says, expressive with his hands. "Taking care of Grandma and Pop-Pop's farm. They needed some extra muscle now that Pop-Pop's getting older. Old man hates to admit he needs the help, but since his hip surgery, he hasn't gotten around the same."

We look at each other as if there was more we both had to say but didn't know how.

"Thinking about taking a couple college classes though online," he adds and stands up taller.

"That's great, I'm glad to hear. You've always been so smart. Much smarter than I am, we both know that." We laugh together, and his hand brushes mine on accident, but I don't move it away. When he notices, he scratches his beard.

"What about you? Are you a world-renowned baker yet? Should I be asking for your autograph?" he says.

"I haven't been baking much," I say, pushing my hair behind my ears. "Well, I have, but it's the boring stuff. The good ol' daily bread, but nothing else really." I laugh a little and hide my hand in my coat pocket.

"How's Sam?" he asks even though I had hoped he wouldn't. My phone lit up and buzzes in my hand. Sam has texted me.

Sam: *WHAT IS TAKING SO LONG????? HURRY!!!! We are going to be LATE!!*

I swallow a lump gathering in my throat, and I feel my hand growing hot.

"Sorry," I say, shoving my phone back into my purse. "It's Mom," I lie. "We have to get going for the dinner, she's waiting on these peas." I shake the half-melted bag of wet, wrinkly peas in my warm hands.

"Yeah, no. Get going," he says as he starts to walk away and then stops to pulls me in for one last hug. His smell lingers on my coat for a minute.

On his way out, he shouts at me walking towards the check out, "Hey, Happy Thanksgiving."

"Happy Thanksgiving," I wave back to him. "I'll see you around." My voice fades into the distance. I wanted to say, "Goodbye, love you," like I have said to him a thousand times before. But I don't. In my head, I say "I love you" repeatedly. My mouth wants to say it, too. I know I won't see him around. I live in a different state. I don't know when I will ever see him again.

"Congratulations on your engagement!" I yell over my shoulder as I head towards the door. By this time, he's halfway into his pickup, and I am sure he can't hear me.

"Who was that?" Sam asks as I climb into the car.

"Oh, just someone that I grew up with. An old neighbor."

"What are yelling about, I couldn't hear."

"He's engaged. I was just saying congratulations."

Sam nods and turns out of the parking lot.

I look back at the pickup truck, "He didn't hear me though," I whisper to myself.

THE NEXT MORNING, I wake up in my childhood bedroom to a text.

> **Paul:** *Are you still in town? Do you want to grab a coffee and hot cocoa?*

A smile cracks on my mouth. My eyes tingle into my nose, and my chest tightens. I roll over to Sam. I look at his face and feel disgusted like I've had a regretful one-night stand, except we hadn't had sex and he was very much my husband. I imagine myself sneaking out of bed and meeting Paul. I imagine coming back in quietly before Sam is awake. I think about making an excuse, like needing to run to the pharmacy for tampons or allergy medicine, just to leave the house and meet up with Paul.

Instead, I try to ignore it. Every time I go to the bathroom, I pull out my phone and start typing, just to erase it.

> **Me:** *I can't… I wish I could…. I miss you.*

I erase "I miss you" but didn't want to.

> **Paul:** *I'm not engaged anymore. I just thought you should know that before you leave.*

"Jade, we should scoot out early today. I have to help my mom put together a few things at her house," Sam says, his breath lingering of cheap beer he drank with my father to make him happy. Later, Sam will complain the cheap beer gave him a migraine, and somehow, it will be my fault.

I roll over and make a face that pretends to look happy. "Mmkay." When Sam has his eyes closed for a good few minutes, I text Paul again.

Me: *I'm sorry to hear that... what happened? I wish I could take you up on that coffee and cocoa, but we have to leave early this morning.*

Paul: *Figured you'd say that.*

A few minutes pass and Sam heads to the shower.

Paul: *Ps. Check your mailbox.*

My heart begins to race like it did nearly fifteen years ago. Before I talk myself out of it, I pull on an old, hooded sweatshirt from the drawer, surprised it still fits. I tie my shoes tight and head out to run. I haven't ran in so long that I worry my legs might not remember how.

While Sam showers, I run out to check the mailbox. Inside there's a note that says,

Meet you at the stop sign?—P

It will take longer than ten minutes if I don't run, and I know I don't have much time to spare without Sam knowing. I need to run as fast as I possibly can. Once I'm out the door, I start lightly jogging, casually, normally. Once I'm out of anyone's sight, I sprint as fast as I humanly can. I realize I don't know if I have ever run quite this fast for anything ever.

At the halfway point, the road turns from a forgiving flat surface to an angry uphill. It's at this point where I always lost steam and would start walking. With walking not being an option today, I instead push myself harder and harder up this hill. My cheeks slam down hard on my jaw with each powerful step on the dirt road, gritting my teeth shut so that don't rattle in my head. The cold, fall air burns my lungs with each inhale.

Once over the hill, I see Paul, standing there next to the stop sign, waiting with his hands in his pockets. When I see him wave at me from the place that once meant so much to us, everything stops hurting, and I slow down enough, reminding myself that I need to make it there to him in one piece. My stiff knees start to buckle, which makes me limp a little on the slow down. When I get close enough to walk, I throw my hands over my head and try my hardest to not look nearly as dead as I feel. I imagine this is the kind of victory a marathon runner might feel after a race. Insanely stupid, yet full of overwhelming joy. Everything melts away as I near closer and closer. I can see Paul laughing a little. He yells out at me, "Did you do that on purpose?"

"Do what on purpose?" I ask, bending over with my hands on my knees, sucking in sweet, sweet oxygen as fast as I can.

He points at my sweater, and I look down. It's the one he gave me when we met. I hadn't even noticed, I just grabbed one from the drawer.

"It still looks better on you than me," he says.

I walk up to him, holding on to the stop sign, afraid that if I don't, I might collapse. His golden eyes meet mine. This time when I look back, I investigate them, searching deeper, trying to see if they'll tell me something words can't say. Words I want to hear. Words I'm afraid to hear. Words that would melt me.

"Hi," he says, smiling. His beard is still the same as it was yesterday, modestly overgrown. He's wearing a flannel jacket half-zipped, dark jeans and a clean pair of boots, ones that don't look like they belong on the farm. His hair looks a bit groomed, pushed off the side just slightly, and he smelled exceptionally better than he did yesterday. Teakwood scented and minty fresh. He has tried to impress me. It's working. And here I am, un-showered, out of breath, rosy-cheeked and quite positive I hadn't brushed my teeth or hair. I am a mess, and he is a work of art.

"What did you want from me? Why the note?"

"Why did you come?" I get another whiff of his fresh, cool breath as he speaks and moves his body closer to mine.

"I just wanted to see you. It has been so long. Too long, hasn't it?"

"*Just* see me?"

I push him playfully. He steps closer, puts his hand on mine.

"I mean, I'd take a kiss if you'd let me. Like old times." He smirks. "But I know you're a married woman now." He says, pulling my hand and ring up to his face to examine.

"Holy smokes, Sam did good." He lets out a forced breath of air. "That's a mighty fine rock."

I pull my hand away and put it on my hip.

"I'm sorry it didn't work out," I say. "Your engagement."

"I'm not." He steps closer to me. "Doesn't everything happen for a reason? Isn't that the saying?"

"Does it? I'm not so sure."

He shakes his head. "She wasn't the one."

I look at his eyes and look away before he can say it.

"You are."

My heart beats twice as fast. I want to vomit. I want to scream into a pillow. I want to be his.

"Paul. I... I can't."

"You know you want to kiss me." He learns his shoulder towards me. His scent turns my insides on fire. I close my eyes as I breathe him in.

"How do you know?"

"Did you see how fast you ran?" He laughs. "If you ran that fast in high school, you would've gotten a full ride track scholarship."

"You're full of it." I push him again and laugh. He smiles at me and gives me an adoring look.

"It's cute. I love it."

"I love you," I blurt. "I'm sorry. I didn't mean…" Paul pulls my face into his and kisses me like I was the only one.

When he comes back up for air, he whispers, "Don't. Don't be sorry. I love you, too."

"I'm sorry. I don't know what I was thinking. I really should go. We are supposed to leave to help Sam's mom, we should've left over an hour ago. If I'm gone too long, Sam will wonder where I'm at."

Paul looks around at the wide-open, empty cornfields surrounding us.

"Is this just always how it will end for us?"

"I—don't know…" It comes out almost like a whimper. I don't want to hurt him again.

"It seems like it, doesn't it?" he says, still looking away. A flock of crows fly to the left, his head follows. "It doesn't have to always be this way."

"Maybe not always, but right now it does."

"What do you want me to do, Jade?"

"If I had an answer, we both wouldn't be here right now."

"Jade, what if we don't have as much time as we think? What if this is our last shot?"

"What does that mean?" I ask, afraid to hear his answer.

"I don't know. It just kind of came out," he says, "Life is short. And if it is as short as we know it to be, why are wasting a single minute not together?"

"Paul, I'm really sorry, I have to go…." I squeeze his hand tight before I pull it away to start running back. "I'll talk to you soon, okay?" I yell out. I start jogging backwards a bit towards the hill so I can still see him. "I promise."

Paul stands there still, looking as though I had just tipped him upside and emptied him out. The run on the way back is now twice as painful as it was on the way there, for more reasons than just physical. Now, the aching I feel is inside and out. Seeing him made it worse for the both of us. Knowing that after all these years, there is still very much something there but also feeling the impossibility of it now. I am married. I chose Sam. It's too late.

I ARRIVE AT the front door; my mom is standing there with her arms folded behind it as if she were waiting for me.

"What was that all about?" she says under her breath.

My cheeks are red and hot from windburn and the heat of guilt. She cocks her head and squints her eyes. "Jade?"

"I went for a quick run," I say, pulling off my tennis shoes. "It's a nice day for it." She looks at me and nods as if she knows exactly where I was. She will have her word with me later, it's written all over her face.

"Sam out of the shower?" I ask. She nods again. Mom has always been good at keeping my secrets, but only for so long.

"He's packing the bags and loading them into the car," she says quietly. "He asked where you were—"

"What did you tell him?" My eyes widen in fear.

"I told him I saw you went on a run. I didn't know Sam never knew you tried out for the track team for a short while. He didn't know you were a runner. He said you never mentioned it."

Sam walks in. "Hey, track star. How was your run?" His arms are full of our bags. My cheeks still red and my breath still out, my mind still replaying Paul's tongue rolling over mine. My lower half is still swelling and aching to be touched by him again. I try to swallow that down.

"Fine. It was cold at first but warmed up after I got going."

"You look sweaty. Did you want to shower before we head out?' His face looks a bit disgusted as if I'm looking too Ohio for him right now.

"I'm alright." I head to the sink to grab a drink, open the freezer, and toss a few ice cubes in it.

"I'll cool down in a minute." *Sweet lord, please let every part of me cool down.* I think to myself. My tongue still tastes like the sweet inside of Paul's mouth. I swish around water in my cheeks like mouthwash.

"Sam, it's always so great to see you." Mom wraps her arms over Sam's shoulders, hugging his neck. "You don't work too hard now, you hear?"

Sam laughs. "No promises, Diane. It's no easy task to give your daughter the world." He winks at her, kissing her cheek.

"I know it. You're a good man, Sam. I know Jade can be difficult. Just ship her back home if she gets to be too much," she laughs.

Mom has always taken his side to please him. That's just her way. Keep the man happy, make them feel pure and innocent. The man does no wrong, ever. I was always glad I didn't have a brother for that reason. When she was pregnant with my little sister, I worried if it was a boy, she'd let him get away with murder and pacify him into an awful, irresponsible man child. The world didn't need another one of those. Thank God, lucky for her and all the women in the world, she had daughters. Women she could toughen up by making them accountable for their own actions, responsible for everything. Even the things they shouldn't be responsible for.

"I think I'll keep her. As long as she doesn't run away like she did this morning." He winks at me, and every part of my body wants to disappear.

CHAPTER SIXTEEN

PAUL CONSUMED MY brain the entire drive home, but you wouldn't know it by looking at me, listening along to some long-winded podcast with Sam about real estate investments. Boredom had painted over my post Paul glow, and any shadow of excitement could not be traced. Later that night, after travelling back home to Chicago and helping his mother move her new furniture, it was Sam's idea for us to take a weed gummy in the rooftop hot tub. Apparently, a colleague gave the gummy to Sam after his complaints about his neck hurting. Sam blames me for his pain in his neck. Tells me he carries the weight of everything on his shoulders and it's no wonder it hurts. Says he's joking, but that's his usual word track after saying anything rude, hurtful, or insulting. It's always "just a joke" and I'm the sensitive one that just "didn't get it."

Even though Sam isn't always great, I find myself beginning to feel awful about the fact that I had swapped spit with another man just hours before this. And just any man, Paul. Luckily, after the gummy kicked in, the guilt dissolved along with my consciousness. It's clear it has kicked in for Sam, too. His eyes are more googly and he's smiling, which is quite the sight. Sam rarely smiles a true smile anymore.

"You're the most beautiful thing I have ever seen," Sam says, smiling wider at me with his glossy eyes. He leans in to kiss me, his smooth wet chest presses into me. I haven't liked kissing Sam for what feels like years, our last enjoyable kiss was on our wedding day. He put his lips on mine and the sensation was quite pleasant, sensitive, and soft. The edible made our faces feel like they were melting into each other's. It wasn't exactly erotic or sexy, but it was fun. I could've made out with a log and had just as much fun. Fun was what Sam I needed more than anything. We have become so dull, so serious, so boring. It wasn't like Sam to suggest the gummy and it wasn't like me to be spontaneous about mind-altering substances, especially since I tend to become paranoid on the stuff. If it wasn't for me needing to take my mind elsewhere and off Paul, I would've declined. Instead, I now find myself more confused.

When Sam and I have moments like this, it feels like picking him was a no-brainer. He has these moments where he is fun, exciting, sexy, daring, and charming. All the qualities I loved about him when we met. On paper, Sam is a catch. It's just that over time, that paper has disintegrated, worn thin and the words have become hard to make out.

Once we came down from the high, we were still giggly but able to think and communicate a little, we head back down to the condo. I make salmon and wild rice for us for dinner and we both log on to our laptops to prepare for the work week ahead. Another busy week at the office for Sam makes another lonely week for me at home. I'm working from home, so the office doesn't get too political about Sam's wife supporting their team. No one knows I'm Sam's wife and I work under an alias name, Bren Hanner. Part of me doesn't mind, it keeps me out of the office drama and uninvolved in all the schmoozing I know I would hate anyway as an introvert. The other part of me hates being a secret and even worse, hates being so alone. My options are slim until we find a bakery, and until then, we both need to save up as much as possible. And the fastest way to get there is to support Sam and his team with these next few big deals.

FROM THE WINDOW I watch the setting sun meet the water, our condo has faded from its orange sunset glow to being lit up by the million white flecks of tall city buildings. As promised, I snapped a photo of both for my mom. When she received the text she replied right away, as if she were waiting for it:

Mom: *Am I ever jealous? What a perfect life. Enjoy!*

She sends a picture back. The same orange sky with a scene that used to be home. Wide open grassy yard, a pond with a small flock of birds flying over it. Peaceful nature scape full of memories. Some good, many not. And then I remembered why I left.

ON WORK NIGHTS, we're in bed before nine so Sam can wake up by four thirty in the morning to work out before heading to the office.

"I wish I knew you were a runner. What else don't I know about you?" Sam says, spitting toothpaste into the sink. He wipes his mouth.

"I wouldn't say stomping down a few dirt road runs makes me a runner."

"I just didn't know you ever enjoyed it, even for a short while. I guess I would've been curious to know more about that side of you. I've always ran in the mornings, had I known you also enjoyed it, I would've asked you to tag along."

"I was sixteen. What other side of that teenage girl do you want to know about?"

"What else did you like to do?"

"What did *you* like to do?" I say, almost reverting to that angsty teenage girl all over again.

"Why are you changing the topic? I just wanted to know more about you. It feels like sometimes you had this whole life before we met that I know nothing about."

"Well, I didn't," I say, scrubbing the facial cleanser off my cheeks with a warm washcloth. "It was a boring life in Tiffin, Ohio. That's why I left." I pat my face dry, burying it in the towel for an extra minute to hide my face.

"Except you liked running."

"Can you let it go?" I mumble from the towel. "Jesus, Sam."

"Aren't you curious about what I was like? You've never asked once about what my life was like before we met. I've just told you things without ever realizing you never really asked or shared much back."

"I didn't think it was important. To talk about who we used to be. I'm not that person anymore. I let that person go."

"You sure about that?" he says. "Because you sure are acting like someone from Tiffin Ohio right now."

"Oh my god. What does that even mean, Sam?"

"Like there's still something about that place that is eating you alive every second you're away from it."

The thing about Sam is that often, he isn't wrong. It's not Ohio and it's not the places there eating me alive every second I'm away from it. It's the person. It's Paul.

CHAPTER SEVENTEEN

S AM HAD THIS brilliant idea to test drive an SUV after work. I quite liked my car; it was a black Audi A4 Sam bought me for a college graduation present. Yes, he bought me an actual car for a graduation present, like it was no big deal. His mother lost her mind when he did, too. That was the first time she let me have an ear full about how unworthy I was for her son. On my graduation day, she called me. Sam had graduated five years ahead of me and had already began earning a great deal of money working in the real estate brokerage with his father, the man his mother hated more than me.

For the last six months or so, it has been very clear that Sam is ready for a baby, but I haven't quite caught up to him. After many arguments about it for months, he's convinced me to shop around for a bigger car, just in case it changes my mind. He took me to a dealership hoping that I'd leave with not only a bigger car, but a new desire for a child.

"Just to try it on for a day, see how it feels," he says with shrug. "Can't hurt."

"How what feels? Driving a mommy mobile?" I roll my eyes and cross my arms.

Within the first few minutes of scanning the cars, I felt nausea and regret. The first one the dealer pulled up was a minivan to test drive, not just a bigger car, but it was a car made exclusively for moms. When I saw the doors slide open, I could picture it.

My weathered skin, tired purple bags hanging under eyes, French fries dried into the floorboard. I could hear the wailing dreadful screams of "Mommmmmmmy!" and something within me broke.

"Absolutely fucking not," I say to the salesman as I uncross my arms, shooting an evil glare at Sam. Rage bubbled up from my stomach and I can feel the eruption about to blow. I know this means war to Sam, me having an opinion. Sam laughs and spoke sweetly to the salesman, "Sorry, she doesn't know a good thing when she sees it. She'll warm up to it." He uncrosses his arms, put them in a power stance on his hips and glares at me. I know this look. The look of *You better do this thing I'm suggesting or else I'll put you through hell later.*

I wonder what his retaliation would be like if I didn't. He nods me into the car, and I take a seat on the driver's side. The ass of it is so wide I feel like I have gained weight by just sitting in it. I reach below my feet adjust the seat forward, forward, and forward a bit more. I wiggle the mirrors in their correct place to somehow safely operate the machine that felt too big for my small body. This purchase would feel like I would be doing and driving a rather big thing for everyone but myself. Like the car wouldn't really be mine at all. It feels like a loaner car that I'd suffer through until I had to give it back. Seventeen, eighteen years? I take the minivan onto the highway and drove extra slow and careful, imagining I had indeed a child or two in car seats behind me. I wonder if this is what motherhood would feel like? Loaning out my entire identity until God only knows when I could return to myself? The thought shakes me. My life not really being my life. My car not really being my car. I wonder what else moms might lose out on. Up until this point, I never have to consider that feeling of selflessness and it worried me that maybe perhaps I never feel ready to let parts of myself go. If this is a small glimpse of motherhood that I am getting and I already don't like it, who is to say I wouldn't love it at all. Any of it. That worries me, too.

"SAM, I CAN'T—DO this," I say, parking the van back into the dealership lot. I can tell by the way he furrowed his eyebrows into his pointy nose that he isn't happy with how the day went. He gives me the silent treatment on the drive home, and I can tell he is silently fuming. When we get home, he tells me I am right: I probably am not ready to be a mother. That I am immature and too selfish. That I have some major growing up to do.

"For starters," he says, "You could think about finding a steady job on your own. Not one that I gave you out of pity. And not that I really need you to work much longer or need your money, but for the simple fact that you aren't reliable, and you need to grow up. You have no track record of staying in one place for very long." He sighs. "I don't know... maybe you're too flighty to be a mom, anyway. Crazy of me really to think that you would be ready. You can hardly take care of yourself."

"Okay, even if I'm flighty, I still know what I want. And it's not a baby. Not right now." Sam huffs and then grows quiet again.

The rest of the day and into the evening he stonewalls me, pretending that I don't even exist. If I am walking into the kitchen, he will quietly walk out. If I enter our bed, he turns out the light as soon as I peel back the covers. When Sam isn't exploding, he gets eerily quiet. He shuts down and shuts off. I find it almost worse than when we argue outwardly. Because when he breaks his silence, I know he's about to unleash a verbal lashing onto me. It's this ticking time bomb waiting to go off that destroys me worse than the bomb itself.

"You wouldn't be you without me, Jade." Sam shouts, breaking his silence.

I say nothing. And that's the part I hate the most. Because I know he's probably right.

CHAPTER EIGHTEEN

T HE NEXT MORNING arrives, and Sam is still quiet. It isn't until the following evening where he broke his silence and was ready to throw his verbal punches.

"YOU WOULD'VE ENDED up dropping out of school, making some stupid business decision on your own. You would've tried to open a bakery and you would've failed miserably. You would've given up when things got too hard, and you'd be flat broke right back in Ohio like everyone else still there that you know. Probably married to some Joe-schmo mechanic without two pennies to rub together."

I watch Sam's reflection in the bathroom mirror from behind him as he adjusts the cuff of his dress shirt. He's looking at me as if he wants to slap me. He doesn't, but I wish he would. Anger is always brewing in his silence, and for some reason I would rather see it on the outside.

I stand there and take it. After everything else I have been hiding with Paul, my feelings, the kiss, the texting, I have no room to speak. He isn't perfect and neither am I. And I've learned the hard way; speaking up doesn't always get you the outcome you're looking for, especially when the person you're speaking to is incapable of fully hearing you. Besides, he's not wrong. I wouldn't have half of what we have if I were to try on my own. I don't have the business acumen, the experience, the capital. Sam does, and even if I hate to face the music, Sam is mostly right.

"You've always been predictably unpredictable," Sam shouts. "You're a pretty girl, but you are so young, so naïve. So—stupid." He throws his hands in the air, paces back and forth as he yells. "You think you can be miss independent, but you can't. Look at your own mother for God sakes. Do you really want that for yourself? The girl I met would say no, but the woman I'm staring at looks glossy eyed and clueless. I don't even know this person anymore. This girl right here has gone crazy." He points his long finger at my face.

"I don't know you anymore, either." It slips. And instantly, I regret it. He cocks his head slowly at me as he makes a snarling, sour face.

"If you want to leave, leave. The door is right there, Jade. I'm not stopping you. You think I can't find another pretty girl to keep your side of the bed warm at night?" He shakes his head, pacing back and forth. "You're not irreplaceable. Maybe that's some business advice for you that might help. Be irreplaceable or find out how easy it is to be replaced." Sam slams his whiskey down hard onto the table, spilling some onto the marble. *Did he just threaten to leave me? Did he just give me the permission to leave?* Without thinking, my body throws my purse over my shoulder and walks towards the door. When I go to open it, Sam's hand slaps down on the doorknob. He stands in front of me, blocking my way out.

"Where are you going?" he asks.

"You just told me to leave, I'm going…"

"Where? Where do you think you're going?" He pushes his body against mine, towering over me.

"I don't know yet, can you let me open the door?"

"Look. I didn't mean it. Alright?" His face turns from angry to anxious, as if immediate regret has consumed him.

"Come on. Can we just talk? Like adults?" he says.

I stare at him blankly. My eyes say no, we cannot.

"I'm sorry. Let's forget about this stupid fight." He puts his arms around me. "You know how it gets sometimes when I'm stressed from work. Don't overreact."

"Get off me!" I shout at him, as I force his arms away from my body.

"Stop it," he says, hugging his arms around me even tighter. "I'm trying to give you everything. Can't you see that? I love you Jady bug." He kisses the side of my head; his bourbon breath blows into my face.

"Come on. You know I didn't mean it." He takes the keys from my hands. "Go take a hot bath, I know you've been tired. I bought you some fertility tea; I can steep that for you. I can't have the future mother of my children stressed out. Go rest." He puts his hands on my shoulders softly, walking me towards the bathroom. "I'm sorry. I love you. Let's forget this." After all of this, babies are on his mind. How could the thought of a child be on his mind when it is so clearly removed from mine? I know what Sam is doing right now. He's trying to smooth things over well enough for me to have sex with him.

Two things I know that I don't want in this moment. Sam's baby or Sam. He has been tracking my menstrual cycle on an app, saying he was curious about my fertility. I didn't mind at first because it meant he knew when my period was coming and that meant he knew when to also leave me alone. To be honest, I also found it attractive that a man wanted my babies so much he was willing to take interest in my body on the cellular level, even if I was entirely uninterested in his offspring. The feeling of being desired is one we all crave. I'm not on birth control other than condoms, but that has not mattered since my body has not allowed sex in forever. It wasn't just the lack of sex that was bothering Sam, but every month during my fertile week he becomes angrier at the lost opportunity to make a child. The pressure to make a child or not has also contributed to my body shutting off sex.

Numbly, I let my purse fall to the ground in surrender and I walk into the bathroom. Sure, I can fight back, but each day that passes I find myself much too tired, too numb to consider it. It's easier this way. I drop my clothes onto the floor and step into the cool tub replaying the night before my wedding all over again. Once the water stops and the silence begins, everything hits me all at once. Tears spill down my cheeks as a muted cry chokes on its way out. I take my bath towel, fold it in half and explode violent heaving sobs into it. When I get out to look at myself in the mirror, my eyes are so swollen and pink, it looks like I'm having some sort of an allergic reaction. They're so puffy that I can hardly open them. I notice my face hanging sallow and long as I press my cool hands into my temples. My voice feels dry and hoarse from the series of muffled screams that I exploded into the bath towel. Breathing in air feels so painful that I need a cough drop to pull in oxygen without agitation. Still looking at myself in the mirror, lifeless in a bath towel, I unwrap a cherry flavored lozenge from the medicine cabinet and pop into my cheek. Everything hurts. *How did I get here?*

Using my voice was a struggle in more ways than one, so I kept quiet the rest of the night. My throat was so agitated that even breathing in air alone was too much, I needed a cough drop to breathe without pain. I unwrapped one and popped the cherry flavored cough drop into my cheek. Everything hurts and I feel helpless. How did I get here?

In bed, though I am under the covers, I'm frozen. I can't

speak. Can't think. Can't move. My body has become a shell of itself, empty and hollowed out.

I sit there being completely denied of my reality. I lie here awake but half conscious, questioning my denied reality. Second guessing my sanity as I wonder if maybe I am dreaming it all up. If I made things a bigger deal in my head. If Sam isn't as bad as I make him out to be. If I'm the problem. I have been told how wrong I am, how crazy I am enough times that I am starting to believe it. That I was wrong, and he was right. I was crazy and he wasn't. That how I feel is all my fault. Maybe Sam is right. That this is love, this is just how it is, and I should be grateful.

CHAPTER NINETEEN

AFTER TOSSING AND turning for hours, I finally break. I can't sleep. I wait until Sam has started to snore before rolling out of bed. I tip-toe to the elevator to make my way down to the garden. As I walk out into the main entrance, I look down at my feet and realize I forgot to put shoes on. I'm too anxious to care.

I being to pace back and forth barefoot, feeling the cold dewy ground on my soles.

With my hands over my head, I stare up into the night sky. For a few moments pull at my lower lip as I consider mustering enough courage to act on an impulse. The one that has kept me awake for one too many nights. The one that still rattles me from the inside out.

I pull my phone from the pocket of my robe and stare at the blank screen for a minute. *This is a bad idea.* With his name and number just beneath my thumb, I can feel my hands tremble. A surging feeling of apprehension hits me hard in the chest. *It's too late to be calling.* I press his number and wait. *I'm sure he won't answer.* Until he did.

"Paul, it's me," I say, and my voice cut out a little.

"Hey. You alright?" he says, he muffles, vis voice still half asleep.

"I know, it's late. I'm sorry." I sit down on a bench, clutching my robe shut.

"Is it late? I haven't looked at the clock. I've been sleeping."

"I didn't mean to—I'm sorry…"

"Don't be. What's going on?" His voice is deeper now and concerned.

"Everything? I don't even know where to begin, Paul." Tears attempt to surface, but I clear my throat and swallow them. "Sam wants to have a baby, and I just—I'm worried. I just don't know…"

"You don't want to be a mother? Or what is it?"

"I do—I think. Just not… right now. Just not…"

"With him?" he says. He knows.

"Yeah." A sigh of relief pours from my chest. "Because what if I do and the shot at us, if ever, is over," I say, surprised at what just came out of my mouth.

"It'll never really be over," he says. "I don't think that's how a love like this one works."

Those words from his mouth made my heart sink into my gut.

"I'll love you even if you have a Brady bunch of babies before making your way back to me," he says, laughing reassuringly.

I laugh and sniffle into the phone.

"I think you'll be an amazing mother by the way. I really do," he says. "But I would be lying if I said I wanted you to have your babies with Sam." He pauses. "I want to have your babies with you. I'd give you the whole Brady bunch if you let me."

He continues, "I don't want to wait forever. I can't. You know I have to get on with my life, too."

Paul is right. How could I expect him to sit there and wait for me, even if he says he will, why would I want him to? It's not fair and I know that. I find myself in this place often. Knowing I need to make a move forward yet feeling stuck and paralyzed by fear. "But I'll always be here when you're ready. I'd take you back with four kids or no kids"

He laughs. "Hair or no hair. Arms or no arms. Legs or…"

"No legs, huh?" I smile. "You'd love me even I looked like Lieutenant Dan from Forest Gump?" We both start laughing.

"There's something about you… I just can't say no to you. I'd carry you around like a baby if I had to," he says. We both laugh again. I love the way he makes me laugh even when I don't want to.

"Maybe I'll just be a big baby then, that's the easy thing to do."

"Look, I'm here for you, no matter what, Jade," he says.

"You're too good for this evil world. They don't make them like you anymore, you know?" I say.

It's true. I don't deserve him anymore and yet here is, loyal and unconditional. His love never wavering, never judging, always available.

He is quiet, and in his silence we both knew it was an admittance to the fact that he was too good to wait on me anymore. In this moment I know I have less time than ever before to make a choice. Paul and the life I never wanted in Tiffin or Sam with the life I've only ever dreamed of in the city.

"Thank you for everything, always," I say.

"Good night, sleep tight," he says before hanging up, just as he always had when I was his girl. I clutch my phone to my chest and sit on the bench for a few minutes soaking in all that I love about Paul. Imagining a life in Tiffin. Would it really be so bad to never leave that town?

WHEN I GET back upstairs, I notice the lamp is on in our room and Sam isn't in bed. He is awake. My heart begins to race, wondering if maybe he had been listening to my conversation from the window. I hear the toilet flush. Maybe he has just gotten up to pee and noticed I wasn't in bed. I wipe my grassy feet before he comes back into the room. When he walks in, he looks at me as if maybe he heard every word. I expect rage, but instead I am met with silence and a mumble goodnight. He turns out the light and crawls back into bed. I roll over and grab my phone. A text from Paul pops up.

> **Paul:** I forgot to say it when we talked just now... but I love you. I hate ending a phone call with someone I love and not saying it before I hang up. You never know if that's the last you'll ever hear from me, and if it was, I'd rather say I love you than just good night.

As I read his text, a jolt of heat wooshes in my body. If this is the last time we were to talk, I owe Paul the truth. Finally.

> **Me:** I love you, too. Always have. Always will.

It's true. I've never stopped.

> **Paul:** Let's do something about it.

What does it look like to do something about it as adults with two separate lives in two separate places? The thoughts keep me awake all night.

CHAPTER TWENTY
(Three Months Later)

S AM AND I have a rooftop dinner party with our new friends and neighbors we met in our complex. All of that was fine and then I just couldn't do the other part after. Play happy wife with Sam without an audience. We're in the elevator back down to our place when he starts to feel me up. His hands on my body feel snaky and cold as they slide up my skirt.

"Jesus, Sam, what are you doing?" I say, swatting him away. "We're in the elevator. And you're drunk."

"I know, I know… you just look so sexy tonight." He squeezes at my thigh before pushing me hard against the wall. "You never dress like this anymore. I can't keep my hands off you." He starts to kiss my neck; it sends a haunted painful ache down my spine. I know there is no way I can avoid him tonight. He pushes me against the elevator wall with one hand wrapped around my throat. He sucks on my neck and as he unbuttons his pants. With two fingers, he forces my panties to the side and shoves himself inside of me. A moan pours out from his mouth along with his hot cigar and whiskey breath.

"Oh my god. You feel so fucking good." He presses my wrists tight above my head and rides into me, pulling me down onto him hard and fast. His cold golden watch slaps down onto my thigh with each fast stroke.

I spit in his face just before the elevator dinged open and he withdrew. Unfortunately, Sam liked it.

Once we get to bed, I surrender again. I just want it to be over. I want to close my eyes and dream. My body has become so repulsed by sex over the last year, that Sam suggested I get help from a sex therapist. I've been seeing her a couple months now.

"The sex therapists suggests that maybe you should try some of the small asks I journaled in my last session to warm me up. She suggested a foot rub, or something," I say as I take my heels off, running my thumb along the flat part of my foot and closing my eyes.

"A foot rub isn't foreplay." He laughs. "And you know I hate feet." He grimaces. "And the feeling of lotion all over my hands." He makes a gag noise in his throat.

"It was just a suggestion. A small place to start," I add. "I like foot massages, they feel nice. I think it was suggested to help my body relax, the therapist thinks I'm wound up from stress. The move, not being in the bakery right away."

Sam says the rent is still astronomical and no one is selling at the right price. It's a seller's market, making every option extremely expensive and keeping me in limbo. I didn't say it, but the therapist also mentioned the emotional tension between Sam and me is the blame. That my central nervous system no longer feels safe with him. The fight, flight and freeze response completely shuts me down. Of course, Sam would see my nervous system problems as my fault, therefore making it harder to explain to him. I don't even try.

"Pass," he says nibbling on my neck. "What else did she suggest? Any fancy lubes or toys?" He half smirks and leans his body over mine.

"She's not a sex worker, she's a therapist for god's sake." I shake my head, "No, she wants to look at the deeper root cause of this... sexual shut down."

"Root cause?" he huffs. "Sexual shutdown? How long will this last?" he says as he peels his shirt off over his head.

I shrug.

"This just happens to some women. It's okay," he says, and rubs my arm softly as if trying to coax me into believing he has a gentle side. Years ago, I'd see it as genuine, now I know it's subtle manipulation.

"You're not the first and only woman who doesn't love sex. It's perfectly normal." That is where he was wrong. I do love sex. When he's not around, I self-pleasure. I am still orgasming several times a week, just not with him. I don't have the heart to tell him that it's not me, it's him. He kisses my shoulder. My body shudders cold.

"Why am I paying her $100 an hour for her to not help solve your problem?" he mumbles to himself. "We should fire her."

He pushes his body heavy onto mine. "I've been waiting a while. This isn't fair to me. Men have needs." He unbuttons his pants, slides my hand over his erection.

Laying on top of me, he slides his tongue into my mouth, pins my hands over my head with one hand and he removes my underwear with the other. He slips his dry finger up inside of me.

"How are you not wet? Do I not turn you on anymore?" His eyes are fixed on mine.

"I told you—It has been hard for me to *get there*…" and by there, I mean *with him*.

"I'm not having sex with a dead person. If you can't be into it, into me then…" he starts to raise his voice. My eyes widen and a very real fear that he might in fact shove himself inside of me to make a child against my will comes over me. Instead, he takes my hand from his grip and rolls off me and onto his back.

"Fine," he says in defeat. "We don't have to have sex today, but if you wouldn't mind—helping me out." He makes the blow job gesture with his tongue in his cheek. I think about how many women would like to have sex with him or even feel lucky enough to blow him, how many women he might work with who would beg for him. And here I am, repulsed at the sheer thought of him.

"I've been so stressed at work. I could use a—happy ending today." My stomach sinks and a hot wave of nausea consumes me. If I don't suck him off, I know the argument would be worse than the act I'm dreading. I duck my head down and promise myself that I'll make it fast. I use all the techniques to make it end as soon as possible. I moan and pretend that I find it enjoyable. I squeeze his balls simultaneously as I bob my head up and down. He grips the pillow over his head for the first half, and the second, he slams my head down hard with his hands, gagging my throat over his flesh. The pain in my face and the tears in my eyes must arouse him enough to release all over my face. I wipe myself off with a towel in the bathroom.

"Your birthday is next week. Don't make plans for next Thursday," he says, kissing the side of my temple. "I can't wait to see your face."

CHAPTER TWENTY-ONE

"CLOSE YOUR EYES," Sam says, placing a blind fold over my eyes. Sam is wearing a tailored grey suit with a tie that makes his ice blue eyes pop. He makes a point to tell me to dress nicer than average, which meant I'm wearing an emerald cocktail dress I wore to a wedding once, the golden diamond necklace he bought for my last birthday and nude Louboutin heels. I pressed my long dark brown hair straight, making subtle waves around my face. Ran a rose-colored lipstick over my lips, puckered them in the mirror and checked my teeth minutes before we had hopped into the car to head downtown for my birthday. We parked in an alley where he said there was a surprise for me, but I'd have to spend the rest of the car ride blindfolded. When we arrive, Sam opens the door, takes my hand, and helps me out. The warm thick air smells sulfurous and peppery. We're near restaurants, that much I know.

"Okay, okay... keep walking," he says, guiding me gently with his hand on my lower back. I hear keys jingle from his pocket as he opens the door.

"Okay, almost there. Hang on. Wait just a minute." The room is warm and has a sweet scent. He takes his hands, unties the blind fold.

"Open your eyes," he says. When I open them, Sam has the most adorable and charming smile on his face. The face that swooned me years ago. It had been a while since I'd seen this face.

I almost forgot what it looked like. He's holding a set of keys in his hands and places them in mine.

"You're going to need these."

I cover my mouth, "No." I shake my head. "No, you didn't. Are you serious?"

"Yes. I'm serious." He puts his arms around me and hugs me tightly. "This is why I've been working so hard, have been so stressed. I wanted it to be perfect for you." I walk around the bakery, holding his hand. I brush my hand on the empty glass cases, picturing my breads, tartlets, cakes, immaculately frosted and curated creations.

"But isn't rent crazy? Aren't there no available spaces for sale?"

"I was able to pull some off market strings. Honestly, I got lucky; it was a rare deal that I couldn't pass up. Especially knowing how much this means to you." He smirks with his hands in pockets. Takes them out when he says, "It's all yours, Jade." He pulls me into his body again, and I hug him fiercely. I try not to cry, but seeing my dream come true has it near impossible to hold it in. Tears flow out of my eyes; I cover my mouth in awe. I look up at the beautiful golden chandelier, every detail is perfect, exactly how I had always pictured it in my head. And here it was, a reality.

"I, of course, have a few details to work through," he says. "Staffing, ordering, and all of the logistical pieces. I'm hiring a management team to come in and get this place going."

"Yeah?" I say, still scanning the room in wonder, imagining my hands frosting and decorating behind the marble counter.

"Wait until you see the sign, it might be my favorite part." It read—le mélange parfait. "It means the perfect blend in French," Sam says. A familiar tingle runs through my body. *Our honeymoon. The wine. That sour, bitter, awful wine.*

"You remembered," I say, forcing a smile, rubbing my hand over the back of my arm, feeling a phantom pain from where the pinch was. The pinch he clearly forgot about.

"You hate it, don't you?" he says, looking down at his shoes.

"Why would I hate it?" I ask, wondering if this is the moment he remembers and apologizes for the pinch, the fight, all of it.

"Well, because we argued over it. You got mad that I wanted to order a nice bottle for our honeymoon. And that I didn't let you pick."

Pretending I don't remember the actual details, the truth of what really happened to not spoil the moment, I say, "Was that it? I can hardly remember. It was such a beautiful night."

"So, you don't hate it?"

"It's—perfect. How could I hate it?" I pull him into another embrace, looking up into his blue eyes, searching them for honesty. *Was this really happening?*

"Thank you, Sam." I am thankful. Everything I've wanted is officially in the palm of my hand. When Sam is good, he is heroine. But even if it feels good in the moment, even if I am addicted to these highs, I always worry about what comes after this. When the bender will spiral out of control and when the next relapse will be. This roller coaster ride with Sam is a wild one, but it's too late to get off now, isn't it?

CHAPTER TWENTY-TWO
(Two months later)

CHICAGO HAS LOST its charm.

Everything that once glittered with hope and possibility is now tainted, ugly and murky. I can no longer see the shine of this dream life that I cherished so deeply for so long. Even our condo's view lost its appeal. What once used to mesmerize me looks as unflattering as a traffic jam. There's nothing glamourous anymore about sad people wearing overpriced peacoats, living in sad empty houses. Even the bakery isn't what I had hoped for. Sam has me hoodwinked. Completely hoodwinked. I thought owning the bakery would mean that I would be the one leading, the one designing and creating. And at the very least, I'd be the one baking. No. None of that. Sam had simply invested in this bakery, dedicated it to me and then hired a full staff and team to run the business. The part that hurt the worst and cut the deepest was hiring a baker. Yes, the bakery was growing into a massive success. This part of town was alive and happening, and the local news couldn't get enough of this place.

"Did you see Channel 6 news?" Sam says, slamming the door open. "You did it again! They can't get enough of you. Tom says he thinks it'll all go national soon, the press is obsessed with the creative vision." He kisses my head. "You're a genius." When Sam is good, he's so good. When he believes in me, I believe in me, too.

Last week I had an interview about the bakery that aired today on the morning local news. I read a script the management team had written for me, apparently one of them knew a guy in PR and hooked Sam up with all this positive press. Since Sam isn't one for the camera, he asked if I would be the face of *Le Mélange Parfait*. Holding the script in my hands I whispered to myself: *even my own thoughts aren't mine*. None of this is mine. Not in the way that I had hoped.

My phone vibrates from my pocket.

> **Paul:** *Heard the news...your mama was shouting it from the rooftops at the farmers market this morning. Didn't know you finally had the bakery you've always wanted...you forgot to mention that.*
>
> **Paul:** *Congratulations, Jade. Always knew you had it in you. I'm proud of you!*

Punch to the gut all over again.

> **Me:** *Thank you.... It's a long story. I'll tell you more soon.*
>
> **Paul:** *Call me tonight?*
>
> **Me:** *I can try. It's hard with Sam always around, but I will try...*

Paul doesn't respond. He doesn't have to. I know that his silence is saying more than his words ever could. And I wish it were easier to do what I know I need to do. *Please keep holding on, Paul.*

SAM PROMISES THAT once the online success and it's 'Insta fame' calms down, I can step in more. That after the professionals have set the bakery up with its blueprint for success, that I will have a bigger role. The only time I see my bakery is when I flip on the news or scroll through social media. The bold colors of the cakes, the exotic flavors, and the artistic vision the managers have for the bakery are inspired by my many mood boards I'd shown them and the photos of cakes I had made. But still, they weren't technically mine. They were knockoffs. The press doesn't excite for those reasons alone. The success isn't mine even if my face is plastered all over the news as if it were. Sam is beyond thrilled, though. He thanks me repeatedly for the idea of a bakery. He never knew my dream could create such a cash cow for us. But this isn't my dream. I am still his virtual assistant, living in isolation, with my dream half in my hands and half out.

SAM SENDS A text.

> **Sam:** *Meet you at my mother's house? She's making dinner tonight and asked us to come.*
> **Me:** *Are you coming home before, or will I meet you there?*
> **Sam:** *Work is nuts. I'll just have to meet you there.*

I ARRIVE AT Sam's mother's house first. Sam's father is remarried. They divorced when he was eleven and he hasn't been around much for much of Sam's life ever since. However, Sam works for his father's business, so they are on good enough terms now, but his mother is still very much a bitter woman about it. His father had several affairs and she later divorced him after the last affair he had when she was pregnant with Mary.

His mother opens the door, looking the other way. "Come on in," she says. "You can put your shoes over there." She points to the neatly organized shoe rack. "I can take your jacket." She extends her freckled hand out. The house is quiet, sterile and smells like citrus. "Mary hasn't arrived yet. "Care for a glass of wine? Some water?" she asks, adjusting her gold necklace to fall neatly over her collar.

"Sure. I'll have a small glass of wine." She nods and walks to the bar in the living room, reaches into the cabinet, pulls out a few glasses. It's never been just the two us alone in a room before, so of course it's awkward.

"Sam should be here any minute," I say. "He's been caught up with work a lot lately."

She pours the wine into my glass and hers. "Sounds like his father after all. He has always been a hard worker, just like Stewart. That's the one quality I'm glad he got from his father." She hands me my glass, takes a sip from hers. "Everything else, I pray that he didn't." I take a sip and decide to fake a laugh and say, "Oh, only the best ones were saved for Sam."

"You can't fool me, dear. He's my son. I'm his mother." She looks at me and arches her pencil-thin brows.

"What do you mean?" I cross my arms.

"His taste in women is the same as Stewart's." She swallows her wine again, licks her lips. "Young. Naïve. Wide eyed to the world like a freshly born baby."

"I don't see what you're trying to say." The door opens.

"Someday, I think you will."

Mary yells down the hall. "Mom! The food smells delish. Your girl over here is starving. What's in the oven? I brought a bottle of wine!"

She rests her hand on my shoulder and leans in to quietly say, "We'll continue this later. In the meantime, he's my son, and I will always choose him. Even if he's wrong, he's blood, darling. You're water." She turns and heads towards the front door. "And I don't think you're entirely innocent, Dorothy. I can smell an affair as easy as a canine." She purses her mouth, the currant color ripples into the crack of her old dry lips. "I can't say I blame you, especially if he's anything like Stewart. Doesn't make it right and it doesn't mean I approve."

She turns towards the door. "If I were you, I'd click those heels and head far way, back to Kansas." She waves her arm behind her head as if she was swatting a fly. "Or Ohio, or whatever." She walks away before I can speak.

"I'm not... I..." I mutter, almost positive that she didn't hear me, but figured it was worth trying to say something.

Sam walks in next. "Sorry, I'm late." He takes off his shoes and coat, walks over to me and kisses my forehead. "What did I miss?"

"Your mother's finest mood. That's all."

"She's a bitter old woman. You know it's nothing personal."

We gather in the dining room. The table is set with fine china, crystal stem ware, linens, silver dinner ware and a small floral arrangement his mother gets delivered weekly.

"Mary, I made beef bourguignon. Granny Jaqueline's recipe."

"Sam's favorite," Mary snuffs.

She smirks and shrugs her shoulders. "It's almost done."

Because Sam went to college in Ohio, I didn't spend much time in Chicago with his family. Most people know their in-laws well before marriage, but I'm getting to know them after the fact. Sam knows more about my family, has a better relationship with them and has spent more time with them. Sam always avoided bringing me to meet his parents, especially his mother. I didn't meet her until after the engagement. She and Sam were always "too caught up."

When we finally met, she shook my hand and said, "Congratulations. You made it this far." I never realized what she meant, but I may be starting to figure it out now. Lasting in this family would take some serious survival skills.

"Mary, do you mind bringing out the chopped salad and the sourdough. I picked up a loaf from Dominick's." Sam is seated, opens a linen and places it on his lap. Pours water into our cups and himself a glass of wine.

"Do you need some help, Mary?" She looks at me like the request of help was foreign.

"Okay," she mutters. "Yes, Mom has a few more things in the kitchen to bring out."

I take the container of whipped butter and place it a glass dish with a butter knife and place the loaf of bread onto a wooden serving board. His mother has baked brie and has asked me to serve it along the bread too. Sam is at the table with his head down, clicking away at his phone. He loosens his tie and shakes his head with annoyance at an email. Once the food is on the table, Mary pinches Sam's arm before she sits down. "Off the phone, no work at the dinner table."

"Don't be like your father, Samuel. Put the devices down."

Sam shoves his phone back into his pocket. "I hate when you say that."

"It's bad enough you work with him. Next thing you know, you become him." He unfolds her linen aggressively onto her thighs, adjusts her silverware, clinging them against her plate.

"He had an affair; he didn't commit manslaughter."

"There's more than you will ever know, darling boy," she says. "The affair was the tip of the iceberg. The rest is none of her business," she looks at me and looks away. "Or any of yours."

"Oooookay. This got heated quickly. Is there more wine? I get the strange feeling this dinner might need it," Mary says, swirling the last bit in her glass before drinking it down.

"If you don't want to become your father, try your best to make your wife sincerely happy and put her before work, before yourself. And do so without expecting anything from her in return."

This feels less about me and more about her.

"You didn't divorce over his career or because he was selfish, you divorced over Evelyn and the affair," Sam says, reaching over the table for the bread and brie.

"A strong woman never tells you all the reasons why. She just presses forward, emerging from the surface to rise above the water, like an iceberg. All you see is the tip, you don't see what caused her to move. I can assure you it's more than one push. It's a series of a thousand microscopic pushes that only she knows."

The room goes silent.

"Better yet, do nothing." She uncorks the wine, pours a little in her glass. "Do nothing and watch what happens to your marriage.

CHAPTER TWENTY-THREE

SOMEWHERE ALONG THE course of togetherness, the lines blur. We become so much of our partner over time that I start to question which is me and which is Sam. Do I really like colonial style homes or was that just something I grew to like because of Sam? Who am I really? What do I like? I'm not even sure anymore. Today, I realized I'm not sure if I like tomatoes when I've always liked tomatoes. Anytime I order an Italian sandwich I say, "No tomatoes please." It has become second nature. I wonder if it's because I've said no tomatoes for him, for Sam, for six years now years. I have said it so much that I now say no tomatoes for me, too. Over time, I believed I did take a disliking to tomatoes. I'm not sure how or when that happened, but today I wonder if it's true or if I had come to believe something that wasn't true. When you lie about something so much, you start to believe it. Today's the day I started wondering about the lies I've been telling myself.

This afternoon, while I ran out to grab lunch for Sam's office, I make a point to ask for a tomato soup and salad with sliced tomatoes with my lunch. I take a bite, the slimy skin and squishy gel of tiny tomato seeds slide through my teeth. My mouth waters from the acidity, but I don't love it the way I remembered always loving it, but I don't hate them, either.

This confused me more.

This bakery reminds me of the one I met Sam in. A stuffy

bakery filled with the overly pretentious type that wouldn't be caught dead drinking drip coffee. They're always the ones that request the pour-over and ask about the gluten-free options. Of course, Sam always went to this one to study for his exams, and I happened to work there. If you were to ask me then at nineteen, I of course would've told you it was fate that we met. Jesus, everything was fate. Romanticized in that teenage way. And yes, I was happy then. Finally getting paid to do something I enjoyed doing. The job before that I sorted packages at a warehouse. Even spending a full shift in a place with windows and sunlight felt like a major life upgrade, the sweet smell of cinnamon rolls and coffee wasn't anything to complain about either.

It was a rainy fall day when Sam walked in. The bakery was charming, but it was severely understaffed for a college town. I was making croissants one minute, pouring coffee and working the register the next. After a full day's work, my feet would ache, and my hair would be so greasy I had to wash it immediately when I got home.

When I brought Sam his order to his table, he reached for my arm and said, "What do you like to do?" The question was awkward, and I wasn't sure why he was asking.

"Bake," I said quickly, turning away towards to register. "And I should probably get back to it. Enjoy."

"Wait," he said. "You don't have to say that just because you're working, you know. I'm genuinely curious about you." I smiled and stood behind the counter. I was too busy for small talk, but I was intrigued. No one had ever told me they were curious about me before. He was tall, dressed preppy in a collared shirt with a cashmere sweater over the top. Gold watch, nice pants. He was dressed like a trust fund kid. In Ohio, they're easy to spot. He followed behind me, leans over the glass dessert case. "What else do you like to do?" He looked at my name badge and then up at me with those piercing blue eyes. "Jade."

"Who are you? Why do you want to know?"

"I said I was curious about you." He bit his lip a little, and locked eyes with mine. "I'm Sam. When do you get off work?"

"At six," I said, shuffling away from the counter and back to take orders. He looked at his watch and shouted over the counter. "That's in three hours. I can wait. I have studying to do anyway."

Sam waited for me. As I untied my apron after my shift us up, and Sam was standing behind me when I turn around.

"So, you really like to bake?" he asked.

"I do, actually."

"Are you a student, too?"

"Taking a semester off. Not sure what I want to do yet. Figuring myself out I guess." I took my hair down from the ponytail it was in all day and put my coat on.

"That's a lie," Sam said.

"What's a lie?"

"That you need to figure yourself out. I think that's a lie."

"What do you mean?" I asked, knitting my eyebrows together. Who does this man think he is?

"I think you know what you want, you're just afraid to let yourself have it."

I glanced at his golden watch and back at him. "Easy for you to say."

He nodded as if he knows his privilege is written on his face.

"Look. A girl as pretty as you deserves to *own* a bakery, not just work at one. Don't you think?"

"Well, that would take a lot of money and skill. Both of those I don't have yet."

"Someday, you might." He smiled a knowing smile. "Do you want to grab a drink with me? Or dinner? Or both?"

I agreed to dinner and drinks. Sam swooned me and it was

easy to do. He was gorgeous, smart, and seemed to have a genuine interest in me and my future. I found Sam to be refreshing. His dreams were far away from Tiffin and so were mine.

"You have the potential to run the show, don't you think it's time for you to have that cake and eat it, too?" Sam smirked, and when his ice blue eyes met mine, I trusted him. He had that way about him. Sam was effortlessly convincing. He could've talked me into eating a handful of broken glass if he said it smooth enough. Every word he spoke made sense, and of course because he was older than me, it was clear, he knew more about life than I did. I followed Sam's plan for me and never looked back.

Sam was the first person to see my dream and breathe life into it in a helpful way that felt like a push in the right direction. He became my mentor and my boyfriend shortly after. He advised me to meet with the business school counselor office, set up my appointment for me and everything.

It's true, Sam has had some of the most positive influences in my life, especially when it comes to my career. He just—gets it. But it's also true that he's equally had the worst.

I DROP THE sacks of lunch to Sam's office. When I arrive, he is extra braggy about how amazing I am. How great I support him and his team. I look around the office, the big shiny windows, the glossy marble floors, the tall expensive cologne scented men, polished dress shoes, clean suits, and perfectly groomed hair. I wonder how I got here. How I have blurred and blended into Sam so much that somehow, I became him and somehow this is the life I had chosen.

On my way out, I get the overwhelming sensation to stop into the restroom and look in the mirror. I want to see myself in this moment, the one where I do not recognize my own life anymore. When I see my reflection, it's exactly what I thought. A confused, tired woman waking up to her true desires after years of stuffing them away. What I need to do next is the very thing I've been avoiding.

When I get home, I change back into my sweats and bury myself into my screens. I try to seek connection with the outside world by staying further away from it. I feel less alone when I detach from reality than when I participate in it. I check the clock and scan the house, making sure everything is in its place before Sam gets home to complain about how lousy of a housewife I am, even though it's physically impossible to do two things at once. To work for his company and keep a perfect house and have the time to make the perfect meals.

"The house should always be prepared for company," Sam says. With his job, he often brings clients back to our house for dinner, often without notice. To the rest of the world, I have it all together. I am the perfect wife to the perfect husband living on the perfect side of town in our perfect condo. And the way we keep the house and everything around us, no one would know otherwise. Everything is shiny and in its place. But if you look close enough, you can see it. The lamp has a dent it from one night I threw it after he screamed so hard in my face, I could see the details of his tonsils. A couple vases are glued together if you look close enough. From a distance, it's perfect and so are we. It's the things you wouldn't notice until you look at them closely, but the thing I realized is that rarely anyone ever does.

CHAPTER TWENTY-FOUR

I T'S MID-JUNE AND the weather is gray, moody, and confused in Chicago. Somedays it wants to be a pleasant late spring day and others, it wants to open the door to hells front porch. Today, it has decided to be a rainy spring morning. I'm out running errands at the corner supermarket when my phone rings. I look down. It's Paul calling. I hadn't heard from him in so long, I wondered why he'd be calling now. I answer the phone in the produce aisle as I throw a bag of apples into my cart. When his voice hits my ear, I feel weak.

"You don't have to come. I know it's far from where you're at now, but I thought you should know." He pauses for a second, his voice lowers. "Grandma Lo passed away last night."

I cover my mouth. "Oh my god. No. Paul. I am so sorry. What happened?" That feels insensitive to ask, but it slips anyway.

"Blood clot to the brain, I guess. When she wouldn't wake up, we called the ambulance right away and…." His voice cracks and he clears it.

"Wow." I shake my head. "I can't imagine…" I throw a few items in my cart and head for checkout as fast as I can. The cashier is scanning my items quickly, seeing the hurry all over my face. He points when it's time to run the credit card though and nods goodbye before I leave. It was an unspoken exchange that I wouldn't be speaking because I couldn't give energy to anything else but Paul in this moment.

"I thought I should be the one to tell you. Services are on Saturday at 4pm if you wanted to try to make it. I won't be mad if you don't. Really. I know it's been years and all—"

"This is all so horrible. God. Are you okay?" I say, stuffing the full paper bags into the backseat of my car. He doesn't answer.

"Paul, of course I will be there. She was a very special woman."

"She is. She was…Won't Sam get mad?"

"He is so busy with work…he will hardly notice I'm gone," I say. "Don't worry, I'll be there, alright?"

"Thank you." He says softly.

"I'm really sorry for your loss, Paul. She will be missed." In my head I think of the lie I plan on telling Sam. I decide that I'll tell him my mom is having Lasik and needs my help for a couple days. She had Lasik last year, but Sam would never remember that.

"I'll see you in a couple days."

Oh my god. I will see him in a couple days.

TIME DOESN'T MAKE sense when Paul and I come together again. It has been years, but when I hear his voice, it always feels like I've never not heard it. I realize now that the reason I've never been in a hurry to make things move forward with Paul is because it has never fully felt like we weren't still it for each other. Just felt like we were passing time on our way back together. Is there ever any urgency to get back what already belongs to you?

Driving into town reminds me of all the reasons I wanted so badly to leave it. Where would I work if I stayed? How would I spend my time in this town, especially after now knowing how big the rest of the world is outside of it? All that's left here is an old grocery store, a neighborhood pharmacy, Dollar Tree, City Bank, Gerald's Funeral home next to the State Farm Insurance office and the local police station. I remember when it was a big deal that McDonald's came to town, because there was only one other restaurant. I wondered who would appreciate the kind of bakery I wished to have, the kind that Sam promised me, in this town? No one. That's who.

Sam calls as I pull into the funeral parking lot.

"How's Diane?" he asks, concerned.

"Oh," I say, trying to remember the lie. "She's fine," I whisper, watching everyone from the car window dressed in black head inside. I look at the clock, it starts in five minutes. "She's asleep right now."

"I won't bother then. Tell her I said to take it easy."

"I will…"

"Love you. See you tomorrow, right?"

"Right. Alright, I better go…love you, too." I swallow hard and hang up. Every lie inside of me begs to come out, but instead I open the car door, smooth the wrinkle from my skirt, apply a subtle lipstick and walk towards the door.

Paul delivered a beauty eulogy, and it was then that I remembered how brilliant and smart he was, especially when it came to words. For a small-town boy who didn't finish college, tonight he proved he didn't have to. I had to wipe tears away and a laugh a little when he talked about her biscuit recipe that only one other person knew about. Sitting tucked away in the back corner so the ones who still hate me didn't see me, but visible enough for Paul to know I was there. When he found me, his face lit up and I knew then it was worth all the lies I've ever told. His sorrow is mine. His joy is mine. His peace is mine. I will carry him with me forever.

ON THE STAIRS of the funeral home, once everyone has left and hugged goodbye, I sat next to him. I tried to keep my distance, especially knowing I have been forbidden from this family for so long, I wanted to remain respectful.

"You alright?" I ask.

"I just lost the only woman I knew as a mother, and not too long before that, the only man I knew as a father." He hangs his head between his knees, holding back tears. "I know it's silly, because I'm not a kid anymore, but I feel like an orphan all over again."

It was easy for me to feel his heavy heart. I can feel it all so deeply. I can hardly separate his feelings from mine.

"It's okay to cry, you know." I rub my hand softly on his shoulders.

"Trust me, I have. I just don't think I have any more fluid left in my eyes," he says, his voice muffled into his trembling hands. I rub his back soft and carefully with my hand. I've never seen him like this, so I'm careful with how I respond.

"I wonder what she might think if she knew I was here. She hated me, you know. It feels a little wrong to show up to her funeral. Even though I never hated her, even if it tried to."

"She didn't. She hated the thought of you ruining me the way my parents were ruined."

"If your pop-pop were still here, he would've shooed me out at the door."

He laughs a little. "True. But I'm a man now and I would've told him that you deserve to be here, too." He grabs my hand. "Grandma Lo loved you. She just loved me more and, in the love, got carried away with protecting me from all things she thought might ruin me, too."

"I wish you would've said that when we were younger." I look away, watching the cars pass by.

"What?

"That I deserve to be with you."

"I tried, I really did. It wasn't easy then—they were all I ever had. All the love I'd even known, until I met you…"

"Why didn't we fight like hell to save us?" I ask, shaking my head. He looks down again, shakes his head, too.

"I don't know. Maybe it's because when you're young like that, you don't have the strength or the courage to do what you know is right. All you know to do is what you've been told is right. We only learn the truth when we're old enough to identify and accept it. And often by then, it's too late." He lifts his head up and turns to look at me. "Unfortunately, most of the lessons we need to learn happen after it's too late."

"I wonder where we'd be if that day never happened."

"I think about it every day. I've never stopped wondering." He looks at me with aching eyes. "I don't think I could ever stop wondering either. Believe me, I've tried. The what if's have kept me up at night for years."

"Do you have to rush out of town?" He looks at me, his hand touches mine." Or do you have a couple hours to cheer up an old friend?"

I smile. "You know, I think I can spare an old friend a couple more hours."

"I want to show you something. Follow me behind my truck."

Down the same dirt road, we grew up on, I follow him, passing the fields and flat grassy farmland. A melancholy pang strikes me as I pull into his grandparent's driveway. The barn paint has faded over the decade since I last sat on the old wrap around porch and stared at it. Still, it feels oddly like home. Worn in and cozy, like it knew I would be arriving right on time. It welcomes me in with its old familiar charm.

"They left it all to me," he says as he opens the front door, the house echoes in its emptiness. "The house, the farm. All of it."

He scans the house, everything still looking the exact same way I remember it, nearly in its same place. "They would've left it to my parents, but—."

"What are you going to do with it all? Sell it?" He opens the fridge and offers me a beer. We both crack the can and start sipping quickly. I pick at my fingers, knowing this might strike a chord.

"Sell it?" he says, taking a step back. "That thought hasn't crossed my mind once. I'm going to keep it, build upon the legacy my pop's built." He turns away, not knowing where to look. His gaze wanders as he runs his palm through his hair. "I'd love to raise a family of my own here, teach them the lessons only that only this farm can reveal."

I LOOK AROUND the house, swipe the smooth wooden kitchen counter tops with my hand.

"The market is hot right now. And everyone is going crazy snatching up these farmhouse style homes." I walk around, knocking on the wooden beams to examine its structure. "You could probably tear this wall down for an open floor plan. This is a classic, too. A little work and updating could make you a significant return," I say, surprised with how much real estate knowledge I've learned from Sam in passing. Surprised with how much I sound like Sam.

"I'm not selling." His mouth falls open as he crosses his arms and leans against the doorway.

"Sam could get you above asking, he's a shit husband, but he's a great agent." I laugh a little. "You could use the money for going back to school, do something new and different with your life."

He looks at me, deep into my eyes, concerned and gentle. He walks closer to me, puts his hand on my shoulder. I feel myself unwind just then.

"What did you say?" he asks, drawing his eyebrows together.

"I said you could use the money for—"

"No. Before that. Sam is a shit husband? Why didn't you ever tell me?"

Up until now, I have kept my feelings about Sam to myself. Paul's touch makes my body shudder and begin to melt by his warmth.

"He isn't the best." I take another sip looking away from his eyes as I find myself back pedaling, defending Sam as I have always done. "He could be better."

"Has he hurt you?" He turns my chin towards him softly. "You better tell me the truth, Jade. And if he has, I'll drive up there and kick his ass right now," he says, his eyes still connected to mine. And he would. That's Paul. Overprotective and unafraid. I missed this masculine sense of security I feel when I'm with him. When I'm with him, I know I'm safe. When I'm with Sam, safety doesn't always exist.

I turn away to look out of the farmhouse window.

"No. Not really," I say, cradling my arms. My body felt suddenly chilled.

"What does that mean? Please be honest with me." He lowers my chin softly towards his face again.

"He hasn't even *really* hit me."

"Jade. If he has, he's a dead man..." His voice deepens to a pitch I've never heard from him before.

"He hasn't. He's just...." I take a minute to think about how to explain Sam when I hate him most. "At his worst, he's not my favorite person. Alright? He's unkind, empty, unavailable, and, yes, maybe a little hostile. But he's never hit me." I defend him again. Even though I am sure that if I told him about the pushing, pinching, or shoving, he'd have the keys to his truck in the ignition faster than I could stop him. That wasn't technically hitting to me, but to Paul, he would have no tolerance for a single finger laid on me.

"Jesus, Jade. What on earth are you still doing with him?" He slams his beer hard down onto the counter. "I will never get it. I never thought he deserved you...." He shakes his head and pulls out a cigarette, fumbling to light it.

"You will never understand, Paul. And I don't expect you to," I say, pulling the cigarette from his mouth and flicking it into the trash.

"Have you lost your mind? Who are you anymore?" I say, blinking at him rapidly.

"Wouldn't you like to know?"

"Yes, I would actually."

"Interesting," he says, shaking his head as he tries to conceal a thin-lipped smile. I wonder what he's thinking. Instead of asking, I attack him more on the cigarette subject.

"How dumb are you to smoke? It could kill you, you know."

"Dumb? Was that a shot at my intelligence? Just because I didn't finish college doesn't mean I couldn't have easily done it. And what would you care if I was dead or not."

"Paul. I would be absolutely destroyed if you died. I think you know that." I look at him then, those golden eyes set my body on fire. My chest aches even thinking about the possibility of it. "And trust me, I know you're a bright man. However, on the subject, I do wish you would've finished school, you could've been anything..."

"So, what do think I am because I didn't? Nothing?" He takes a heavy sip of his beer.

"Oh god, Paul. Stop it. I never said that—I..." I pinch my

lips together as I can feel myself getting frustrated and my stomach hardening. My defense mechanism has subdued to yelling fits with Sam, but with Paul, I find myself reaching for the tenderness that somehow still existed in my calloused heart.

"Please, I didn't mean that, and you know it…"

"I gave up school for my family because they needed me. I'm sorry that's not the kind of man you want. Some low-quality uneducated man who will never meet your high standards." Paul looks down with his hands tucked into his pockets.

"Paul, you are quite possibly the most brilliant and beautiful man I know. It's not that at all. I just wish—" I take a second and look around the farmhouse again noticing all its flaws. "I wish you wanted what I wanted."

"What does it matter? The most important thing I want and have ever wanted is you, Jade." His voice is desperate and pained. "It's simple. I want you, this farmhouse, the barn we spent so much time in. Hell, I could fix it up, we could get married in it. Have one of those fancy barn weddings. I'd do it for you. Give me six months and I'll give you everything you've ever wanted."

"I wish it was that easy, Paul." I look down at my two-carat ring that quite possibly costs more than his pickup was worth when it was brand new. He can't give me everything, not exactly, though I know now isn't the time to dispute the details. Paul is hurting and when Paul hurts, I hurt, too.

"I know I can't give you everything that Sam can," he says. "But I know I can give you everything Sam can't."

His hand brushes on my shoulder and down my arm with his fingertips. My eyes close and my body pulls into his. "Tell me I'm wrong, Jade." He grabs my hips and leans into kiss me. His golden eyes stare longingly into mine. "Tell me I'm wrong and I'll forget it all."

A lump collects in my throat, blocking any words from coming out.

"Regardless, I will always love you. You'll always be my girl, alright?"

Fear takes the words from me, but the look on his face pulls them from under my tongue.

"You're not wrong..." I whisper, startling myself. Knowing the fire I'm about to start within me, feeling the flames rise from the ashes again.

"What was that?" he says, with a smile. He cuffs his ear. "I didn't hear you. The cows couldn't hear you; the frogs and the worms underground couldn't hear you." He looks at me like I'm the only girl that has ever existed and he smiles.

I yell into the empty house, "I SAID YOU'RE NOT WRONG!" I hurl myself into his arms, grab his face firmly and devour his lips. With his effortless strength, he twirls me around. Hikes up my black Versace dress, holding my thighs tightly. *Damn it. Damn it all.*

"I love you." The words fly out of my mouth.

"I love you, too. I've never stopped," he says. I slug my heels across the kitchen floor. He carries me to his room, the room we have made love in many, many times. Paul stumbles into the doorway, knocks the lamp off the nightstand with my feet. In between kisses we laugh at the mess we're making. Luckily, the old dusty lamp didn't break, but the shade has a nice dent in it now.

"Ooops," he says. "Your fault, totally your fault." He tosses me onto his bed, forcing my legs open. "You have to redeem yourself."

He kneels onto the floor, pulling off my black knee-high tights, kissing the inner edges of my thighs. He looks up at me and smirks confidently as if he had just remembered exactly how this body works and just what to do to it. His confidence makes my mouth open slightly, eager for his tongue.

Paul pulls my panties to the side, slides his finger inside me, slowly at first and then more intensely as my hips grind into his palm, begging for more. If I were an oyster, by now I would be fully cooked. Tender, warm and wide open, ready to be ravaged and enjoyed by him. But Paul wasn't done with me, not yet. He takes his finger, draws it in and out of me slowly, carefully, lips locked onto mine. The pressure of his tongue intensifies as moans hum from my neck. I shove myself up and down, trying my absolute hardest to not finish before we've even gotten started.

"I'm going to come if you don't stop—" I say, in between sudden bursts of moans.

"Good, I'd like to see you come more than once," he says as he traces his fingers down my ribs. "We have a lot of time to make up for," he whispers.

He stands up to unbutton and pull off his shirt. His chest broader and his body is finally a full entire man, making it feel like the first time all over again. I watch him undress slowly, as he keeps his gaze onto mine. Everything feels like we're in slow motion, like we are both taking still life photographs as a memory we want to hold onto forever. I stand up to peel off the rest of his clothes.

For a moment, I wonder if I'm about to do this. Cheat on my husband. With his buckle in my hands again, I realize exactly what I'm about to do. It's one thing to kiss another man when you're married, but an entire new ball game once I let another man inside of me. Right now, I don't worry about hurting Sam. He's hurt me enough, and to me, he deserves this. He deserves Paul's hot body dripping all over me, digging and writhing into me.

Paul's beard is now damp with sweat and the love letter he has written with his tongue between my legs. He strokes me gently; my body gives way, shaking and losing control. I arch my back and moan, trying again not to climax without him. He gives more of himself to my every curve and fold relentlessly, stroke after stroke with his mouth. He wipes his face and with his lips, he kisses me up slowly from my legs to my chest.

When he penetrates me, I'm tender and overflowing, begging him not to stop. Paul pushes my knees into my chest, plunges gently in and out of me. I forgot this about Paul. How his passion for me is kind and gentle unless we're in bed—where he pleasures me without mercy.

My hands pull him into me deeper, moaning with very thrust. *More. More. More. Please, more.* My legs shake with intensity under his strong body, surrendering to him fully. The thought of Sam's angry face walking in on Paul deep in his wife sends a haunting thrill through my body, making me even more drenched with arousal. I could come to Sam's pain alone, but I know I'd come a lot harder if he were here witnessing my deep pleasure by not just another man, the only man I truly love. I want him to see the orgasmic desire for Paul all over my face. I want it to scream, *fuck you, I'm being fucked by a real man.* The thought makes me feel like exploding. *I'm so bad.* I repeat in my head over and over as he pushes deeper into me. Pulsing and throbbing, I grab his wide shoulders as I climax, screaming into these sheets I've screamed into before. As I come, a blissful wave quivers though my entire body hard and fast. My pleasure sends Paul over the top and he finishes with me.

After, we are both breathless and flushed red with desire-warmed skin. Tears come out of my body like it's had some sort of spiritual release, as if my soul had just met God. As the tears come out, I can't help it but to let out a laughing sigh. My body must find it hysterical that it has finally had real sex with the right man. Real incredible, amazing sex. With a real incredible, amazing man.

I have never once felt this way with Sam. It was obvious to me that body was so perfectly made for Paul's. When he is inside of me, we fit perfectly like a puzzle meant to be together. I may not be Paul's wife, but after that, I can feel what it might be like if I were.

For a moment, I feel a sickening envy that Paul has slept with other people, even though I have no reason on this great green earth to feel that way. Something about knowing the quality of women he's been with since me makes me feel queasy. The women after me didn't deserve sex this good. They didn't deserve *this*. The thought of another woman mounting Paul for a ride makes me ill, churns my stomach a little. I hate imagining how Paul has gotten so great at sex since me. And how many women he's been with. I do not try to answer my own stupid question in my head, because the thought of it breaks my heart.

We lie there in this quiet old room a while, my head on his chest. He strokes his hands through my hair, kisses my head repeatedly, as if I were going to disappear if he didn't.

"Can you picture it? Me and you. Waking up right here next to each other."

I look around the room, everything is old and dated. It smells like 100-year-old chipped paint, nature, and dust. I picture myself here, waking up in this old house next to Paul. His sweet coffee breath in the morning. The smell of dirt, gasoline, and farm as he hugs me before dinner. I make him dessert that I've baked all day, and he's overjoyed and full of warm compliments.

I realize as I doze off that I am falling asleep without dinner, yet I feel completely full and satisfied by the sheer feeling of his arms holding me safely in the dark. Tonight, I belong to Paul.

CHAPTER TWENTY-FIVE

WHEN I WAKE up before him, I watch as he breathes slowly. Quietly, as the sun begins to rise, I slip through the crack of the old wooden door to the house I wasn't sure I'd ever see again. I don't know what to do from here, but I do know Sam was wondering where I am and why I haven't called. Twenty-five missed calls lit up on my phone, ten voicemails. By now, I know that Sam knows I've lied. I'm sure he has called my mother, investigating my whereabouts. When I get into the car, I make sure to back out slowly and quietly. And when the tires hit the pavement, I take a deep breath, let it out and do what any girl in trouble would do—I call my mom.

"MOM. I DID something very, very stupid." I rehearse out loud before she picks up.

"Hello?" she says.

"Are you home?" I ask, instead.

"No, why?" her voices lowers.

"Never mind. Has Sam called you?"

"Jade, you're acting like a lunatic. What's the matter?"

I wait for her to answer my question. She's right, I'm acting like a lunatic.

"No, he has not. I don't talk to Sam that much on the phone, you know that. Unless something is wrong. Is there?"

I sigh a bit of relief, my shoulders sag.

"Have you ever been unfaithful?"

She pauses for a minute and clears her throat before whispering into the phone. "Who told you, Jade?"

"Wait. Who told me what?"

"I'm assuming you found out," she whispers again. "About Ron. Was it your sister? Did she tell you?" We both pause. "Look, this isn't a conversation I'd wish to have on the phone."

"Well, I'm actually in town…funny enough."

"You are?" Her voice sounds confused, yet undeniably excited to see me.

"I have something to tell you, too."

"I'll be home in twenty minutes, just finishing up at the grocery store."

"Okay."

"Oh, and by the way, Mrs. Thompson passed away. Did you hear? Her service was last night. I was going to go for our family, even if we didn't see eye to eye after… you know… but I got caught up…"

"I'll see you when you get home, mom."

I arrive before my mom, but use my old house key to let myself in. I plop down on the living room sofa. A few moments later, my mom walks in with two coffees and a sack full of raisin bagels.

"You hungry?" she asks. "I am, actually."

We sit at the dining room table, she slices my bagel, cracks the lid to my coffee and stirs in two creams.

"Let's get to talking before your dad gets home."

"You go first," I say, tearing into the bagel like it's the first thing I've eaten in days.

She takes a sip of her coffee. "Well, it's true. I met someone. His name is Ron."

"Really?" I just…can't picture it… I stuff another bite into my mouth. Somehow, I'm more enamored by this than my own dirt I dug myself into last night.

"So, yes, I have been quoting 'unfaithful' but God, I am happy. I am loved by a wonderful man…and sweetie, let me tell ya. There ain't nothing that feels better than that."

I nod and raise my eyebrows; feeling all my lies bubble up to the surface. She looks at me with her knowing eyes.

"How did this happen? When?" I say, noticing my voice shake.

"At work. We worked together 15 years ago. And then of course he moved away, and that was that. I always felt that spark when he was around, and you know me, I sure wasn't going to act on it. I'm a married woman with two daughters. I didn't have the time back then. And well, when you moved out, I was lost, empty. And don't you know it, Ron moved back to town—"

I stare at her blankly, cradling the warm coffee in my hands. Feeling oddly guilty and responsible for her affair. I don't want to make her feel any worse, but I know my turn to tell on myself is next and I'm not ready. Maybe I don't have to tell her or anyone—ever.

"I know it's wrong. I wish every day for something to take this love away from my heart, it would make everything a lot easier." Ouch, I felt that. Definitely felt that.

"Are you going to leave dad? Because I don't really blame you…" Though I can't picture it, I try to for a moment.

She shakes her head. "If I was going to leave your father, I would've done it years ago."

I nod and take another sip of coffee. "So, you're not with Ron anymore?" I say, half my face tucked behind the cup. If I hide behind it, maybe I'll feel better.

She sighs. "I never said that. Ron is married, too, you know.

It's all so complicated, sweetheart. Sometimes we worry that leaving what we've got already might take away the romance, that spark. Until Ron and I absolutely cannot go another day without being together, until we feel that every night should be spent together, we won't leave our marriages. It's not all that bad being married to your father. A lot of what we have is good. We are a great team and it's easy the way we do things. There's just something small missing, and for now, Ron fills that. Right now, I am whole. And I'm happy with that so long as I can keep it going without hurting anyone."

"That sounds—messy…" I say, but I know I can't judge. My mess is messy, too.

"You ever hear that saying? *Men marry a woman hoping they never change, and women marry a man hoping they can change him.*"

I shake my head.

"Well, I went wrong ever thinking I could marry and make your dad a romantic man. He's never once showed me love in that way. Ron? Oh, he's a big time romantic." A blush catches her cheeks then. "Flowers, gifts. Sunset walks, you name it. It's all magical." She smiles as if the thoughts of Ron instantly took her to a better place. But I knew after some time that I can't change the man I married. I can just change how I respond to it. I know your dad loves me, even if his way of showing it is different. I love him, too. That's the complicated messy part, indeed." She stares out the window with a longing in her eyes. "But true love can be a selfish act, and I've never been one to be selfish."

She takes a bite of her bagel and picks at her sleeves. "Anyway. What did you have to tell me?"

"Honestly, it was nothing." She gives me the side eye. *Mom's always know.*

"You went to the funeral, didn't you?"

"Yes." I cover my mouth, afraid of what might spill out next. "And can you please not tell Sam. He wouldn't understand, and I don't feel like going into it with him…."

"Your secret is safe with me." She sips her coffee looking down her hands. "So, where does he think you are?"

"I said I came back home to help you out."

"With what?" She laughs, taking another bite of her bagel.

"I said you got Lasik and needed help."

"Baby, I got Lasik last year…"

"Yes, I know, but Sam doesn't know that."

"I sure hope not. I'd hate to see you ruin a good thing over a selfish spark."

"Is that what Ron is? A selfish spark?" I ask. She takes a minute to respond as she struggles to answer it honestly.

"Might be." She shrugs like it's not a big deal, but we both know it is. "Which is why I'm careful not to hurt anyone."

"Wouldn't it hurt if dad found out?"

She nods. "Which is why we won't be telling anyone, right?"

"I guess it looks like we're taking this one to the grave then, aren't we?"

She stuffs the last bite of the bagel in her mouth, takes a sip of coffee and winks.

"So, the funeral was yesterday afternoon. Where did you stay overnight?" Her eyes widen then as she realizes. "No. You didn't—with Paul? No. You didn't—did you?"

"You have no room to judge, mom…"

"I'm not judging… I'm just…" She's judging. I roll my eyes and cross my arms.

"You know, I knew you saw him over thanksgiving. That run you did? I knew…"

"How? How did you know?"

"You had *that* look on your face," she says.

"What look?"

"The same look you had when you were 15 years old." She pats her hair. "The same look you have right now."

I catch myself smiling even though I try hard not to.

"I think I might leave Sam for Paul. I think—I still love him," I blurt out without trying. Her face hardens and her eyes narrow.

"No. Absolutely not," she says, shaking her head firmly. "Nope. You have an amazing, dream life with Sam. Do not throw it all away for this fleeting fantasy moment with Paul."

She grabs her phone out of her pocket. "Look at this. Look." She swipes quickly through photos. Do you see that?" She points to the last photo I sent of the Chicago skyline at sunset. "Paul would never give you that."

I stare at the skyline and wonder what it would be like to never see it again. To give Sam the keys to the bakery, the condo, the car.

"Look out the window here. This is it. This is all Paul could give you. He will never leave this town. *Never.*"

"So. Maybe I want to come back—" I say, trying to convince even myself.

"Sweetie, is it really all that bad at home? With Sam?" She looks at me as if she needs to know the truth. But of course, I can't tell her. I can't tell anyone. Even if I told her, she wouldn't think it was that bad. She wouldn't believe me. No one would.

"But I love Paul…Can't it be that simple?"

"It's not. It's not that simple," she says, scanning around the room. Her eyes look heavy as if a tear might fall any minute. "If it were, I'd be with Ron." She swallows hard and looks at me. "It's not that simple."

I nod and decide it to be best to stay quiet. I realize then there is no convincing her. I've made up my mind anyway, with or without her approval. I love Paul and he is my home.

ON THE DRIVE back to Chicago, I attempt to call Sam only for him to now ignore them all. This only tells me all hell will break loose when I arrive. When he's angry, he's loud. When he feels absolutely anything else, he's silent. The silence scares me more than his anger. I try to distract myself from the variety of feelings plaguing me at once. The sadness of saying goodbye to Grandma Lo, the thrill and excitement of being in Paul's arms again, the rush of hot passion still pulsing through my body, the fear of what Sam might be brewing up when I open the door. I could never tell the truth. I could never tell Sam about Paul. Any of it. Ever.

I rehearse the story in my head. *My mom had Lasik, she needed more help than I thought. My phone died, which is why I missed your calls.* I say it out loud enough times until I start to believe it. This is what happened, and even he can't convince me otherwise. During the four-and-a-half-hour drive back to Chicago, I also have time to think about Paul. Even if I tried not, Paul was occupying parts of my brain that he hasn't occupied in a long time.

WHEN I OPEN the door to the condo, Sam is sitting there reading a book. Sam hasn't really read a book since college. This isn't good.

"If you're seeing someone else, please just tell me," he says, his eyes still locked inside the book. "My mother has been insisting you're having an affair, which up until now I have felt was entirely impossible." He looks at me then. I use every muscle in my face to hold it in place, unemotional, unflinching. I wonder if what Paul and I had was technically an affair. It didn't feel like an affair, it felt like I had always belonged to Paul. And for a short while was just being borrowed by Sam.

"Your mother has never liked me, of course she would tell you that."

"Are you?" he asks again.

"Sam. I was with my mother for her post Lasik care. You can call her if you'd like?" I hold up my phone, waving in the air. Lying so well that it terrifies me.

"I thought she already had Lasik."

"No." My heart pounds so hard, I'm almost sure he can see it through my shirt. *Stay cool. Stay calm.*

"Why didn't you answer my calls?"

"My phone died. I fell asleep on the couch away from the charger, didn't see all the missed calls until this morning." He looks at me and takes a deep sigh out, shakes his head in relief.

"I was worried about you."

I crawl into his lap, praying to God that the smell of Paul is not on my body any longer.

"I know," I say, pushing his hair back, kissing his forehead. Playing his dear sweet perfect wife. "I'm here now." He pushes me off his body, revolting me off his lap.

"Not to mention I needed your help for a couple things happening at the office. We needed our assistant."

"It was the weekend anyway, I don't normally…"

"Well, this was an important weekend, Jade. One where I needed you. And you weren't there," he says, standing up. "Do you know how bad that makes me look? To close one of the biggest deals we've had, only to not have my assistant there, *my wife*, to back me up. Embarrassing. A real slap in the face. I gave you this job because you had nothing. And this is how you treat me?" He huffs and slams open the refrigerator.

"You're being ridiculous, Sam. My mother needed me." I realize I'm turning into him. The gaslighting, the denial of his feelings.

"No, she didn't. You have another sister and a father who could've helped. You left for another reason, and I'm going to get down to the bottom of it."

If I was worried before, I'm full-on panicking now. *Would he hurt me if he knew the truth?*

"Don't waste your time. Because that's all that would be. A waste of time."

Stay cool, stay calm.

CHAPTER TWENTY-SIX

W HEN SAM WAS on his best behavior, he was heroin. Anyone could become addicted to him. How could you not? He was charming, absolutely stunning to look at. But over time, his beautiful threads unraveled, and he became just another awful person I wanted to forget.

A couple weeks passed, and Sam and I had never felt more distant. Our sexual shutdown was still very much a real thing. I kept my communication with Paul minimal, even if my whole body craved a simple hello from him and when I did hear from him, I deleted any trace of a text, and by now he knows better than to call. And after my Irish goodbye, I'm almost sure he's fed up with me and with waiting. I seem to only be good at one thing: making bad decisions.

Things have been quiet with Sam and I for months, but they were a calm quiet, not an angry silent. It was almost nice to operate as roommates versus a married couple. I finally felt peace and realized what my mom was saying might be right. Maybe I didn't have to leave Sam. Maybe the spark I feel Paul is selfish and juvenile. Maybe it's just another phase that will soon pass. What I have here with Sam is too hard to give up entirely. Maybe what I should do is figure out a way to have both? At least until I know for sure I can't live without Paul. Though most days it does feel like I've nearly arrived there. The only thing keeping me here is the bakery and this city I love. If I could get Paul to move here, to see what I see, maybe then things would be different? Maybe then we'd have a compromise we both love.

AT MY LUNCH hour, I decide to leave the house. It has been days since I've left the house and interreacted with another adult. I'd be happy just to smile at the receptionist. It's then I realize that desperation is sinking in from my severe social isolation. Work has been busy, but an hour away from my computer would serve me well.

I lace up my shoes, put my hair up into a clip and run out the door. Today, I decided I felt like running. Running feels like freedom, it feels like leaving something behind that I don't have to turn towards and think about in this moment. The gym is about a mile away, and about a half mile in, I see Sam's car serving through lanes to beeline to the sidewalk I'm on. He rolls down the window, throws his neck to hang out of it.

"Where are you going?' he yells out.

"Oh, hey," I say breathless. "I'm headed to the gym."

"Like hell you are—dressed like that. Get in the car." I look down at my outfit, yoga pants and a cropped tank top. *Dressed like what, someone on a run?* Sam is losing his mind.

"What is the matter with you? How did you know where I was?" It was at this moment I realized it was very likely that he was tracking me. I pull out my phone, removed my ear buds and search for the tracking app. I found it. "Holy shit, you're tracking me!" If I was ever to be afraid of Sam, now would be the time.

"Get in the car, Jade."

"No, you're a lunatic. Get away from me!"

"Do not make me get out of this car and put you in it." His face reddens as he curls his lips.

"Now you're threatening me? What the hell is this?"

Sam jumps out of the car and grabs my arm, twisting it until my skin began to burn. Though all of me was consumed with fear, my body froze in place. My eyes widened and stared into his. The burn of bile stings the back of my throat as it blocks out any noise, I want to make to stop him. A hard thudding races through my chest. I turn and twist my body until I'm loose from his grasp.

"Let go," I shout, my breath coming in short bursts.

"Come on, we're leaving." He tugs again at my arm. I look around for a bystander, but there's no one in sight.

"Let go! Get off me!" My voice cracks. He puts his hand over my mouth. My hands tremble as I stare vacantly at him.

"Stop it. Stop it," he says, shushing me. "You're acting crazy, Jade. Why do you like to draw so much attention to yourself? Just stop and get in the car. Let's talk like normal people. I'm your husband, not a criminal."

I follow him into car before he gets angrier. I sit inside quiet, afraid, frozen, avoiding any eye contact with him. Time seems to slow down as I realize what just happened.

"Okay, yes," he admits. "I was tracking you. And I panicked, alright? I was worried you were going out to cheat on me. Alright? I love you, I'm sorry." He presses his fist into his lips. "You know this is not me. I'm not a monster. I just don't want to lose you. Can't you see that?" Out of frustration, he slams his fist into the steering wheel so hard it honks. My body jolts and springs forward from the noise.

"You're scaring me! Why are you doing this? Why are you hurting me?"

"Oh my god. Are you crazy?" He laughs. "You are delusional. You are hallucinating if you think I hurt you." He laughs again. "That didn't happen. What are you even saying? If you call that getting physical, you are crazy. I have never laid a hand on you."

He shakes his head. "Everyone was right, you are dramatic."

"Alright, Sam. Guess I'm just being dramatic." There's no convincing him. He's right, I'm wrong. Always.

"I hate to say it, but yes, sweetheart. Drama follows you everywhere."

I nod my head to appease him, though inside I'm planning my escape. My divorce. My way out. When he falls asleep that night, I text Mary. Someone needs to know. Someone who will believe me.

Me: *Something horrible happened today with Sam*

She replies within seconds.

Mary: *I've been waiting a long time for this text...*

Mary: *I'm so sorry... What happened?*

Me: *He got physical. He has been tracking me. I'm actually really scared.*

Mary: *Christ. My mother has gotten into his head; she thinks you're cheating on him.*

Mary: *She thinks everyone's cheating on someone.*

His mother is right, but I know this is still not warranted. I need out. A safe out.

Me: *I don't know what to do.*

My hands tremble. I really don't know what to do.

Mary: *I would say you could come stay with me, but I know Sam and that would only make things worse*

She's right. It would. She is his sister after all.

Mary: *I'll help you figure this out, okay? My brother has always been awful... Didn't I warn you?*

Me: *He wasn't always this way. I swear it only first began on our honeymoon. It was like marriage changed everything...*

Mary: *That makes sense. The divorce affected him the hardest. He had behavioral issues at school, would get into fights. He got kicked out of his private school over it. That's why no one in the state of Illinois would accept him into college. He's a fucking hot head, dude...*

I decide to leave the conversation unanswered. I don't know how to respond to Mary. I don't know how to respond to Sam. I don't even know how to respond to Paul. I know I need to figure this mess out, but I also know I need just little bit more time. I need to be strategic with my next move. I need to get out of here.

CHAPTER TWENTY-SEVEN

I FEEL SAM'S cool hands on my waist from behind me. He leans over my shoulder and kisses my cheek as I pour a cup of coffee. "Look behind you," he says with a nervous laugh. "I bought you flowers, just because."

"Is it maybe *just because* you assaulted me yesterday?"

"Assault?" He huffs and shakes his head with a laugh. "Jade. I'm not a monster. You know this. Can we please stop being so dramatic? Can you please let me love you?"

He pulls me into his body. "I can feel you pulling away and that scares the shit out of me." I look at him blankly, wondering if he could see the emptiness inside of my eyes. "For god's sakes, you won't even have sex with me anymore. That alone can make a man crazy. We have needs. You know this." He rubs my hand on his zipper.

"Can't you feel how badly I want you?" His coffee breath, his whole existence, makes my body ill.

"I just need a little space, okay." I pull away from him grasp.

"So, what? So, you can cheat?" He slams his coffee cup hard onto the countertop so hard a piece of the marble chips and falls to the floor. "I wish you would admit it. That you don't want me anymore. That it's not me, that it's someone else you want. Why don't you just say it already?"

"Because," I say swallowing a lump in my throat. Deciding whether I want to tell the truth now or continue to live this very comfortable lie. "That's not what I want." I choose the comfortable lie.

"What do you want?"

"Space. Please. Just let me breathe." What I want is what I've always wanted. And that's Paul. But it's not that easy and saying that could make Sam grow even more dangerous. Even Mary thinks so.

He tosses the flowers down on the counter and walks out the door. Tucked inside the plastic they're still wrapped in was a card. I open the card which said:

I wish you loved me. I'm sorry I failed you. Let me spend forever trying to get it right.

Please.

Love, Sam.

My restless body is frozen, it doesn't know what to do. Do I leave the house and see if he's tracking me? And what if he is? What can I do, especially since he's my husband? It's not illegal for a husband to know where his wife is. Is it? Sam does have very real and valid concerns of cheating. We're both wrong and bringing anyone else into the picture might only make it worse.

I decide it's time to text Paul.

Me: *He's onto us...He thinks I'm cheating.*

He doesn't respond right away. My hands shake until he does a couple hours later.

Paul: *Does one time count as an affair? Who knows if you will ever see me again? I haven't heard from you since.*

Paul: *Which by the way, was not fair to do me...again.*

Me: *I know. I want to see you again. I just need more time...*

Paul: That's what you always say

Me: This time is different. He knows I love someone else more

Paul: This doesn't concern me. Not until you do something about it

Me: You have no idea how hard this is for me...it's not that easy to leave

Paul: Yeah well, it's not easy for me to wait, either

I start typing a reply and erase it when I see him start typing again.

Paul: But I've waited this long... why not a little longer.

My heart flutters and warmth pours into it. I close my eyes and smile for a minute—taking it all in. Paul and his patient love.

Me: Do you mean that?

Paul: I wish I didn't, but I do... Though every day without you I swear die a little more

I can't bear the thought of him hurting another day.

Me: I love you. I'll be yours again soon.

Me: It'll be us this time.

Paul: Promise?

Me: Promise.

I picture us running back into each other's arms again at stop sign. That golden boy and his arms around me again.

Paul: Ps. I love you more

CHAPTER TWENTY-EIGHT

I'M OFFICIALLY A rich woman.

Maybe not by most people's standards, but from my perspective as a small-town girl from Tiffin Ohio, I've made it. Between Sam's success at the brokerage, and the new success of the bakery, we have more money than I ever imagined we would. I'm still not in the bakery, but Sam constantly assures me that it's almost time for me to get in there and do my thing. In the meantime, I've been baking cakes on my lunch hour, practicing my icing, creating bold new color palates and unique flavors.

Today feels different. A longing and restlessness for Paul has set fire in my brain, consuming me. As an attempt to take my mind off him, I take it out on the cake. Swirling blood orange butter cream over the lemon thyme sponge and mascarpone layered cake, imagining my tongue running across his body with every slide. Getting lost in the art of it is half the reason I fight for the dream. After dressing the cake with real orange wedges and thyme sprigs, I step back to admire the masterpiece I created. A twinge of sadness sinks in as I think of Grandma Lo in this moment and wonder what she'd think of me. She did turn me into a baker after all. Feeling pleased with the finished product, I snap photo of it for some reason and send to Mary.

Me: New cake! You like?

Mary: OMG! GIRL! WHAT?! Yesssss. I need this cake. Almost too pretty to eat

Thirty minutes later, Mary tags me on her booming social media account to her four hundred thousand followers. "My sis did this! Would you eat this?"

The comments poured in. Thousands of red hearts lit up her post.

Mary texted me almost immediately.

Mary: *Umm, your cake has gone viral*

Me: *I've noticed…*

I could hardly believe it, actually. I imagined how busy her phone must be on the receiving end of that.

One comment read: *I'd sell my soul for this cake.*

Mary: *You need to get into that bakery ASAP. What's the wait?!*

Me: *Sam…he says that they're just preparing for me…*

Mary: *Preparing for you? What does that even mean?*

Her question makes me wonder. I have trusted Sam's every move that I never even question him anymore.

Mary: *You should start your own social media account for these cakes you're baking*

Mary: *If you don't, I will. Because the people love them!*

Me: *Maybe. I'll think about it.*

Mary: *I would. It would show Sam who's right and who is wrong.*

Sometimes I forget I'm talking to Sam's sister and when I remember, I realize I still should be careful with how I respond.

Mary: *He should've bet on you from the beginning. You're amazing.*

I go back and forth before I ultimately decide to take Mary's advice and open an account to share my cakes. My hands tremble before I click to upload and I'm careful to remain anonymous. The last thing I want is for Sam to think I'm creating a secret account to cheat. I decide my intention is to share my cakes with the world, if I'm moving back to Tiffin to be with Paul, I'm going to need an outlet to share my baking. And even if I convince him to move here, I could use this page for my new business. I couldn't imagine Sam giving me our bakery without a fight.

Within the first two weeks of having the new account, I had already gained a few thousand followers from Mary's account after she'd repost them. Thankfully, Sam is not active on social media. Says he doesn't have the time and is not interested in wasting what he has left on his free time to concern himself with other people's problems.

"When I wake up, I don't even want to check my emails first thing. That would be me responding to other people's problems before my own. That does everyone good except me," Sam says. In some ways he's right. "My father has surrounded his whole life responding to other people's problems. Even Mary, who despises him, is doing it every time she logs on. It makes no sense to me. She'd cry for hours for him to be a part of her world only for her to barely live in it now herself."

I'm not like Mary and I consider my social media use to be moderate. I don't post often, maybe a photo at every major event, and I probably have about twenty photos total from when I started the account when the app was first created. My over exposed, smudgy filtered photos are still there. The ones of me and my family dog. Me at my cousins wedding in Colorado in a sundress on some mountain view. Me and Sam, our new keys in hand to our new condo. Me at a rooftop party for my engagement. My ring shining over the city lights. Me when I'm trying to convince the rest of the world that I'm good at life. No, great at life. I am the best at life and here is my tiny square as proof.

My account is private, only my friends and family can see what I post. Up until now, I've mostly use my social media accounts as a form of entertainment, to see how everyone I once knew is doing. And to pass the time. To daydream. To connect with real people in a fake world. In many ways, I am a real person in a fake world. Maybe this new account will be a new beginning. Maybe it will open a door to a real-world connection with a real person. Maybe that's what everyone is hoping for anyway, even the fake people in the fake world.

A TEXT FROM Paul lights up on my phone. I lick buttercream off my fingers.

Paul: *Are you free to talk?*

I scrape my hand up and down my leg. This could be a talk that makes or breaks everything between us.

Me: *Yes...*

He calls me immediately and I answer with a nervous knot in my stomach. Afraid he might be done. Done with waiting. Done with me.

"What are you doing?" He asks with haste to his voice.

"Baking...why do you sound like that?"

"Because I'm this close to driving to Chicago right now to scoop you up. I can't live without you another moment. I'm dead serious, Jade. I can't." he says. I hear the keys rustle in his hands and the ignition start up.

It hits me then. Fifteen years. Fifteen years stand between me and the biggest mistake of my life. It wasn't that day with Paul and I in the bathroom, it wasn't Paul, and it wasn't the act I regret. It was getting caught. Somedays, still riddled with shame and confusion, I wonder how we let our guards down. *How did we get here? How did we let it end up like this?* We were so careful at first. I try to pinpoint when we got so relaxed in our sneaking around. Certainly, we had concerns, we knew what might happen if weren't careful. And for a long while, we thought we were careful. It makes me wonder if my mom was right. That maybe it did all boil down to fate. That maybe we weren't supposed to be together. That it was supposed to end. But everything in me in since that day cannot accept that as a fact. We were two people very much in love who very much wanted to stay together. We have unfinished business. Forces outside ourselves pulled us apart. And now the magnetic force within us has remained strong enough to somehow always bring us back together. I lost him once, and I knew that I didn't want to lose him again.

If my mom's theory on fate is true, then why is she messing around with Ron while still married to my dad? Why did Ron come back into her life, and why did he move back to town? Why can't they quit each other? Maybe I wouldn't be where I am without Sam, but even after fifteen years, I can't help but wonder what my life would be like if that day never happened.

"Are you serious?" I ask cautiously, peeling my apron over my head. The time has come. He's ready for me to leave and so am I. It's different this time, I can feel it this time.

"Do you want me to be serious?" He laughs nervously, but I know he means it.

"Yes...of course. But Sam..."

"I hate even hearing his name. Can we call him something else? Dr. Robot. Alien man. Donald duck. Literally, anything beats hearing his name out of your mouth. Saying his name makes it real and reminds me that you still belong to someone else."

I laugh. "Okay, okay. Well, Donald Duck is coming home soon. Let's make a real plan…"

"My real plan is to scoop you up, toss you into the back of my pickup and marry you. How's that? Does 7:30pm work for you? Works for me." Another call comes in as we're talking, I pull the phone from my cheek to see who it is.

"Keys are in my hand. Just tell me where to find you and I'll be on my way."

"Shit," I said. "It's Sam. On the other line. I mean… it's Donald Duck."

Paul sighs. "Do you realize how hard it is to share the love of my life with a man who doesn't deserve her?"

"You're hardly sharing me, I promise." It's true, we don't even have sex. "Okay? Please. Don't do this… I'm trying, just…hold, please."

I click over to answer Sam's call. I try my best to act normal. *Stay cool. Stay calm.*

"Hello, darling. I'm calling because I can't hold it in anymore. I have a surprise for you." Sam says, his voice high pitched and eager.

"You do?" I say, surprised.

"I will be leaving the office soon. When I call you, come outside, okay?"

I click back over to Paul.

"Apparently umm—Donald Duck has a surprise for me."

"Wow. He's going to do anything he can to keep you now, don't you see that? I swear, it's like he knows we are this close…"

It's not possible. I'm yours. Please, believe me. I want to say those things to him, but instead I don't say anything, because he's right. He will do anything to keep me, and it takes everything in me to leave.

"Where do you live? Just tell me. I won't come today, but I need to know where the princess sleeps and where to rescue her when she's ready."

"Since when are you this romantic?" I laugh a little.

"Since we started our own Romeo and Juliet story fifteen years ago."

"Thirteen forty-four Riley Boulevard. Big building. 22nd floor. The door man's name is Leonard."

"Jesus. A door man. Is it beautiful? It's fancy, isn't it?" I can tell this makes him feel inadequate, but it's still him that I want.

"All that glitters is not gold," I remind him. "His family has millions. What do you think?"

"I think I might have to rescue you in something nicer than my old muddy boots then, won't I?"

"You can recuse me naked, and I'd still come with you."

"Especially if I was naked—then you'd literally come with me."

"You're an idiot." We laugh and I shake my head. This man and the way he makes me feel like a kid again. How could I not pick him this time?

"A sexy idiot."

"Alright, naked prince charming. You can come rescue me any other time you want, just not today."

"How about tomorrow?"

"Deal."

SAM ARRIVES EARLY and when he calls me, I take the elevator down and look for him from the street. He calls me again. "Can you see me?" I squint my eyes, looking around.

"No, where are you?" I say, my hand over my brows, searching.

"I'm waving. To the left." I look to the left. Sam is driving a brand-new white luxury SUV. He hangs up, drives around the cul-de-sac, parks in front of me and steps out.

"It looks like I earned my girl another set of keys. Here you go. It's yours," he says, tossing the car keys into my hands.

"Wow. Oh my god—It's so… nice," I say, walking around the car. "It's big though, don't you think?"

"Jade, you're a thirty-year-old woman now. You left everything small back in your twenties. It's time to think bigger," he says, putting his arm around my waist and his hand over my lower abdomen. "And by bigger, I mean family." He leans in to kiss me. "I know you weren't in love with the idea of a bigger car, but it was a great deal. I traded in your old car, and it brought the price of this one down significantly." He runs his hand over the hood. "We're going to need this eventually when you get pregnant."

Is he crazy? "You traded in my old car? Without asking me?" I shake my head and blink a few times as I try to process what's in front of me.

"We are a family, Jade. This is our family car," he says, looking down. "I thought you'd be happier about it…"

"And I thought you would let me make any of my own decisions. I thought I would have at least a little say in my life and in this marriage." It came out whether I wanted it to or not.

"Will you ever be happy when I do something nice for you? Why are you always so ungrateful?"

"Something nice? You practically stole my car and sold it."

"Your car? So, what? What's yours is yours and what's mine is also yours?"

"I never said that. I'm just saying, that would be like me selling our condo without asking you first."

"Are you being serious right now?" He shakes his head, rips the key from my hand, shoves me out of his way. "Fuck it. I'll take it back then," he says.

"Sam, stop. I didn't say that. I don't want to fight." It's true, I am so tired lately, so drained, the last thing I have energy for is another blow up with Sam. The car is nice, but that isn't the point. The point is that Sam never lets me take the wheel to my own life. And quite literally now, he has taken the wheel yet again.

"It's wonderful, okay? I love it," I say, walking toward him before he steps into the driver's seat. "I love it." I smile. "And I love you," I tell him using my most convincing voice.

"You do?" He leans in to hug me.

I nod and bury my chin into his collar bone. The smell of his cologne lingers on my nose. "Yes, I do." The tricky thing about saying "I love you" to Sam is that I do love him at times even though I can't stand him often. None of that makes sense. Part of what is so hard about leaving him is the very real fact that sometimes I do love him. I love who he was and who he could be, and I love the life we have built. Sometimes I worry that I might make the mistake of leaving before giving us a real chance to get better. Before I let him prove himself just one more time. I equally worry about waiting too long to make my way back to Paul and forever missing out on the greatest love of my life. It always comes down to this. One minute I'm sure it's Paul and the next, I'm convinced I can't live the life I've always wanted without him.

When I see Paul tomorrow, I'll know what to do.

CHAPTER TWENTY-NINE
(Tomorrow)

I SHOULD'VE BEEN aware that hearing from Ashley meant major news, but I had just pulled out my laptop, logged into work and was successfully distracting myself. The thoughts of seeing Paul again were becoming all consuming, I can hardly focus on anything else. I open her message with hesitation.

> **Ashley:** *I'm really sorry, girl. I can hardly believe it. I wish I could hug you right now…*

What? What does she mean?
My hands shake as I open the link to the news article.

A photo shows two cars collided, one smashed under the other. Flashing police lights, a black night sky. *Roll over crash on I-94 kills one man, injures two.* Chills run down the sides of my arms and down my spine. My soul could feel it before I read further. It knew.

My hands tremble uncontrollably. When I see it, the world starts spinning in slow motion. It hits me in the stomach first before hitting me everywhere else. The feeling fills me up and empties me out all at once. A vacancy takes over my body as my reality is quickly painted dark. And before I could say a word, my knees gave from under me. My chest tightened, denying me another sip of air. My body melts into my hands as I stop breathing for what feels like a week. When I open my mouth and come back for oxygen, everything starts to hurt. My bones, my organs, even my flesh feels as if it was immediately hanging loose on my face, like I had just seen a ghost. In many ways I had.

I clutch the trash can, feeling as if I would either faint or vomit, or both.

"Hey, hey, Hey." Sam sees me from the hallway, rushes to my side. When he's concerned, he sucks his bottom lip into his teeth and his mouth caves in a little.

"What is it, what's wrong?" Sam rubs my shoulder as he kneels to me. I couldn't even say the words. My mind didn't want to accept it. But then it came out cold and hollow.

"He's—dead," I said. Hearing those words come from my lips broke me open. It didn't even feel like I was speaking, it felt like my body was being borrowed.

"Who is dead? Who?" Sam asks. I hand him my phone. My mouth can't say his name. My head can't believe it. My heart can't handle it.

"Wait. Was this the friend I met at that St. Patrick's Day party that one time?"

I stare off, numb, sick, and empty. I can't move. I can't speak. I can hardly exist. I can't even blink. I just—can't.

"Didn't you date him when you were younger?" he asks. His voice echoes into my chest painfully.

What I want to say, I don't. I don't say that the love of my entire existence is dead. Even if I wanted someone else to know the gravity and feel the weight of this loss in this moment, because anything less than the truth feels like an abomination to what this man meant to me.

I haven't told Sam enough for him to realize this. If I want to keep the peace, I need to control my grief, stuff it far enough down so that no one can see it. Even if right here, right now, I have also died.

I nod and close my eyes, trying to desperately hold back my tears, the tears that I know would confuse Sam. I shouldn't be this upset over a young love, an old friend, in his eyes. Especially one he thinks I have lost touch with. For all he knows, that's all it was. But none of that is my reality.

"I need to take a drive, okay?" I wipe my hands over my leaking eyes, swallowing back the waterfall of tears begging to flow.

Sam nods and runs his fingers through my hair. He's treading lightly, knowing that I'm half in and half out of our relationship. One wrong move and he knows I could be gone. A bouquet of flowers wouldn't cut it now.

"I'm sorry, baby. He seemed like a nice guy." He brushes softly against my hand.

A nice guy? He wasn't a nice guy. He was the very best one. And now, he's dead. And I am the idiot who waited too long to claim what my heart desired since I was a sixteen-year-old girl.

Paul Thompson. Gone forever. It is officially over.

I swipe the keys off the counter and run to my car like I have somewhere to be. Once I shoved them into the ignition, I could feel the tears bubbling up to the surface.

It hits me then. *He was on I-94. He was on his way back to me.*

CHILLS COVER MY arms as every part of me wants to be erased. This was my fault. As my car leaves the neighborhood, I know I'm free to let it out. All of it. A heart shattering sob and belly burning scream pours out of my mouth, tears stream down my cheeks, making it hard for me to see through the blur. Between the blurred vision, puffy eyes and wailing coming from my body, I decide it's best that I find a safe place to park. I pull into a coffee shop parking lot and let myself entirely crumble in the sight of no one. I find it hard to breathe, to open my eyes. When

I look around, nothing around me feels real anymore. There's a sick feeling settling into my stomach that won't leave, like I've been punched in the gut repeatedly. Everything hurts.

Paul died. He's dead because of me. This sentence spins around in my head like a heavy load of wet laundry tumbling to dry.

Right now, in this moment, I hate everything.

I hate death. I am angry at it, and I'd like nothing more than to shout at it like I could it could hear me. It's not just death, it's the permanence of it that makes me want to combust. A new sudden envy takes over me. A maddening bitterness as I realize how many people still have what I don't – their person.

I HATE EVERYONE. The people who are inside this coffee shop, ordering their mocha chip Frappuccino's with a smile on their face and their world still completely intact while mine is exploding piece by piece alone and broken-hearted inside of this car that I also hate. It baffles me, really. How could they, these people within a few hundred feet of me, carry on with their life when the most important person on earth just left? My mind doesn't seem to connect the reality of how everyone else can carry on as usual, when the same world we all share just isn't the same anymore and it never will be. Why can't anyone else feel that?

Bitter with God, I question him.

How could an asshole drunk uncle be alive still, or rapists, or murders, or mosquitos, or killer bees, or pointless living things like parasites, but not my Paul? None of it makes sense. And all I want to do is make sense of it.

I wonder why natural selection failed to do a better job at weeding out the bad ones. Shouldn't it be the criminals that don't have a pulse anymore. Why not take them? Why did my Paul have to be the one to go? The what ifs are sinking in, and I hate them, too. *What if I had just let him come when he first asked? What if I never married Sam and chose Paul all those years ago? Where would we be now?*

HE WAS RIGHT. I shouldn't have married him. And now it's too late. And more than anything, I hate myself for letting this happen. Paul never deserved this. He deserves to be alive; we should've been together. I should've chosen Paul and I will never forgive myself for it. Inside I'm unalive, and on the outside, I'm taking on a new identity. I decide from here on out that I'm invincible, because even if I'm not, I don't care what happens. I could walk into oncoming traffic unscathed. For a minute I imagine it. I picture myself as a translucent outline of where a human is supposed to be colliding my body into cars to see if I could feel it. I can see my milky white hands slip through the crashing metal without so much of a drop of blood.

I don't know how to be me without him.

CHAPTER THIRTY
(Two months later)

THERE ISN'T A funeral. And even if there would have been one, I can't face his body.

Not after what I've done. My coping mechanisms have all deserted me, too. I've stopped sleeping, kitchen therapy fell by the wayside, and food has started looking like some foreign object I don't have the interest in participating in. I had even stopped making my weekly sourdough. On the days I hated Sam, which was every day, I'd knead at the blob of dough and pretend it was his face. How could I hate a man and be too afraid to leave? How could we be so great, but also so terrible. Beautiful and ugly. Good and evil. Oil and water.

Now that I have nothing left, I convince myself there's no reason to leave Sam anymore. I don't have the energy to go if I tried. I am hollow. Empty from the inside out. Paul's death has destroyed me. I've lost him many times before, but this is what losing him forever feels like. And it's a feeling I was never ready to accept.

I'm left physically and emotionally depleted—and it shows. My face has become gaunt and haggard, my sallow skin formed shadows etched beneath my eyes, that no amount of makeup could disguise. Looking in the mirror seems to serve one purpose and that was to remind me of what happened. I decide to take Mary's advice. I pull myself out bed and drag my sad ass to a

Botox appointment. I will try anything to lift my face back up, especially as I've noticed it's constant decline from the ugliness of grief. I also had the thought that maybe if I don't look dead, I won't feel dead. If there's anything about Mary's advice that I agree on, it's that she's right—I am too young to look like this.

In the waiting room I cross my legs as I read through the pamphlet depicting a woman with dewy white taunt skin smiling at me with her perfect fake face. *I want to be her*, I think to myself. *I want to be anyone else.*

"Young people need Botox, too. Especially the ones with a story. Something tells me you've got one."

What is this man, the oracle? How does he know?

"We wear our life experience straight on our faces, for better or worse," Dr. Stephen, the board-certified plastic surgeon says to me as he prods at my face. He takes the Botox syringe and squirts a little into the air while pinching at the thin skin around my eyes.

"But unlike marriage, you don't have to settle. You can do Botox." He laughs and the irony in his words sends a dull ache into my stomach.

He picks around at my face and continues.

"The reflection we get in the mirror doesn't showcase our age, but also what we've been through." He looks at me as if he's looking through me, like maybe I had become hollow. His eyes lower at mine, questioning and seeking. He clears his throat a little.

"Hell," I tell him. "I've been through hell. I just lost the love of my life." It felt like taking a breath of oxygen to say that out loud to someone else. I didn't even want to say it, but it came out anyway.

"Well, I have a vial for that." He injects my face with juicy tiny needles, but even that wouldn't remove my great loss. The pain has made a home in every cell on my face, even if we smooth out the lines, the hurt goes deeper than skin.

I think about what my mother said that day when she told me I had a certain look on my face when I'm around Paul. I wondered how differently my face looks like without him. And not just without him for a moment. Without him forever.

I convince myself that smoothing out the sad lines might remove the hurt. That maybe by bringing back my old face, it might trick the rest of me into believing my old life was still here.

"You said Mary recommended you? She didn't say her brother passed away. I'm sorry to hear this news.—"

"It wasn't him." My voice weakens. I tell him because I can't tell another soul, and neither can he. No one else but me, my mom and Dr. Stephen know.

He nods. "Oh. I see. That's a different kind of loss, isn't it?"

"Yeah...." I try to hold it in, but a tear begins to fall against my will.

"Let your eyes leak a little. Tears won't ruin the results." He pats me on the shoulder. "You'll still look amazing. You might feel like hell, but you'll look amazing."

WE DON'T HAVE a real backyard, not like the football field sized backyard I'm used to in Ohio, but we do have a small courtyard garden lined with arborvitae that is shared with the other condo dwellers that I can see from my kitchen window. I always hated this, though I can admit it is beautiful.

Privacy is something I have missed and longed for since arriving here, and it's not something we've had much of since moving in. Sam despised the idea of having a yard to maintain and no one could talk him out of all the amenities we'd be getting by living here. The doorman attended lobby, the valet, the dry cleaning, on-demand housekeeping, the rooftop with panoramic views of the city of Lake Michigan and the Chicago skyline and cabana style furnishings.

He says he won't move to the suburbs until I am pregnant, because he's not going to commute in rush house traffic just for me to have a backyard herb and vegetable garden that made me feel better about the pizzas I wanted to make with them.

I spend a lot of time looking out of my kitchen window like an amused child staring at a snow globe. Wondering how all that pretty stuff got there and wondering if I could somehow crack the glass open to play with it from where I was standing.

Today, I'm staring out searching for Paul. Not in the sense that he will rise from the dead, though I wish more than anything that he could, but in the sense that I cannot explain. Something in me wants to find him even though I know he isn't going to be anywhere that I look.

I find myself searching for a trace left of him. Flipping through old notebooks, trying to find a page with his handwriting. A bird, an animal, a penny, anything. I search for peace in pieces. Pieces of his clothes, a piece of paper, a piece of jewelry he bought me. I rummage and rummage, seeking, and searching for anything that had any bit of a memory of him. I do that until I can't. Until the floor calls in my aching body and becomes my favorite spot to exist. Lying on the marble floor brings more emotion out, as if the hard cold ground had magic powers to pull everything out of me all at once.

When I'm down there, it's easy for me to wretch my body violently into a ball and cry for hours—listening to every song that made me think of him. The same songs we danced to, made love to, laughed to. Sometimes, I'd fall asleep down there clinging to something of Paul's and I wouldn't open my eyes even if I was wide awake. Most days I feel like there's nothing left to see.

In the mirror, I look like I haven't eaten in days, because if I'm honest, I haven't. I wish I was the emotional eating type—it would certainly help my constant anemic body from trying to kill me. But no. My body decides that food is the enemy when it's in a state of misery. I want so badly to wake from this nightmare, for it to all have just been a bad dream. But the truth is this nightmare is real.

Sam tries to be remorseful. He even tries to understand what this news might feel like for me. But no one prepares you for the death of an ex-lover. There is no guidebook on how to mend that kind of broken heart. No one knew what to say to me, not my mother, not Sam. Especially not Sam. He knew Paul was my ex, but he didn't know what he meant to me. He didn't know the extent of us, the stories, the depth. The truth. And the truth is that Paul was mine. He was a part of me. And that part had just died, too.

I'm holding myself together like a Band-Aid underwater. I can keep it together, but only for so long. I save the keeping it together for when Sam is home. But as soon as he turns a corner, as soon as I am alone in the shower, as soon as I have a mere minute to myself, I let the grief to seep out of me like hot lava.

HE'S GONE. AND even though he's been gone before, for years at a time, this time meant he was gone with no going back. This is the moment where I finally understood what being what being gone really means.

Gone means his red pick-up truck would never make its way the farm again. Gone means that his left hand would never wear a ring. Gone means he wouldn't have any children with his golden hair. Gone means his woodworking saw would never spin again.

In the many days after this, I try to make sense of all that was now lost. Even his half-eaten groceries in his fridge feel like a tragedy. I imagine his favorite bag of honey mustard pretzels— half gone. And then I wonder what else was wasted, what else was half gone and unfinished. All the things that were fully gone or not started at all. The grief inside of me wants to stuff everything leftover and half empty into my body all at once. I imagine stuffing everything left over into my body to fill the gaping hole of his absence. The reality of that makes no sense but picturing it in my mind makes me feel whole and complete. Like a task on a checklist, all I wanted was everything back in its wholeness. If it couldn't be Paul, it could be everything left over.

I think about his lost opportunities to pick up where he once left off. And that of course, and most importantly, includes me. I spend days putting together conversations in my head that we would never have again. And then at times I threw in the conversations we did have, wishing they would've gone better. How I would've spent the last time I saw him, what we would've done differently. I have lost something I knew I could never replace.

DAYS HAVE PASSED and I'm still searching for him. I look for him outside of my kitchen window as I scrub dried ketchup off a lunch plate. I search for his face at the gynecologist waiting in the lobby for my pap smear. The faces of husbands waiting with their pregnant wives remind me of his, like the world was becoming a house of mirrors game I didn't want to play in. I search for him when a bird lands on a tree. I search for him when any insect crosses my path. Every day I search for him, and in the desperate moments, I ask him to come to me. I plea and I beg for him to show up, cross my path, send me a message, speak to me, something, anything—would you come back to me? *Please.*

I search for him in every sunrise and sunset. Drops of water on a rainy window, which is easy to do. This year, the year he died, has been the rainiest one this nation has had since 1930. And because rain was our thing, I like to think the world was weeping with me. That comforted me for a while. Along with sleep. I would've spent months in bed asleep if I had the chance, but I found ignoring what I felt on the outside made me more pleasant looking on the outside. If I ignored it, it wasn't real. I told myself that lie as long as I could, until how I felt on the inside would meet me on the outside unexpectedly.

CHAPTER THIRTY-ONE

HIDING GRIEF IS hard. This is the first month I have forced myself into social interactions. Ones I haven't taken part in since being married.

After work parties and happy hour cocktails with Sam. I even throw myself into working harder, working late, which of course pleased Sam. I try to bury myself in responsibility and being busy. Because if boredom found me, or stillness or solitude, they'd be the ones to bury me first.

For the last two days, a cardinal has been coming to my windowsill as I'm logging on for work, the same time each day. I believe there to be a nest in a potted tree in on our neighbors' balcony, though I can't see far enough from where I'm standing to confirm. To comfort my sadness, I have told myself this bird is Paul. Even though I know better, something inside of me feels solace in thinking it's him making connection with me. I have even started to talk to the bird when Sam is at the office.

Today, I ask Paul, "Where are you *really*? You know, are you in heaven? Or someplace else? Are you okay?" When the bird flies away, I feel anger boil up inside of me. I don't get the answer I expect, but I guess that's what you get when you ask a bird questions through a window and when birds can't talk.

"No, don't!" I cry out to the bird. "Don't! Don't fly away…. Please. You stupid fucking bird."

Then, it happens all over again, being swept under the wave

of grief. The constant reminder that he's dead. I fold in half and the tears are wringed out of my body like a wet towel. For whatever reason I had the thought that Paul would rather take the form of birds over anything else if he could. And I often convince myself that he does. Sometimes, I picture him as ladybug, a moth, a butterfly. Whatever it is, it always has wings. I'm not sure if I really saw and felt Paul as these things or if I missed him so badly that I wanted to. I try to see him as just about everything. Each day I became more desperate for a sign. I search the entire day for proof that maybe he wasn't entirely gone. And when a day came up short with clues, reality would strike me again and I'd grow gauntly fatigued from the endless hunt. The search was over.

WHILE SAM WAS in the shower, I took the elevator to the rooftop. Something about being above the trees makes me feel more alive. I walk to the edge and look down at how small the people look from up here and for a minute I wonder if this is what it's like to look down from heaven. Though I'm not religious, Paul was, and I learned a lot about his beliefs spending time around him and his family. A lot of the stories I found hard to believe and wondered if maybe the point of them weren't to be taken as literally, but maybe to be used as metaphors. But Heaven? That's a place I want to exist. To think there is a better place than where we are on earth, a place where we can meet the ones we love after they die, a place that feels like paradise once we arrive? Well, there is nothing to lose in hoping it is real. I tell myself Paul is in heaven even if I don't know what that means. I picture paradise. But a paradise without us together is hard to imagine.

"Be careful, you could fall," I hear Sam's voice shout through the wind.

"How did you know I was up here?" I turn to look at him, the wind blows my hair around behind me.

"Wild guess," he says. "What are you doing up here?" His blue eyes sparkle like a summer pool when they reach mine.

"Sometimes, I just come up here to think." I look down at the city beneath my feet, feeling larger than life. Invincible. A sudden surge of adrenaline comes over me and passes just as quickly.

"About what?" He comes closer to me.

"Life… Love," I say, turning my head back to absorb the skyline.

"And what comes to mind about either?" He hops up behind me, holding me against the metal rail. My stomach drops and my heart begins to beat faster and faster. An image pops in my head of him throwing me over the railing, I see my body free falling. I try to move away from the edge and out of his embrace, but he's too strong and one wrong move could send us both over.

"I'm going back down now," I say.

"Did I spoil your moment?" he whispers. "You don't want to see the beautiful view with your husband? We never come up here together anymore." He grabs my face. "If I were crazy, I'd say my wife was trying to escape being near me." I look into his icy eyes again. "Am I crazy?" he says, his voice reverberates through my spine. *Yes*, I say in my mind. *Yes, you are crazy, and I am terrified of what you are capable of when you're angry, which seems to be more often now than ever before.*

"No," I say, instead, breaking free with my left foot, and pushing my body out of his arms. "You're not crazy," I say. "But I am if I continue to stay with someone who scares me when they get close to me."

"I wouldn't be so scary if would just stay close to me. Instead, you're always trying to leave. Just like my father did. He was never happy just being with his wife, his family. He always wanted more. Nothing was ever enough for him," he says. "It doesn't seem like it will ever be enough for you either."

"I'm not like your father."

"You loved him, didn't you?" he says, shaking his head as he looks out over the railing. "The guy from the article. He meant something more to you, didn't he?"

"Why do you want to know?"

"Because ever since I met him that night at that party, you haven't been the same. It was like I had all of you until he came back in the picture that night. And after that, I began to lose you inch by inch, slowly over the years. And since he's been dead? You've been as good as gone, too."

I shake my head and cross my arms. "I should've known," he says. "I told you I loved you that night. And you were so weird about it. Maybe I was too drunk to see it then, but I see it now."

"It's him. He's the one you wanted."

"That's not true," I say. Tears begin to build, and my chest begins to ache, the words, the truth coming from his mouth felt like tiny daggers to my heart. I try to hold back the tears by looking away.

"Tell me you didn't still love him. Tell me that I'm just being crazy. Tell me it's all in my head. Tell me I haven't been slowly losing you all this time. Tell me that your whole heart didn't leave when he did."

I can't. I cannot in Paul's honor deny my love for him again.

"You're right," I say, pushing past him, walking away towards the elevator. "I did love him. But you are still crazy."

"So, now that he's just some dead guy, where does that leave us?" he says, hopping down from the ledge.

The very real urge to shove Sam off this balcony comes over me. Every bit of me is set on fire with rage. Instead of moving, I am frozen in place. Even once the elevator door opens, I find myself unable to step inside of it. He walks near me, put his hands on my shoulders. Just then my phone begins to vibrate. I pull it out to see that a text from Paul's estranged aunt Kathy rolls in on my phone.

> **Kathy:** *Since services weren't available for Paul, he has been cremated and the family will spread his ashes in places he loved to be. His sisters said to reach out to you, they thought you should know...*

When I read it, my heart sinks deep into my body, into a place that only exists for it to fall into and dissolve. A craving for his ashes consumes me and I contemplate asking for even the smallest amount of him so I could spread them all over me. The person he loved most.

"I just want my wife back. Can we forget this guy ever existed and move on together?" Sam says, as he breaks down sobbing hanging his head over me.

"Please." He begs.

"I love you, Jade."

"I know you do," I say.

There's no man more romantic than the man that knows he's about to be forgotten. Sam knows he is fading for me, and that only makes him want me more. At first, I was delighted his over-the-top expressions of love. The lavish wedding, the luxury home, the cars, the flowers, the bakery.

Right now, I know two things to be true, even if they don't make sense. I didn't want Sam to be with anyone else, especially now that Paul is gone. I know there is no one else alive that loves me this way, but I also didn't want to belong to him anymore either. Because that's what being with Sam grew to feel like—belonging to him.

SAM AND I step into the elevator and on the way down, he grabs my hand to hold, leans his head on my shoulder. As much as I hate Sam at times, I also hate seeing him hurt. I don't have it in me to break another heart. Not right now.

So much of me believes that Sam is right to feel the way he does. So much of his pain and anger towards me is warranted. Paul has always consumed most of my heart and that was never fair for me to try and love them both. When we make our way back to the condo, I walk into the bathroom alone, pull out my phone and text Kathy back.

> **Me:** I still can't place it in reality. I'm so sorry. I love you all. Thank you for telling me.

I hesitated to say it, but I don't regret it. Saying I love you sort of feels natural now, even if for years it didn't because I hated her. I hated his whole family. They all despised me after what happened and so I despised them, too. You know, for doing what teenagers do. Grandma Lo finally stopped hating me when I moved away to college and started dating Sam. I wondered if this was only because I was longer a threat to her or her grandson. I was taken and I had moved away. Sometimes I'd see her when I'd come back home for the holidays at the only grocery store in our small town, and she was cordial. It felt like progress and a slap in the face at the same time.

As the years went on, she had started to wave or smile at me. She even sent me a friend request on social media, which I found funny to imagine her on social media. Sometimes she would like my posts and comment nice things. It appeared to be like an olive branch or an unspoken apology for ruining my life. Somehow along the way she had forgiven me, and I had decided to accept it. But by then it was too late. Maybe that was intentional on her end. Maybe I still hate her a little bit for it, especially now.

THE WHOLE THING was like a modern-day Romeo and Juliet to me. I obsessed over this rebellious and forbidden love. I read the lines of their poetry with tear filled eyes before I fell asleep every night for at least a month after we broke up. I wanted to be validated and this story felt beyond validating. It was the only way I could make sense of my heartbreak. I'd crack open the old and tattered book I bought from the used bookstore in town. The pages were so old they smelled like aged cheese; and I was careful with them as if they were the very fabric of my heart. I pictured me as Juliet and Paul as Romeo, of course. I even imagined that if one day we got back together, we'd have two dogs and name them Romeo and Juliet. And we'd live to see our story take a different turn, and the dogs would remind me of how hard we fought to be together. The lines kept me awake and I'd write out the ones that made me feel equally shattered. My favorite ones made their way to my school notebooks and on the back of my homework assignments.

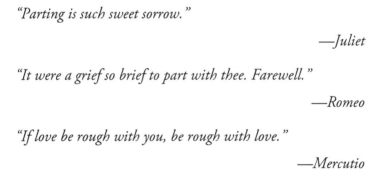

"Parting is such sweet sorrow."

—Juliet

"It were a grief so brief to part with thee. Farewell."

—Romeo

"If love be rough with you, be rough with love."

—Mercutio

CHAPTER THIRTY-TWO

I FIND MYSELF beginning to crave the taste of his ashes just to have him on my mouth one last time. The loss of him I feel so deeply, I would swallow what's left of him whole if I could, just to keep him alive within me.

After going back and forth, I text Kathy. I knew I needed a final goodbye. This closure was important enough to risk looking crazy over.

> **Me:** *I know this might be strange, but would you mind sending some of his ashes? I would like to do something special with them.*

Kathy doesn't respond until the next day, which has me feeling like a fool for the last twenty-four hours. When she does reply, I feel sick as I read her message.

> **Kathy:** *Sure. Where should I send them?*

I give her my address and pray that Sam doesn't get to them first. Paul will be back in my arms again, but in a way that I never wanted to experience.

THE ASHES ARRIVED a week and a half later.

When I hold the envelope in my hands, they tremble. I consider not opening them in the house so Paul wouldn't have to witness what goes on here, the things I never got the chance to tell him. How unloved I really am. Holding his body in this envelope bring equal parts comfort and pain. I'm just as close to him as I ever will be, and just as far apart as I will ever be. I'm not with him or without him at this moment, not entirely. Somehow, the bird must be listening as I heard it's sing-song chirp outside the windowsill again. Even if I tried, I couldn't hold back the tears now. I wave at the bird. "Hey, you," I say, wiping the tear from my cheek.

"That's not what you think." Sam catches me, shaking his head with a laugh as his eyes cut to the bird and then back at me.

"What are you trying to say?" I ask, still looking at the bird.

"That bird isn't the dead guy you are so in love with." He laughs again as he pops open a small bag of chips. "Is that what you think? He has turned into some bird, coming to say hello?"

"Sam, Stop." I say, hiding the envelope under my thighs. "What, are you jealous? Of a bird?" I force a small laugh as I shout at his body walking away from the kitchen.

"It wouldn't surprise me if you were, you know…" I say. He's doing what I hate, putting salt on the wound. "What? You afraid that I love this bird more than you?"

"Whatever." He stuffs a few chips into his mouth. He mumbles, "Go be in love with some bird, I don't care."

Saying those words out loud make me question myself. Am I in love with a bird?

THE FIRST MONTH he passed away, I self-pleasured myself more than I had in a long time. I'd sink down into the bathtub, close my eyes and I swear I could feel him on my skin again. I had never wanted him so badly. After I came, I'd lie there full of both orgasmic euphoria and bitter grief, that the combination would send me into a dry heaving cry. My body knew he was gone more than my mind was willing to accept. My mind somehow missed the memo—that he's gone forever. But my body, her genius anatomy, didn't forget what he felt like inside of me. She and grief reminded me every time I saw myself naked in the mirror. On my worst days, I'd undress in front of his ashes, picturing his eyes on me again.

Lately, I'm surprised by what images haunt my mind as I grieve the life of Paul. Sometimes, out of nowhere, flashbacks giving him another blow job, my lips wrapped around his erect flesh, and pleasuring him on my knees.

A soft smile stretches on my face at the thought, a rush of heat swells into my stomach and until I shudder cold when I come back from the daydream.

He's dead. He. Is. Dead.

If I close my eyes right now, I can see him. I can feel him when I trace an outline with my fingers over my hips and breasts, feeling the heat of his hands over mine.

With Sam gone at work, I begin craving Paul again. It's the only time I can allow myself to wander into another world where we're together again.

I close the curtains and undress in my bedroom. My left-hand caresses my neck, slides down my chest and stomach like hot oil, my warm palm becomes his touch. I squeeze the thick edges of my hips tightly, rocking them up and down. I lean down into my floor mirror and find myself taken over with arousal, licking the neck of my own reflection. I stick my finger in my mouth and close my eyes and suck. In these moments of grief, desire still ravaged my body. I want him no less now that he is dead than I ever wanted him. I throb in places I always have whenever I thought of his hot body on mine. On my knees and rock back and forth, slipping my fingers inside of me softly. I flip my hair and ride the outline of his ghost. I moan quietly and say his name over and over. If I kept my eyes closed, if I breathed deeply, he came to me. And I came with him.

Sorrow, lust, and desire haunted me and followed me everywhere. If my eyes were closed, my body somehow could feel his heat. Somehow his heat was still running over me like a warm waterfall. I wondered if maybe he were there, witnessing me, making love to me, even if I couldn't see him. It didn't matter how I felt him, all I wanted was to feel him again. And again, and again.

I thought I could close my eyes when I was with Sam and pretend that he was Paul. But his heat was different, in fact, there was almost no heat at all. Sam's skin was colder, and his scent was so deeply Sam, that my mind and body knew I could not be tricked. It was only when I was alone that I could still feel him. Sometimes I could hear him. I swear I could hear him telling me I was beautiful. His whispers were so real and honest that I couldn't tell if it is my head going crazy or if I was just dreaming, or if there was some veil he has been hiding behind that I just can't see.

The door behind me pushes open as I finish. I turn my head to see Sam. Even though he's my husband, it still feels like an invasion of privacy.

"That was…" he says, stepping into the room, eyes wide in disbelief.

"What all did you see?" I cover up, embarrassed, as if he hasn't seen me naked before.

"All of it," he says and swallows, his hands shaking. His face is aroused but his body is set on fire with rage. I can feel it.

"Why didn't you say anything? Why were you watching?" My voice trembles.

"I wanted to see… I wanted to know… what could be better

than being intimate with me...what was missing for us..."

What did he hear? God. Tell me he didn't hear me moaning his name.

"No one wonder you don't want me...You've been fucking off... alone..." He shakes his head. "And the worst part is, even with him, dead, he's still getting more of you than I am..."

He heard everything. I begin to pull my clothes on quickly. He walks over to me, pushes me to the floor and balls his fists in my face. He doesn't hit me, but I wish he would. I really want him to hit me. I want to feel his red-hot anger against my cheeks. I want another reason to hate him. An unforgivable excuse for me to leave and leave for good. But what would I return to if he did? Where would I go? How could I survive without him? He's convinced me so many times that I couldn't, I started to believe him.

"I wish I knew I married such a whore..." he says, slamming his fist onto the ground, just missing my head. I shake underneath him, but I try to be still. He straddles me then, leans over me and pulls my face to his.

"What will it take for you to love me again? How can I get you to see me...When all you have seen is him—" He shakes his head, his eyes fixed on mine. I swallow hard, fear has stolen my ability to speak, but I push through anyway.

"You're... hurting me..." I whisper. The weight of his body crushes me from underneath.

He half smiles, a dark look glazes over his ice blue eyes. "How does that feel, darling?"

He licks his lips and sucks on the bottom of my lip before biting it a little, enough for me to taste blood. "Does it hurt?" he says. I can feel him hardening over me and I begin to fear that he will force himself inside of me again.

"I'm sorry," I mutter anxiously. "Please, Sam. I love you." I lie. "Don't hurt me."

He climbs off me, rolls over and cries hard into my hair.

"I'm sorry, too." He sniffles and muffles into my shoulder. "Let's forget this day ever happened, okay? I didn't mean to hurt you…"

"I know, you're hurting, too."

"I hate this guy and I'm glad he's dead." Those worst cut deeper than what happened minutes before.

I love Paul and I hate that's he's dead.

From that night, things have been escalating until one of us broke first. I find it easiest for the fights to stop if I cried first. As soon as tears were shed, the fight was over. It wasn't hard to do anymore, I could cry anytime I thought of Paul at the first sign of defeat, my weakness would surrender me. Yelling louder didn't do anything. If anything, it makes him angrier. Crying or rage were the only white flags. I'd cry or I'd throw things. I've broken lamps and stemware glasses. His mother's vintage heirloom vase. Throwing things against the wall fills my body with a sensation like warm honey flowing through me. I'm running out of things to break, but keeping them whole hurts, too.

"You have an anger problem!" Sam shouts, after I threw his shoes across the room.

"You need help." He spat in my face. I was never an angry person before Sam. It's hard to know if I've always been this way but didn't know it, or if Sam had turned me into a monster.

TONIGHT, I TOLD Sam I wasn't up for a rooftop meet up with his friends from work and he lost it.

"You never want to do anything anymore. You've turned into such a boring old brood since that dead guy came into the picture."

It wasn't something I wanted to do, but I felt my body throw its arms around his neck. If you've ever caught a large fish and held it with both hands, you almost know what it feels like to choke a man. At least that's what it feels like to me. His cold flesh, squishy veins against my grip, bulging eyes staring right into mine. I couldn't believe this was happening, almost as if I was watching it happen instead of it happening. I didn't feel real, but it was. I had snapped and wound up with my hands around his neck. I realize in this moment this could go one of two ways as his eyes remains glued onto mine. Sam could fight back, or he could profusely apologize, claiming he was all wrong, and then later use that to attack me in other ways for a long time to follow. Sam is always the victim, even when he isn't. I pull my hands from around his neck, and he gasps for air. He looks at me then as if he knows what was next, and there was nothing he could do or say to stop it. Staring at me blankly, he wipes the corner of his mouth, and walks away.

He knows that I have had enough.

AFTER THE CHOKING incident, I stay up late, go online, and Google how to get a divorce. We've only been married for two years, but somehow, it already feels like twenty. Time has a funny way of bending when you're miserable.

As for the paperwork I print out, it's laughable. I fill out a desperate e-document from a one-off site. I click away at it with bleary eyes and shaking hands. I fill out my address, my birthday, and any information I could remember about Sam. Everything else, I pretend I knew even though I don't. Without having any access to my banking information and so on, I have no idea how much we shared in assets, what the value of what we own together is. It didn't matter, because when I got all the way through it, I paid the $6000 processing fee and pulled the trigger. I'm done. I don't know what's next, but I do know that change is around the corner.

It took all this time, all these years, and my hands around his neck for me to realize that Sam didn't want me to love, he wanted me to own. He wanted to use me. When two people are in love, there is equal give and take, yet all Sam wanted to do was take and take until I was empty. He married me to be his helper, his maid, his servant, his secretary, his sex doll, his housewife, his everything he asked me to be—which was always everything I never asked for. When he appeared to be showing me love, they were just illusions.

To be honest, it feels like a hasty thing to do without trying more counseling first. But my nervous system wants to turn it all off today. I just want it to be over.

I never wanted a relationship to end bitterly. What I hate most is feeling lonely, but what I didn't realize was how lonely it can also feel when you're with someone. A person who doesn't make you feel alive, seen or heard. I was becoming a ghost of myself the longer I stayed. But I didn't want to burn any bridges or anyone, either. What I want is to leave quietly and painlessly. To slip away in the night after a good day. I don't want to give up on a bad day. I want the recency effect in full bloom. To be remembered as a beautiful flower, the best damn wife. Not who I really am and who I've become.

So, tomorrow morning, I will make Sam a brunch he always loved—stuffed French toast with sliced strawberries and maple syrup. I will ground organic coffee beans—French pressed and poured it in the Crate and Barrel mugs we got from our wedding registry. I will hold him tightly before he leaves for a meeting and when he's gone, I will pack my bags and slip out the door. I will leave on a good day. I didn't know yet where I'll be going, but I do know, I won't be returning.

CHAPTER THIRTY-THREE
(November)

I PACK WHAT felt like mine, and left what didn't, which was almost everything but my clothes, a few pair of shoes, toiletries, and Paul's ashes. If I was leaving this all behind, it meant that I couldn't take who I've been with me. I was starting over and that means a clean, fresh start. I scan around the condo and give a last look. Saying goodbye has never been my strong suit. I kiss my hand and touch it to the ground. Before I leave, I write a note. I'm careful not to tell Sam where I'm going, or anyone for that matter.

The point is that I don't want anyone with me. In my note, I say I went camping, but I've never been camping in my life, so I don't think they believe that's what I'm doing. I don't say where because I don't want company. I gave my mom a few vague hints, so she didn't send a search team, but I didn't give as many to Sam. If Sam was going to find me, I'd want him to have to hunt me down like an exotic animal or pretend that I was as good as dead.

"Jade, sweetie I haven't heard from you in a week. You alright?" my mom asks.

I mumble into the phone, "I'm fine. Just tired lately."

"You aren't—" she whispers with shame in her voice, "Depressed, are you?"

I haven't put a label on how I feel because I haven't felt like this before.

"No, mom. I'm not. I've just been feeling tired."

"You're probably low on iron again—you've always been borderline anemic. Are you eating enough? Taking your vitamins?"

"Mom. I'm fine. I love you. I'm really fine." I push onto my stomach with my hands, I probably should be eating more. I walk over to the pantry and grab a handful of pretzels. The bag ruffles into the phone.

"This isn't about Paul, is it? Honey, it has been forever since you both—" She pauses and breathes deeply into the phone. "You couldn't be upset still, right? You've been over him long before this…"

"I think I'm just tired, Mom. I'll take my vitamins, again. That's probably it."

"Well, how's Sam? I need grand babies. You two have been married two years now."

"Oh, I wanted to tell you, I'm headed on a little girl's getaway in a couple days." I spin open a water bottle and take a sip. "Camping."

"Camping? Good lord. Can Anemia make someone crazy? You hate the outdoors. Bugs, and dirt, and animals. Should I call a shrink? Now, I'm worried."

"Nature is good, I think. Maybe it'll give me some energy back. I'll take my vitamins in the woods. Anyway, all is well. I'm good. I'll tell you when I get back." I stuff a few pretzels in my mouth.

"Alright, well I'll be checking in. Lions and tigers and bears. OH MY!" She laughs. "Bye bye. Love you."

I PULL OUT a pen and write Sam a note.

Sam,

I can't do this anymore. We're getting divorced. I've gone camping, and I won't be coming back.

Jade

Before I leave the city for good, I decide to stop by Mary's apartment. I have no one to tell, no one who would understand, and I also had no idea where to go. All I know is that I feel like running away and I feel like doing it now. When she buzzes me up, my eyes are pink and swollen. She knows before I open my mouth.

"You're leaving him, aren't you?" she says, scanning my bags. She throws her arms around my shoulders to hug me tight.

I nod. "I hate this," she says, wiping the corner of her eye.

"Great. Now, I'm tearing up again," I said with a laugh.

"Where are you going?" she asks.

"I don't know." I shrug and can't help but let a little sad chuckle out. Going somewhere without a clue does feel funny.

"You seriously don't know?" She looks at me, her eyebrows knit together confused.

"I have nowhere to go except back home."

"Where did you tell Sam you were going? You can stay with me, you know?"

"I said I went camping."

"Camping!" she laughed. "With who? You don't think Sam will believe that do you? I mean, I love you, but I never pegged you as the outdoorsy type—" She adjusts a golden watch on her wrist and spins a ring around her finger anxiously.

"I'm not really going camping—I don't know why I said that."

"I think we sometimes say things we mean without realizing

it," she says. Even though she is what most people wouldn't call smart, she can have these moments of profound wisdom.

"What do you mean?"

"I mean I think you *should* go camping—" she says. "And I think you know deep down you should, too. But here's the thing, tell no one where you're going. Not even me. Sam will ruin this for you. Even though you're like a sister, I am Sam's real sister, and I don't want him to call me asking where you are, pressuring me to tell him. I'm a horrible liar, and that wouldn't be fair or helpful to you."

I respect her honestly more than ever. She does care and that stings a little to know she won't be my sister-in-law anymore.

"Where should I go camping? Do you know any places?"

She squints, pouts her lips, and gives the 'are you kidding me' face. Suddenly, realization strikes her.

"Well, I used to date this guy in Asheville. He was actually an influencer for a few outdoorsy brands." She takes her phone out to show me his profile. "See? Here he is on some mountain wearing this brand that literally pays him to hike for a living. Ugh, he was so cute. That beard kills me." He was attractive, but of course he was. She's gorgeous.

"Why did it end?"

"Long story. Distance to sum it up." She picks at her nails. "Also, I'm not outdoorsy."

I nod and she laughs at little.

"Maybe try North Carolina? The Appalachian Trail is beautiful this time of year I hear."

It's decided. I will hike the Appalachian Trail and for added motivation, I will do it for Paul.

I don't know the first thing about hiking, or the nature of surviving the trail, but I do wonder if Mary's right. Maybe I should go to North Carolina.

BOOK TWO

CHAPTER ONE

"WHERE ARE THE hiking boots?" I ask, rubbing my eyes, my vision still foggy from the heavy fatigue and grief. As it turns out, losing a person you love beyond comprehension is exhausting. I stop at a sporting goods store off the highway. Saw a mountain in the logo and figured that must be the place Mary was talking about.

A long man with a long face wearing a flannel shirt and a headset points to the back of the store. A row of boots line the back wall from top to bottom.

"And the camping stuff?" I ask.

He lets out an aggravated huff.

"Well, 'camping stuff,'" he says in air quotes, "is what you see all throughout the store. Anything specific you're looking for?"

I shake my head, lick my upper lip and shrug. "All of it. I don't know. I've never been, and I want to go. Like today. What do I need?" I pick up a package of wool socks on an end cap and examine them for a second before setting them back down.

He laughs, "What are you running away from? The law or your life?"

I force a croaky laugh. "Just kind of feel like exploring."

"The wandering type, huh? You're in the right place." He walks me around the store. I try on a pair of hiking boots and lace them up tight. I roll my ankles around in them as I sit on the bench. When I stand up, I walk back and forth on the carpet.

From what I read online—I should size up to prevent blisters.

"I'll take them, thanks."

He shows me where the tents are, sleeping bags, survival gear. The word survival makes my stomach turn a little as I start to wonder what in the actual hell do I think I'm doing.

"How long are you going camping for? You might need a portable shower?"

I shrug, "Not sure. Until I don't feel like camping anymore, I guess."

He shakes his head and laughs as he, too, is in disbelief that I'm doing this.

"So, you might need this too then," he says, he puts it in the cart. "Unless you're hiking, then you won't want to carry this." He looks at me.

"I will be hiking." He pulls it back out of the cart.

"This will be too heavy to carry, and depending on where you're going, there could be checkpoints to shower at. Where are you camping and hiking?"

"North Carolina."

"Any idea where at?" he asks.

"Haven't decided. Around Asheville maybe."

"You haven't decided?" This time he looks at me like a lunatic. "You know most people who do a hike in the mountains, plan it out pretty meticulously. The natural elements can be gnarly. And without proper gear, you could get screwed out there. Hurt—killed even."

"Oh," I say, and my voice shakes a little. "Do you know anything about hiking, gear, or North Carolina terrain?"

"Lucky for you, I do. Probably wouldn't work here if I didn't."

He looks at my left hand.

"Your husband going?"

I look down at it, too. Forgetting up until now that I had my ring on. "No." I clear my throat. "He's not. It's a long story."

He nods. "Say no more," he says, as if it were an unspoken thing he already understood.

"Welp, let's get you the gear and on top of that mountain." He laughs.

Throughout the store, he thoroughly guides me though everything I need and sends me a few educational articles to read.

"I realize now that I only have today to prepare and that likely isn't enough time, so I plan to learn as I go."

He nods. "If you have the proper gear, you can learn as you go. That's most people do."

I can't help but feel as though maybe Paul was behind this. As if he had some bit of this man, being in this exact store, at this exact time, to help me as much as he is. I find comfort in pretending he is regardless.

AT CHECKOUT, I grab a few power bars and a handful of these red glucose liquid filled pouches to slurp down in case I get lost and can't find food. Or if I just didn't want to die, but didn't want to eat, either. As of late, that's been my mood. I didn't eat until 2:30 in the afternoon yesterday, and 4pm the day after that. Eating feels like a chore I never feel like doing anymore. I only know it's time to eat when it feels like my feet want to give way from underneath me, or when my head feels full of dizzying air that makes me light and woozy.

I wonder if this is what depression feels like or if it's the sadness in my body fighting against any traditional joys, like glazed donuts or greasy pizza. Not having an appetite would usually scare me, especially as a person who finds comfort in baking and in food in general. Though I find the emotion of fear to feel distant and untraceable. A further continuation of invincibility, or maybe a realization of not caring what happens to me either way.

At the checkout, I pay for the items with our joint credit card. Everything is shared equally with Sam, including our money. And since the divorce isn't finalized, I'm not terribly concerned if he comes looking for me through my receipts. Its finding me in the woods that'll be the hard part. I want to get so lost that even I don't know my own way out. And I don't want to come out until I feel like coming out. Maybe it'll be the weekend, a few days, a few weeks. Months. Who knows? I am not trying to plot timelines. I am just trying to get lost.

I'VE BEEN READING about people who take what's called a Thru Hike. Where they hike all the way from Georgia to Maine. I know I likely couldn't do that without preparing for months but considered not stopping until I cleared the state of North Carolina. I wonder how long that would take me. I also wonder how long I will last out there. I didn't feel like setting a goal, especially one I couldn't achieve. The only goal I felt confident in doing is disappearing. So that's what I'll do.

After leaving the store, I decide to make a list on the back of my receipt full of my grand plan for my last shakedown with Paul. If I had a plan at all, I was to release his ashes in the forest and say my final goodbye to him forever. The list includes singing with the windows down to Paul's favorite songs, drinking Budweiser, smoking a cigarette like he was the last time I saw him, eat Cheez-It's with spray cheese from a can, drink gas station coffee and hot cocoa like we did when we were kids. As I'm writing, I stop to laugh at the irony of me creating this list with a branded pen stamped with Sam's business logo. I write down the last couple things and toss the pen out of the window. Anything left of Sam won't be coming along with us.

If I'm going to celebrate Paul's life, if I'm going to fully remember him, I'm likely going to come close to dying myself. If it won't be the mountain lions, maybe it'll be the cigarettes. If it isn't that, maybe it'll be the Budweiser. And if isn't that—I'm sure enough it'll be the heartbreak that will do me in.

I do a little more reading about the Appalachians in the parking lot before leaving—I find that it breaks the dry spell for my tears. Something in the way the mountains are explained makes me feel something. Something new. Their description as "gentle, easy and unchallenging" and even understated—it all feels like a metaphor for who Paul was and what his love was like. Vistas are said to be extremely rare, meaning you often can't see through the thick of the forest, much like this feeling of grief. If Paul was the gentle Appalachian, then I knew Sam was Mount Everest. Loving him was a constant uphill battle. It was work. It was unforgiving, challenging, difficult. Love should not feel like summiting Mount Everest, love should be a gentle Appalachian Mountain.

CHAPTER TWO

I WASN'T HEADED to the mountains to die, but I also wasn't headed there to fully survive it in one piece either. I knew with my lack of experience, this place could destroy me, and since that is a feeling I'm becoming familiar with, I'm probably more prepared than I think I am.

Paul still consumes my mind daily, and even more so on this ten-hour drive down to North Carolina. I start to spend less time thinking about being with him physically, or intimately, and have begun to crave his stillness. I don't just daydream about the parts that sparks a passionate flame anymore, I daydream about sipping coffee without exchanging a word. Sitting in his peace. Exchanging nothing but calm. *God, I miss his calm.* That feeling of home I got when he wrapped his arms around me. That feeling was my drug. It wasn't thrill or taking myself to a new height. It was an anchored moment of peace in time.

As I drive, listening to the wheels turn, I wonder why I have kept myself in the state of suffering. Vacillating between sad movies and sad music, locked away in a dark room, even more isolated from the world and the people in it. I realize that maybe it's because deep down I wanted these things to take me deeper into my sadness. For some reason, I don't want to forget that sadness, I don't want to stop feeling. I am afraid to stop hurting. I worry that if I stop hurting, it means that I stopped caring, stop loving, stopped longing. It hurts worse to keep holding on to the hurt, but what I feared most was what it would feel like to let go of it. So, I kept him alive by suffering and antagonizing myself with more pain.

THE ACHE INSIDE of me follows me still everywhere, and right now I couldn't get rid of it if I wanted to. And I can find it when I'm not even looking for it. Sometimes I do look for it, just to let it out, like an overly full tire. To let it hiss out before it bursts, to keep moving forward. This trip is my big release, I can already feel it.

I'M AT THE gas station when I check my phone for the first time all day. I'm careful to keep it off in the event Sam is tracking me. I've parked my car at a campground that allows hikers to park for free as they summit. Once the car is parked, I will only travel by foot everywhere else, which starts to terrify me the harder I think about it. I log into my social media accounts for a final time and that's when I see it. The photos that were uploaded to Kathy's Facebook page today at 2:38pm.

Her caption read: *The weather is finally nice enough to do what Paul would've wanted.* The photo shows Kathy wearing a bright pink t-shirt studded with rhinestones and dark blue jean shorts. She's standing high upon a rock with her brown frizzy hair blowing in the wind behind a sleepy gray sky. It looks like it might have rained on her, too. The second photo at first looked like a river dusted with glitter. When I click on the image and looked closer, it broke me all over again.

The caption read—*His sister and I spread some of his ashes here. He loved this place.* Seeing that was like a bullet to the chest. She didn't do this to torture me, but that's all it did. Another upload came in minutes later. My heart shatters before caving in as I watch the video that destroys me. Kathy and her husband Dale had shared a video of pouring Paul's ashes into the river near the farmhouse. The river where we first said, "I love you."

Without a sound, they remove the lid to a Mountain Dew bottle and emptied his remains. I watch as everything he ever was pours out of the opaque green plastic container. How it felt slow motion to me, like time stopped as his dust flew out into the river below. My mind couldn't make sense of it—how such a small bottle could contain all that he was and all that he had. Anger began gnawing at my insides, making my legs restless and my body shudder. I drop the phone from my hands and hold my breath. And when I exhale, it feels as though my soul has left my body again. And I know that every moment spent in these mountains, I would be trying find it.

The man I love with the depths of me, the man that loved me, and was trying to save me was inside of a Mountain Dew bottle. Thoughts of us making love again swirl in my brain. Images and echoes of his laughter. And then I imagine how I might feel if I knew then the last time was with him, that the next time I saw him, he would go from a full-grown perfect man to a handful of dust collected and contained.

We used to talk about what we'd be when we got older, and if I only knew he'd turn to ash and be poured out from a bottle before thirty, I can assure you things would've been different. If I only would've known that then, I would've fucked him harder, loved him deeper and I know for certain, I would've chosen him over Sam.

Because he loved me so deeply, and my love matched his, there was never an urgency to act on it, to be together once and for all. "Once and for all" was so forever engrained in us, that it paralyzed us from forward motion. We thought because the love was always there, it wouldn't go away. Or that somehow fate or fantasy would choose the perfect moment where we belonged to each other again. That I wouldn't have to carry this regret around as a burden anymore. And if I knew that I was going to, I would've picked a better container for him. I felt a deep responsibly to press rewind on this moment.

Watching that video stirred something ominous within me, shredding at my insides and changing me forever. A person I loved more than the air in my lungs was dust. He was faceless. He was glitter on water. I throw my pack onto the dirt and my water bottle over a tree. The ache has turned into anger that bubbles from my stomach to my chest, and I let out a painful scream. It just came out. Sometimes the ache brings tears, sometimes rage. Sometimes both. But this time I feel something new. I feel like running.

"Ma'am?" A voice calls from the campground admissions cabin. "Everything alright?" Her slow Carolina accent draws closer.

"I didn't think anyone was watching." I wipe my cheeks. "I'm sorry I hit your tree." I say, embarrassed someone witnessed the lashing I gave to their property.

"Well, it's better than a bumper hitting it. Trust me, the trees have seen worse."

"Is it still okay to park my car here?" I say, pointing to it.

"Depends. Where you headed?"

"I don't know. I thought I'd just start walking and see where I end up."

She shakes her head like I'm the silliest person she's seen all day. And I realize now that maybe I am.

"Well, you better hurry and get somewhere. Sun's going down soon."

I look down at my watch. She's right. Sundown is after five

and it's four right now.

"You can stay here for the night if you want?"

"How much is it a night?" I start to dig around for my wallet.

"Eighty bucks," she says.

I hand her my card.

"Cash, sweetheart. Credit card machine is down right now. Electricity has been on and off all day from all this crazy weather, I apologize."

I don't carry much cash with me. I look into my fanny pack. *Shit.*

"I only have fifty."

"I'm sorry, miss. You could try the motel up the road, but I'd leave your car before the lot fills up. Most hikers get here before sunrise to park. And everyone attempting a summit over the next month is starting early to get ahead of all this rain. It'll be crowded before you even wake up." She scratches an itch on her arm. "You're lucky you even found a spot."

"How far is the motel?"

"About ten miles."

"By foot?"

She nods. "That's correct." I consider staying overnight at the hotel, but something inside of me wanted to choose this over the familiar comfort—it also made me feel closer to Paul.

"Can I sleep in my car?'

"I wish I could let you. Unfortunately, it's a liability because we lock it up at night. Say you had to use the bathroom, there would be nowhere for you to go because you can't get out."

"I don't normally pee at night," I say, even though that's a lie. I have been waking up at night to pee more than normal, which is largely why because I haven't been sleeping very well.

"I'm sorry, ma'am."

I look down at my ring.

"Can you do trades?" I slide my ring off my finger out of desperation. "This ring probably costs as much as this entire campground and could pay a couple employees for the next few months at least."

She tightens her lips and looks around. "Hmm. I haven't never done a trade before."

She opens her hand and walks me back to the cabin.

"You sure you don't want it? It's awfully nice..." she says observing its sparkle. She's right, it is a beautiful ring and I'm crazy for giving away, but something tells me it would just hold me down.

"I don't have any use for it anymore."

"Ahh, you're one of those hikers," she says.

"One of what?"

"The newly divorced kind." She tips her down in knowing-ness at me.

"I suppose that's a fair assumption. Are there a lot of *my kind* out here?"

"There are lot of hurt people trying to heal something out there in these mountains, that's for sure." She walks me to the cabin, has me sign in on the clipboard and hands me a map of where my site is located.

"I gave you the one with the nicest view." She smiles. "It's a bit of a hike up the trail, but it's worth it."

"Thanks. I'm here to hike anyway." I half smile back, realiz-ing it's one of the firsts I've had. *Maybe this place is already working.*

"If you decide you want the ring back when you come to pick up your car, just bring the eighty bucks with you."

"I meant a trade as in it's yours to keep."

"I know what you thought it means, but I also know the mountains can change your mind."

"It's likely I won't," I say, tucking the map in my back pocket. "But I do appreciate it. Thank you again for everything."

I walk all the way to the windy top and already regret my decision to do any of this at all. I'm feeling muscles I haven't ever used before ache, and I've only gone up a small hill. I laugh out loud at myself. *What was I thinking? This was a horrible idea.*

Considering I've never gone camping before, setting up my tent should also be comical. Thankfully, that woman was right. The view up here is stunning, the light shines through the trees and onto the deep green rolling Appalachians. I'm tucked away far away from the campers. The site I'm on would be considered the honeymoon suite of all campsites, I'm sure. Once my tent is up, I boil a bit of water over the fire pit to pour into my cup of noodles. I keep my phone off and plugged into the portable charging port. I am quite impressed with myself for getting this far. *Jade, mountaineer, master of the wilderness, day one.*

The sun is beginning to set over the mountains. It reminds me of a Bob Ross painting that doesn't fully feel real. My mind is quiet and still for the first time in a while. I wondered if it was because of all the distractions, like the act of setting up camp of being captivated in the present moment by a sunset. The busy work has already taken so much space up in my mind that it hasn't had enough time to catch up with the reasons I came here.

That thought lasted about as long as the sunset, and once it went down and I am alone in the dark for the first time—the fear creeped in. Not for the bears that are likely scattered around these mountains nearby. Not of the other campers. But the fear of wondering what Sam was doing, how angry he would be that I left, and if he was out there trying to find me or not. I pull the sleeping bag over my face and try to get the image out of my head—the one of him racing down here as fast as he could to find me and destroy all of this.

I picture him on this journey, rummaging through the same sporting goods store, buying the same things I did just to track me every time I turned the phone on. And if he was tracking me, would he be able to find me? The thought sends a chill through the tips of my toes. I need to wake up early tomorrow morning and get moving. I can't let him find me.

CHAPTER THREE
(Three days later)

THANKSGIVING IS THIS weekend.

That wasn't a part of some grand plan, but now as I think about it, it feels somewhat like divine intervention. The last person I needed to see what Sam's mother on another bitter holiday. I think to myself, *This is great—I can hike over the weekend, find a place in town to eat a thanksgiving dinner alone, in peace and head back to the trail.*

More than anything, I notice that I am starting to gain an appetite again, which makes me feel the most alive I've felt since Paul left. A gnawing hunger begins as soon as I wake up, and it seems to have officially awaken after being on the trail a few days, as if my body somehow knew that once it was away from food, it wanted more of it. The absolute opposite of "out of sight, out of mind." It was an absence makes the heart grow fonder situation. And I want a turkey dinner something fierce. Since I can feel my anemia settling in, I know the meat might help. My plan is to hike the next three days towards town. I'm not certain I'll find a turkey dinner, but I know I will find warm food. I'm nauseated by the thought of eating another cup of noodles, instant mashed potatoes, instant oats, trail mix and dry power bar.

All the research suggested not to pack too much additional food, because there would always be a town close enough with food. It wasn't like hiking out west where you needed to pre-ship food boxes at checkpoints. It was supposed to be simpler to survive on these trails, but still I knew that simple didn't always mean easy. Not when you're in the wilderness. Nothing about it feels easy. The bugs, the mud, the elements, the rain, the aching, the pain.

Each day on the trail, I discover a new weak part that would give out by the end of the day—some days it would be my feet, somedays my shoulders would feel rubbed raw from my pack, and today, it was my back. My lower back throbs with each step. It's a day where all I can do by the end of it is crawl into my tent and collapse. I see a lot of collapsing in my near future.

One thing I know for sure—nature knows grief better than I do.

The fog is constant and hangs over the mountain's stoic and ghostly, reminding the trees to remain patient for the sun. The rainiest year since 1930 perhaps wasn't the best hiking weather. Everything is wet and has stayed wet since I've been here. I quickly realize how much I despise sloshing around in flooded shoes and falling in the mud after slipping on my first wet root. Not to mention how dangerous the fog was. At times, I am hiking headfirst into misty clouds, not only blocking the vistas, but often I can only see the cars behind me or to the sides of me, even the road signs were too fogged over to read.

MY APPETITE IS ramping up wildly today and I can feel a shakiness take over my hands. At this point, I have no choice but to nourish myself with something other than cup-o-noodles or red gel glucose packs. I know at the pace I was travelling I won't make it down the mountain and into town by sunset. My only option is to do something I was quite sure I would be able to avoid. Hitchhike. *Desperation can make you do strange things*, I think to myself with my thumb sticking out on the side of the road.

Each time a car doesn't stop, it splashes muddy rainwater over my boots and the bottoms of my pants. I try backing up a little bit further, but the way the road curves, they wouldn't see me, and I don't want to risk getting hit. I know I'm not as invincible as I feel. The thing keeping me alive now is completing the journey for Paul and finding a better spot for his ashes. After what feels like sticking my thumb out for too long, I start walking into the direction of town, hoping maybe a car might stop for me. To my luck, a car stops.

"You need a ride, miss?" a man calls out.

A pit grows in my stomach as I consider avoiding the lessons, like everyone else, I was taught my whole childhood. *Do not get into a car with strangers.* But I am teetering so closely on the edge of my life already, running from chaos with a starving stomach that demanded real, hot food didn't sound half bad.

"I'd love one, thank you," I say, hopping into the front seat. I considered sitting in the back like a taxi but thought that might be rude considering this person after all is doing me a favor. I figure manners might help keep me alive.

"You don't smell as bad as the rest of them," he says with a grin. He has dirt brown shaggy hair and dark turtle green eyes. I try to remember every detail about him in case I have to tell the police what his face looked like. You know, in the event this goes south, and I have to do a tuck and roll escape out of the car. Sam's right, I can be dramatic. *Light blue baseball cap, prominent eyebrows, long narrow nose, thin build, maybe 5'8, ripped jeans and flip flops.* Yes, flip-flops in the middle of November. Pretty harmless looking guy, strange yes, but appears mostly harmless. Then again, don't they all at first? I have watched one too many crimes shows, and it has clearly made me prepared for the worst.

"The rest of who?"

"I pick hikers like yourself up all the time," he says. My shoulders sink a bit in relief. I assume this probably makes him a nice guy instead of a serial killer. "I used to be one myself before my knee injury. I like to think of it as good karma. Help someone out if you can, and when you need it, you'll get help, too."

I nod. "Karma."

"Where to?"

"I was just headed into the nearest town with food."

"You're in luck, because I'm headed to grab my pickup order from Tommy's."

I don't know what kind of food a place like Tommy's has, but it sounds like warm food and right now I am not feeling picky.

"You got a trail name yet?" he says. "You know, like a nick name. Mine was always snacks, because I always carried the most snacks and always had extra snacks to share."

"No, I guess don't have one yet," I say.

"You hiking alone?" he asks.

"No," I lie. "I'm actually meeting my husband in town."

"Oh, I didn't see a ring—wasn't sure."

I look down at my bare hand. "I don't like to wear it when I camp and stuff," I say.

"We should think of your trail name on the way into town," he says. "What's something you like to do?"

I think for a moment.

"I don't know. Bake…"

"What's the first thing you ever baked," he says, scratching his chin.

"Biscuits," I say.

"I think we just found your trail name, biscuits." He laughs. "You'll get used to the new name, it's fun. Besides, didn't you come here to forget who you really were anyway?"

I nod. He had a point.

"You making good time even with all this rain?" Snacks asked.

"I've been nearly crawling, if that's what you mean."

"The rain can do that," he says and chuckles. "Unfortunately, the rain means you need to move a bit faster. Especially when it has been coming down like this."

"Really?"

"Of course. If it's not the freezing temps that could threaten your life, it's the landslides that come this amount of water."

"Landslides?" I ask, a nervousness drops into my stomach.

"The creeks and streams, once they overflow, they make the mountain slide down like a kid at water park. Scary, to be honest. Trees come on down right with it. It's like nature's way of getting pissed off, having a tantrum."

Again, nature and I are fully synced.

WHEN WE ARRIVE in town, there's a drag show parading in the streets.

"The south is changing," Snacks says, shaking his head pulling into Tommy's restaurant. "This new president has everyone thinking they can use whatever bathroom they want, wear whatever they want." If I knew him better, I'd tell him to mind his own business. Paul's family grew up in the south and that's largely why I couldn't imagine living life that same way. Snacks is right, the south has changed, and I'm here for it.

"I ordered pick up, but we could go on in and sit," he says, adjusting his ball cap. "Unless your husband won't like that. I'm old school, so I understand. I wouldn't let my old lady do that."

"He's a few hours behind me, I won't see him for a bit." I sit down into the booth on the outdoor patio. Golden clouds rest over the blackness of the mountains. "He's not the jealous type anyway." I laugh a little on the inside because Sam is most definitely the jealous type, and he is technically still my husband. The mountain views from this restaurant make it feel fancy, but it's just a mom-and-pop diner for hikers. I'm so hungry my hands tremble as I hold the menu.

"You feeling alright?" he asks.

"Yeah, just starving." When the waiter comes, I order a cheeseburger burger, fries, chocolate milkshake and extra pickles.

"Boy, do I love a woman who can eat," Snacks says. "With a name like biscuits, I guess I can't be too surprised now, can I?" He laughs as he sips his beer.

"With a name like Snacks I expected more from you."

WHEN MY FOOD comes, I can't help but to shovel it into my face. Everything tastes holy. Warm, satisfying, sweet and salty. "This has got to be the best burger I have ever had in my life," I say, moaning orgasmically in between bites. "And this milkshake. Wow. It's like a dream come true."

Snacks laughs again. "I remember that feeling. Like you're born again, everything feels brand new. That's a good feeling. Enjoy it. That's the magic of the trail."

Dusk is setting in and I start to feel a wave of anxiety. *I wonder where Sam is? I wonder if he is in North Carolina.*

"You see him?" Snacks says. I can feel the milkshake in my stomach begin to rise. *How does he know I'm looking for Sam?* For a moment I wonder if Sam has hired Snacks to find me. To hunt me down.

"Who?" I say.

"Your husband." My eyes widen and I begin to feel nauseous.

"You said he's coming into town. You were looking around, I thought maybe you had found him." I must be losing my mind. *Sam isn't here. I have nothing to worry about. Deep breaths.*

"That's right. I think I'll just meet him at a hotel in town."

"If either of you get lost, here's my number," he says, writing it down a napkin. "If you need help, need food or need a ride, I'll be your guardian trail angel." He winks and folds the napkin into my hand.

"Thank you, Snacks." It's in this moment I realize we haven't exchanged our real names and for the first time in my life I'm happy to have a new identity.

I DECIDE TO spend the night in a hotel. Unlike most serious hikers on steep timelines working against the clock to summit specific mountains by specific hours, I find that I am more of a meandering hiker. No timeline, nowhere to go, nothing specific to see and no big goals to achieve.

I have spent most of my life trying to get to the next chapter, always climbing in one way or another to make it to my next destination. or once, I crave the freedom of having a destination that leads to nowhere.

The most serious hikers are the Thru hikers. They are waking up early and moving fast towards Katadhin, the highest mountain in the United States. I didn't set out on this journey to break personal records; I don't even know the name of the first mountain I summited. I have no intention even of making it out of North Carolina. All I know is that I felt like running, making a movement away from where I was towards something new. What that something is? I don't know yet.

When I open the door to this hole in the wall hotel, an over-whelming sense of gratitude washes over me. There's a bed, the most luxurious thing I have ever seen. No, it's not the California King with Egyptian cotton sheets like I'm used to, but it's a soft place to land, and right now, I'm happy to have anywhere else but the ground to sleep. I take a long warm shower, change out of my layered dirty clothes into my shorts and t-shirt, which have yet to be worn. I haven't felt this clean since I've left. Fatigue begins to swallow me up, but before I shut my eyes for the night, I pick up my phone from the charger and to decide it's time to call my mom, who I know has likely talked to Sam.

The phone hardly rings before she picks it up.

"Jade? Are you alright?" she says anxiously.

"Yes, I'm fine." I clear my throat. "I'm still camping."

She whispers into the phone, "Jade, you are not camping— are you? Sam is worried sick. He even drove down here looking for you. What is going on?"

"He drove to the house?" I feel the nausea creep up again as my biggest fear is coming true. *Sam is out there hunting me.*

"He's looking for you. He said that if you weren't here, you might be with another man."

"Jesus, he has really lost his mind."

"Lost his mind? I have never seen him so worried about you. He *loves* you, Jade. Where are you? You can tell me."

"I don't want Sam to find me, mom. I needed this get away." *I needed to get away.*

"Was this about him wanting babies and you not being ready? Because sweetie, this isn't the way to go about it. You don't just leave on a whim with just a note as a goodbye...after years of marriage..."

What I can't tell her is that I'm afraid of Sam and I can't tell her why.

"I'm almost out of battery mom, I have to let you go—" I pick at my fingernails and stare at the TV.

"Please, keep me updated a couple times a week at least. We are all worried."

"Don't worry, okay?" I'm safer now than where I was, I mumble under my breath.

"Call me soon. I love you. You know that right? You know that I love you?" I can hear her sniffle into the phone.

"Mom, please don't cry. Everything is fine. I just ate a giant milkshake and cheeseburger, took a hot shower. I'm in a safe hotel for the night. Everything is okay. I promise." I can hear her relief sigh then.

"If this is about Paul… if you're…. *depressed….* We can help you," she whispers, and the words choke her on the way out.

"I'm not—I'm okay," I say out loud for the first time since his death, and I wonder if it's true. If I am not depressed and if I am okay. Regardless of if it's true or not, I want to believe it.

"I love you, mom. I'll see you soon."

"You be careful, alright? Call me if you need anything."

When we hang up my fatigue seems to have transformed into an alarming sense of awareness about my surroundings. My peace is gone, my breathing begins to shallow. Sam could be close by now, especially if Mary alluded any clues to him.

Maybe I did need to make my way to Katadhin as fast as possible. I set an alarm for an early morning; I need to get moving and get out of this town and back into the woods as quickly as I can. I need to make it impossible for him to find me.

CHAPTER FOUR

T WO WORDS—HUNTING SEASON. Even after an early start on the trail and a strong attempt to be organized in my quest, I am completely lost, despite the soaking wet map I have in my hands. My keychain thermometer attached to my pack says it's 40 degrees, but with the rain and wind chill it feels at least ten degrees colder. The worst of it are the gunshots going off around me. Each time I hear an echo, I imagine Sam with a rifle. Not that he has ever owned a gun, but I can easily picture him with one. Hunting. For me. And that sends a chill down my already frozen spine. I often have these moments where I think, *Okay. If I can get out of here alive, I can make it to Katahdin.*

The rain that everyone has warned about is here as well as lightning everywhere. I slide down the slippery trail more than I walk. The mud and the rain are so cold, my limbs have started to tingle. I try not to complain—I put myself here in the first place but bitching out into the ether seems like half of the survival skills I need right now.

When the weather cooperates, it's hard to be angry at the views: mountainous creeks surrounded by rhododendron, mountain laurel, and hemlock glades. I try not to focus on anything else but my next step forward. Not the hollowness of my stomach, my heart, or my life.

I START A journal. Isn't that what sad girls do? I was surprised when it was one of the first things the man at the sporting goods store had suggested; to document my trek. I didn't think I'd use it but bought one anyway. Turns out, I was wrong. More than anything, the longer I'm alone, the more I desired to talk to someone, even if that someone is myself. And since I haven't really talked to anyone about this deep sadness, I figure it wouldn't hurt to take it to the page. I try talking to myself on the trail, but it turns out the sound of my voice annoys me, and I enjoy the quiet too much to hear anything at all.

Somedays, I write out to the abyss. To the universe, or God, or whoever was with me. Somedays, I'd write a letter to myself, but most days, I'd write to Paul. I'd ask him questions, and I swear within minutes, I'd see a clue. One morning as I was journaling Paul, I asked where to find fresh water. Within ten minutes of my pen touching the paper, I met hikers with canteens and they lead me to a stream. Not only did they help me, but they also offered dinner and a game of scrabble at their campsite before going our separate ways. I am physically alone most of the time, but oddly I never feel half as lonely as I did in my Chicago condo with Sam. Not by a long shot. Which had me wondering how Sam might be reacting to not having me around.

CHAPTER FIVE

G RAY.
Gray hills. Gray sky. Gray fog. Gray bark. Gray leaves. Gray dirt. Though I have walked all over them all, I couldn't tell you the names of each mountain I summited. Fifty-nine miles in and the biggest thing I have learned is that the trail sets the pace, the trail sets the agenda, and all I have to do is listen.

To my untrained eye, everything blurs together as the same and I was just grateful to make it up to the top and as far away from the life beneath me that I once knew. Even if I am here doing nothing significant, I can feel myself approaching a destination to somewhere new. And that was a feeling I didn't know I needed until now.

When I do summit the top, the views often render me speechless and during these moments, it all makes sense why I came here. It makes sense why anyone would be here. The vastness and the bigness of the space allows mother nature to teach the lessons that only she could. Every step is a struggle up the mountain. Today, I feel like sitting longer than I usually do once I summit the top. I pull out my journal and decide to write a little as I watch the fog swim across the black tops of the trees.

Dear universe, or whoever is in charge out there-

I am ready for a sign, but I quite literally hear crickets. I hear a long pause. The pause that breaks down tension the way that meat does when you chew it in your mouth long enough. The inevitable breakdown before digestion.

Perhaps I'm not ready for a sign and to that point I wonder why. More learning and growing to do, I imagine? It's tiring now waiting for things to happen, but I'm not just waiting, I'm working too. These gray hills are exhausting. So, I guess, the crickets tell me to rest. Is that my sign? I will rest and be still and be quiet again. Until it's time to get back to work, and while I'm at it, I better get patient.

Maybe the crickets are hungry – I wonder what crickets eat? I wonder what my crickets need. And why the hell are they still chirping at 3:46 PM on a Sunday afternoon? Was it the rain last night? Are they confused? I can't ask crickets questions. But I can ask the Internet. I always ask the Internet. But the Internet isn't available now and it doesn't predict the future and that's sort of what I'm asking for. For someone to tell me what the point is for crickets. The long pause for all this restless tension. For feeling the need to be here now. Can you give a sign? A clear sign, please. I miss him more than ever.

Thank you,
Jade "Biscuits", Mountaineer Extraordinaire, Day 15

CHAPTER SIX

M Y EYELIDS GREW heavy early after making it halfway down the mountain today. Some days are moving days where I make a lot of progress forward, and others are resting days, where I don't do a lot of anything.

On resting days, I make it a point to stay deep in the woods. The closer I am to town, the more likely I am to be found. I pull Paul's sweatshirt over my head and scrunch it into a ball. I nestle it against a log, take a sip of filtered muddy river water and close my eyes. I rest my head into his sweatshirt like a pillow.

The fatigue lingers between my eyes with a crushing intensity that begs to keep them closed. I fight to keep them open most days, but right now it feels extra. A noise, a rustling through the leaves and sticks forces me to open my heavy eyelids. My heart begins to race, I stand up and start walking towards the rustling.

In the distance there is a small, abandoned shack. The white paint is chipped, the wood siding is rotten, and the windows are all broken. I inch closer slowly, peeking into them. I jump back when I see a shadow and the silhouette of a man inside. Even though I find myself afraid, I can't help but draw my body nearer. I put my ear close to the broken glass. There's a voice. *Someone's inside.*

I walk around the front and find an open door. As I enter the dark empty space, it creaks with each step forward. Every corner I turn the voice grows louder. Just then, I begin to race through the house. I bust open doors with my cold tired fists, yelling out to it. "Is that you? Hello…" I turn into another dusty cobwebbed corner. "Where are you? Hello?"

The voice begins to fade into soft whispers. The whispers fade into silence.

No one is inside of this house. *Am I losing my mind?*

I walk out of the house and sit on the damp front porch. Just then, I notice a deer approaching me through the half-lit forest. I stand and walk towards it slowly. The deer lifts his rack up from the ground, turns its head towards me as if like he's carefully looking for something. When I'm close enough, I stare into his shiny black eyes. The deer lifts his rack up from the ground, turning it like he's looking for something carefully. Stupidly, I ask Paul if it's him. "If this is you, would you come to me? Would you look at me? Would you give me sign? Make it known this is you." I whisper quiet enough to not startle the deer, but loud enough that it must've heard me. I hold my hand out, the deer walks closer, close enough for me to embrace it, yet I'm afraid if I do, I'll spook it away. We are both mystical creatures in awe of each other. At any moment this deer could decide I am a threat and bulldoze my body with its horns. Instead, it tries to understand me. To discover what or who I am. Maybe it can sense my broken heart in the way that my family dog always did. Maybe it's some animal sense that knows. I reach my hand out closer to let it know that it's safe. But by the time I get close enough to touch, the deer runs off quickly, leaping over mossy fallen trees. The pursuit to search for constant avenues of connection with Paul will likely never leave me, but the strength and the many efforts to try, do. Could he be the bird in the window and the deer in the forest? I want it to make sense. I want it to be him. *Is this my sign?*

SPENDING ALL THIS time in the I thought I'd find my strength, my stamina, and my energy. That I'd grow new muscles in new places and become stronger. That being farther away from Sam and closer to Paul would make it easier. That having his ashes in my possession would revive me. Instead, I find my body more fatigued, fragile, and barren than ever before. Instead, I find myself sad and ugly in the rare company of other ugly people. Un-showered scraggly hikers walking along wet highways and through soggy state forests. I think back to the plastic surgeon and what he said about wearing our experiences on our faces. I wonder what my face says about me now.

Without a mirror, I decide to turn my phone on for a moment and snap a quick photo of myself. Even with the horrendous rain and my numb wind burnt cheeks, I'm curious to see what I look like. I stretch my arm out and center the camera in front of me. I see it then. My hood over my damp hair, my face ghostly white and my tired eyes with deep shades of purple bags hanging underneath them. Dr. Stephen and Mary would tell me I look like shit. That I am too young to look like this. And they would be right.

This afternoon I decide to move my campsite since the sun is out and it's feeling much warmer, the warmest it has felt yet. I've sat at this rock on top of this mountain for two days now. Though I found it comforting to be in my nothingness, I also felt like moving today. I walked for several hours before my heels ached and bled. I didn't know they were bleeding until I stopped at a creek of running water, took my boots off and washed my feet.

The cool of the water feels soothing to the irritation and stopped the bleeding. The smell of them, however, did not quit.

Sunset seems to be coming early tonight. After trekking up and downhill on steep trails with aching shins, I knew I would be sleeping hard tonight. The trails gave me no mercy and today felt draining in a new way. It didn't matter how long I hiked; the voyage remained unchanged. The same towering trees on the same dirty path and many sleepy grassy hills met my every turn. For the most part, the weather was descent and that was my only comfort. I was lucky to discover a few areas that allowed more sunlight to poke through and I was able to steal sweet, happy pockets of warmth. The real killjoys were always under the trees where it remained three shades darker and cooler. The dark spots are always the hardest.

Before daylight runs out, I fill my canteens with water and begin my search for a place to sleep. I often like to find a place alone where I can release an incredible number of feelings all at once. This usually involves screaming as loud as possible into the empty echo of the forest. Sometimes, when I see hikers with families pass by, I second guess my screaming fits. Usually after a good emotional release, I like to pull out a cigarette from the pack I bought in town. I take a long puff in, cough my brains out and then I consider yelling some more. Lather, rinse, repeat. Sometimes it helps, the other times it destroys me more.

With a sore throat from all the screams and cigarettes, I decide to dig around in my pack for cough syrup. When it's in my hands, I examine the bottle and think about what might happen if I decide to drink the whole thing. The pain I feel for Paul today is constant and it is begging to be witnessed. I consider screaming again, maybe even at the trees, like they've done something wrong to me. Instead, I jump up and down, stomping my feet into the dirt.

I don't question why, and there is no one around to judge me, so I let my body convulse on the ground. While I'm down there, I welcome many powerful chest bursting sobs as they make their way out. Since being here, I give myself full permission to let the ache out in any avenue my flesh will allow. In many ways, I feel safe now that I'm finally alone to unleash it in the ways that it wants. My grief has peaked, and I will let her be.

The ache follows me around like a shadow. It settles in my stomach and rests there until it grows large enough that it forces its way out in the form of tears, screams, or rage. Against all control, the release finds its way out somehow. I'm learning that instead of judging it, I let it be. If anything at all, that is something these mountains have taught me. How to "just be."

Occasionally, I have dreams about Paul that are so real I don't want to wake up. When I do wake up, the nightmare called 'life' begins all over again. Tonight, it was no different. The sound of a gunshot pulled me from my dreams, reminding me to keep moving. This time only faster, farther away from where I started.

CHAPTER SEVEN

D AY SEVENTEEN, AND I've walked over a hundred miles alone.

It's a cold can of beans for dinner tonight that I try with everything in me to force down before they come back up. And when they do, I pop a red gel glucose pack in my mouth and dream about the warm mouthwatering food that waits for me at the bottom of this mountain.

I can always count on plummeting temps when the sun goes down. And when it does, the fantasies of a sweltering hot July night creep in. Nothing sounds sexier to me than sleeping in just underwear and a tee shirt—thighs stuck together from humidity and sweat dripping in places it shouldn't be. I'd give anything to trade that in for sleeping in the many damp layers of cold clothing clinging to my body. Feelings of dry warmth are almost a distant memory.

The rain has decided to let up and the clouds have melted away along with it, making the night sky the most visible it has been since being out here. I stare out of my translucent tent canopy and gaze in awe at the million tiny flecks above me. I wonder which of them would be Paul if he were star.

In this moment, I realize that while this experience has posed nothing other than challenges, it is equally plagued with beautiful moments like this. Tomorrow, I will eat hot food and life will better. It has to be.

My sleep was as restless as the wind, which rustled my tent all night long. This morning my body took convincing to leave the warmth of my quilt. While it had been calm and cozy at camp, the wind was now blowing aggressively on the ridge. The only way to keep warm now is to move. If it wasn't the rain making life feel like a pain in my ass, it was the wind. By now, it is hard to tell which element I hated more. They both made me work for comfort.

At the beginning of my hiking endeavor, I made it a point to avoid people, but over time a deep longing for outside connection became all consuming. When I notice people walking down the trail this time, I make sure to speak up when they wave at me instead of actively avoiding them as I have been doing. I realize now that ignoring people who have more survival skills than I do isn't the brightest move.

Today, I pass a group of hikers on my descend and decide that I am going to try my best to join them on the trek down into the city. I am starting to get low again on food and all the food I had left made me physically ill at the thought of it. I have a serious aversion to oatmeal, cup-o-noodles, cold beans, and anything that looked like it could be made from or into granola.

"Hey, where are you guys headed?" I ask them as I pause to lean against a tree.

"Linville falls today," the only female backpacker responds. The other two men are talking to each other while adjusting their gear.

"What's your name?" I ask.

"Dizzy," she says with a straight face. "This is Cheese and Rat Tail."

Trail names. Right. Nearly forgot. For a minute I was judging her parents for naming her Dizzy.

"I guess I'm Biscuits," I say with a laugh, extending my hand out to shake. "Nice to meet you."

"New to the trail, eh?" Dizzy asks.

"Is it obvious?" I look down at my boots. She holds her finger into a small pinch and laughs.

"A little," she says, removing her pack. "My real name is Carmen. And that's Rael in the yellow shirt and Guss in the black shirt."

"I'm Jade. Though biscuits is a much better alias. You guys start this hike together?"

"No, this is my new tramily...trail family," she says, putting her arm around Rat Tail and Cheese. "We met on the trail back at mile post 60, early on. I was struggling and these guys are seasoned enough to help me thru. Hence the name Dizzy. I was looping around trails getting lost more times than I could count. We decided as a tramily that together we can make it to Katahdin. There's no way I could do this alone. You alone?"

"Yeah. But I've just been section hiking. I'm not a thru hiker."

"Do you want to be a thru hiker?" she says, throwing her pack back around her shoulders.

I haven't given it that much thought. Afraid if I say no, they wouldn't let me tag along, and afraid if I say yes, I will have to commit walking my sad ass all the way to Maine.

"Haven't decided yet." I'm not a serious hiker, but I am trying to survive. And maybe even enjoy this a little more than I have been.

"You're welcome to tag along," Cheese says.

"Even if you don't make it all the way to Katahdin, you can stick around as long as you'd like," Rat Tail adds. I picture it. Walking though the woods together at a faster pace. If something isn't working or if I'm feeling exhausted, the guys could help me set up my tent and pack it up. And I bet they have better snacks.

Different equates to better when you're eating the same things every day. A loud, sharp bang goes off and the echo pops against the trees.

"Hunting season," says Cheese.

"Still scares me shitless every time," Dizzy says, clutching her chest. "Who's to say they don't miss an animal and get one of us?"

"You worry too much, Diz," Cheese says, shaking his head.

"We better get moving, we all know it'll be dark before we know it. It's easier to miss your target when it's dark, too. I don't want to be hunted."

"Can you imagine being hunted like an animal? Tracked down to every footprint—just to POW! Crack you one right in the head," Rat tails says with a finger trigger to his temple.

It's then that I imagine Sam out there, rifle in hand hunting me like an animal. Second thought, I may need these guys to protect me. If Sam's out there, he's gone crazy. A crazier Sam is not a Sam I need to face alone.

Cheese, Dizzy and Rat Tail start making their descend as I think about joining.

"Wait up," I say. "I'm coming, too."

THE TEMPERATURE FALLS quickly as the sun hides behind the clouds. Then the rain comes again. Luckily, we are on the descend today. I find that walking through the haze and mist of water is easier on the way down than it is on the way up.

"I'm afraid that we might get swamped in if we sleep too close to the falls," Dizzy shouts over her pack. She decided we should set up camp at a shelter tonight, a luxury I haven't yet experienced with all this rain. Another reason I'm glad I said yes to walking with them instead of alone.

An abandoned leaf-filled path leads us toward our protected abode. Even the word shelter sent a warmth through my numb toes. When we make it to the shelter, a deep relief sinks into my bones. Is it a nice place? No. But do I have to pitch a tent in this horrendous violent and unwelcoming rain? Also no, which feels like a real treat.

The wooden walls are drafty, and Cheese ironically enough is shooing away the mice. It's not a pretty sight in here, but I was in the company of people under a roof, and that gave me a familiar feeling of comfort that I didn't know I'd miss this much. We stretch our sleeping bags open and huddle next to each other to keep warm. Dizzy makes us cups of instant hot chocolate, while Rat Tail cooks us some hot herby instant mashed potatoes. The taste of butter and herb, albeit from a bag, is a combination I didn't know I'd ever miss this fondly.

"Oh. My. God," I say, spooning another bite in my mouth. "This is crack. I could probably eat three whole bags."

"You can have another bag if you want, but I only have the plain kind left," Rat Tail says, waving a bag from his pack.

The thought of anything else plain and bland in my mouth made me queasy.

"I'll just save some room for the restaurant tomorrow."

"I can't wait to smash all that warm food. I'll probably eat so much that I'll pass out," Cheese says, licking his bowl clean.

A gnawing sense of hunger occupies the inside of my stomach until I fall asleep. I can hardly get food off my mind. Somehow my love for baking has grown with each passing day and at night, all I can think about is that sweet vanilla smell of warm cake coming out of the oven and licking buttercream off my fingers. Because thoughts of food have crowded my brain along with thoughts of basic survival, I have hardly had time to think about my sadness, especially in the company of new friends, though I know she is still there unaddressed.

This entire time I have carried Paul with me—his ashes still inside of my pack. I have carried him hundreds of miles and with me for so much longer than that. I haven't once considered what it would feel like to let him go.

CHAPTER EIGHT

MORNING COMES QUICKLY and these guys aren't wasting time. Our hike began in the dark, luckily, I have my head lamp packed. We didn't even eat breakfast before rolling up our sleeping bags and leaving the shelter, which made my already empty stomach growl in agony.

The plan is to hike to the falls and make it into town by lunch. Food was the best motivator to keep our pace up. *"Mc.Donald's. Mc.Donald's. Kentucky Fried Chicken and a Pizza Hut."* This became the singsong anthem they would chant when we felt fatigue set in, or when the temperature was chilling us again. Even though I didn't like fast food, it didn't sound half bad after days without a warm meal.

The hike is beautiful, even if it was fueled by two dry granola bars that I had to slam sips of water in between bites just to choke it down. The trails to the falls crossed several small streams, grassy balds with wild black horses walking through the morning fog. We wind and loop though multiple low-canopy forests and overgrown fields.

The heavy rainfall over the last few weeks has created a dangerous environment for hikers. Soggy leaves, dense ground and waterlogged trails make slipping and falling easy to do. The last thing we need is a broken bone in the wilderness.

To even my untrained eye, it appears the reality of a landslide was beginning to look more and more likely. Many fallen mossy trees have shifted from their original ground as evidence.

I look around the sunny landscape the trail has carved through and in this moment I'm grateful I joined the group. The pace and journey are the refreshing push forward I didn't know I needed.

We finally reach the sun-drenched summit with towering pine trees standing as tall and proud as we are. I forget about my hunger and fatigue as I watch the falls cascading below us. A feeling of peace surrounds me as the sun permeates through my skin. Fragrant floral smells of wet earth and fresh rain fill me up with each breath in. Birds chip back and forth.

Rain was our thing.

When I close my eyes, all I can see is Paul. I feel him closer than I've ever felt him as if he were embracing me right on the edge of this cliff. While the other three are taking photos of the falls and washing mud off their boots, I take the bag of Paul's ashes out of my pack and examine it closely in my hands.

The small bag filled with gray bits of dust, ash, gravel, and bone. *What if I let him go, right here in this waterfall?* I think to myself. I long for him so deeply in this moment, my hands begin to open the bag without thinking about it. I pour a small amount out onto my palm and close it shut. My heart begins to thump, a lump collects in my throat as I ignite both feelings of comfort and pain. *This could be our final goodbye. The absolute end of us.*

I look down into the water as I imagine him being carried by that instead. Envy grew as I pictured Paul enrobed by anything or anyone else other than me. Without effort, tears stream down my cheeks. I rub his ashes over my arms, my neck, and my face, feeling the bumpy bits of him over my lips.

"I will never let you go," I whisper with my eyes staring up into the endless blue sky. "I will carry you with me forever."

"Are you alright?" Dizzy walks over to me, placing her hand

on my shoulder.

I nod and wipe the wet ash from my leaking eyes. She helps me off my knees and pulls my body against hers into an embrace. "These mountains have this ability to crack you wide open, don't they?" she says, understanding a sight that's impossible to understand.

"It's not an easy journey, but here you are, moving forward every day, no matter what. That's pretty bad ass." The words to respond in any profound way are lost on me, so I pull my pack back up over my shoulders.

All I can say is, "Thank you."

"Who's hungry?" Cheese says as he does a little dance rubbing his belly.

Dizzy laughs. "Food always helps. Let's make our way down and into town."

"*Mc.Donald's. Mc.Donald's. Kentucky Fried Chicken and a Pizza Hut,*" Rat Tail sings out.

"THE WAY DOWN the mountainous trails is usually pretty easy, but with all this rain, it's slippery as heck," Dizzy says. "But if you grab a hiking stick, it helps a little." She snaps a tree branch over her knee, handing me the sticks. "I have these for balance and stability." She pulls trekking poles from her pack.

"The guy at the sporting goods store didn't think I'd need them for my recreational hike, so I opted out."

"He didn't check the North Carolina forecast then. This rain is a doozy," Cheese says.

"Where did you come from?" Dizzy asks.

"I'm from Tiffin, Ohio, but I have spent the last few years in Chicago... with my umm... my husband." I swallow. The word husband feels like hot sauce on my tongue.

"You came all this way without your husband. What does he think of that?" Rat tail chimes in.

"Um. He hates it," I say quickly. "Because he's also not really my husband anymore. Or at least he won't officially be soon. I'm getting a divorce."

"Man. Sorry to hear. Pretty brave of you to come out here solo. Diz did the same thing."

She looks at me and smiles. "I didn't need no man," she says, flexes a muscle and smiles a brave independent smile, "but once I got on this trail, I started to see the value in one." She laughs. "A good honest man, that is. I'm glad I found these two or I'd still be making dizzying circles around the same lonely wet trail."

"I didn't leave a marriage behind, but I did leave the man I loved, but didn't love me. He had commitment issues, didn't want to face his own stuff. So, I left. Best feeling ever," Dizzy says.

"I hear you," I affirm, jabbing my sticks forward into the mud. "It's a good feeling to run away from it all."

"Nothing like the great outdoors to make it all better," Cheese says.

"First thing I'm ordering is bacon, regardless of where we go. I'd eat bacon on a burger, by itself, on a sandwich, with eggs. Doesn't matter to me. I just want to feel that salty greasy crunch in my mouth," he adds.

"As long as the food is hot, I'm happy," Rat Tail says.

CHAPTER NINE

A S WE APPROACH a Dollar General in the distance, we realize that we have officially made it. Weaving through the back trails, we make our final descent into town. Dizzy and the guys wanted McDonald's, soda, and fries. And since that was never a place I enjoyed, I walk across the street to a Waffle House instead.

My shoulders sink in delight as soon as I see the sign. The sweet smell of pancakes, sausage, and maple syrup is bliss. And the thought of a cold glass of orange juice quite literally makes me weak in the knees. My body is craving fresh fruit like it never has before, and I know I have a better chance of finding it here over McDonald's.

Before heading inside to stuff myself silly, I decide to smoke a cigarette to stave off the nausea from starvation. The last thing I needed was to waste any of this delicious food as it made its way up and out of my body. Especially after waiting such a long time to be acquainted with it again.

I pull my pack off my back and lean against the side of the Waffle House. My hands shake as I pull the lighter to my lips.

An old man in a red flannel shirt stops me outside of the Waffle House diner.

"What are you doing with those cigarettes, pretty lady?"

I shrug.

"You're too pretty to smoke, dear."

I nod, half smile and look away.

"You know why people smoke?" he says, walking in front of me.

I shrug again and shake my head. I stuff the cigarette between my two fingers.

"Nope. Not really."

"Grief." He taps on his chest. "Grief is stored in the lungs. People smoke when way deep down in here, they're sad. Grief and sadness directly affect the lungs. If we are unable to express these emotions or are being overwhelmed by them, it will weaken the lungs and compromise their main function: respiration."

"Are you a doctor or something?" I say, puffing down on the cigarette slowly.

"No, ma'am, I just know a lot about livin' and a few things about dyin'," he says. "What are you sad for, darlin'?"

I could feel my face light up by the question. No one other than the plastic surgeon has asked me this. No one has asked me how I have felt. People have criticized or made assumptions, but not one person close to me has asked me this question, let alone a strange old man at a diner. The question instantly perks me up, and it's then that I realize it's because I finally get to talk about him. I get to tell someone his name, who he was. Talking about him brings him back to life, if only a few minutes. And when he comes back alive, so do I.

With a smile I say, "His name was Paul."

"Was?" he says curiously. "What happened to him? How'd he get away?"

"That's complicated." I grin and draw in another puff. "He died. So, he's gone forever."

"Is he?" he says. "That's not what I believe."

"Where is he? Heaven?" I laugh again, shaking my head looking at my boots.

"Well, I don't exactly know. But I do know he's watching over you. If he loved you like you love him, he's not going anywhere you aren't." The man walks over and puts his hand on my shoulder.

"I lost Betsy back in '83. I know she's still with me though. A love like that doesn't stop because their heart stop beating. If anything, it continues to deepen in a way you might not understand yet."

"How did you get over her?"

"Who says I'm over her?" He laughs. "I'm just as crazy about her as I was when I was 21. The only difference is our love is larger than life, so it lives on."

"So how do I move on?" I ask, surprised it even comes out of my mouth.

"You keep breathing, knowing you're still loved anyway."

"Bill, your to-go order is ready." A waitress opens the door with two Styrofoam containers wrapped in a plastic bag.

"Grief lasts as long as love does, sweetie. Don't waste another breath feeling unloved." He turns and walks away. "Or another breath on those cigarettes."

I knew he loved me forever, even if his forever only made it to twenty-nine years. Even if his forever didn't make it to grey hair and spotty hands. The thing about Paul is that he never said, "until death do us part," –he never got the chance, but he also never had to. We knew it would be a forever kind of love. Even if it didn't make it to thirty years alive, it was impossible for our love to ever die.

I smirk and begin to walk towards the door inside.

"Where are you headed around here anyway?" the old man turns around to ask.

"Why do you want to know?" I ask.

"Well, I think I might a know a place that might help fix you back up."

"Who said I'm broken?"

"I know a broken human when I see one," he says, scratching his chin. "Would you do anything to talk to your Paul again?"

I think about that for a minute, wondering what that might mean.

"Yes, of course I would."

"Then I might know just the place for you." He takes his receipt from his pocket and an old pen from his flannel and starts writing. "Here are the directions," he says. "Be careful up the winding roads, it can get slippery after all this rain. Might even want to wait until it passes. It's quite a hike, but you'll be glad you did it."

"Look, if you're thinking about sending me directions to a church, I don't need that right now."

He hands me the receipt and reaches for my ear. He whispers, "Where I'm about to tell you to go is more like heaven than church."

He reaches for my ear to whisper into.

"On top of this mountain, there's this... magic sort of phone. And It's only meant for the grieving to connect with their loved one who passed on. I went after Betsy passed."

I pull my head back in disbelief and look at the old man who I now believe to be crazy.

"A magic phone?" In my sadness, I find it hard to find the humor of this make believe. My voice reflects my annoyance and anger.

"This isn't funny to me, I'm sorry, sir. I'm just not in the mood for pranks."

"Shhhh," he says, quieting me down. "I know, I know. I look like some crazy old mountain man from North Carolina, but I've been around a long, long time, seen a lot of things. I have never seen something like this, I wouldn't have known about it if my friend Johnny didn't tell me about it after he lost his father. Betsy had been gone 15 years by then and still, just like that, she was there when I arrived. Like she had never even left." His face is peaceful and honest. "The hardest part about it is, even though we've found our paradise, we aren't supposed to tell anyone else about it. Only the grieving mourning a loss can know about this phone," he says.

"There are a few very important rules with it, I'm just the messenger, I didn't make them up, so I don't know what they mean or why they're rules in the first place," he says. "The first rule is that no one else can know about this phone, other than another grieving soul. The second is the most important rule, you can't pick up the phone after you've made your one and only call. It's just one call and that's it."

"Why? What happens to them if they break the rules?" I ask.

"No one really knows, but I've heard stories about those who have broken them. Most people are afraid to take this hike in the first place, because it's been all over the news. The people who don't make it back are misreported as missing people, but the grieving, we know otherwise. We know the truth. We know that they are likely the ones who didn't follow the rules. After a while living around here, you start to notice a pattern. The grieving are the ones who went missing in this area."

"Where did they go? What happened to them?" I ask with an eyebrow raised.

"Honey, I'm afraid I don't know, and I don't want to find out." He says with a modest chuckle. "There's speculation that unearthly complications may arise after making that one call. There are all kinds of theories. Who knows which one of them is true? Or if they are true at all."

"What are they?' I ask.

"One theory is said to be that the light beings, you know, angels, and our loved ones who have crossed, only have enough energy to push through one call. And that the other times, it could be dark, evil forces posing as light. They could be pretending to be Paul and have something sinister in mind."

"Alright. Stay away from the dark forces, noted," I say sarcastically.

"What's the other theory?" I ask.

"That the second time they picked up the phone was to go back to paradise with them and never return back to earth."

"You mean, they'd kill themselves?"

"Not exactly. They just wouldn't come back to place they've been living after being in heaven with the one they loved." He clears his throat.

"Here's what I know. We have no way to be sure if that's true, the only way to know is to pick up the phone again and see what happens. But I've lived here a long time and see the weekly missing person's report. I've been paying attention to what happens on that mountain. If I were you and I went to The Phone of The Wind, I'd go alone, and I wouldn't pick it more than once."

"Why doesn't anyone tell the authorities or make this a big deal? Aren't missing people a big deal? Doesn't anyone want to go looking for them?"

"And what? Risk our chance to talk to the person we love most one more time? Risk that rare opportunity to connect again, to hear their voice, their advice, their comfort, their wisdom? I don't think so. There are too many grieving souls that know about it. It's highly protected by us," he says, his voice cautious and gentle.

"Look, I wouldn't tell you if I didn't think it could help."

"What happens to those who tell other people, the non-grieving people?"

"I don't know, and I haven't wanted to find out. Like I said, too many people went missing. Too many people protecting it. All I know." He says, adjusting his sleeves.

"Well, thank you, I appreciate the idea." I take the receipt, fold it into my pocket. "I should really be going; I need to get to something to eat."

"Enjoy your visit," he says, walking off and waving from a distance.

I contemplate this mountain for a minute. *What if he is the town's crazy old mountain man and everything he said is not only crazy, but also false. What if he is poorly misinformed? What if there is no phone, no portal to the dead?* And then I wonder, *what do I have to lose? What if it's real?*

CHAPTER TEN

ORANGE JUICE HAS never hit the spot quite like this. Drinking it down was like itching a scratch that needed to be itched. As I'm sitting alone in the booth next to the window, oinking up as much food as I can, I see Dizzy and the guys across the street finishing up their meals, throwing their cups and crumpled paper McDonald's bags into the trash can. Dizzy is reorganizing her pack with its contents spread out on the front lawn, the other two are glued to their phone, likely sucking up all the free WiFi while they can before going back off the grid and into the forest.

I try to shovel the rest of this breakfast into my mouth without a bite of it wasted as quickly as I can, so they aren't waiting on me any longer. I realize now that I need to make a choice. Do I continue this hike with them? Do I push myself to Katahadin with my new tramily? Or do I head back out alone, away from people and protection and into the abyss of uncertainty to look for this damn magic phone that may or may not even be real? Do I stick with the people I have grown to quickly trust, or do I trust this old mountain man with my next move? As much as I loved hiking with Dizzy, Rat Tail and Cheese, carrying Paul was always something I have done on my own. Deep down, the solitude was difficult, but it was what I craved, especially with how I left things back in Chicago with Sam. The person I need most was myself and the person I wanted more than life itself was Paul. To think I had even a sliver of a chance to see him again felt worth it to me to make the trek anyway.

"Biscuits, how was your breakfast?" Dizzy calls out.

"Heaven sent." I laugh at the irony of what I just said, walking over to them as they sat on the grass.

"Right on. We're just about to head back out. You ready?" Cheese asks.

"Actually—" I pause and look back at the Waffle House. "I think I'm going to head in a new direction. I don't think I'm ready for Katahdin. Not this year anyway."

"Aw man, you sure?" Rat tail says with his hand on his hip.

"I'm so much slower than you guys, I hate to drag you down anyway. You don't need my dead weight."

"Nah, you aren't dead weight. You just needed a little extra love, and we were happy to give it."

"I'm really glad I met you all. Thank you. For everything." They all pull me in for a hug goodbye.

"Not that you need it, but good luck making it to Katahdin," I say.

"Here, take this," Dizzy says as she hands me a small bag of beef jerky sticks. "Protein, in case of food emergencies."

"Wow. You sure? This is worth its weight in gold," I say, squeezing the bag tightly in my hands. "I don't know what kind of trail magic brought you all my way, but I'm grateful it did."

"Good luck biscuits, searching for whatever it is you're searching for," Dizzy says.

With their packs on their backs, they walk down the road disappearing again into the blackness of the forest. I head into the Waffle House and order a meal to go before making my ascend to The Phone of The Wind. While I wait for my order, I decide to tell my mother I'm alive.

"Mom," I speak into the phone.

"Jade, are you alright?" Her voice is relieved by the sound of mine.

"Yes, I'm still alive. Still doing alright."

"You by yourself?" she asks with an inquisitive voice.

"Actually, I made a few friends. We've been hiking together."

"Oh, thank Jesus," she says. I always found that funny of her to say for a woman who didn't identify as religious. I don't tell her I just left them to hike alone to a magic phone on some spooky mountain where people often end up missing, I let her believe I'm still with them.

"When will you be home? Has Sam made it to you yet? He's been calling me, ringing my phone off the hook asking where you are..."

"What did you tell him?"

"The truth. That I truly didn't know."

"Where did he say he was?"

"He said he was trying to find you; said you haven't been answering his calls."

"Well, I haven't been answering anyone's calls. I've had my phone off most of the time to save battery. You know that."

"You should give him a call, Jade. At the very least, hear the man out. You know he loves you. He deserves to know where you are and when you'll be home and such. Please, call him after this, okay?"

There's so much I wish I could explain but even if I did, I know she would never understand and see it as it is. The man will always win in her eyes, there is no point in trying to alter that now.

"I'll call you at my next stop into town. I'm headed back into the mountains."

"Be careful. Alright?"

WHEN I HANG up, my phone flashes with dozens of missed calls and voicemail notifications. A few from my mother but at least fifty of them from Sam. My hands tremble at the thought of hearing his angry voice. A large part of me wants to ignore them and pretend I never saw them, but the guilt inflicted from my mom has me curious. *What if he has changed? What if he is worried? What if he is sorry?* Just then several texts appear in a row from Mary.

> **Mary:** Jade. I'm sorry. Sam asked where you are. He was crying and shit—I told him you went to Asheville. I didn't know what else to do. He seems so worried.
>
> **Mary:** He left last week to look for you. Bought hiking gear and everything. Which honestly has me shook. Can't even picture him hiking. Or you either. What in the world...
>
> **Mary:** Can you please respond to me...
>
> **Mary:** Are you mad at me?
>
> **Mary:** Are you alive? Hello?
>
> **Mary:** Where are you?

What did I expect? Mary is his sister. I was a fool for completely trusting that she wouldn't tell him where I was. But at the same time, how could she? She knows her brother and his violent tendencies. I put the phone to my ear, swallowing the fear that has been building in my throat to hear Sam's voicemail.

"Jade—It's me. Look, I'm sorry. I fucked up. I know I did. Please. Tell me where you are? Let me make this right. I love you."

I listen to the next one.

"Are you really not going to answer my calls? After all I have done for you? How could you do this? Please, answer me. Please."

"This is fucked up. How dare you leave without telling me

where you are. I'm worried about you. Call me. Please."

"Why are you being such a bitch about this? We could've just talked like adults. What the hell is wrong with you? You can't just leave. You made a promise at that altar and now look at you.... I will never forgive you for this."

The next one was more apologetic.

"Look. I didn't mean that. Just tell me where you are," he says, crying into the phone. "I need to you know are okay, Jady bug. It's me. I love you. Please, don't do this."

The next one was as mean as it gets and sent chills down my entire body.

"Two weeks. You have left me in the dark for two weeks. I swear to God, I will find you. And if you're with another man... the both of you have a huge surprise waiting for you. I will not be disrespected and made a fool of by my lying cheating wife. I will find you. Mark my words. I will find you."

The final one made me sick.

"Paul is dead, it's time for us to get back to us now. When I bring you home, we can start over. Things can be the way they always should've been before he was ever brought back into the picture."

I power my phone down quickly, pay for my to-go order, throw my pack on my back and my thumb in the air. I can't avoid it—I need to hitchhike my way to the trail. Sam is hunting me like an animal, and I need to get lost quickly before I get found.

CHAPTER ELEVEN

W HEN A DRIVER stops, all of me wrestles with getting in. *What if Sam is inside? What if it's someone Sam has hired?* If I want to become untraceable, I need to bury myself deep into the black tops of this mountain faster than I can walk. Hitch hiking is the only answer.

"Where you headed, ma'am?" A man with a tattooed neck pops his head out the window. Why do they always have to be men? And then I remember that I'm a woman and there's no way I'd ever feel safe picking anyone up from the side of the road.

"To this mountain," I say, pointing the old man's scribble on the receipt.

"Big bear mountain? You got a death wish, young lady?" he says with a concerned chuckle, raising his brow.

"What do you mean?" I ask, looking to my left and right.

"Well, if the bears don't get ya, something else might." He laughs again. "That's what they say, anyway. Though I have had a couple friends who did the hike and had nothing but good things to say about it."

"Something else?"

"Who knows, maybe it's a person up there. Someone who knows that a pretty girl is goin' all the way up that mountain alone, on a dark foggy night. All by her pretty self."

The hair stands stiff on my arms.

He laughs and smacks the side of the car with his hand, "I'm just teasin', I didn't scare you, did I?"

I shake my head, even though I've never felt more afraid and on guard in my life.

"Beautiful view though, one of the best. I think it's worth it." He flashes a creepy half smile with stained teeth. "Some might say it's breath taking. Be careful though, keep any food either inside a sturdy house or hang it in a tree. The bears are hungry this time of year. They are getting ready to hibernate."

"Okay, thanks for the heads up. I'm not sure I'm going yet."

"I did scare you, didn't I?" He asks again, making me wonder if he was trying to scare me.

I look down at my feet and suck my lip into my teeth, trying my best not to say it. *Yes, I'm terrified.* I put on my brave face instead. The one I've had to use most of my life.

"Well, head on down then before all this rain. You aren't going to want to come down this slippery, muddy mountain after the rain."

"Okay, thanks. Noted."

"One last thing," he says. "Don't forget. It's colder at the top of the mountain. You'll be going from fall to winter in no time. No one is really headed up right now, most folks are on their way down. You sure you're going still?"

I have nothing to lose, and I have my supplies.

"I move quick," I lie. "Thanks."

I PRETEND TO walk in the opposite direction and wait for his truck to disappear before I turn around to head up the mountain. I turn on my phone for a quick minute, but there's no signal. If I want to call Snacks to hitch a ride, I'd have to hike all the way back down to town for the Wifi, which risks time and being seen. I turn my phone off and begin my ascend to big bear mountain by the only way possible right now—by foot. By myself.

Sure enough, fall has turned its back on me yet again as winter temps began to creep in by sundown. It's not that I don't think about quitting, I do nearly every day. It's just that the days I'd feel like quitting, the sun will poke through, and the comforting warmth keeps me on the trail. I stare at the ground a lot while I'm out here. And eventually start talking out loud to myself. "I think moss is pretty. It's sort of nature's best fashion accessory. Nature always seems to be on trend. I wonder why people choose to wear animal fur instead off moss. I'd rather wear moss."

The wet leaves are dressing the ground making each step upwards a slippery challenge. Normally I love fall and wish it was longer. Often it feels too short season of season, which is ironic because it's also the one that's most honest and true. It reminds me how beautiful change can be, even ugly things, like letting go. Even death.

I find a warm rock that has been baking in the sun all day. I take a seat on it, rest my pack on the forest floor and pull out my journal. I take a breath in before talking to the empty lines.

I'm so used to seeing the trees online, I think I've I forgotten what real trees look like. My head has been down so long I forgot what things really look like when I decide to look up and out. While that sounds crazy, I can assure you it's a curated world in small squares that has us all disillusioned. It has become hard to decipher what is happening. And once removed from the digital world, your world also feels oddly digital. It's hard to separate the false realities from the real. This will be an experiment, my own experiment. I wonder who misses my small squares, or the words under my photos. Who is missing my presence, my proof of existing? My life. Would I ever exist again to anyone else if I didn't log back in online? Would people forget me? Would friends lose touch or forget my birthday without a social media app reminding them that I'm alive. Who would check in on me if they hadn't seen a square photo upload in a while? To leave that square world behind feels lonely and scary, isolating and socially lethal. But staying feels the same too. I've completely fallen off the planet, at least that's what it feels like when you check out of social media island and ground yourself into reality. The real living and breathing things start to look artificial. There's no way this tree looks so perfect. Surely it must be bought. Surely some model purchased it for her home at a coupon code discount. Surely there is a filter placed over it making it so vivid. Those are things I'm glad I don't have to concern myself with in this moment. In this moment I feel reality. The earthly elements brushing against my cheeks. I died when Paul did, but slowly am becoming revived by this mountain, even if most days it feels like it's killing me. I'm the most alive I've ever felt. This world feels wild and free. So much so that I find myself feeling somehow nourished and fed by it.

Food. God, I miss food. I've hardly thought about the lefto-ver food I packed from the Waffle House until this moment. I take the hour's-old burger and floppy cold fries from the Styrofoam box and sink my teeth into it like a hungry dog. I forget to save any extras just in case of food emergencies, which I realize now is a rookie mistake. I'm careful to take modest sips of water from my canteen as I remember that I'll soon be off the common trail and into the backwoods. Being uncertain of where the water sources on the trek, I know I will need to ration what I have until I find more.

I thought trail hiking was hard, but I hadn't hiked off the grid like this. Before, there was a path laid out for me, rest areas, shelters, camp sites and people. Now, I'm heading into no man's land. But it's only thirty miles, I tell myself. Some people walk that in a day. I don't have much farther to go, I tell myself. I'm closer than I think.

I'M NOT SURPRISED when I feel drops of water drip onto my head from the trees towering above me. The rain last night drenched everything again. Wet mud, soggy leaves, and vibrant green moss dressed the path ahead. A few times I slid and almost fell, and each time I kept thinking how horrible it would be to break a leg or get injured out here alone. Those thoughts, however, are much outweighed by the thoughts of Sam finding me, shoving me into the SUV and whisking me back to the life I hate. Walking up and away on black bear mountain feels like my only hope.

Thoughts of embracing Paul one last time makes the worst of this worth it. Soaked socks, damp clothes and hiking in muck for days on end is hardly the worst of it. The weight of my pack has my feet, ankles, shoulders, and legs aching in places they've never ached. Not to mention bug bites, slivers, cuts, and blisters have become more and more frequent. Comfort is still nowhere to be found on the trail and by now I've peace that it likely won't be.

I've met runners who clear some fifty miles a day, homeless hikers, stoner hikers and people who call the trail their backyard. While I can't say the whole journey so far has been pleasant, I can say that with certainty, there is something rather special about belonging to these woods. Every time I sink my hands into the dirt, I can feel the pulse of the earth as it untangles the knots in my mind and body.

ON THE SOLO treks, when everything but nature surrounds me and the silence consumes me, I can hear him. Paul's voice and his laugh flow into my head uninvited, both triggering and comforting. It's my constant reminder that though he isn't physically with me, he is always there. I swear in the stillness I can hear him whisper to me, *"You're so beautiful."* And I still hear his jokes echo through my head so clearly, as if my brain gets hijacked by his voice when I need to hear it most.

I find comfort knowing he is somehow always protecting me—in ways that weren't possible when he was alive. On the lonely walks, my head takes me to places my heart has avoided going since he left. Thoughts about what our life would've looked like if I chose him. How I wore swollen eyes every day for about a month me as it hit me all at once—the sincere and permanent pain of regret.

Because even if your mind doesn't want to go there, your heart knows things that your mind can't explain. Loss hits different when you lose someone you chose to love. I remember grieving the loss of my aging grandparents and how that still hit hard, but it felt different. This love I had for Paul was one that I willingly tattooed on my soul. I had never lost someone like that.

CHAPTER TWELVE

W ITH THE BEGINNINGS of a dehydration headache, I know I
am running out of time. I'm almost out of water. I have
drunk nearly all the water left in my canteen and knew this was
not looking good for survival. I beg Paul again for a sign. I need
water and I need it soon. For now, I have resorted to only
drinking a mouthful after every mile. It's an unequipped uphill
battle as it is, add in dehydration and it's a losing one. *Waiting for
a sign. Any sign, please. Help me find water.*

About every five miles I turn my phone on for a quick minute
to check for a signal. At this point, I am hoping to call Snacks to
hitch a ride. The more I wind up this mountain, the more alone I
become. Rather than being alone on the common trails, being
alone up here feels different. Scary different. I wave my phone
around searching for a signal. And when I can't find one, the
panic begins. *This is not good. Why did I do this? Why did I come
up here?* The land surrounding me has begun caving in. The
mudslides I was warned about are starting to happen around
me – roots are pulling away from the ground, the edges of cliffs
and roadsides were crumbling on my ascend and it was only
getting worse by the hour. The trails are blocked by fallen trees
and piles and piles of brush. Historical heavy rain fall has over
saturated the terrain causing flooding so intense that even the
earth feels like giving up.

The ground vibrates beneath my feet—another tree has fallen

not too far ahead of me. Thankfully, I jump out of the way before I collapsed along with it. I couldn't help but feel like asking Paul again for another sign. *I need help. I need him.* Everything around me seems to be giving up and unraveling, and I too, was syncing up with nature again.

"Paul, if you're out there, and I mean *really* out there, like that old man said you were, send me just one more sign."

Tears began leaking from my eyes and within minutes, I see a cardinal poached on a branch looking at me. I had my sign, and I couldn't give up now. I had to keep going, keep trusting. Moments later, I found water. A lucky slip on an ice path led me to a stream, which gave me another clue—I had more cold weather to endure. Tonight's sleep would be next to impossible, but at least I'd still be alive with something to drink.

When morning showed up, I knew I could make it there by sundown if I moved fast enough. The trick is moving against unwelcoming forces like wind, rain, fog, and the crushing fatigue that feels worse today than it ever has. I wasn't hungry for what I had in my pack, but I knew I needed to eat something for energy. To not die before I get there.

When Dizzy gifted me the beef sticks, they looked incredible, but this morning my appetite for processed meat tubes just wasn't there. Still, I forced one down anyway with very small sips of water and made myself eat an energy bar that gagged me with each bite. It's still moderately dark since it's just before sunrise, so I make sure to put my headlight on as I pack up the last camp site before making my way to Paul. Strangely, I feel a pang of nervousness about seeing him again. What if he can smell how terribly sour I am from the lack of consistent showers? What if he doesn't still love me? What is he blames me for dying? For dying unhappy? Or worse, what if doesn't remember me now that he is wherever he is?

As I walk upwards, I makeshift two trekking poles with sticks like Dizzy made for me. Weakness has taken over my body, making it hard to stand upright, let alone move forward at a brisk pace. Leaves and twigs crunch under my heavy feet as the squashy mud attempts to hold me back with every step.

Every element in nature appears to be working against me and every element in my body has also received that message.

Once daylight shows her face, I am disappointed that the sunlight wasn't showing up along with it. I find myself looking up as often as I look down today. Between the falling branches, gunshot ricochets and loud crashes from the mudslides, I have no other choice than to remain hyper-vigilant. The world around is quite literally crashing down. Again, nature is in sync. I can tell I'm making it higher and higher when my breathing shallows from the altitude, making each step also feel heavier. Tiny bits of snowfall melt onto my half-numb cheeks. The forest is eerily quiet—even the birds aren't messing around with this cold haunted mountain.

I don't have any time to waste. I know I need to push myself faster to the phone. I pull my map back out as I try to make sense of where I'm going. The thickness of the fog poses many challenges with navigation and visibility, making the act of moving forward faster a much bigger struggle. I'm close to running out of water again, but if I want to make it to the phone today, I know that I can't make any stops. My greatest motivation in this moment is the constant reminder that with each step I am moving farther away from Sam and closer to Paul.

I'm almost there, I can feel it. I take another sip of water, pull my pack back over my shoulder and push on more than I've ever pushed on in my life.

I MAY HAVE slipped, stumbled, screamed, and fallen my way up this mountain, but I have summited. There are no more steep rocky hills to fight against, there even appears to be a trail and a map that shows where the phone is. The trail feels so worn down, so open and public that I begin to wonder if I am dreaming. This was the closest I have been to an actual trail since I left Dizzy and the guys in town. I walk up to the map and see that not only am I close, but I have also almost arrived.

The map on the wooden sign shows a pay phone with a carved heart and an outline for directions. I start with a left turn and follow a series of wooden arrows hammered into the muddy ground. A bit of fear seeps at this moment, worrying me about the man with the neck tattoos. *What if he was waiting for me at the phone? What if I wasn't alone?*

Those thoughts quickly fade as I peel away the branches and thick brush, clearing a path to catch my first glimpse at it. The Phone of The Wind.

CHAPTER THIRTEEN

I DON'T KNOW what I was expecting, but this wasn't exactly what I had in mind. To the naked eye, nothing about what's in front of me is bedazzling. The phone does not appear to have any sort of supernatural powers attached to it all. In my mind, a magic phone would look a bit more magical. I walk around the area and examine its structure—bright green moss travels along the sides of the old wooden post. Quickly, my disappoint grows as I realize it's just an old rotary phone nailed to a large oak tree.

I stare at it for a minute, examining it cautiously. Maybe there's more to it than it seems. I wonder, *what is supposed to happen when I touch it? Would I see him? Would I hear his voice?* Even more than that, I wondered deeper. *What do I say to the person I never thought I'd speak to again?* Slowly, I trace my fingers down its spiral cord and run my ice-cold hand over the hard plastic. I pick up the phone, the tips of my nails are turning purple, my hands nearly frozen.

With the receiver pressed against my cheek, I take a deep inhale, close my eyes, and imagine his face. Nothing happens. I wait a minute more, before I exhale my grave disappointment. But just as I was about to remove the phone from my face, I begin to feel something. A warmth starts to envelop me. The center of my forehead begins to buzz, as if a bee was somehow trapped inside of it, swirling wildly inside of me. A weight comes over my eye lids, and by force, I feel the intensity of strong hands pulling the fabric from my coat and into an even warmer space. I notice swirls of light sparkling around the empty room. The brightness of it all forces my eyes closed.

I can feel myself somewhere else, but I'm too afraid to open my eyes to see.

"You can open your eyes," a woman's voice spoke softly. "He's waiting for you."

CHAPTER FOURTEEN

"I DON'T WANT to." My lips tremble. "I'm afraid." My cold hands tingle as my blood rushes warm.

"Don't be afraid," she says, as her voice draws near. Another intense flow of heat pulses through me.

"You wanted to connect to a soul on the other side, yes?" She echoes as if she was walking from a distance.

"Yes." I open my eyes, a bright misty light cast in front of me. I squint as I try to block it with my hands.

"Where is he?" I ask, as I try to search for him past the light. As I stand here in this room, I realize my body no longer aches. My pains from the trail were gone. My skin is warm, and my arms are flushed again with color. I even feel energized and full as if I had just eaten another Waffle House meal. A complete sense of wholeness consumes me. Faint ambient sound of chimes and soft piano echo off in the distance.

"He's waiting for you. He's been waiting for you," the woman says as she appears to step out of the light and into a tunnel. "I'm Anika, your spirit guide." Her voice is angelic and sweet.

"I've always been with you, but it's nice to finally meet you in the flesh." She smiles, her bronze skin luminous and glowing. "Over 500 years to be exact. Our journey began during your past life in Egypt. Then we made our way Africa, France. We've been everywhere together. Of course, you may or may not have known I was there." With her hands she swipes through images of my many lives. The lives I've never known existed. Her wings glitter and flutter on her back like a fairy. Her black curly hair coils elegantly like a halo over her head. "I've always been here to keep you safe. To keep you connected to yourself and to the universe." She laughs and flutters around me. "Well, I try anyway. There's always freewill involved. I do my best to pull you and sway you in one direction, but you still ended up in Chicago." She rolls her eyes and smirks. "Right?"

I find it hard to speak as she gains an unspoken credibility. I press my lips tight and look around. A warm glowing empty room. This goddess woman. My spirit guide, apparently. And me. *Where am I?* I wondered. But there's an even bigger question nagging on my heart.

"Where is he?" I say, looking around for Paul.

"Patience, dear one. I have a few things to show you and explain. The other side is a bit of a learning curve," she says, extending her hand. "Come with me?"

I give her my hand cautiously. Without a blink, I'm transported my bedroom in Chicago. Together we hover over my body like a dream. She points to my bed.

"It's okay, you're safe," she says. "Lay down. I want to show you something." I look at her confused. "It's a gift from your person who passed. He wants to show you this before he sees you."

As I lay next to my sleeping body, I can feel myself sink into in the softness of my bed, the city lights twinkle in the night sky through the half-open curtains. The familiar comfort of it makes me close my eyes. I feel a brush on my cheek that makes me open them. "He wants me to tell you that he holds you every night while you sleep, stroking your hair and your cheeks softly like this."

I smile as I imagine him doing this to me every night, a tear falls down my cheek.

"I thought it was just a dream."

"You aren't dreaming. That's his soul reaching out to you. He's still very much with you."

"Can't he just tell me this when I see him? I will see him, right?"

"That's precisely why I'm here to explain a few things. Sometimes, it's hard for those on the other side to speak with words. Often, they use signs—birds or animals or coins. Or they manipulate electricity, a light flicker, a song on the radio, or for convenience, they will contact your spirit guide directly with a message. That's where I come in. He has always asked me to tell you these things."

"I don't understand how you can speak, but he can't?"

"Energy is complicated, I'm afraid. I'm a spirit guide and he is not yet. He has tried to conserve a lot of his energy so he can hold you every night. It takes a tremendous amount of energy to do that. He also has not fully let go of his earthly life, or you for that matter," she says. "He must really love you."

I nod and swallow. "That sounds like Paul."

"Even this connection today will cost him a lot of energy. But it appears he's willing to drain it all for you. Most souls who accept this phone call are willing to take the risk, even if the consequences place him in waiting even longer."

"What's the risk? Will he die all over again?"

"I'm afraid he cannot die twice," she says and laughs again. "But it will take him some time to regain any energetic strength to continue to communicate with you or spend any time on Earth in his spirit form. He will essentially be trapped here until he's energetically charged enough to leave."

"Is it not good, or safe, to be here?"

"It's perfectly fine to be here, it's just a lot of work for souls on the other side. He will have to rest a while after this communication, that's all," she says calmly. "And it may be some time before he makes it to where he's supposed to go. He's been with you every day—guiding you. After this connection, it might be a while before he has the energetic bandwidth again. It might take some time before he's able to connect with you in the same ways as he has before."

"Okay. I think I understand."

"He might not be able to speak, but you will know what he's thinking and feeling. Do you want to see for yourself? Do you still want me to bring him out to you?"

"Yes," I say, A Christmas morning feeling drops from my belly to my feet. "I'd do anything to see him just one more time."

"Take my hand." She whirls me into another room.

The room reminds me of one from a luxury hotel. Cool marble floors, coved white walls, glowing beams of white triangular lights up ceiling. I look around but see no one else with me. Even Anika has disappeared. When I look again, Paul walks slowly from around the corner. *There he is.*

Without a beat, I run and leap into his arms. The feeling of his skin on mine again is sacred. I squeeze him so tightly, afraid to let him go. Real or imagined, I'm with Paul again.

"It's you!" I laugh a little, in disbelief, running my hands over his forearms. The hair running against my fingertips. "Oh my God. You're really here!"

He nods and smiles. He's younger than I remember him last, and when I investigate the mirror to my right with his hand in mine, we were both different. Our reflections are both clean, dressed in white and appear to be much softer. Unblemished and pure, as if every bad thing was erased and all is perfect now. Our sense of age and time isn't real. I can hardly tell if I've been here ten minutes of ten seconds. We're moving quickly, but it doesn't feel fast at all, if anything, time feels as if it has slowed down or decided to stop for a bit. I'm wearing the same dress I wore on our first date, except it's white and bright. Paul's skin is tan and glowing, his golden eyes shimmer in all this vivid, breathtaking light.

He takes my hand, whisks me out and away through two golden doors. As we walk in, a magnificent garden stands before us. We're surrounded by the most beautiful exotic wildflowers I have ever seen. Shades of pink, bright yellows, bold hues of deep violet and lilac pop vividly under the sun. The air is dense and warm as if we have just walked into a tropical paradise. With his hand in mine, Paul walks me through a tunnel of white roses. Lush green boxwood bushes line the walkway with flower petals dusting the brick beneath our feet. He's got that look in his eyes when I look up at him—the look that could make me do anything. I can tell by his grin that he's excited to show me what's next.

I squeeze his hand tight, afraid to look away from his face. When we get to the end of the floral tunnel, I notice a small table set with two chairs and a white linen tablecloth lying neatly over the top.

I sit down in my chair, feeling the warm wood against the backs of my thighs. A sunlight glow beams above us. I slide my hand over the soft silk linen, pick up a silver fork and spin it around a few times before setting down and running my fingertips over Paul's hands. *This is real. It all feels so real.*

A cup of coffee and cocoa are waiting for us at the table in delicate fine china. Paul smiles at me then, waving his hands as he signals me to drink it.

Paul laughs then, yet I can't hear his laugh with my ears. It's a laugh only heard in my head like a memory replaying. A euphoric sensation fills me up from my chest down into my belly as I take a sip. An inebriating sweetness rolls over my tongue. I lick my lips and close my eyes –savoring every minute of bliss. I'm careful not to keep them closed too long just in case I were to fall asleep and this all be a dream. I didn't want to wake up yet.

Birds chirp loudly from the trees in the garden and a tropical humidity fills the air. Every breath feels cleansing and easy, each one better than next. Butterflies fly all around us. One lands on my hand as it holds his closely.

IT'S CLEAR. WE are not on earth, but wherever we are feels familiar, even though I'm certain I've never been here before. As the sun shines, its light continues to expand brighter and brighter. Paul points down, instructing me to look next to my chair. Beside me, there is a small wicker picnic basket with a white satin blanket stuffed inside. A red cardinal sing songs on top of the basket. It flies away as I begin to open it. Paul holds my hands as I look into his golden eyes. He is more beautiful now than he ever was. His smile is perfect. His skin is perfect. His face rested, relaxed and peaceful. Copper hues from his hair shimmer in the sun. Paul is golden from the inside out.

"I have missed you so much," I say to him, gazing into his eyes deeply. He smiles and nods, squeezing my hands tighter. Even though he can't speak directly to me, feeling his presence again in this beautiful, perfect place has made all the hell I've been ever been through worth it.

"You're showing off, you know," I say to him with a smirk. "This is by far the most romantic thing anyone has ever done. You outdid yourself, sir." He laughs again, shrugging his shoulders. And though I can't hear it, I can feel the emotion of his laugh; it penetrates through my entire soul. Happiness. Wholeness. He takes his coffee cup, holds it up to mine and clinks them together. Paul takes my hand again, kisses the top of it gently before he whisks me away to another world.

The thundering sound of falling water crashes around us. He's taken me to the exact waterfall where I almost poured his ashes. He holds me, rubs his hands over my arms, my face, my lips and pulls me into a kiss. When his lips are pressed against mine, time stops again, and the hair raises on my arms. My eyes roll into my head as I melt into him. An electric knowing comes over me then.

"You were with me?" I ask.

He nods and pulls me closer, holding me against his chest tightly. I close my eyes and when I open them, I hear a voice in the distance.

"You have two choices now." A cool breeze swirls in from above, my hair whips around my face. "Love or fear?"

I look around to see that Paul is gone. The light has disappeared. The sun has turned to snow. It's just me, standing here alone in the faded reality of where I was moments ago. Up until this moment I realize I have only chosen my path out of fear. I can sense that I don't have time to think much longer. Here, I realize the choice must come quick and it must come easy.

Love is all I need.

This time, I will choose love. I will choose Paul.

"Wait. Paul, wait." I yell out to him. "I'm coming!" I can see him walking near me from a distance. He turns to me, hands me the picnic basket. When I look up from it, he has disappeared back into the tunnel of light. As I try to open the basket, I feel a violent shove down the tunnel. I fight against its current and stand back on my feet, chasing Paul back into the light.

"Paul, wait! Please…"

With each step forward, I feel my body tugged down further and further as if I'm running through quicksand. With each push back, the temperature grows colder. It happens abruptly—I drop all the way down and into my earthly body, the phone still resting against my cheek. My hiking boots still pressed against the cold muddy forest floor. My hands icy hands stiff, and my toes fully numb.

I got to be with Paul one last time and everything in me wanted to go back to that beautiful place with him again. The old man from the Waffle House was right. This was real, and it is entirely worth protecting so the grieving could experience this. I am frozen, but grateful. Had this place not been as protected as it is, who knows if I would've been able to experience this at all. Even still, just as the old man said to, I decide to hang up the phone and say goodbye. My numb lips quiver and my teeth begin to chatter. I whisper one last "goodbye" into it. And as I do, a tear falls and freezes instantly onto my face.

Upon placing the receiver back on the hook, a crippling fatigue takes over my body. I slid down the payphone like a heavy bag of sand. Every ounce of vitality I felt in that bright glowing place is now gone. Somehow, my fatigue has gotten worse, as if whatever life was left in me is now trapped inside that phone. Maybe that was my small price to pay—an exchange of my last bit of energy to be with Paul one last time.

I CLOSE MY eyes for a while as it starts to rain down over me. The weather has grown colder and my body shivers violently under its chill.

I don't want to leave Paul. I tried to stay, but I couldn't. I had blown my chance when he was alive, but now that I had Paul again in my grasp, I can't find it in me—the strength to fully let him go.

This time goodbye would be forever.

I'm not ready for that. I never will be.

CHAPTER FIFTEEN

OURS PASSED, AND the sun has gone down. My thermometer reads that it's below freezing. By now my body has become so cold, the bones in my fingers and knuckles cramp and ache when I move them. I consider reaching for the receiver again, even though I was told I shouldn't. Knowing that if I do, I could risk it all. I need to make the right choice this time – I need to choose love over fear.

When I breathe, my breath is milky and visible, reminding me I'm still alive. But when I look down, my hands have turned ghostly white and so stiff that bending them hurts, reminding me that I'm closer to dying than I've ever been. I have lost almost all the sensation in them by now. So much of my body feels numb, it's hard to feel as though I'm here. I'm fading from this reality, too.

Surely, it has been this cold throughout this journey, but the difference was that I have always been moving. This time, I haven't moved for hours. I have hardly eaten in days, and whatever has plagued my body on and off during my quest, has plagued me again. There is no sign of warmth, no sign of light, and not a shred of energy left in my body that can pull me out and away from this phone. I will die here if I don't do something.

But doing something requires more energy than I have.

I reach for my cell phone and consider powering it back on, knowing that in doing this Sam may be able to track my location.

On second thought, I'd rather die here than give Sam permission to come and find me. I reach my cold stiff arm back up to the phone, rest it gently against my face. I take a deep breath in as I close my eyes. I imagine Paul's cheek against my face again, it sends a gentle smile across my lips. Nothing but my foggy cold breath surrounds me.

Time is running out, and there is nothing else to lose. I could die here on the mountain, freezing to death alone and empty from the inside out. Or I could die in Paul's arms. My shivering hands tremble as I press the receiver against my face.

"Paul," I speak into it. My words were just as slow and frozen as I felt. "I—I am so cold." My teeth chatter as I try to make more words out. "Take – take me with you. Bring me back—to the other side."

In this moment, an electrifying surge, a current of radiant heat jolts through me as if the phone had been struck with lightning, and with it we both came alive. I can feel Paul, his warmth, his presence, his stillness and calm, his safety. I can feel my second heartbeat begin to thump again. My hands soften, my cheeks flush once more with radiant warmth. I take another deep breath in and this time it feels lighter, easier. When I open my eyes, Paul is standing before me. A glow casts from his body, angelic and light. A tunnel of brightness forms behind him. This time, his spirit form is even more beautiful, more irresistible than it was the first time. His face is still perfect, unblemished, and smooth. His eyes were still glistening. He holds his hand out to me and he speaks calmly.

"It's okay," he says. This time he's speaking to me with real words, real sound and I can hear his voice clearly. It's different.

It's not just a replay of his memory in my head. It's real. "It's me."

"Paul. I need you." I reach out to grab his hand. "I'm so cold here, I will die if you don't take me with you. Please..."

"It's warm where I am. Come here, let me hold you," he says. He stretches his arms out open to me. For a second, I wonder if this is real. *Did I die here already? Am I dreaming? Is this a dark force posing at light?*

"Where are you? Where are we? Where... is this place?" I ask. My body shivers as I back away from it. The brightness is intense and hard to look at directly. A shudder of fear comes over me, afraid that if I go, I might not come back again. That I, too, may die and never be able to return. Though staying isn't offering me peace or comfort, and in my current state, I will likely die either way. I need to choose Paul this time.

"I'm on the other side," he says. More cold rain begins to fall, and a chill shakes through my bones. My fingertips and toes begin to lose complete sensation again. I can feel myself flickering in and out of consciousness at this point, making it hard to communicate clearly or think rationally. I need his warmth, his love in this moment. Nothing else matters. If those two things are delivered to me now, I have won. I have fought this fight. I have carried Paul until I couldn't carry him any longer. I'm ready for him to carry me.

"Other—side—of what?" my fading voice whispers. I reach for his hand. The sensation of it in mine feels warm, euphoric— like I've just taken the most intense form of ecstasy.

When I touch him, it turns something on inside of me again that has been turned off since he left. I can feel myself feeling again. I can feel myself smiling, laughing without knowing why. I feel so good, so alive and so real. Even if it meant I was dead or dying, there was no way I could turn back from this feeling, even if I wanted to. I'm joining him again, even if it's forever. Especially if it's forever.

"We can be together here; I've been waiting for you," he says, scooping me off the ground and into his arms, carrying me like his bride. The bride I never got to be. The warmth of his glow surges through my body, warming me up instantly. *If this is death, then why do I feel so alive?*

"Am I dead? Did this phone kill me?" I ask, a faint laugh forces through me.

He laughs. God, I missed his laugh. His smile.

"You haven't died... not yet," Paul says.

"But you did. You left me. I needed you." I look at him, and I mean really look at him. He needs to see how much this hurts.

"I have always been with you." He runs his hand through my hair. "I will never be able to leave you... even if you can't see me. I'm still there. Just as I showed you I was."

Paul walks closer to the tunnel of light—each step feels warmer and happier. It's the same feeling I get when I lay on the beach on the most perfect sunny day. Where I close my eyes and feel the sun penetrate through my skin. I can feel a surge of powerful endorphins fill me all the way up. Relaxed and unbound from anything that has ever hurt me. A full body peace I haven't felt in far too long, if ever.

I look up at him and hold his face in my hands, "You," I say. "It's really you." His vivid angelic body lights up even more, glowing brighter and whiter. The warmth feels like paradise, like I've finally landed on the island of my dreams with the one that I love. Exactly as I'd imagined heaven feeling like.

"Is this...heaven?" I ask.

"It feels that way, doesn't it?" Paul replies. "But something is missing. I arrived here alone, and I'm supposed to meet others here. I'm not in heaven, not yet, but I'm almost there. I'm so close I can feel it, I can almost see it. But I don't think I can go without you. It was hard enough for me not having you there on earth, but it's even harder to be here, in paradise, without you."

I think for a moment about the old man, the dark forces posing as light as one of theories to make sense as to why some people go missing, but nothing about this experience could have a shadow of darkness. This is pure light, all of it. It now makes sense to me now why so many have gone missing upon discovering this phone. Once they have reached paradise with the one they love, there is no point to go back to the cold dark earthly world below.

I think for a moment about what I have left on this earth. A terrible husband who has made it feel impossible for me to escape him. The dream bakery that only exists if I stay with him, and if I don't, I have nothing. Sam has made it easy for me to easily slip away without anyone but him noticing. If I stayed, I'd need to leave Chicago. Having nowhere else to go, I would likely move back to Ohio again. Nothing would ever come of my dreams, and I would be reminded every single day that I didn't choose Paul. Sam is probably right; I couldn't do anything as successfully without him. Everything on this earth at this very minute feels underwhelming, hopeless and easy to leave. I know I'll miss my family, even if they are imperfect and frustrating. But I also know I'd see them again someday in a much better place, and that nothing else matters but love. With Paul, I have a warm spot in paradise with our names written in the sand.

"Take me with you," I say as I close my eyes, knowing that up until this moment I've been afraid to die. But now, I am eagerly welcoming it. I will soon be warm and at peace on the other side. Hand in hand with the love of my entire life and thereafter. The other side of this frigid cold forest and this weirdly enchanted phone.

"Take me with you," I say. With my eyes still closed, I feel a tugging and pulling at my arms. A vacuum suction sensation attaches to my chest, compressing into me. More and more warmth and love fill me up, I open my eyes now, fully accepting my submission to the other side and my decision to join Paul forever.

Paul tries to carry me into the light with him, but I notice him begin to struggle as he pushes against a force of energy. He releases my hand, dropping me onto my feet. The warmth fades quickly—my face, arms and hands are stricken again by the cold that I was trying so hard to escape.

"Jade, I—I can only take one person with me."

I cry out to him confused. "Paul, please, it's just me, no one else is here. I'm so cold, please! Take me with you—"

"I can't—there's two of you." He points to my stomach and hands me the picnic basket. When I look inside, an image of a sleeping baby appears. I grab ahold of my stomach with my hand, looking down at the baby in the basket and back up at him. My eyes widen as I begin to panic. *I'm a dying mother to an unborn child.*

"I can't take you both," he tells me again.

"Can you just take me then?"

"If I take you, the baby won't survive," he says, his voice echoes. "If I take the baby, you will survive only on earth, but the baby will join me here on the other side."

"Or," he says carefully, "I can let you both go on to experience life together on earth. And when it's time, I'll see you two again."

The freezing cold engulfs me. I need to leave this cold before it kills me, but I also need more time to decide. Time that I don't have. I knew one thing for sure, I was not ready to be a mother, but I had never thought about what might happen if I had no choice—if becoming a mother chose me. I knew Paul would keep the baby safe, but it didn't feel right to leave a baby behind before ever meeting it. Energy leaves with my body as each second passes. My consciousness wanes in and out, making it impossible for me to reach a decision. I stretch my hand out to Paul, the warmth cradles me again, the brightness nearly blinding.

"Paul, I don't want to die. I don't want this baby to die, either...but I can't be without you. Not again." The words shatter me on the way out. The closer I get; the further away Paul becomes. I can feel myself fading, collapsing into a grey area. No longer with Paul, yet no longer in the freezing rain of the forest. I let out a breath, letting go of all that is and all that was and could ever be. If there's a God, I have surrendered. I open my heavy eyes and I'm somewhere new. Somewhere bright, somewhere warm.

CHAPTER SIXTEEN

"YOU NEARLY DIED," a voice says. "You could've frozen to death from hypothermia. It could've killed you both. What were you doing out there, anyway?"

"Us both?" I ask, my voice foggy and confused. *Am I pregnant like Paul said I was? Was that real?* My eyes struggle to open and when they do, I notice that I'm in a hospital bed. A doctor hovers of me, checks the beeping monitors over my head.

"The baby." She squints her eyes at me in concern. "You do know you are pregnant, right?" I shake my head no, feeling woozy and dizzy when I do.

"I didn't want a baby," I croak. I notice a man sitting in a chair at the corner of the room, wearing a raincoat and hiking boots. He tries to avoid eye contact with me. The doctor fumbles through a stack of papers, "It looks like you are about twenty-two weeks pregnant to be exact. That's what the baby is measuring at."

"The funeral—" I mutter with hardly a voice at all. The last time I saw him. "It's Paul's baby," Even though my brain is clouded, and it takes extra effort, I manage to calculate the math to identify that it is indeed Paul's. After his grandfather's funeral, it was in that window of time. This was during my sexual shut down where my body refused to be intimate with Sam. The only person who could've gotten me pregnant was Paul. It is clear now in this moment that I have major decisions to make, though my body craved and cared for nothing but rest. And food. As much food as I could possibly eat.

"Congratulations, ma'am. I know this news might be a bit jarring. Makes sense why a pregnant woman would do a solo hike in the Appalachian Mountains in such extreme weather as this." The doctor chuckles and adjusts her glasses. "Because she clearly didn't know she was pregnant. Have you not had any symptoms? Surely the fatigue and the anemia could've been your first clue. Your ferritin levels are dangerously low." The doctor looks at me again. "Any fatigue, food aversions?"

Still feeling numb from the cold of the forest, my neck, and shoulders still pained, I begin to trace back over the last few weeks, searching for a clue that I was pregnant. Nothing jumps out at me.

"I've always been on and off anemic," I moan. "And I lost— someone I loved." I wondered if all those feelings of new life maybe went hand in hand with grief.

"It completely missed me." The doctor nods and punches away at the computer, taking notes.

I think that confused some things for me. Was I tired because he was dead? Or was I tired because I was with child? It seems easy to mix up. I've never been pregnant before, or this sad in my entire life. How could I know it was one or the other, both felt so new to me?

"Being tired is like as normal as breathing right now. And as far as food aversions go, everything but a hot Waffle House meal sounded like bad news to me," I say. I notice then the main in the raincoat raises his head and laughs a little, still looking down at his boots.

"Any unusual cravings? Anything…" She looks at me bewildered, scratches her head as if she could recall some clues for me.

"I did have one big craving that stands out at me now that I think about it. Cold orange juice. But I just thought that was from being food and drink deprived on the trail."

The doctor takes out an ultrasound scanner out, rubs cold gel onto my lower abdomen and waves it around slowly. There I see it on the screen, a tiny jumping jellybean. A baby. Paul's baby.

"That right there is your baby," the doctor says, moving around the wand, the cold jelly gliding to other parts of my stomach. "Baby looks good, even with all that you've been through, but is a little sleepy. Not as active as I'd like to see." The man in the chair looks at me, locking eyes with mine for the first time. "And you look rather small for being twenty-two weeks pregnant. When was the last time you've eaten?"

I try to remember what I ate last, but it feels like a lifetime away. I can hardly remember what day it is, let alone what I ate. "I had a small beef stick," I mutter.

"Maybe that was yesterday. I'm not sure, I was running out of food..."

The man in the raincoat is still watching me when I look back up at him again, "Excuse me—but who are you?" I ask.

The doctor wraps up the ultrasound wand, wipes off my belly with a handful of paper towels. "I'm going to give you two a moment. The nurses will bring a menu—you need to eat. Do you eat meat? If not, I encourage it."

I nod.

"And I ordered an iron infusion, it'll be here in an hour. Let's get some food in you first before we discuss moving forward with the baby." She smiles, walks out, and closes the door behind her.

"I'm the man who saved your life. But you can call me Greg.," he says, his voice is deep but has a sweetness to it.

"You saved my life?" I say, raising my eyebrows.

"I found you, yes."

"Found me?"

"I was hiking, too. It was dark, foggy, cold, wet. I was lost, also. And then I saw you, clinging to the phone. I wasn't sure if you were dead or sleeping or almost dead..."

"Wait. You carried me all the way down that mountain by yourself?'

"Yes, ma'am."

"You must be really strong," I say. He laughs. I try to get a better look at his body and his arms. It's hard to see the rest of him from the hospital bed, but I can tell his arms are strong.

"It was that or let you die. I didn't have a choice," he says, almost fighting against the superhero complex.

"Thank you—for saving my life. Though, I will say. I was halfway to heaven before you showed up. It was pretty nice there, and I didn't want to come back—"

He looks at me silently as if he didn't know how to respond to that. I realize that likely sounded a bit suicidal but explaining what really happened would only make it sound worse.

"The phone... it was really there?" I ask. Greg looks at me puzzled.

"Are you sure you're alright?" he says, standing up from his chair walking over to me. When he stands, I catch a better look at him. His back and shoulders are broad, and his long legs also appear strong. He must be to have carried me all that way.

"I mean, maybe the phone was real, I don't know. Maybe I was dreaming up the rest. Maybe I had just fallen asleep," I say, trying not to sound even crazier to this man who is definitely attractive the closer he gets to me.

"What was the rest?" Greg leans in, his rubbery raincoat squeaks a little with his forward movement. As he stands before me, his light brown eyes sparkle under the florescent light.

"Nothing." I shake my head. "It was probably nothing."

"You said you lost someone. Is that what brought you to hike all that way?"

I nod, looking at him as if maybe he knew about the phone, too.

"A lot of grieving people find solace in hiking," he says. "I should know, that's why I was there, too. In the woods, looking for peace." He folds his arms. "Closure. Anything, really." He shakes his head a little and makes a disappointed smirk. He leans into my ear and whispers, "I know about the phone. It is real. I was headed that way to use it, too."

He clears his throat and looks up and into my eyes. "I just lost my daughter a few weeks ago."

He looks down, pulls his lip in, and shakes his head a little. "It wasn't a dream." His eyes meet mine with a familiar light inside of them. A warmth, a kindness.

"Who told you about the phone?" I ask.

"A buddy I work with at the shop. He had lost his father last year. He knew about it and told me as soon as he found out she passed."

"We both have a big secret to keep now, I guess," I say. "Did you get to use it? The phone?"

"No, I made it all that way…then I saw you…and…"

"I'm so sorry. I ruined that for you…"

"Don't be," he says. "She would've wanted to me to save you. My daughter loved a good Disney princess and prince charming story." He smiles and laughs a little.

"Are you saying… you might be my prince charming?" I ask, my sarcasm makes him laugh again.

"Well, I did save you…"

"But not with a kiss…" I say, surprised that it came out of my mouth.

He blushes a little and picks at something on his coat.

"I'm so sorry for your loss. I can't imagine a pain like that.

301

How old was she?"

"She was four," he says, as he chokes up. I can feel my eyes wanting to turn misty. "It happened suddenly."

"How are you holding up? It's all still so fresh…"

"Well, I'm pretty terrible, actually. Which is why I was hiking up that mountain regardless of the weather. I would walk through fire just to see my baby girl again." I have never related to any stranger more. A tear leaks down my face, he wipes it for me.

"When did your person pass? What were they like?"

"He was like—" I think for a moment how to accurately describe Paul. "An organ inside my body. The kind of organ you don't realize you need, because you have more than one, but without it, you aren't the same. You aren't really as strong as you thought you could be once it's gone, and you wish more than anything you could feel complete and put it back where it belongs."

He nods and inhales slowly. "Was he your husband?"

"No, he wasn't," I say. "But he should've been."

"He sounds like he was a good man," he says, putting his hand close to mine before removing it quickly.

The door opens and the doctor is back. "Alright, we have your meal arriving in about twenty minutes. I want to wait to do the iron infusion once you have a full stomach. It can make you feel pretty nauseous on an empty one." The doctor looks at Greg.

"You the husband?" Greg looks at me and as he does, the door swings open again.

"I am. I'm her husband." Sam walks into the hospital and shakes the doctor's hand.

My mouth hangs open as I sit here frozen in disbelief. *Sam found me.* My eyes widen and blink rapidly as they try to make sense of what they're seeing. *How is the possible? How did he find me?*

"Congratulations! You are expecting a baby," the doctor says to Sam. "Jade is pregnant. About twenty-two weeks along. Funny thing is, she didn't know she was until now. What a happy surprise."

Sam looks at me, smiling. "Wow. I can't believe it. I'm a dad. We're parents!" He covers his face in excitement. "I guess that makes sense why Jade went a little crazy." He laughs and playfully rolls his eyes, "Pregnancy hormones." He walks over to my side and kisses my forehead. "We're having a baby." He says calmly, too calmly. I recall his angry voice mails and replay them in my head, knowing that inside Sam is raging at me. Before I can speak, he looks at Greg begrudgingly. "Who is this, Jade?"

"Sam, what are you doing here?" I ask, my eyebrows knit together in concern.

"What do you mean? I came here to take care of you."

"How did you find me?" Sam looks around the room, his cheeks flush with embarrassment.

"How did I find you?" He laughs. "She must still be a little out of it."

"I'm not out of it. Who told you I was here?" Greg looks at Sam and then back at me.

"I am your emergency contact, sweetheart. Of course, the hospital called me right away upon admitting you. And your mother did as well, but don't worry. She knows I'm here now and that you are alright. I can't wait to tell her she's finally a grandma," he says, sliding his cold hand over mine and squeezing it so tightly that it hurts.

"This is Greg," I say, looking up at him. "He saved my life." I catch myself in a half smile then.

"Greg, it's an honor to meet the hero who saved my wife and our unborn child." He extends his hand to Greg to shake. Greg looks at me before he speaks.

"It was my pleasure. I'm glad she's okay." Greg smiles at me then as if he's known me longer than just today. As if he can feel the tension between Sam and I. Between us all.

"She'll be even better now that I'm here," Sam says sternly. The doctor sneaks out of the door as if he could also feel the tension building. "You can leave now, Greg. Thanks again for all your help. I got it from here." Greg takes a step back, looks at the door and then back at me.

"Sam, we need to talk," I say, looking into his steel blue eyes. His outfit is put together, business casual and clean. Dress shoes and slacks, button down collared shirt, blazer. Classic Sam.

"I know, I've been trying to talk to you for weeks, sweetheart."

"No. Not about that or about us. About the baby."

"What do you mean? Is the baby alright?"

"Yes, the baby is fine," I say, taking a breath in. "But the baby isn't yours."

"What are you saying? Of course, the baby is mine. Who else's could it be?" He looks at Greg. "It's not this guy's baby, is it?"

Greg laughs a little. "Afraid not."

"Sam." I take a long inhale in and hold my breath for a moment before blowing up his entire world. "The baby is Paul's."

"That dead guy you've been so sad over? How could it be his baby? He's dead!" He laughs as he paces around the room. "And he didn't even live nearby.... That's impossible. Jade if you don't want to be with me, fine, just say that, but you can't make up stories. This is our baby."

"I'm sorry," I say, my voice cuts out a little. I swallow before confessing two of his greatest fears. "The baby is Paul's. I was last with him twenty-two weeks ago." It hits him then. His face melts in disgust.

"So, your mom didn't get Lasik? You were off fucking some guy instead?" He throws his hands in the air. "Un-fucking-believable. You know what?" He shakes his head over and over. "I knew it. I knew it, and the whole time you had me thinking I was crazy. I even started acting crazy because you made me feel crazy. And all along, I wasn't crazy. You were cheating. My mother was right."

Greg backs away towards the door.

"Greg, wait." I look at him with desperate frightened eyes. "Don't go."

"Oh, come on, are you planning on fucking this guy, too," Sam says, raising his voice.

"Jesus, Sam. What the hell is wrong with you?"

"Wrong with me? What's wrong with YOU? I have never once cheated on you. I have been faithful from the moment I said I do. I meant it. You broke our vows, Jade. YOU."

"Let's not raise our voices," Greg says, looking at Sam. "The poor girl almost died, just discovered she's with child by a man who is no longer alive to be this child's father. I know a lot happened for you, too, but can you try to be gentle with her?"

"Gentle with her?" he says. "Oh, fuck off! She doesn't deserve gentleness. She has absolutely destroyed me. She deserves all the hell in the world for it. And if you get close enough to her, she'll destroy you, too. If I were you were, I'd stay far away from this woman."

"Sam, you should go," I say. "I'm leaving the marriage, I told you this already. This isn't healthy for me anymore." I put my protective hands over my stomach. "Or for the baby."

"So, that's it? You're just done? After all we've been through?" He looks away at the window and then back at me. He huffs, "After all I've done for you? I have given you everything. I have busted my ass to give you a life you could have only dreamed of.

The home, the new cars... the bakery. I did all of that for you. Did it mean anything to do? Or was it all for nothing?"

"No, it was not all for nothing. But I should never have tried to give you even the smallest fraction of what was left in my heart...especially when most of it belonged to someone else."

"That dead guy?" He shakes his head in disgust.

"His name was Paul," I say. "I fell in love with him fifteen years ago and if I'm honest, I never stopped. It was never fair to you from the beginning. But you're right, Sam. You did give me life that was only a part of my wildest dreams."

Sam stares at me blankly. "But out of all of those wonderful things you gave me, something was missing." I added.

"What?" he says.

"True love," I say. "You didn't love me, either."

"Of course, I did, Jade. Why else would I sacrifice and work so hard for you?"

"Because you loved the idea of me. You loved how it felt to say you had a wife, but you never loved treating me like one."

"That's not true."

"Sam, you got scary. You were loud, hateful, rude and honestly... abusive." I said, surprised that I did. "You don't treat someone you love like that."

"So what? You were perfect?" He does his pissed off laugh. "Fucking some other guy makes you a perfect wife?'

"I was wrong. I was never perfect. I have never claimed to be."

"You sure as hell are acting like it now," he said.

A couple knocks tap on the door before it opens. It's the nurse. "Hello, I'm here with your meal."

"Thank you," I say. Realizing all this commotion has yet again removed the thought of food from my brain. The nurse places a turkey sandwich, apple sauce and bag of saltines onto the table next to my hospital bed and walks out.

"Look, Sam. I am sorry for the hurt that I have caused. But I think the damage is done on both sides. Don't you agree?" I don't know why I ask him this. I know his response already.

"No," he says. "I don't agree. I have messed up, too. I know I have. And I'm sorry." He looks up at the ceiling for a minute as if he's collecting the right words. "But I can't leave you. Not like this. I want to take you home. Let's raise this baby together. Even if its's not…"

I look at him and then at Greg.

"It won't be easy, but I can learn to love it as my own. Let's give us one more shot. We owe it to each other." He touches my hand. "We can move to suburbs, you can have the garden that you always wanted? Make a pizza with the fresh vegetables. Spend more time in the bakery. Just like you wanted."

For a minute, I picture it. I can see him pushing a stroller in his work slacks and Ralph Lauren shirt. His baby blue eyes locking mine from the window. Sourdough stuck to my hands. I'd smile and wave with my flat gummy palms. Our grass would be green and fertilized. The brick in our home would be tall, wide, and sturdy. This baby would have a private school education. Sam would be there for sports and plays. He would wink and walk on in the stroller. And I'd be in the kitchen, still daydreaming about what's real and what's missing.

"I—can't," I say, removing my hand from Sam's.

"So that's it?" he says, shaking his head, tucking his lips in.

I nod. "I think you should go."

Sam walks towards the door, gives Greg a smug look on the way to it.

"I will leave," he says, "but you will pay for this. You will pay for everything. You will be sorry." He pauses, his hand on the door. "You just made the biggest mistake of your life. Good luck raising some dead guy's baby with absolutely no money. I hope you both end up on the streets."

"I think you better go, buddy," Greg says. "Before you open your mouth again with words you can't take back, or before I show you how to treat a man that disrespects a woman."

"You know what? You can have her. And the mess she made." Sam says, slamming the door shut.

Greg walks over to me. "That was... a lot."

"I'm sorry. It is a lot."

"Sam is a lot. Why did you marry him?"

"He wasn't like this until after we got married. It was like after that day, literally on our honeymoon, someone hit a switch and he was different..."

Greg nods. "If it helps, I left Kianna's mom a year ago. I know it's not easy to stay and it's not easy to go."

"Yeah," I say. "You're right."

"You should eat, you know?" Greg says, pointing at the food.

"It's hard to eat when all I can think about is this giant disaster that is now my life."

"How I see it," Greg says, "You're alive. You have an entire new life with new possibility. A second chance. And a shot at something I'd give my life for."

"What's that?"

"A child."

Those words pierce through me, and I feel a tenderness pulse through my veins. *I am a mother now.* And even though I have been one for twenty-two weeks, this new discovery of motherhood was creating a softness inside of me that I hadn't yet felt before. An overflow of instantaneous purpose, love, and direction.

I grab Greg's hand, and he strokes the top of mine with his thumb, gazing into my eyes.

"You're right," I say. "This is just the beginning."

CHAPTER SEVENTEEN

U PON BEING DISCHARGED and throughout the iron infusion, Greg stays with me. He never left my side at the hospital, and as he sits next to me, I feel safe. A feeling I hadn't felt since Paul had left. When it is time to leave the hospital, Greg offers to drive me back to my car at the campsite.

"Where are you headed now from here?" he asks.

"Well, I haven't thought that much through. Coming here to North Carolina was an impulse decision," I say, shrugging my shoulders. "So was leaving everything I had ever owned back in Chicago."

"It was easier to leave on a whim when you didn't know you were with child. Now that you know, where will life take you? Not back to that awful husband, right?"

I laugh. "No. Never again." I start to think about where I'm going and where I might end up, but the future beyond North Carolina looks murky. I can't see myself in Chicago or Ohio, especially without Paul.

"Maybe when I get back to my car, I can figure it out. I could always go back home and stay with my parents until I find a good place to stay. I'd need to find a job, too. I worked for Sam's company."

"I can drive you back to your car, but before we go, I was hoping maybe we can have a cup of coffee or tea. I don't feel ready to say goodbye to you yet—I don't know why." Greg says, holding the car door open for me.

"You aren't asking me on a date, are you?" I say with my eyebrow raised. "I am still smelly from backpacking for weeks, dirty in places dirt shouldn't be, and oh, I don't know if you're aware, but I'm pregnant." I laugh as my newly nourished body sinks into the seat of his truck. Greg laughs and shuts the door for me.

"I guess—maybe I am. Baby and all—" He grins at me from the driver seat.

"I guess it takes a lot to scare you away, doesn't it?"

"No, it's not that." He looks at me, moves his hand over mine.

"Why are you so nice to me?" I ask with genuine curiosity.

"Well, I find being nice rather easy," he says. "It's not hard to be kind to you, regardless of what your last husband made you believe. And also—" he hesitates. "I know this might sound silly, but I think Kianna brought me to you for some reason."

"So, I take it you don't believe in coincidence?"

"Not when heaven and angels are involved, I don't," he says, locking his eyes again with mine.

I stare back into his gaze, smiling as he takes my hand.

"That's something Paul would've said."

Acknowledgements

How could I possibly take credit for such a story without honoring the very person who first cracked my heart wide open and showed me love? To Wil, thank you for showing me how to give and receive love. Even if people doubted us for being young, we both knew it was real. Because of that, I will always have a Wil sized hole in my heart. And I will carry you with me forever.

To my mom, thank you for always speaking life into my dreams and having unwavering faith in me. And for answering all my phone calls when these boys would break my heart. To my dad, thank you for instilling the drive and courage within me to dare to dream big. To my sweet boys, Julien and Jean, you are my greatest teachers, healers and have shown me the greatest love there is through motherhood.

Claire, thank you for always being there to listen, honor my grief, allow me to speak his name and share our story well and often. You will never know how much that meant and still means to me.

Audri, thank you for saying yes to my spontaneous North Carolina research trip to Big Bear Mountain. I will cherish our memories there and the friendship we've built for a lifetime. Thank you for also taking the time to help me read, review, and revise my work as I was struggling in the pit of my grief and thick of my divorce to finish this novel. I couldn't have done it without you.

To Steffany and Katie, my two grade school besties that have been there for me from day one—your ongoing support means everything to me. Thank you for standing by my side after all this time.

To my ex-husband and the others who failed me, thank you for not believing in me and teaching me what love was not. Because of you, I now have a second chance at the real thing.

To my writing mentor and friend, Rob Hart, thank you for the guidance and tough love when I needed it most. To Cara Lockwood, my editor, thank you for pulling strings to help me to get this book out so quickly.

To Mason, for showing up serendipitously and reminding me how there is no such thing as coincidence—especially when heaven and angels are involved.

To the BookTok community on Tik Tok, and to my loyal and loving Instagram community, thank you for your never-ending support and encouragement. I wouldn't be here without you. I'm forever grateful. Thank you. I love you.